SMOKE
IN THE
GLASS

D1495118

90710 000 397 763

SMOKE
IN THE
GLASS

Chris Humphreys

FOUR LANDS. THREE HEROES. ONE WAR.

GOLLANCZ

LONDON

First published in Great Britain in 2019 by Gollancz
an imprint of The Orion Publishing Group Ltd
Carmelite House, 50 Victoria Embankment
London EC4Y 0DZ

An Hachette UK Company

1 3 5 7 9 10 8 6 4 2

Copyright © Two Hats Creative, Inc 2019

The moral right of Chris Humphreys to be identified as
the author of this work has been asserted in accordance
with the Copyright, Designs and Patents Act of 1988.

All rights reserved. No part of this publication may be
reproduced, stored in a retrieval system, or transmitted
in any form or by any means, electronic, mechanical,
photocopying, recording, or otherwise, without the
prior permission of both the copyright owner and the
above publisher of this book.

All the characters in this book are fictitious, and any resemblance
to actual persons, living or dead, is purely coincidental.

A CIP catalogue record for this book
is available from the British Library.

ISBN (Trade Paperback) 978 1 473 22603 6
ISBN (eBook) 978 1 473 22605 0

Typeset by Deltatype Ltd, Birkenhead, Merseyside

Printed in Great Britain by Clays Ltd, Elcograf S.p.A.

MIX
Paper from
responsible sources
FSC   FSC® C104740
www.fsc.org

London Borough of Richmond Upon Thames	
RTR	
90710 000 397 763	
Askews & Holts	
AF FAN	£16.99
	9781473226036

DISCARDED FROM RICHMOND UPON THAMES LIBRARY SERVICE

To Karim and Amanda

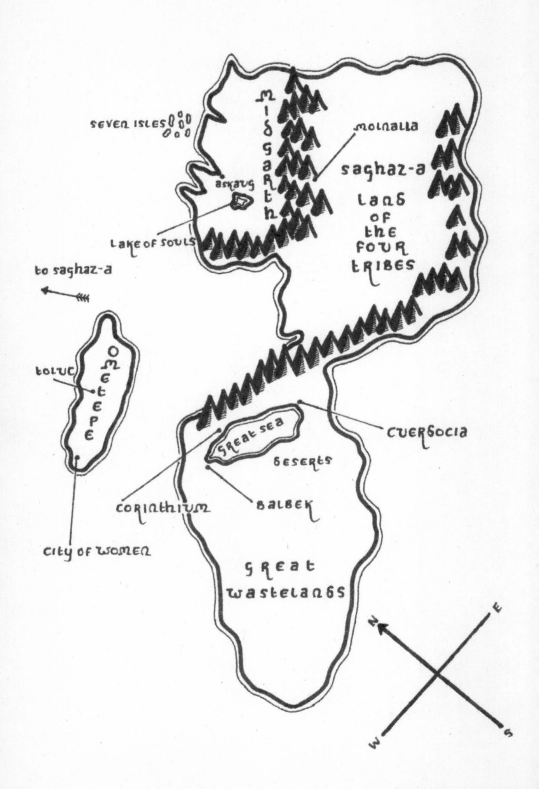

OMETEPE

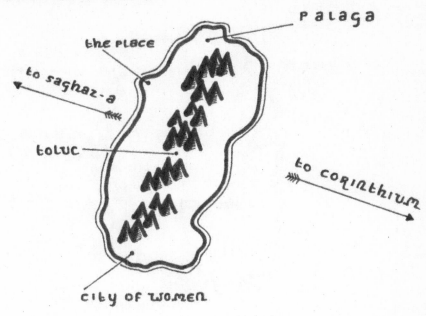

PALAGA

THE PLACE

to saghaz-a

toluc

to CORINTHIUM

CITY OF WOMEN

saghaz-a — land of the four tribes

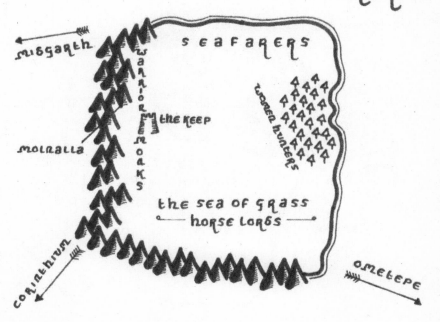

misgarth

SEAFARERS

WARRIOR OAKS

THE KEEP

women hunters

molralla

CORINTHIUM

THE SEA OF GRASS
— HORSE LORDS —

OMETEPE

miSgarth

SEVEN ISLES

saghaz-a

askaug

molnalla

Lake of souls

galahur

lorken

to corinthium

corinthium

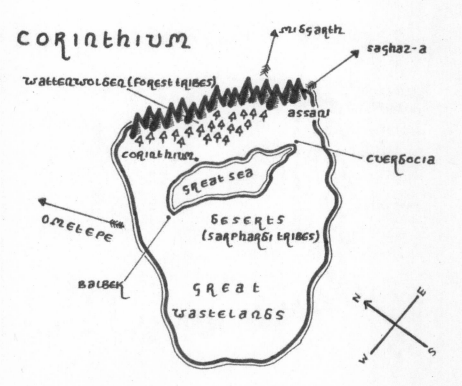

miSgarth

saghaz-a

wattenwolden (Forest tribes)

assani

cuerbocia

corinthium

great sea

omelepe

deserts
(sarphardi tribes)

balbek

great

wastelands

N
E
W
S

Dramatis Personae

Corinthium:
Ferros
Ashtan
Megaloumos
General Olankios
Lara
Aisha – Lara's younger sister
Gan, Tutor – Timian monk of the Southern Xan tribe
Mikon – ship's captain, Arcrana Isles
Streone Lascartis – Innovator of the Great Theatre
Lascartis, Gonarios, Trebans – old families of the city
Lucan – Leader of Council of Lives
Roxanna – his daughter
Graco – Lucan's servant
Maltarsus – workers' leader
Marya – his wife
Andropena – whore
Parkos – general
Carellia – former whore
Gandalos – Cuerdocian officer
Smoke
Caradocius – legendary leader of the northern (forest)
Wattenwollden tribes

Stephanos – young man at cult ceremony
Traxia – old woman at cult ceremony

Ometepe:
Atisha
Intitepe
His daughters:
   Tolacca – priestess, 300 years old
   Sayana – Youngest, 70 years old
   Amerist – Warrior, 150 years old
Asaya – Atisha's childhood friend
Old Gama
Fant – dog
Saroc – priest king, immortal
Nak – mountain guide
Bok – guide
Poum – the One
Muna – governess of the City of Women
Besema – formerly 'the One'
Natara – maiden of the marana
Yutil – formerly 'the One'
Novara – formerly 'the One'
One-eared Salpe – warrior
Ravaya – maiden in city
Tokat – Intitepe's commander at City of Women
Santepe – last defeated son

Midgarth:
Luck
Freya
Hovard
Bjorn Swift-Sword
Einar the Black

Agnetha
Stromvar
Gytta – Luck's wife
Ulrich the Smith
High Priest
Peki Asarko
Petr the Red
Ut the Slayer

Four Tribes:
Priests:
    Anazat – High Monk
    Alon – assassin
Hunters:
    Gistrane (in Ometepe)
    Karima – huntress
    Korshak – Horse Lord
Serimaz:
    To Horse Lords, he was Wind Rider
    To Seafarers, Shield from Storms
    To Huntresses, Moonlight Hunter
    To Priests, The One before the One

In the time before what some in their own tongue would call the cataclysm, and others the awakening, the planet was divided into four worlds.

Separated by unclimbable mountains and by unsailable seas, for many thousands of years the people who lived in each world knew nothing of any other, thought that they ruled the planet alone. Yet eventually in every world there was a story that linked them all: of a visitor who fell from the sky or who came from the ocean, half a millennium before our present days.

The visitor brought gifts. Gifts that many, in their own tongue, would call curses.

The one who came appeared differently to the different peoples – as man, woman or child. Was called Gudrun Gift Bearer in the North, Andros the Blind in the South, Tasloc Wave Rider in the West. And the first gift given, but only in three of the worlds, was immortality. A small number amongst them would be born and live for ever. They would discover it only upon their death and their rebirth. It could be neither chosen nor willed. Old men and young, women and babes, it could come to any. It was not inherited, although from time to time immortals did bear immortals. Most would watch in sadness as the one they'd married when young or the baby they'd given birth to grew grey, passed them and died. Thus everywhere was immortality seen as both blessing and curse. And it changed each world utterly, according to their separate ways and customs.

The second gift the visitor gave to every immortal changed it more. For it was the gift of possession – possession for a time of another's body and life – and again it was different in each of those three worlds.

In the Southern lands, that would become Corinthium, immortals could possess another person, a mortal. Dissolve into them for a time, their own flesh gone, their spirit and mind transplanted. Wise men and women over the years believed that the visitor gave this gift so that immortals would themselves grow wise, having lived in another's skin, in their minds and hearts – felt their pains, learned their longings, discovering how another needed to live, so they could be as shepherds to the flock and help all to live well.

It is not what happened. For in that land it first became a sport, and then a way not to help but to control.

And thus the gift was squandered.

In the land of the North, that came to be known as Midgarth, the gift of possession was different – there the immortals could possess only beasts. All that ran, flew, swam or slid on their bellies across the ground were available to them. It took but sight, a moment of sinking, before their bodies were gone and human became animal. Again, for those who first received it, it appeared to be a gift for learning. To discover, for the brief time of possession, that animals were not lesser because they did not reason as man reasoned. That each – furred, feathered, scaled – deserved their place in their world as man did, with as much respect. Yet here, as in the South, this gift swiftly became a game, a chance to make a tale to be told before the hearth-fire on long winter nights.

And thus the gift was wasted.

In the third world, Ometepe, one immortal killed all others before the power of possession – which would be different there – was discovered.

And thus the gift was lost.

Yet what of that fourth world, the largest of all worlds, itself divided into four tribes, that would be known as *saghaz-a*, or Land of Joy? The visitor also came to it, though much later, only a hundred years ago. There she was called *azana-kesh* or 'the one who comes before'. She gave each of the scattered, warring peoples of that world a different gift. Not immortality, not possession.

Hope. Hope in the form of prophecy. Of someone who would come to unite all worlds – but only if the four tribes first united themselves.

It took near one hundred years, of war and hatred. Until they were ready. When they were, *azana* – the One – was born. Not in their land. Far away. Yet by then a united people had found ways to climb unclimbable mountains, and sail unsailable seas.

Now is the age of prophecy fulfilled. Now is the age of the darkness that gives way to the light. The end of the dominion of the Immortal. The beginning of the dominion of Man.

The age of *azana*. The age of the One.

(From scrolls found in a cave on the mountain of Gorach. Attributed to Smoke, the Hermit)

I

Trial by Death

Of the two men who lay beside each other on the ridge, watching the kidnappers' camp, one was to take a mortal wound that night, the other a wound that would make him live for ever. Neither could know it, for the gods had not cursed them with the far-seeing eye. Neither would have cared if they had known. 'Half odds are good odds' was a law they lived by in the hills of the Sarphardi, where death was so easy to come by. Both would have taken the bet and gone to grave or immortality with a gambler's accepting smile.

Neither cared about anything other than what they did next. About that they cared a great deal and because of it the two men, closer than brothers, did what they rarely did: quarrelled, in short, angry whispers.

'Because I claimed it first.'

'Only because I did not think you would be so stupid as to do so.'

'Stupid?'

'As the chicken without a head. As the donkey following its tail. As the—'

'Ashtan!' Ferros held up his hand to halt his friend's comparisons before he went round the farmyard. 'How often must I prove it? I am better at the closework.'

'Better?' Ashtan reached to make a gap in the grasses before him and spat carefully through it. 'You base this outrageous boast on one night in Atrau?'

'And that other in Quba, plus the dawn raid on Temir.'

'Pah!'

Ashtan hawked another impressive amount of phlegm, bent to spit, and Ferros used the brief interlude of silence to deploy his winning argument. 'Besides, brother, when I run from the camp dragging the girl and the boy with five screaming Sarphardi a pace behind, who is the more likely to make at least three shots in the dark?' He smiled. 'For I will reluctantly concede that, at night at least, you are better with a bow than I.'

Ashtan, about to spit, swallowed instead. 'By night, by day, in my sleep or drunk, I am better with a bow than you.' He grunted, then shrugged. 'Well, brother, if you are so keen to court death in the form of a spear up your arse, so be it.' He still had the grass parted for the spit and peered through the gap again. 'This is how it goes. I will be behind that pile of rocks there. You run straight from the fire towards me. When you reach that bush that's shaped like a crouching leopard, you throw the kidnapped down. I take two of the bastards then, backlit by flame, you a third with your taka.' He tapped the throwing knife, sheathed on Ferros's forearm. 'Drop, draw, throw. If the other two stop there long enough to wonder what is happening, I take them then. If not, see if you truly are good enough at closework to hold them off till I get there to save you. Again. Agreed?'

Ferros thought of continuing the argument – but they didn't have time. 'Agreed.' He grinned. 'Though one wonders who is the officer here, and who the mere soldier.'

'This, in your mother's milk.' Ashtan spat again, and grinned back. 'Come! Let's go kill someone.'

'It doesn't worry you that they could be your cousins?' Ferros asked, as they slid down into the gulley and checked their weapons.

'These? Did you not note them by their fire? They are clan *gelcha*. Renowned fuckers of their own livestock. A disgrace. Besides,' he inserted an arrow's notched end into his mouth, pulled it out, its feathers now glistening and smooth, 'one of them is Tamin the One-Eyed. He once laid his hand upon my sister Sorani's arm.' He placed another arrow in his mouth, drew it out. 'Him I might just wound and make his death a long, slow pleasure later.'

'No.' Ferros checked that his short sword slid easily from the sheath on his back, that the knives, one on each of his forearms, the cutter and the thrower, were secure. Then he drove three arrows tip first into the soil beneath the lip of the gulley and laid his own bow beside them. 'Do not take the risk. There are five of them to two of us. They may fuck their own goats but they are still Sarphardi warriors. Besides, the girl and boy will be terrified. We must get them back to the city and their family swiftly. No time for slow pleasures.' He rose to a crouch. 'And that, soldier, is an order.'

'Sir!' Ashtan placed his arrows in the quiver, picked up his bow by its buffalo-horn grip. His lips parted over teeth brightened by the light of Horned Saipha, the hunter's moon, a crescent in the sky. 'And again, in your mother's milk.' He spat, and rose too. 'Go well.'

'Give the quail's call when you are in position. I'll reply when I am.'

'It had better be soon.' Ashtan gestured with his head. 'They have begun on the girl.'

Ferros turned. His friend's hearing was superb but even he could now hear the girl's faint, desperate weeping, the boy's pleading, cut off by the back of a hand struck hard across a

7

face. His own face went ugly. 'Go with the gods,' he muttered, already turning away.

'And you, brother.'

Sounds came clearer as Ferros emerged from the gulley and, crouching low, ran in a circle around the edge of the Sarphardi camp to its far side. The girl's pleading, the boy's weeping, the kidnappers' mocking laughter ... which halted for a moment as one of their horses snickered when Ferros ducked into their lines, and resumed when he'd calmed the beast with his hand and a whispered word. He could see the single tent clearly now over the mount's shoulders, a dozen paces away. The fire on its far side made silhouettes of those within – two distinct figures crouched on the ground, the five tribesmen one monstrous blob above them. Then one detached, moving to the tent's entrance, declaring his intention to piss before he got down to anything else, more mocking laughter following him. Ferros could hear the slur in it now – the merchant's wagon they'd stolen along with the children had carried a large barrel of date brandy. So close to the city, this girl's father had thought he would only need one bodyguard. But the raiders had been getting bolder of late and the bodyguard would have died first and fast, the merchant swiftly afterwards.

It had been chance and a jackal's howl that had led him and Ashtan, out for a morning hunt, to the two bodies poorly concealed in scrub beside the road. They would have buried them well enough to protect them from scavenging animals, then brought a wagon from the port – if it had not been for what the dead merchant was gripping in his right hand: the doll of a soldier in full Corinthium armour. 'They have a child,' Ferros had said. There had been no time to do anything for the dead now, only to chase the murderers, and hope to save the living.

The Sarphardi might have had a night's head start but they also had the wagon with the profit and the two riders had overtaken them by sunset. Now, by the one moon's rise and the other's fall, they would deal with them.

This one first, Ferros thought, as the man walked a dozen paces off and lowered his breech cloth. He let him get midstream, let the ribald song start in the tent about acts to be performed in the famed brothels of Makat, before he drew his curved slicing dagger. By Saipha's light he could make the throw with the other knife, but the man might fall noisily and he needed to be sure that Ashtan had reached his position before he startled the other four.

Slamming his hand around the man's mouth, Ferros pulled him close, even as the blade bit. Two sprays now, one diminishing, one fountaining. The warrior was large, bigger even than him, and the man bent, braced, stood tall, lifting Ferros from the ground. For a moment Ferros thought he might lose him, pressed his hand tighter against the mouth, wrapped his dagger hand around the huge chest. The man stumbled and Ferros rode him to the ground, lying atop him till life left.

He rolled off, crouched and turned, dagger before him. But he didn't think he'd made much noise, and the same reassuringly nasty song and sounds came from the tent. Then, from beyond it, came the quail's cry – Ashtan, in position.

There was no point in delaying – especially since his own warrior's blood was up with his enemy's sticky on his hand. He tipped back his head, echoed the cry – poorly perhaps, because the men's voices stopped within the tent, while the girl's and boy's sobbed on. It didn't matter much, not when his signal was immediately followed by his comrade's voice.

'Attack!' Ashtan yelled. 'Soldiers of the Ninth, advance!'

The shout had the instant and desired effect. The four warriors snatched up weapons and ran out of the tent's front entrance. There wasn't an entrance at the back but Ferros swiftly made one – jabbing the tip of his curved dagger into the hide wall and slicing down fast. Pausing only to sheathe one weapon, he drew another, the short sword on his back, then stepped through the slit. The girl and the boy – she maybe fourteen, he perhaps half that – were still crouched on the floor, clutching each other. Their eyes shot wide when they saw him but they didn't scream. He might not have been wearing the full uniform of an officer of the Ninth, but he had the breast and back-plates, decorated with the unit's serpent gods, and the green tunic beneath. And though the desert sun had tanned his skin as dark as any tribesman's, it had also bleached his hair near white. Unlike her black-haired captors, she could tell in an instant that he was a soldier of the empire. 'Up!' he commanded, in a whisper. 'Can you run?'

The boy just stared at him. It was the girl who answered, 'Yes! Oh yes!'

'Then on my word, fast as hares. Straight past the fire, straight down the path.'

He stepped to the front flap and a swift glance showed him the Sarphardi half a dozen paces away staring hard into the night. Only one had a bow, with arrow nocked, the others their curved swords, the swordsmen also holding kite-shaped shields to cover them all. Ashtan began shouting more commands but even with these efforts, it would only be the matter of a moment before the tribesmen realised they faced a few men, if that, and not a squadron. The moment was his.

The shield of the man he'd already killed was on the ground. Snatching it up, thrusting his arm through its hide grip, Ferros bent to the boy and girl. 'Wait ... wait.'

An arrow, driven from short range into one of the raiders' shields, knocked the man holding it a half-step back. 'Now!'

They burst out, the boy stumbling, the girl fast. Ferros grasped the sword grip in his shield hand, used his freed one to grab the boy's arm and propel him forward. They were three paces past the fire when the shouts came. 'Faster,' Ferros cried, shoving the boy after his sister, turning in the same moment to thrust the shield out. An arrow thumped into it. Immediately he turned and ran again. When he reached the bush that resembled the crouching leopard, he grabbed both of the children and dropped with them to the ground. As they hit it, he heard a shriek from behind him, did not turn to look, did not need to. Good shooting, brother, he thought, rising, dragging the children up, running. Another half-dozen paces and instinct made him turn again, shield braced. Another arrow hit it, and he let the force turn him to run once more.

He caught up with the children at the rise where they'd studied the camp. The children slid over it. He made a tally of the enemy: one dead at the camp, one dying on the path, three following. Three to kill. Odds nearly even. Smiling he stepped over the lip, dropped sword and shield, reached for his bow.

Which wasn't there. Or it was, but not on the ground where he'd left it. He saw it then as it rose, with one of Horned Saipha's moonbeams glinting on the iron arrowhead, and he realised, in the instant of life left to him, that he'd erred back in the tent. That there had been three warriors sheltering from Ashtan's arrows, not four. And that the fourth was raising his own bow against him, the string already drawn all the way back.

As the arrow entered his right eye, his last thought within the shock and the fear was that, after all, it should have been Ashtan who had done the closework, not him. His friend would never have miscounted. And because he had, he had killed them both.

Some last thought, he thought, as he died.

Ferros woke, naked, freezing, as the second of the moons, Blue Revlas, she of Night and Morning, was chased from the sky by her would-be ravisher, the sun.

They had stripped him of his clothes and left him for dead. He understood why when he turned his head and the arrow, which had burst his right eye and gone on through his skull and stuck there, dragged across the earth beneath his head. It was the strangest sensation he'd ever felt, wood grinding on bone, accompanying the strangest sight: the feathers of a shaft the other side of his nose. Though he knew that it was his only wound, a mortal one, it was not the source of the awful pain. The rest of him was. His whole body was burning, inside and out.

He'd heard about the agonies of this second birth, far exceeding any that could have come at the first. People gossiped about it, speculating, wondering how they would face it if they were chosen. Books were written, of philosophy or tales, plays enacted in theatres exploring the theme. So few were born again, perhaps half a dozen a year it was said, to add to the small pool. Yet those few could come from anywhere, from the fleet or the army, from gutter to palace. In the central city of Corinthium, in one of the smaller cities like Cuerodocia or in his own home town of Balbek. A gift in the blood. It was said that two immortals conjoining had a better chance of having a child who was like them but it was never guaranteed. While the suicide cults that thrived and died out over the centuries were both illegal and unproductive, it was said that of all those who killed themselves in their rites only three had ever joined the immortal ranks.

It was said, he thought, sitting up, swaying with the rush of blood to the head. Not by him. His parents had certainly not been immortal, dying in the last great plague that had killed one fifth of Balbek when he was five. The army, where orphans were sent, had been his life for the eighteen years since. And there, all speculation was discouraged. Handle what's in front of you, the drillmasters pounded into every recruit. One life is good enough for a soldier. Seize its every opportunity – for glory, riches, honour. For love, if you can find it. Nothing else matters.

He had never sought to be immortal. And now he was.

What would he do? What he always did. Handle what was in front of him – an arrow embedded in his skull. After that? Discover the source of the weeping that was coming from just over the rise.

He touched the arrow on its feathers, moved it slightly. A shudder of nausea went through him. He was tempted to pull it all the way through but he knew just enough about immortality to know he mustn't. Pulling any blade from a wound often killed the wounded. Even if he was immortal now, he could still succumb to death as he'd done when he was first shot. Hours more would pass before his immortal body healed itself again. And waking to the agony of rebirth was not something he wished to go through twice. It would also mean he wouldn't find out who was crying so desperately, and why.

Careful not to jog the arrow, Ferros raised his head above the lip of the rise.

They were in a group, the living, the dying and the dead, clustered around a glowing firepit. Two Sarphardi warriors were on their backs, hands crossed over their torn and bloody chests, eyes closed but with open eyes painted on their lids. Sitting beside the corpses were the ones he'd sought to rescue, the boy and the girl. They were the source of the weeping. The three other men, each one clutching a knife or a burning, sharpened stick, were standing before a fourth. He was hanging upside down from a tree branch.

Ashtan.

He was alive, barely. The wounds on his body caused by blade or fire, the blood pooling below him, showed that he had no right to be. Ferros could see his torn lips moving in prayer or curse. Curse, knowing him. He could not be far from his end, for even as he watched a warrior, the one with a single eye – Tamin, Ashtan had named him – thrust a flaming stick into the dangling man's ear. His friend's eyes went wide, but no sound came other than another muttered curse.

Tamin threw down the stick as if it was its fault. 'It is time,' he growled. 'We eat his heart and we go. The slave market at Buzuluk starts tonight and if we ride hard we'll make it. These two will fetch a good price.'

'Better, since you didn't have time to take your pleasure with her,' said another.

'More interesting things to do.' Tamin leaned down to the dangling head. 'Is that not right? Did we not do *interesting* things to you, jackal of the Corinthians?'

Ferros had always known that Ashtan could muster twice as much spit as any man living, and dispose of it more creatively. He did so now, expelling a wad into Tamin's one good eye.

'Blood of snake!' Tamin stepped back to the others' laughter, rubbing his eye furiously. 'Now I think there is time for one last interesting thing.' He turned to his men, snarling. 'You! Cut him down. You! Bring my horse.'

Ferros heard the words but didn't see them spoken because he was moving in a crouch along the rise using the protection it offered him. He circled swiftly to the tent. As he suspected, his armour, tunic and weapons were in it. Clothes could wait. He slipped on his two knife sheaths, picked up one of the Sarphardi kite shields, drew his sword and stepped out.

The man with the horse had just returned, holding the bridle. Tamin and the other man were attaching a rope to Ashtan's neck. So focused were all three on this task that they didn't notice Ferros approach, though he made little secret of it. The girl did see him and screamed. He couldn't blame her. He could imagine what he looked like.

14

It was awkward, fighting with the use of only one eye. Perspective was wrong, and he missed blows he should not have, cut parts he'd not been aiming at, was cut on arm and side, not deep. Two of the warriors survived his first assault, and both had managed to get weapons into their hands. But maybe it was the fact that they believed they were fighting a dead man that weakened them. Or maybe immortality compensated for his poor vision. When he'd killed the first man, he took the second's overhead blow on the top edge of his wooden shield, let the blade bite deep, twisted then wrenched the shield down and to the side, and so pulled the curved sword with it. Then he thrust hard and straight, driving his point through the man's neck.

Tamin scythed a blow over his head. Ferros ducked, stepped back. Shrieking, the one-eyed man dropped his sword, turned and flung himself over his horse. 'Yah!' he cried, kicking his heels in. The horse, superb as all Sarphardi mounts, went straight into a gallop. But as his opponent mounted, Ferros too had dropped his sword and, even as the man's heels dug into the horse's flank, he drew his throwing knife. The horse had gone five paces when the taka took Tamin in the neck. He fell, though his mount kept going.

Sound, which often went away when he fought, came back to Ferros now – the diminishing fall of hooves on earth, the rising cries of the boy, the weeping of the girl. What concerned him most, though, was the softest sound there – breath on the ragged lips of Ashtan, trying to form words.

'Quiet!' he snapped at the girl, who obeyed instantly, drawing her brother to her, both staring at him in silent horror. In a gentler voice he said, 'Fetch me water,' and as they scrambled up and ran off, he turned back to Ashtan. Holding him, he used his slicing knife to sever the rope at his ankles, lifted him carefully down and laid his friend's head in his lap. 'Brother,' he said, studying the havoc the Sarphardi had wrought, 'I have to tell you, you do not look well.'

One of Ashtan's eyes was caked shut with congealed blood. The other was missing a lid. This eye moved nonetheless, taking Ferros in. A whisper came, though the Corinthian had to bend to hear it. 'The monkey accuses the man of having a bare arse?'

Ferros smiled. 'How badly did they hurt you?'

'Those inepts? Hardly at all.' A cough came from deep inside him, pink flecked the lips. 'But they have killed me nonetheless.' The one-eyed gaze moved over him again. 'Is this a wound?'

'No. It is a death blow.'

'And yet you live.'

'And yet I live.'

'So. At least one of us will.' Ashtan shook his head very slightly, winced and wheezed. 'I think they've broken all my ribs. Other things. I am not going to be much help to you, my captain.' He swallowed. 'You should leave me. That horse you let go may lead others back.'

'Which is why we leave now. All of us.'

When he heard the brother and sister's footfalls, he ripped away one of the dead warriors' head cloths, tied it swiftly around to cover his nakedness. The girl carried a water skin. But she did not hand it over, just halted, stared ... started when he reached and lifted it to squirt some water into Ashtan's mouth, then some into his own.

'The wagon,' he said, 'are the horses near it?'

It was the boy who spoke. 'They are in the traces, sir. They were planning on leaving, when they ... when they'd finished with ...' His gaze went to Ashtan and he shuddered, turned away.

'Do you know anything of healing, girl?'

She would not look at him but she did reply. 'I have completed my first two years with the Healers' Guild. I hope to be a healer one day.'

16

'That day is today. Do what you can. There are some unguents and herbs in my saddle rolls, wherever they may be. Cloths too. Battlefield medicine.'

He rose, took a step towards the wagon, and her voice stopped him. 'Thank you, sir. For following, for coming back. For—' She broke off and he turned to look at her. She regarded him directly now, not flinching from his wound. A bold girl, then. 'Can I ... can I try to help you with—'

She gestured and he lifted his hand, tapped the arrow, felt the shudder through the bones of his skull. 'This is beyond your two years, young one. If I am to get us back to Balbek, this must stay where it is.'

He turned, kept going, even when the boy's voice came. 'Are you ... are you an immortal, sir?'

'I am now,' he said, walking on. 'May the gods pity me, but I am.'

Immortal or not, it was the limit of his strength to get the wagon and its occupants to the city. Ashtan died not far from it, as night fell, Balbek's lights already standing out against the purple dark of the great sea beyond. The girl could have done nothing more, his wounds too severe and too hidden for even the most experienced of the Guild's healers. She wept, nonetheless, in great wrenching sobs, and Ferros was too tired to comfort her.

The gatekeepers, two soldiers he didn't know, tried not to show their shock, failed, let them through fast, dispatching a third to run a report ahead to the fort. They moved swiftly enough after that. It was reasonable timing, the hour of their arrival. The good citizens of Balbek were largely at home for their supper so the streets were not busy. It was the less good citizens who were about, soldiers off duty, frontiersmen, mariners, miners on leave from the copper workings at Ganhar. These spilled out before tavern or brothel doors and sometimes blocked the way. A whip flicked between the horses' ears and close to a wine-reddened face moved most. Only once did a man, a barrel-chested docker, hold his place and curse Ferros – until he saw beneath the hood that really covered nothing. 'Trachamea's tits, boys, but look what we have here!' he shouted, and others advanced to gawk and curse in turn. All could recognise a mortal wound when they saw one – an arrow through the head being one of the more obvious that any had ever seen. The resentment that immortality often caused, with immortals occupying almost every position in the highest ranks of army, temple and courts, was usually constrained by manners and the watchful eye of the state. Here, it was unconstrained by liquor.

'By Trachamea's tiny tits,' the docker of big chest and limited vocabulary called again, 'soldier boy's not so pretty now. Gods, but look at that split apple.'

Hoots and jeers came fast. Someone seized the horses' bridles and the twin pair jerked their heads, stamped their feet.

All I need, thought Ferros, so weary he'd have liked to lie down in the wagon beside Ashtan and sleep. But his duty was to the girl and boy quivering in the back and to his dead comrade lying beside them, to see him properly burned and his ashes scattered to the seven winds before the sun rose and set again. So he one-eyed the biggest man there, that same docker, still cursing and mocking, and considered.

Though he didn't blame the man. He remembered joining in muttered conversations in barracks, resentments expressed at an immortal gaining promotion over a mortal better qualified. It had happened to him, twice, only making officer at the third attempt. The orphan son of a blacksmith could expect little else. Now, though, he'd been chosen, by which god he did not know. Mavros of the round shield, he suspected.

He coiled the whip back. He was good with it, could pluck

a sparrow off a gate post. Could pluck out a docker's eye if he needed, too, even with only one of his own.

Then he heard it – the rhythmic tread of rivet-studded sandals on cobblestones. Heard next the sergeant's bellow of 'Make way, there! Make way!' A squad twenty-strong rounded the corner, breastplated and helmed, marching in perfect order, shield arms swinging, heavy javelins sloped across their shoulders. The crowd scattered down alleys, into yards. Only the big docker lingered and he but for the moment it took to look again into Ferros's one eye, make an obscene gesture with thumb and curled finger, then slip through the door beneath the sign of a huge phallus pointing at Trachamea's tits.

'Sir! We had word of your coming.'

The sergeant was someone he knew, liked. Megaloumos. The man had fought in twenty campaigns, had seen everything. But even his eyes widened when he saw Ferros's wound and realised what it meant, though it was the only concession he made to surprise. He swung up onto the wagon seat, took the reins and whip with a curt, 'Allow me, sir. Yah!'

As the wagon pulled away, his squad dividing before and after it, the sergeant glanced back, saw the girl and boy, and the body under its bloody shroud. 'Ashtan?' he asked.

Ferros nodded. 'Sarphardi raiders. We killed them, freed their prisoners. Ashtan—'

His name. An arrow through the eye and a life to come completely different than he'd ever imagined for himself. It was suddenly all too much. Tears started to run from the one eye left and he laid his head on Megaloumos's shoulder with a sigh.

The sergeant stared straight ahead. 'Nearly there, sir,' he said softly. 'Nearly there.'

Ferros lay in the darkened room, naked under a thin sheet, his head propped up on a horsehair bolster, listening to the sounds coming through the window – of the fort, and, beyond it, of the port. They'd cleaned him up, tended to all his wounds save the biggest one, though the healer had snipped both feather and metalled tip from the arrow, leaving just a small length of shaft, ends proud each side of his skull which he would return to remove once the draught of poppy had taken a deeper effect. Ferros had been right to guess that its removal would kill him again for a while. Now, of course, he needn't worry that it would. 'We'll keep you asleep for a day and a night. Let the body heal quietly,' the surgeon had said. But when he'd tried to ask the man how it was possible for anyone, immortal or not, to survive an arrow through the head, the man had muttered about specialised knowledge, made the excuse of patients elsewhere, and left.

From the first moment when the girl he'd rescued looked at him, to now and this healer, immortality had made everyone uncomfortable, even fearful. He was different now, for ever ... *for ever?* ... different. And in that cell, with his mind beginning to fog with the thousand questions he desperately needed answering, he knew only this: that he was the most fearful of all. At that point Ferros would have traded all his future life to be back the previous morning with Ashtan, to have never heard the jackal's bark, never found the doll, never followed a stolen wagon's ruts to this fate.

He already felt some of the effects of the drug in the sinking of his limbs, as if each part of his body were a candle, blowing out one by one. Soon he could no longer feel his legs, his hips, his fingers. His mind was calmer, yet still active, sights and sounds of the recent days still playing there, defying sleep: moon glimmer on an arrowhead, the grinding of wood against his skull, a fountain of blood from a man's neck, Ashtan's torn lips, the girl's screams, Horned Saipha waxing in the sky. Blue Revlas fleeing.

His eyes closed at last – then opened immediately when the door was pushed in. He'd have to tell them to give him a few minutes. He truly didn't want to be awake when he died and was born again.

'Do you sleep?'

It was not the healer's voice but another he knew. 'Commander,' he said.

'No, do not try to rise.' General Olankios stepped closer, peered down. 'How are you, Ferros?'

'Well enough for a dead man, sir.'

The general smiled. 'Dead but alive. Dying to live. You have entered the world of paradox, young Ferros, yours to dwell in ... for a long, long time.' The smile faded. 'I pity you, soldier. Some think that immortality is the gods' greatest gift. In my experience, like any thing given, it comes with too many obligations to fulfil.'

'You are? I didn't know.'

'No. Few do. I discovered that soldiers are less likely to obey a suicidal command on a battlefield if they are the only ones committing suicide.' That faint smile came, went. 'I only discovered I was immortal leading such an action. In the north, against the Wattenwolden.' Olankios leaned into the lamp spill, the light reflecting from the dome of his head. 'Could I not have found it out when I was young and handsome like you, rather than this old, bald, paunchy man?'

'So it is true? We do not age?'

'Maybe we do. It's hard to tell. We certainly heal. This eye of yours will return, keener than before. It is one of the wonders of—' He shook his head. 'But I am not a surgeon. Nor am I here to tell you of the ways of immortality. You will learn those when you have recovered enough from these wounds to be sent on to Corinthium.'

'The great city? I've ... never been. Balbek, these deserts, this is the only home I've known.' Ferros swallowed. 'I thought I might stay here, in the army, learn what I need—'

'You cannot. There are none here to teach you. Of duty. Of philosophy. Of … pleasure.' He nodded. 'All of which awaits you when you enter the Sanctum on the Hill.'

'The palace of learning? A rough soldier like me? They will think me a Sarphardi raider.'

'They will cure you of some roughness. They will leave some of it. They will use everything you are to shape you into what they need you to be: a true servant of the empire, under the gods' special favour.'

One question had pressed Ferros above all others. He reached through opiate clouds to find it. 'General, I was to marry in the spring. May I still?'

'She's not immortal, is she?'

'Lara? No. I … I do not think so. Is that possible?'

'It would be as unlikely as … as lightning hitting the same person twice. Which does happen – I knew a farmer in Otrano who—' The older man smiled, yet there was no joy, only sadness in it. 'No, Ferros. You have learned the first price demanded for the gift. If you choose to stay with her, she will age, you will not. At first it will seem a little thing, barely noticeable. Until she begins to run ahead of you, changing, greying. Claimed by time.' He looked up to the wall, beyond it. 'It is … awful.' He focused on Ferros again. 'And there is something else. That goes with Immortality. Perhaps I should not tell you but—'

Noises in the corridor. The general straightened. 'But they come and I must go. The healer will chastise me for keeping you awake. Wait!' he commanded, as the door half-opened. 'I really only came to you for this.'

Olankios raised his left hand. The pale palm was blackened, covered in soot. 'We burned Ashtan, with all the rites of a warrior. He is in the seven winds now – hunting, fighting with his clan, making love to a beautiful wife. He lives for ever in honour. And he travels with you always. Here,' the general bent, drew a black circle around Ferros's heart, 'and here.' He reached up, and drew a smaller circle on Ferros's forehead. Ferros closed his one eye at the soft touch, then found he couldn't open it again. But there was light behind the lid, and he smiled as he watched Ashtan vault onto his fastest pony, spit impressively then laugh before he galloped away.

'Blessings of the gods for your journey,' someone said.

He wanted to make the formal response, but sleep took him before he could form the words.

2

The Temple of Love and Death

In the Palace of Waters, all was ready. For a short time and for one purpose, it had been given over only to women.

Each one there had her task. Four tended the hot water that flowed from the mountain – the gift of Toluc, the fire god who ruled from his molten throne at the top of the world and for whom the city was named. They channelled his blessing through gates and stone sluices, maintaining the perfect temperature in each pool for its specific function – lingering, bathing ...

... birth.

Three more women played music, two on wooden flutes, one on strings stretched over the shell of a turtle, sounds soothing as much as flowing water; whilst two others prepared cordials from the fresh fruit brought daily by runners from the fertile valleys below, mixing them with ground nuts and special herbs.

There was one woman who had a task yet did not move, just sat, in the farthest corner, in the shadows. The others knew she was there – but only a few looked at her, and never more than once. All knew she wore a mask and those who'd seen it hoped they never would again.

Only one woman in the palace had no task, though she was the focus and cause of all the others. Yet if most of them prayed, it was Atisha who prayed hardest of all.

'Toluc, God of Fire, bless me, help me, guide me. Intitepe, King of Fire, husband, lover, bless me, help me, pity me. Alam, Goddess of Childbirth, bless me, help me, protect me.'

She prayed with her hands wrapped across her swollen belly. And though the words were spoken out, to goddess, god-king and god, the yearning of the prayer was all inwards, to that life within who kicked her even now. She knew that many of her prayers were useless, could not alter the child she carried. That had been decided long ago. Yet she could not stop. Stop and she'd think – and glance again into that shadowed corner.

It had been a while since her last contractions. They'd been going to move her into the birth pool but then the pain subsided, the hammering slowed and eased. Her back hurt so much, and the cushions they'd placed behind her on the couch were more comfortable than any submerged tile could be. Yet it was more than that – for from the couch Atisha could look out of the stone window arch at the next hill, at the palace upon it. If she stretched up she could even see the window where her chamber had been. Hers and his. Remember her life there.

Remember him.

'Hurry, Atisha, hurry! Can't you hear his horns? He comes. Why are you always so slow?'

Atisha looked onto the surface of the water in the bowl, away from her own eyes which she'd been painting, into the eyes of her friend. Even in the blurring of the liquid mirror, she could see that Asaya had overdone hers again. The purple stain circles behind them had the reverse effect than the one intended, making the actual eye look small rather than large. But there was no telling her. 'This is how you catch a king,' Asaya had said, compounding her errors with too much scarlet on her lips, the paint made from a certain crushed beetle, and too bright a dusting of gold on cheekbones – which, in truth, were too deeply buried in flesh to save anyway. But Asaya was her best friend and a sweet girl, full of easy laughter when she wasn't preparing for her destiny, and Atisha would say nothing that would hurt her in any way.

'You are a treat fit for a god, my dove. Go swiftly, so you can find a place at the very front. I will follow.'

Asaya took a step, hesitated. 'I'll be by the puma statue, at its left paw. It's where he looks longest, old Gama says. Always.' She bit her lip. 'But the crowds! You'll never push your way through to it unless you come soon.'

'Then I will. Go! Go!'

Asaya went. When her friend's steps had faded, Atisha looked back on the water's surface, stuck out her tongue, picked up a wet cloth and used it to wipe all paint and stain away. Her mother, gone to watch the procession, would be especially annoyed.

Rising, she shed the little she was wearing. Old Gama had also said that it would be an especially fertile year – a year, in fact, of lust, advising that all should dress to emphasise their womanly youth. She had – so now she unwound the chest cloth that had bound and lifted her breasts, followed by the loin cloth that had emphasised the swell of her hips and concealed little else, and dropped both of them to the floor.

The music of the procession was drawing ever nearer. Swiftly dressing in her simple short skirt, her long-sleeved llama-wool shirt, and her scuffed knee boots, she thrust her obsidian dagger through her belt, and went out through the back door.

A growl greeted her, followed by a whine of pleasure. 'Come, Fant,' she said, bending down and releasing the hound's leash. He gambolled about her legs, giving little barks. All dogs were meant to be tethered for the duration of the festival, the penalties for not restraining them costly. She was not going to the arena, though, but the opposite way, up into the hills. And since there had been sightings of pumas, prowling close, daring and desperate after a tough winter and lean spring, she would need her dog. 'Fant,' she said, grabbing

26

him by the muzzle and staring into his velvet brown eyes, 'shall we go and see a god? Shall we, puppy?'

The hills rose steeply from the back of her family's plot of maize, gourds and potato. Deer paths crisscrossed the slopes, but Fant seemed to sense which one she had chosen today and Atisha climbed fast after him; breathing hard, she soon crested a small ridge, turning left along it. This trail ran parallel to her town's main – only – road. She could not see it through its screen of thick brush but she could clearly hear the Fire King's procession upon it: the deep bass notes of the hollowed logs, the wooden trumpets, the strum of thick strings on sea-turtle shells, the beat of sticks on huge hide drums, the drone of organs, their bladders expelling air. Under it all, the bird-like twitter of a thousand voices. She knew she could never distinguish a single one but fancied she could – Asaya's. 'Which one do you think he is? That one with all the muscles? Or him with all the gold? Here, Lord! Look here! Choose me!'

Atisha remembered some of what her friend would be seeing. The musicians, the men of the court, each of them masked and dressed as the ball players they also were, as if for the ultimate game. But she'd been five when the Festival of Choosing had last come to town twelve years before and her memories had blurred. She was looking forward to refreshing them.

Just as the procession began to enter the temple, she took another left path and swiftly reached her chosen spot – a rocky clearing, that directly faced the middle of the wide, many-columned white platform. The back row of stone benches was perhaps the height of twenty tall men beneath her, curving for about the same length, each row in front of it diminishing till the very last, which could seat only the elite of the village, the ten men of the council and their wives. The open space between them and the raised platform was crammed with all the maidens of the town, with still more shoving in. All but her.

The music had built to a huge, tuneless cacophony – which ended suddenly. The silence took her breath.

The craftsmen who had built the temple years before had known their business, had chosen the site partly because the hill on which she sat curved in such a way as to make any sounds performed, any ceremony enacted, wonderfully audible to all. She'd sat up there before and heard, with utter clarity, priests whispering the rites among the stone columns way at the back. Now, even though the dread of silent ceremony held all the people below, townsfolk and paraders, she still heard whispers, mainly from the maidens – 'Is it him? Is it him?' – as, singly, a group of masked men, one of whom had to be Intitepe himself, strode to centre stage. Each of them wore the ceremonial headdress, each face an animal mask – jaguar and puma, snake and eagle, others of fish, fowl, flesh, and all surmounted by a crest of the iridescent green and blue feathers taken from the osako bird; though under this magnificence they were dressed for the game, in simple brown tunics that reached to mid thigh and left the arms and shoulders, those muscular arms and shoulders, open to view and admiration.

All the men were tall, slim, strong – heyame, the game that was also worship, required the build. Well, she admitted to herself with a grin, peering from one beautiful bicep and muscled shoulder to the next, I suppose I wouldn't have minded being at the foot of the stone puma now for a closer look.

The stage, the seats, the open area, all were filled. A settling came, a moment of held silence, not even a whisper now. Then at a signal from one masked man in the very middle of the athletes' line – is that him? Atisha wondered, with the rest – noise burst forth from everywhere, music again from every instrument, ululation from every voice, from all upon the stage or before it, a great wave of sound that actually had her rocking backwards. Fant gave a little whimper, and took off into the bushes. He would scavenge around, not go far. He hated loud noise.

The athletes were tumblers too, the game demanded it. Removing their ornate masks – they wore simple, tight-fitting leather ones beneath, concealing their identity still – to strikes of drum and trumpet blast they rolled, leapt, tumbled, flew. Many used the way-tana, the sacrifice stone in the very centre of the stage, as a vaulting place, springing from it to flip through the air, even through the dancing flames of the brazier that stood beside the stone.

Atisha gasped. She'd been too young to be taken to the temple twelve years before. Now she watched men soar like birds, defying the pull of the earth. She clapped her hands at each feat, stunned, delighted.

'Have you guessed which one he is?'

The voice came from perhaps two arm-lengths away, loud because it had to be to top all that funnelled noise. She cried out, fell back, heels driving her away ... from the man she now saw, squatting as easily as she had been, hanging from his knees, hands folded before him.

'I am sorry to startle you. I did not know any way to make my presence known, other than speak.' He smiled. 'Are you all right?'

He gestured to her legs, which she'd dragged across the rock to get away. She stood, looked down, rubbed off traces of stone. There was one little scrape in three lines, colouring red. 'I'll live,' she grumbled.

'I am glad to hear it.' His voice still had a smile in it though his face was serious. She studied that. It was ordinary, like his dress – a simple if well-made llama-wool tunic that reached to his knees and covered his shoulders halfway down his upper arm. It had a band of deep crimson around each edge, the colour denoting him as a scribe of some sort, a man of learning. A city man, for certain, with features that were leaner than those of the men of her lowland town, a smaller nose and his skin a lighter shade of brown. His hair was cut short in the city style, with a little grey at the temples and dusted through the black. His eyes were grey too, a thing unseen in the town, the province. Her father, his friends ... everyone had brown eyes, including her.

She squatted again, keeping the new distance between them. 'You are of the court,' she said.

'I am.'

'Then why are you not below?'

'I have taken part in so many ceremonies. To be truthful, I find them dull. I prefer to watch only a little – and look for plants. See?' He opened his folded hands. In them were five small prickly balls, the size of sparrow's eggs. 'Do you know these?'

She did. They were a muddy brown but as they grew and put out stems they would change into a range of vivid greens and blues. At this early stage, they were known by a rude name to do with a youth's changing anatomy. She looked up, saw a smile in his eyes, as if he knew her thoughts. Frowned at the idea. 'I do,' she answered. 'Paytaza.'

'When the plant is older, its sap holds healing properties. At least that is what I think. I am experimenting.'

'Are you a healer?'

'Sometimes. It is more a pastime.' He opened a small leather satchel at his waist, dropped the plants in. 'Though I think—'

A deep-throated growl cut off his words – and the next moment Fant was there, teeth bared, hackles raised, eyes wide and filled with menace. The man's own eyes widened – though, she noticed, did not fill with fear and he did not rise from his crouch. 'My,' he said, 'but aren't you the fierce one?'

He stretched out a hand towards the drooling jaws and Atisha wanted to cry a warning. Not for him so much – but it wouldn't do her or her family much good when Fant took a finger, as he had done to someone who'd threatened her before. That had been a fellow farmer though, not a man of the court. The least this would mean was the dog's death. But she found she couldn't make a sound, held, as Fant was held, by the gesture the man now made – a swivel at the wrist and a slow unfurling of fingers, one at a time. 'There,' he

30

said, reaching further, fingers fully splayed now as Fant gave a small whimper, stuck out his tongue – and licked.

She found words. 'I . . . I have never seen that. Fant is not usually so friendly.'

'Fant? A good name.' He shrugged. 'I have had many dogs over the years.' The man turned his hand, palm up, and the dog stopped licking to lay his muzzle upon it.

'Fant!' she called sharply, suddenly annoyed. The dog jumped, then slunk over, dropped at her feet, and lay there twitching.

The man pulled back his hand. 'So we know why I am here,' he said, 'but why are you? You should be below, should you not?'

'It's a better view from here.'

'Not for Intitepe. The fire king has good eyes but not even he could judge you up here.'

Her annoyance, at this man's calm, at Fant's meek surrender to him, was with her still. 'Perhaps I do not wish to be judged,' she replied. 'I am, after all, not a llama.'

She turned back to the temple below, to the men leaping ever more frenziedly to a rising tempo in the music. His voice came. 'No,' he replied softly, 'that you are not.'

She didn't look, but felt his eyes on her, over her. She sat, drew her legs up to her chin and her skirt as far over them as it would reach, wrapped her arms around them, focused on the crowd, swaying in time, clapping, chanting, part of the ceremony too, filling with a tension, yearning for a release.

He spoke again. 'I must return. I have a small part to play in what follows and the king does not like delays. He can be most ill-tempered about it.' Atisha didn't turn, but saw him rise out of the corner of her eye. 'Will you come with me? There is still time to put yourself in the fire king's vision.'

She still did not look, just said, 'I am not dressed correctly. I am not wearing enough paint.'

A soft chuckle came. 'As long as I have known him, I don't think

I've ever known Intitepe's choice to be swayed … by paint.' A pause, then, 'Maid?'

It was a command to look, and though she wanted not to, she found she couldn't resist, just as Fant had been unable not to lay his head on this man's hand. And when she'd turned he asked, 'What is your name?'

She didn't want to tell him. But again she found she couldn't stop herself. 'Atisha,' she said.

'Atisha.' He bowed his head. 'It has been an honour.'

He was gone, slipping through a bush. Fant rose, shook himself from nose to tail tip, went to the bush he'd vanished through, lifted his leg and pissed. 'Oh,' Atisha said, 'aren't you brave now?'

She looked again to the temple below; but her eyes were unfocused, and for a long while she saw only a blur of leaping shapes; even the music, still rising in pace and pitch, appeared foggy to her now. He took my name, she thought. He didn't give me his in return.

The music played ever more frenziedly, the tumblers kept tumbling. Then, suddenly, loud cymbals crashed, the music ceased, bringing focus to her ears and eyes. The athletes moved to the back, and three priests came forward. Two of them held a mountain sheep, a full-grown ram, dragging it to the waytana and up a ramp to the stone's red-stained summit. There the beast stood, its thick horns curling like a crown, king of its world and fearless despite the crowds. It had been kept for the years since its capture in idleness, groomed and hand fed, only for this moment.

The third priest wore long purple robes and an ocelot mask. In his left hand he held a staff of blackwood, his own height tall, surmounted by a face that matched his mask. In his right hand he held an obsidian dagger. Handing his staff to a servant who crouched nearby, he raised the dagger high.

The crowd was utterly silent. The earth seemed stilled, with only the faintest of breezes sighing though the stone columns. The high priest nodded and the two others threw the ram onto its back. Only

32

now did it struggle. But the men were strong and skilled, splaying the beast's limbs, avoiding its sweeping horns. Stepping close, the high priest plunged the dagger down.

Blood spurted in a great arc, reddening the faces of the other priests, reaching the front ranks of the maidens pressed below, who groaned but did not cry out. For a few moments the only sounds were the squeals of the dying beast and the breeze which had strengthened and was now moving in the flags.

The priest delved, sliced ... then ripped the heart out. He turned back to the crowd, raising the organ high into the air as the animal behind him shuddered into stillness. When its last twitch came, the priest lifted the heart yet higher then hurled it into the brazier. Coals spattered, flames shot to the sky. Yet the smoke that came was not grey but yellow and red. The crowd cried out at that, and the priest, taking back his blackwood staff, raised it high and shouted, 'Colours of fire, colours of the sun, colours of the burning mountain. The gods have spoken.' Then rapping his staff three times onto the stone of the platform, he began to intone the prayer all knew.

'Toluc, Fire Mountain,
Mother, father, brother God,
Seed giver, life giver, heat giver,
Hear our prayers.'

Atisha murmured the response with the crowd. 'Hear all our prayers.' Beside her Fant gave a little growl, as if responding too.

The priest stepped back. One of the twelve now walked forward, and the people gasped as one at the approach of their king who was also their god. Strange, she thought, leaning forward. I didn't notice anyone in a condor mask before.

Other than that, he was no different from the other ball players, in his simple tunic. And yet he was completely different. For he was Intitepe, the Immortal, twin god with Toluc the volcano, and Atisha found herself standing with no memory of the action of it, wondering how she hadn't distinguished him straight away from the others, so

33

distinct was his power. She could see waves of colour surrounding him now, as if he had tethered a rainbow. When he raised his arms, purple, green, red, blue and violet wings rose with them, as if the condor would take flight. Suddenly, keenly, Atisha regretted her choice, the need to be apart, beyond another's choosing. Beyond his. For the eyes of the condor, most far-seeing of all birds – else why did it rise in the sky so high? – were lowered now to the young women surging forward, with their arms thrust out in appeal. She could be among them but she wasn't. She was, as she so often was, above, separate, removed.

Still, his words reached her clear and clean. 'It is the time of choice,' Intitepe said, his deep voice flowing. 'A hard, hard choice, when the beauty and intelligence of the maids of this province are so multiplied before me.'

It was a formula, she was sure, repeated in all twelve provinces, every twelve years, when this moment came. And yet he said it as if for the first time.

He gave a sigh. 'Alas, I may choose only one. And I have. I choose—'

The maidens pressed forward. Atisha leaned, as close to the cliff edge as she could without toppling over it.

'I choose—'

His voice sang out. Two of the other athletes came forward, reaching up to each side of the condor headdress, laying their hands on it. Intitepe clasped his own hands before him, as if in a prayer to his brother in the sky, the sun. Then he opened them, and raised them over the crowd. All waited for them to lower in that breathless moment of choice. Instead, they kept rising, up, up, up above all the heads, colour flowing in continuous waves from each arm, focusing like a beam of irresistible power sent up the mountain.

'I choose ... You!'

The coloured waves hit her and she reeled, staggered back, somehow did not fall. Looked again to see the two men beside Intitepe remove

34

the condor headdress in one sharp lift. She could see, clearly again now, the faces in the crowd all turned to gaze up at her in wonder, rage, shock. That shock a match for hers as she looked into eyes that she knew, even if she could not see them from there, were a special kind of grey. For they belonged to the man who'd sat beside her. The man who was also a god and who spoke again now.

'I choose you ... Atisha.'

The cramps hit her, in a gut-twisting, savage, sudden wave, and she cried out. A woman was there, instantly. Atisha did not know her, nor any other in the temple of birth. She knew why that must be. If the decision of the gods went against her, there would be no friend to pity her or, worse, attempt to give her aid.

It did not mean they were unkind. 'How goes it, little doe?' asked the one with lines made by smiling and age around her eyes, crouching beside the couch.

'I don't know. Aaah!' Atisha bent at the sudden force of the pain. 'I think it may be close.'

'Time to bring you to the pool, then.'

The pain doubled as they helped her stand, another older woman coming to support her on the other side. But when the wave eased a little, enough, Atisha pushed her gently away, bent and snatched up the one thing she'd brought from the palace to the temple – a puma, the length of her forearm, made from llama skin and its wool, and stuffed with river reeds.

The older woman smiled. 'I can bring your poppet, child,' she said.

'Thank you. I have it.'

Tucking it under her arm, she let the women help her towards the pool. The pain was intense, but there was one tiny, tiny hope in it: the hardness under her arm, pressed into her side – for within the puma was a dagger with a razored edge.

35

They removed her shift, lowered her into the pool. The water was beautifully warm and eased, for a brief moment, the terrible pains in her back. A moment to pray again.

Please, Alam, goddess, please, she said, but only in her head, the thought directed inwards.

Yet even as she prayed for her child, Atisha also prayed for something different – strength and courage. She knew that, over the years – the centuries! – and in this same place, others would have prayed the same; others might also have hidden, beside the birthing pool, an obsidian dagger. There were no tales of any succeeding in using it.

Perhaps that means it is my time, she thought, and prayed again.

The cramps returned, harder, much harder. She let out a cry – and heard its echo, slipping her again into memory. For the last time she had made love to Intitepe had been in this same pool. Most of the time the building was used for pleasure, not royal birth. Aztapi, the blue moon, had risen and fallen six times since that night …

She'd been atop him as she liked to be, as he liked her to be, the pressure that had been building within her for the hours that they had made love, that had been released in smaller waves before, let go now in one huge surge, like the mountain of water that would sometimes crash upon the coast after an earthquake. Her cry was loud, unrestrained; his shorter, quieter – for the pool opened to the sky and the valley below and he had told her once that he did not think his people wanted to hear their god making love and taking the same pleasure in it as ordinary people.

She loved hearing him, feeling him, seeing the release in his slate eyes. Since coming to the city, after the great ceremony of joining, they had made love often. Though not, at the beginning, often enough; for he had eleven other maidens to accommodate. Yet as the blue moon waxed and waned, she'd been sent for more and more frequently, until it became clear to all that she was 'the One'. He still occasionally took another, had to, to keep the peace in the marana, the house of Chosen Women. On those nights Atisha slept alone and, sometimes, usually, wept. Always, though, he sent for her the next day, and she forgot her tears in their joys, and their joined bodies.

Sometimes, too, he went away. His empire was vast, and in far corners of it farmers got angry or minor lords ambitious. A while before he'd been going to deal with one in Palaga, the northernmost province, and he did not know for how long. She'd wept at the news; couldn't bear the thought of not touching, of not being touched, before he left. So she came to him when she should not have – for all in the house of women knew their most fertile times and were careful. Now, after three full passages of aztapi he'd returned and sent for her straight away. To her great joy. To her greatest fear.

Because tonight was different. While making love with him, she'd been as lost as she ever was, could almost forget. Now, slipping down beside him into the pool, she could only remember.

'My heart,' Intitepe said, opening his arms. She went straight to her place, her cheek against his shoulder, his left arm enfolding her. Pressed against him so she could feel his heart, its rapid beat, slowing, slowing. 'Do you see it?' he said, and she looked up at him, as he nodded again towards the sky. She followed his gaze, tried to pick the one light out of the myriad there this night. Frowned. He laughed, and reached a finger to stroke away the lines on her forehead. 'Remember, my love. Find the Spider, its left eye, the leg below that. Do you see?'

'Yes.'

'Follow the leg down, past the cluster of seven monkeys?'

'I see them.'

'There. The brightest one. The one I named for you. At-i-sha.' He drew out her name, relishing it. 'You are immortal too now, for you will for ever be remembered in the skies.'

When he'd first told her, first helped her trace the stars and find the one he'd chosen for her, she'd been overjoyed. Now, with what she had to tell him tonight, joy had gone. Yet she couldn't speak of it. Not yet. So instead she said, 'I hope my star is far enough away from all the others you have named. I wouldn't want you getting confused when you look at it in a hundred years and think of someone else.'

Sometimes, when she dared to raise his past, he would get ... not angry, he was rarely that, but distant, distant as those stars. Now, though, that laugh came again. 'Ah, my puma,' he replied. 'I knew from our first conversation upon that hilltop that you would never simply accept and let things pass.'

'As other star-named women have done?'

She said it sharply, and he moved away from her a little so he could look at her. His eyes held no laughter now. 'I have told you that I name very few. Only the One, and not even many of them.' He looked skywards again. 'But you also have always known the sweet sadness of this.' He sighed. 'I am the fire king, immortal. Perhaps I age but if I do, so, so slowly, whereas you—' He broke off and looked down at her again. 'I cannot love you for ever. But I can love you completely now, Atisha. And see you for ever in the stars.'

'I know. I know!' she said fiercely, pulling him close again, feeling for his heart. She knew he loved her, as he had few others. So maybe, maybe it was time for her news? But still she couldn't speak directly to it, not yet. She had to ask something first. Had to.

'But you don't only see love in the stars, do you? You see death there too.'

He stiffened, looked up. She thought he might try to push her away, so she dug in deeper. 'You wish to speak of this now?' His tone was cold. 'After we—'

He did not like to talk of it. Tonight, she needed to make him. 'Yes. I need to understand. That's all I have ever needed to do, with everything. It is who I am. It is why I believe you chose me, over all

38

the prettier girls.' She reached up, took his jaw, turned him to her. 'Tell me.'

The jaw in her hand clenched – but he did not turn away. 'I have named a star for each of my dead sons.'

She had to make him say it. Tonight, she had to. 'The sons you killed.'

He flinched but still did not look away. 'The sons I killed.'

She was the one who had to look away. From the pain in the grey eyes she loved. 'Why?' she murmured. 'I do not understand.'

'Of course you do. Because of the prophecy.' He did move away then, rose to look down on her, water running from his long, slim, muscled body. 'You know this.' Yet even though he knew she did, he repeated it anyway, as if repeating it made it even more true. His tone had none of his honeyed warmth now, was as frigid as the snows on the southern mountains. 'Saroc, Priest-king and my immortal enemy, before I threw him into the mouth of Toluc, my brother god, to dissolve his flesh for ever, prophesied that a son of mine would do the same to me – just as I did to my own father.' He took a deep breath. 'So I hunted down and killed every one of my seven sons. Threw them into Toluc's destroying flames – and named a star for each one. I took their lives – and gave them immortality. For now they too live for ever in the night sky.'

She wanted him to stop. Could not let him. 'And if a woman bears you a son, you give that baby to the flames too ...'

'I do not. The priest does. I—' He broke off, looked hard at her, his jaw clenching. 'By Atoc's five wounds why do you talk of this now? Why?'

He was never angry with her – rarely with anyone, that she'd witnessed. What did a god who had everything need with anger? But she saw fury now, quailed before it, the flames in his eye, in his voice, his whole body rigid. She wanted nothing more than to sink back, touch him, calm him, begin to slowly make love to him again, lose herself in that, in him, under the stars. But death was in them

39

now as well as love and she had to know. 'So this is the last of it, that I don't understand,' she whispered. 'Answer me this and I will let it be.' She fixed him with her gaze. 'If you believe in the prophecy enough to kill every son, how can you not believe that it will come true, despite all your killing?'

He was the fire god. Immortal, with the wisdom of five centuries of life lived, and the certainty of countless more to come. She knew he must already have considered this, every time he was forced to, as she had forced him to this night. And looking up into his eyes now, she saw that he had, for there was fear in them, a moment of weakness in one who never showed any. And his vulnerability in that moment overwhelmed her, for though he was a god he was also a man, just a man.

She rose up, engulfed him in her arms, held his frozen body tight to her, tried to melt him. Before she knew him she had accepted, as all in the empire accepted, those occasional sacrifices, the climax of great ceremonies. Indeed, she had believed, as all believed, that his brother gods in the sky had only sent him a son to be sacrificed. A price, a terrible but holy price to be paid for a realm without war, without slavery, with abundance for all. The babies made the lava of Toluc rich with their bones, their flesh, their blood; and the lava enriched the land.

She had believed in it – until it was her womb that was filled. Until it was her who might bear a son, only to see that son cast into fire. From the moment she felt life stir inside her, she believed it no more.

He began to shake. And – a miracle! – he was crying. Yet from his sadness she took a joy. For these tears could only mean one thing: that he loved her enough to do what must be done. To change the way it had always been. She would be a star for ever but their son never would be.

She pulled away from him then, looked deep into the flowing eyes, with love, that love reflected back. She knew, she was certain *now, had seen the man-god's sadness. Was certain too that she had discovered the way to banish it in him for ever. His At-ish-a. So when she said, 'I am with child,' she said it in joy not fear.*

He started. His arms rose and fell. He stared at her for a long moment, his face, his eyes unchanging. She could feel both their hearts now, beating faster. When at last he spoke, there was neither honey nor ice in his voice. 'You are certain?'

'Yes.'

'How?'

She smiled. 'You know how, my love.'

'You mistook your times?'

'I did. It was the night before you went to campaign in the north. You sent for me. I ... I had to come.'

'And will you ... ?' He paused, swallowed. 'Will you have it?'

She'd considered it. There were ways. But she felt the joy still. 'Oh yes,' she cried. 'Yes I will!'

He stared at her for a moment longer. Then he nodded, looked above her, then back down. His eyes were filled with infinite kindness when he reached his hand to touch her cheek. She laid her face in it and closed her eyes, waiting for the words that would change the world.

'Goodbye, At-ish-a,' he said.

She opened her eyes. He untangled from her, stepped from the pool. She watched him, her own words frozen by the ones he'd spoken. Only when he reached the door of the chamber did she rise, cry out, 'Wait! Wait, my love!' But he did not pause, did not look back, and by the time she'd grabbed her dress and run to the door, it was already closing, and the man closing it was a guard not a god, a guard who held a key, turning it now in the lock. And all her lamentations would not open it.

Her cries now in the birthing pool were wrenching, agony and terror combining. The two women, who had slipped in beside her, murmured encouragement.

'Yes, little one! Little doe, little puma. Push down, push. Yes. Push!'

She screamed – and the child came in a rush. Slipping into the waters, tethered to her by the cord, floating free, kicking even, driving itself through the pool, a water creature still. Moving and twisting so she could not see, could not answer the question and know their fate. 'Hold her,' she wept, wish and command both. 'Show me.'

The women were as anxious to know. One reached, lifted. All looked.

'It's a girl,' the one holding her cried in joy.

'No,' the other groaned, 'No, look! It's a boy.'

A new sound came – the scraping of a chair, pushed back. In the shadowed corner of the room, the woman with the raven's mask had risen and was coming forward.

Atisha peered, desperate to make sense of what she saw. Between the baby's legs was a protrusion. But it was rounded, not long, a bulb not a stem. Beneath it were sacks ... that looked like lips.

She shook her head, tried to clear her eyes, looked again. Nothing would resolve. A new voice came. 'Give him to me,' commanded the woman in the raven mask.

'No!' Atisha threw off the women still holding her. Though it was agony to move, though she knew that she would drag the child with her in the effort to reach the puma on the other side of the pool she had to try, she had to ...

'Wait!' the woman with the laugh lines around her eyes cried out. 'I have seen this once before, just once, in my village.' She still held the baby up, and turned her now to the masked figure looming above the pool. 'This child is not a boy. She is not a girl. This child is ... neither.'

Atisha looked again, at the wriggling, pink flesh before her. Saw what the woman saw, and didn't see. What was there and what was not. She half rose from the water. 'Neither. She is neither! See! See!' she cried. 'You cannot take her.'

The masked one bent to look. Spoke, though now her tone was hesitant. 'I will ... I will go to the palace. Keep the mother and ... that ... apart till I return.'

She went. The women did what they needed to do. Cut and bound the cord, helped Atisha pass all that was within her. The baby was taken, fully wailing now, its cries an agony for Atisha who was taken to another pool to be cleaned, then dried with soft cloths, wrapped in others. Though her every instinct made her want to rush across to her crying baby, she knew they wouldn't let her. Besides, now she could clutch the puma they'd brought her, gather her strength. If the word which came from the palace was the wrong one she would take her chance. She had made up her mind. She would kill if she had to, seize her child. Below the temple were paths she knew well. One led to the river. Boats were tied up there.

It didn't take long for the raven-masked woman to return. Atisha would have liked longer but, painfully, she sat up, put her legs to the floor, reached into the mouth of the puma to clasp the comforting coldness of sharpened stone.

The woman came to the middle of the room. 'Bring the child here,' she commanded. She was obeyed immediately, the kind woman bringing the baby, who was still crying. She held Atisha's child up.

But the masked woman didn't reach for it. 'Intitepe, Fire God and Fire King, in his wisdom has decreed ...' she paused a moment and looked straight at Atisha, who gripped the knife even harder, 'that you may keep the child.' To her gasp and the gasps of all the other women there, she continued. 'For now. When you are well enough to travel, you will be taken south, to the City of Women. There you will await,' she glanced at the baby again, 'developments.' She nodded. 'Give the mother her baby.'

Atisha sat, dropped her shift off her shoulders. The wailing child was placed in her arms, and she put it straight to her breast. There was a fumbling, a moment of uncertainty displaced by joy as the babe latched on and began to vigorously suckle.

With the two women cooing beside her, Atisha could only stare at the question in her arms. Yet she had an answer of her own, at least for now, for she had a little time. How much, she couldn't know. She was bound for the City of Women. There she would regain her strength, keep her blade sharp, prepare for any *development* that came. Because this she knew, clearly, certainly:

No man, king, god – all three! – was going to throw *her* baby into a volcano.

3
Luck of the Gods

Far down the fjord, at the base of a glacier – a place the sun had not reached for five months – lay the town of Askaug. Winter still gripped it, snow banked to the height of a tall man against every wall, and icicles the length and heft of boar spears descended from the turf roof of the largest building there.

The occupants of the mead hall were not cold. Indeed, many had thrown off their bear-skin cloaks and wool shirts to expose their red-pelted chests to the huge fires. Some of the men were completely naked, provoking awe or disparagement depending on what was revealed. The ones recently returned from a cooling roll in the snow banks were especially mocked.

Most nights a good crowd gathered in the hall. This night only the very old or very young were absent. Despite the contrary evidence of snow and ice outside, tomorrow would be the first day of spring. It had to be celebrated – in drink, in roasted meats, in tales of war and magic, sung and spoken. As words and liquor flowed, old stories were remade, new ones created. Later, furs would be pressed down by heated bodies and another generation begun.

There was an expression in Midgarth, spoken during the day of preparation, anticipating the night's raucous celebrations: 'The mouse on the roof beam will look down on some fine doings this night.' Like all such Midgarth expressions, it was not meant to be true, merely a representation of something else. Yet this night it *was* true. For there was a mouse up there, gazing upon all the doings below.

A mouse who was also a god.

His name was Luck. He'd often wondered if that was a joke his parents had made when they name-gave him. Or had it been a ward against a doubtful future? That if the scrawny baby born that day with the outsized back, the stumpy right arm and shorter right leg, was to survive he would need plenty of good fortune, so they might as well begin with his naming? He'd been unable to ask them for they'd died shortly before his second birthday, long before he could talk, which he then held off doing till he was nearly ten. Died violently on this very day, the one before the spring came.

Four hundred years ago.

Congratulations on the day, Luck thought, bitterly, as he did every year. Luck was never lonelier than when he was in company; even more so at this feast which seemed a mockery, to him, of all he was. It was everything he didn't like to do. Drink, because he'd learned from too many attempts to disprove it that he did not have his people's traditional capacity for mead or ale. Fatty meat, which revolted him. Tale-telling, which always dealt with heroes, and he was palpably not one of those. And, especially, the carnal acts that followed. There was a freedom on this day, amongst a people who were quite free about such matters anyway. Husbands abandoned wives, wives sought out old lovers or took new ones. Since nearly all was forgotten the next day, there was little need to forgive. There was a reason the celebration of the season's change was known as Oblivion's Feast.

Yet he liked to observe, part and apart too. Many of these people would visit him in the next weeks, seeking to learn their fortune for the coming year. And though he did see visions – in the tala stones he threw, in birds' flights, in the shimmer of light on water – he also knew that visions were only one portion of any person's fate. Who they were now, what they brought to their question, that was also a way in for him. So he watched, and took note of many things.

Now, as Luck gazed down on the crowd, he singled out his fellow gods – the three who lived in the town, and the one who was visiting, Einar the Black. Watched how the Widow Agnetha was keeping his goblet filled, his platter crammed, his back and thighs ... kneaded. If a mouse could smile, he did then, for Agnetha had come to Luck for a telling the week before. He'd cast his tala, and the stones with the different shapes carved upon them had shown him, as clear as fjord water, that if she took a god to her bed during the feast she'd have triplets, each a hulking son. Since her husband had been killed a year before by one of the ferocious bears who shared the land, she would need all the help in her business – the dyeing of cloth – that she could get.

But the resident gods of Askaug would not play their part in this prophecy. Luck's brother, Bjorn Swiftsword – they did not share parents but all the gods in a village were brothers – Bjorn was older by a mere quarter century, and the handsomest being, man or immortal, in the district, perhaps in the whole of Midgarth. He always had his pick of the maidens at Oblivion's Feast – and rarely restricted himself to one. Five were competing for him now. He could have one, all, or none. *Though if he keeps drinking mead at this rate*, Luck thought, *none is the likeliest outcome.*

Luck looked now at his other brother-god, the eldest, Hovard; who, if he was not as handsome as Bjorn, could have twice as many lovers for his silver tongue, his golden laugh and the simple reason that he cared. Listened and cared and

47

so was irresistible. Yet Hovard would have none, even with the dispensation of the night. He would leave with the one he came with. Loved her alone, most unusual amongst the gods. As she loved him.

Freya.

She'd been there a moment before, sitting at Hovard's right hand. Now that space was empty. Luck sought her among the throng, did not find her. Because, he suddenly realised, she was now sitting beside him on the beam. Not as a woman, nor a god, both of which she was.

As a cat.

When a god dissolved their own body into that of a living beast, the thrill of it was in the sharing of that beast's whole being, its lusts, hungers and all. Instincts too. Bears would snarl and charge to the fight when surprised and the god would often let the beast have its vicious way. Hawks would fold their wings and drop from danger, yet turn suddenly to the attack. Salmon would weave and flip through the water, exhilaration for the god within in every turn.

A mouse would run away.

So Luck turned as fast as the creature he possessed yearned to. Yet not fast enough to elude the paw that dropped hard onto his haunches. He felt the sudden prick of claws. 'Do not run off, little god,' Freya purred. 'I wish to talk to you.'

Instinct, once thwarted, soon passed. Now he did not seek escape; welcomed her paw on him, as he would her hand on his crooked back were they in human form. They sat in easy silence for a time, studying the crowd. Until Agnetha rose, took Einar the Black by the hand and led the visiting god from the hall.

'She goes to make her triplets.' Her voice was in his head, the way they spoke when they were animals. 'Did you not think of fulfilling the prophecy yourself?'

He smiled. 'Might that not be considered self-serving? "Find

48

a god to get your babies. Oh look! There's one right here!'"

If a cat could laugh, Freya did, an extended purr. 'Most gods are not so moral,' she said.

'Most gods are not shaped like me,' he replied, his smile gone.

A silence again. Then, 'You should take another. It's ten years since Gytta—'

'I want no other.' He took a breath, held it. I shouldn't speak it, he thought. Spoke it. 'None but you.'

She lifted her paw from his haunch. 'I have told you. You must not talk to me that way.'

'Because of Hovard? Or because I look like I do?'

'I will go.'

She rose, and headed, cat-graceful, along the beam. He called. 'Freya.'

She stopped but did not look back. 'Yes?'

'Do you think it strange that but one god visits us for the festival?'

'A little, yes. But the passes are still so thick with snow.'

'Which a god could fly over as eagle or run over as a winter-lean wolf.' He sniffed. 'Besides, there have been worse snows. Ten years ago, ten gods came. Even last year, four.'

'Maybe there are better feasts elsewhere.'

'Or maybe there are fewer gods.'

She turned back at that. 'What do you mean?'

'I have heard that some gods have vanished.'

'Heard?'

'Seen. In the mirror. In the waters. In my stones.'

A silence, then. 'It is hard for us to die.'

'Hard. Not impossible.'

'Then how are we dying?'

'I think ... I think someone may be killing us.'

She stared at him. 'That is hard too.'

'Hard. Not impossible.'

A longer silence. Then the cat took a step back towards him. 'What is it you have seen?'

He took a deep breath. 'I have not truly ... seen. I have felt ... a shadow only. Something ... something turning our way. In the east. Far in the east, beyond the strongest eagle's flight.'

'You are frightening me.'

'Good. I think you need to be afraid.' He looked down into the raucous crowd. 'I think we all do.'

The cat looked too. 'Shall I tell Hovard?'

'Not yet. He will want answers that I do not possess. Let me ... explore a little more. I may journey.'

'As man or beast?'

'Both. Though, as you know, I move swifter as a beast.'

'But not for long.' She turned back. 'How many days can you remain an animal?'

'A mouse? Many. A bear? Perhaps a day.' He sucked in air, let it whistle between his sharp teeth. 'They struggle to get their lives back, don't they? And the stronger they are, the swifter they expel us.'

'It is just as well. I sometimes think that it is they who possess us. If we sink too deep—' She laughed, but the cat she was just cried. 'Once it took me a week to get Hovard to give up being a wolf. I had to enter the body of a she-wolf in heat to make him.'

The cat cried again and the mouse turned away. 'Well,' he muttered, 'Hovard is Hovard.'

'He is. And see, he is missing me.'

She turned, went to the beam end. He called again, 'Take the cat with you, Freya,' but she entered the loft, didn't pause or acknowledge that she'd heard – though when she emerged a moment later onto a ladder as a woman, she was holding the cat in her arms. She stroked it as she crossed to Hovard, who greeted her with a kiss and filled her goblet. Freya set the cat down, raised the cup to her lover but didn't drink straight away. Instead, she looked up to the roof beam.

A mouse was still up there, cleaning its whiskers, witnessing the doings below. But the god had gone.

It was snowing again, huge flakes falling, already filling the boot prints of the visiting god Einar and his desirous partner. Agnetha's hut lay halfway between the hall and Luck's own on the edge of Askaug, so he began to follow along their path, his weaker right leg as always dragging a little, obliterating their tracks, leaving the long trough of his own. Icy white pressed against him and part of him wished he had stayed a mouse and now had fur to ward off the storm. He thought of going back – but it was hard on the god's body to inhabit a beast twice in a night. Besides, the village cats or a keen-eyed owl would have eyes out for a snack and it hurt to be struck by claws, to feel teeth sink in, the moment before he gave up the animal form and regained his own shape. Harder on the mouse, whose instincts might have warned against attack if it were not possessed by a distracted god.

As he limped along, Luck wondered again at something he'd never ceased wondering at, this power of transformation. He, who'd ever sought to know the world better, how every part of it worked, how those many parts were joined, had never fathomed how a god's body could vanish, how a god's spirit could enter a beast. It was so beyond all the other ways of nature that he observed. But Gudrun Gift-Bearer had left no explanations, only the gift itself. *If* she ever existed, Luck thought, stopping to catch breath and look up into the snow still falling. Sometimes he also wondered if the tale of Gudrun was just another story, invented before some hearth-fire long ago, to explain the unexplainable.

He shook his head. Even the one goblet of mead, the

necessary toast to the feast, had dulled him. And he needed to be clear. He had told Freya all he knew, all he'd seen, and it was little enough. When he got back to his hut, he would ask the stones once more, or seek shapes in a basin of water; try again to give substance to his fears. Something in the east, he'd said to her, but as to where and what, he had no more than his uncertain suspicions. And his dread. When he'd sought before, in stone or water, a sense of dread was truly all he'd understood.

He came to a cross-paths. Agnetha's hut was on one corner, the sign of her profession hanging from the eaves above the door: a twisted cloth, dyed in deepest indigo. As he looked at it, a faint cry reached him through the wind.

Yearning gripped him. Perhaps he *could* have offered himself to her, prophecy and its fulfilment, both. She'd probably have taken him, for the benefits he'd bring to her, the triplets he'd promised. She was also kind-hearted and would have thought it sad that he was alone on the feast night. But pity was something he'd seen in another's gaze from the first moment he could remember, and ever since in every stranger's eyes. Four hundred years of that and still he could not bear it. Only one person had ever looked at him without pity. One woman. His Gytta, a mortal, dead at sixty, and that ten long years ago, after the shortest forty years of his life.

He sniffed, took another step – and pulled up, face swivelling again to the hut. Another cry had stopped him – but this one had nothing of heat and passion in it. And hearing it, Luck moved as fast as his one strong leg would allow him to the hut's door. He did not know much about this Einar the Black, save that he was a god of the southern mountains and had arrived on eagle's wings, his customary transformation. He'd appeared a reasonable sort. But appearances deceived, especially among the shape-shifting gods. And Luck had not made his prophecy to see Agnetha – a decent, simple soul – hurt in any way.

Yet he paused at the door. He had to be sure. Despite his years he was inexperienced in the ways of love-making. With Gytta it had always been simple, easy, fulfilling. But he understood that some people took pleasure in different things, even painful things. So he bent an ear – and heard another cry, a moan of hurt and such terror, it had no pleasure in it, none. He also heard another sound. He'd heard it before, too often in fact, had never got used to it, as some did.

It was the noise a blade made slicing into flesh.

There was no time to call out for help. There was only time to take a deep breath, pull up the latch and throw open the door.

Agnetha's hut was crowded with things for her trade: cauldrons, ladles, undyed cloth and bundles of dried plants. A large bed occupied most of the room. At its foot, on the floor, Agnetha lay, eyes fluttering; a jagged gash across her brow leaked blood. On the bed were two men, joined. Einar the Black was below, face down with a hooded man on his back. It was if he were riding the god for he had Einar's long black hair gripped like a rein in one hand – and a saw-edged cleaver in his other. He was using it to cut the god's head off.

Luck was no more a fighter than he was a lover. But his people were, and there had been times over the centuries when he'd been unable to avoid combat. And he recognised that now was no time to pause – not with the stranger on the bed turning towards him, rising, cleaver held high.

Luck snatched up a pot, and hurled it. His one weak arm made the other all the stronger and the pot flew at the man, who managed to turn his head and take the blow on the shoulder. It must have hurt but he didn't even grunt, just dropped Einar and leapt off the bed to land lightly three paces away. Again Luck didn't hesitate, knew he couldn't. He might be small and misshapen but most of him was muscle, his weight concentrated.

Springing off his one good leg he closed the gap and drove his head into the man's belly.

They crashed back onto the bed, scrabbling over Agnetha who woke, moaned, then screamed. They fell onto Einar. He was unconscious and, in a glance, Luck noted the reason: his neck was sawn half through. The hooded man raised the cleaver – but he couldn't swing down the blade, Luck was too close. So instead he hammered its iron pommel straight down onto Luck's crooked back. He yelped, tried to burrow higher, reaching a hand for the man's eyes, but the shortness of his arm meant he couldn't make them. Another blow came, another, the pain extraordinary. Luck felt himself losing consciousness. Somehow he managed to get one flailing leg onto the bed's end board. Springing off that, he jabbed his fingers into the man's throat.

It wasn't the strongest of blows. But the man gasped, dropped the cleaver, placed his hands under Luck and heaved. He was strong, and threw Luck off the side of the bed. Luck landed hard but grabbed the first thing that came to hand, raised it to stop the blow he felt sure was going to come, as the man grabbed the cleaver again and lifted it high. Yet when Luck saw that he held only a wooden ladle, he also saw death descending in the razor-toothed blade. It was one of the very few ways to kill a god – cut off his head, take it far from the body, fast. He had proved, too late, that someone was indeed killing the gods – and knew that the murderer would make a double kill tonight.

'Stop!'

The cry came loud and sudden from the open doorway. Luck knew the voice. 'Freya!' he screamed. 'Run!'

But Freya was a goddess of warriors and she did not run from a fight. Drawing the dagger from her belt sheath she stepped in and dropped into the knife fighter's stance. At the same moment, Agnetha rolled away, stood, swayed, reached back and turned again with a carving knife in her hand.

The assassin stood on the bed, weapon high, his eyes shifting between the three now opposing him. Then fury took his face, not fear, and he leapt – straight towards Freya, standing before the open door.

'No!' Luck screamed.

Freya slipped sideways, the cleaver missing her by a thumb's width. The man did not stop to aim another blow, just ran on; but as he passed, Freya swayed back up and jammed her blade into his hip. He stumbled, did not fall. Was gone.

Freya stepped straight into the doorway, raised her knife to throw. 'No!' yelled Luck. 'I need him alive.'

He stood, limped towards the door, knowing it was useless, that even a wounded man would outrun him. Freya cried, 'Wait!' then, with her knife, sliced down her palm. Blood spurted and, pressing the red wetness to her eyes, she called once, clearly, 'Hovard!'

Luck was at the door, peering into the still fast-falling snow that hid everything – to sight but not to sound. So he heard the door of the mead hall crash open, the roars bursting out into the night. Heard his brother shout, 'You! Stop there! Stop!' Yet Luck had a raven's hearing and he heard something else too – the distinct sound of a throwing axe clearing the leather of its sheath.

'No,' he said again but he didn't shout it because he knew it was too late. He turned back to the bed. Einar's cut was bad, deep. It would have killed any mortal. But Luck could see, even now, the blood clotting. 'Hold his head,' he ordered Agnetha. 'Do not let him move.' Then he turned and, with Freya at his side, went down the track.

As they hurried side by side, she said, 'I was worried for you, I came to—'

'Thank all our gods that you did.'

Some people had brought rush torches from the hall. A circle had formed and Luck and Freya pushed between the backs to see Hovard and Bjorn, crouched over the body of the god-killer. 'A good throw, brother,' Bjorn exulted. 'Right between the shoulders.'

'Not such a good throw, brother,' said Luck, stepping between them. 'I wanted him alive.' Suddenly he felt immensely weary and he sat, careless of the snow.

Hovard looked down at him, and frowned. 'I assumed he was a thief, which is why he didn't stop. Why was it important to have him alive?'

'No thief,' Freya said. 'This man just tried to kill Einar the Black.'

'Why?'

'That's what I wanted to find out.' Luck sighed, came onto his knees. 'Roll his body over.'

Bjorn did as he asked. Luck pulled the man's hood back. His eyes were open. He looked surprised. His head was shaven, which never happened anywhere in Midgarth. His face was hairless too, also uncommon, and lean – whilst his eyes, beyond the surprise, were beyond dark – they were black. Not just the core. The whites too.

'Not from here. Or anywhere near.' Hovard leaned down to peer at the corpse. 'But where? And how did he get here?'

'Not a god,' said Bjorn, jamming his boot toe into the man's ribs. 'He'd be stirring about now.'

'Oh, he's dead.' Wearily, Luck stood, pulling himself up on Bjorn's arm. 'And how he got here is the first question.' He looked around at the concerned faces of the townsmen and women, spilled from the hall. 'He must have a boat hidden. Find it. Bring me anything in it.' As they moved away, he called after them, 'Open nothing!'

All the mortals scattered to the shore. Only the gods went back inside. They sat at one end of the central table, close to the hearth. 'Mead,' demanded Luck, and the other three raised their eyebrows – they knew his tastes – but Bjorn filled his goblet and theirs. Luck drank fast, then put down the empty vessel. The others didn't talk. They were looking at him, waiting while he did their thinking.

Eventually, a man came in – Ulrich the smith. 'We found his boat. Such a craft I have never seen.' He shook his head. 'They are carrying it up here. This was in it.'

He placed a bag on the table. Made of dark leather, the size of Luck's chest, it had a brass clasp and straps that would slip over someone's two shoulders. There was a shape incised again and again all over it, each the size of a thumb tip. Holding the bag up to the light, Luck saw that every one was a crudely depicted eye. He looked at the other gods then undid the clasp and reached inside.

The first object he pulled out was a small vial, made of thick, green glass, like the kind that sometimes washed up onto their shores, but finer. He could make out a viscous fluid within when he held the vial up to the firelight. It had a stopper fashioned from some pliable wood he didn't recognise. With some difficulty, he withdrew it – and all four leaned their faces away from the sudden, acrid waft. It made him dizzy too, the same mind-whirl he'd get just before a vision came. Luck stoppered the vial again, set it aside, wiped his running eyes, then delved into the bag a little more carefully.

A bundle of dried meat – elk, he thought – appeared next. Then an arm-length roll of soft, cured deerskin. Unrolling that, he grunted and held it up to the others.

'A drawing,' said Bjorn.

'But what are these ... flowing lines?' asked Freya.

'I think ...' Luck peered closer. 'I think they are like the marks

I carve onto my stones. My tala. Each one means something else. Many things else.'

'You are saying this man could look at these and … and comprehend them?' asked Bjorn. 'Like I would read the signs of coming storm in the clouds?'

'I think so, yes.'

'You are right and you are wrong,' said Hovard, picking up the skin, scanning it. 'Some of these marks you speak of could perhaps be understood only by him and the one who made them. But these other lines I can understand.' He tapped them. 'You know that when we plan an attack on another town, or consider an area of mountainside where we wish to drive the game, we trace the land in the dirt before we go?' They all nodded. 'This is like that. But not simple like that.' He spread the skin onto the table, laid his finger on it. 'This is our land. This here, that looks like a mouth? That's our fjord. This,' he tapped, 'is the glacier above us.'

Luck peered closer, whistled. 'You are right, brother. This is indeed a drawing of our land.'

'If that is so,' Freya turned the skin towards her, jabbed her finger near the top, 'then this is the mountain in the far east – the sleeping dragon, Molnalla, guardian and limit of our world. Impossible to climb, too high to fly over, even as an eagle. These waters that lap the northern shores? Impossible even for our mightiest ships to sail through. Many died trying to do so. Your parents—' She broke off then laid her finger on other lines beyond the dragon, before seeking Luck's eyes. 'But this man, or whoever made this, has marked a world beyond, one we cannot know. How could he do such a thing?'

A coldness came over Luck's heart as he looked back at her, then at each of them in turn. 'I think,' he replied softly, 'that someone may have found a way to climb the unclimbable mountains, or sail the unsailable seas.'

All four took sudden, sharp breaths. All four looked to the ceiling of the hall and through it to the skies. It was Hovard who spoke first, after a while. 'All knew this had to be possible. A barrier is just that – a thing that stops us going to the other side of it. There had to be other lands. And we all know our world has changed in the last fifty years. Longer, colder winters. Dryer summers. Storms of greater force than anyone has seen before.' He licked dry lips. 'If Luck is right, someone – this man at least – has used that change to find a way from his land to ours.'

'But this ... this is wonderful!' Bjorn poured himself more mead. 'Our world has always felt too small for our ambitions, you know this. We sail to fight our cousin folk of the Seven Isles with their gods, half a day away. We march for a week to take on the gods and men of the valley townships. We conquer, we lose, we die, we are reborn, we steal back the same old treasures. But if someone has figured out a way to come to us,' his eyes shone, 'then we can figure out a way to get to them. To go, explore ... conquer!' He raised his goblet high. 'Because we are immortal gods and this man was not, they will be sheep. No! Better: worthy enemies so we will win much glory.'

He drank half the draught, beamed at them. No one smiled back. 'Bjorn,' said Luck, 'your courage, as always, does you credit. It is a pity your brains have never been able to keep up.' He tapped the skin, his voice rising. 'They are already here. I suspect they have been coming for years. And, you fool, they have been killing us gods all that time.'

'What?' Hovard reached across the table, shook Luck's shoulder. 'What do you mean by that? How can you know?'

'I did not know. I suspected. The lack of gods at our feasts in recent years? Rumours from other towns? Something stirring in my tala stones, in the seeing waters?' Luck swallowed. 'But tonight I found the truth – when I saw that black-eyed killer trying to cut Einar's head from his shoulders.'

It silenced them all, even Bjorn. Luck reached once more into the bag – and this time his fingers touched something large, hard and so cold it almost burned. He pulled back his hand, took a deep breath, reached again – and pulled the hardness out, laying it swiftly on the table where it rolled before it settled.

It was a globe, the size of two folded fists, made of that same hard seaglass-like substance. Yet its outside was only one part of it – a shell, a skin, a container to hold what was within – which moved, writhed like smoke shifting above a fire, like a sea fog, full of twisting shapes and forms that broke apart to re-form as others.

Luck stared – and instinct took hold of him. Years, hundreds of them, so much time spent seeking what was not yet, in what was now. Predicting fates for gods and men, in the casting of stones, or peering into the seeing waters. The smoke within this globe was like them, a surface to be penetrated, and he suddenly, clearly, knew what he had to do.

The globe was attached to a flat piece of wood a finger thick. Setting that on the table, Luck sat, then reached for the glass vial. His voice when it came was thick, sluggish. He had already begun to sink deeper. 'Cover your mouths. Do not breathe in with me. I suspect that this is poison.' When the others had pulled up scarf or shirt, he unstoppered the vial and poured a single drop of liquid onto the globe.

He managed to stopper the bottle again and lay it down just before he dropped it. Slumping back, he stared into the smoke swirling ever faster within the glass. Shapes came, to vanish in the instant of recognition: a horse's head on the body of a man; the ruin of a ship of a type he'd never seen, scarcely afloat; a hole in a rock face with a bloody hand thrust through it. Lastly, lingeringly, a naked baby. He thought that the smoke was obscuring it, until he realised ... the child had no face. And then in the brief moment before the image vanished, he realised something else.

The child had no sex.

It was the last he saw, before the smoke darkened – then coiled like a column, like a water spout on the sea or a snow devil twisting across an ice field. It thickened – then vanished. In its place was a face. Not a child.

He filled the globe, this man with his bald head, and his black eyes set deep in folds of flesh. When he opened his mouth, he revealed teeth that were also black and sharpened to points. Full lips shaped a word, coming on a voice that was liquid and rich.

'Alon?' the man said.

Luck gasped. He could not speak, could barely think, could only stare, as the shaven man's eyes focused, then pierced Luck's own as if his look was made of needles. Then something contracted at the heart of the blackness. Hissing, the man merged into the smoke, leaving nothing but smoke behind.

Luck toppled back. He was aware of hands catching him, lowering him to the floor. As the darkness came, he realised he had found Oblivion at its feast after all. Though this was not the one all sought, an easeful nothing brought by love-making and mead. This was filled with hideous shapes moving through gloom, and with an evil of a depth and weight such as he had never known. All centred in the face of a shaven, black-eyed, black-toothed man.

'He saw me.'

'Your killer?'

'No, horse king. Alon is dead.'

'How can you know that?'

'Because it was another who saw me. Alon would never have allowed that if he were alive.'

A woman's voice. 'You told us only holy men could use the smoke. It is why you denied it to us, your allies.'

'It is true. So perhaps, in his way, the man I saw is holy too.'

A snort. 'In his way? Do you mean one of their gods?'

'Perhaps. Perhaps the one we've heard about.'

'Blasphemy!' A different voice spat the word. 'There is only one god.'

'We know that, seafarer. The ignorant do not.'

'They will learn.'

'They will.' A silence, then, 'This concerns me. If Alon failed, or succeeded and then was caught, they may have finally discovered that we are killing their gods.'

'Men, I keep telling you! Not gods. Just because they are immortal ...'

'Immortals who can die. And fewer of them now. But enough? Have we killed enough?'

'It was your idea, priest. That if we reduced their number, the few who remained would not be enough to unite a people who never unite, who only fight amongst themselves. Who, disunited, would never be able to resist us.' The woman snorted. 'I never thought it necessary.'

'I did. It was a good idea, huntress. For our northern campaign. Now we will have to hope we have done enough – and accelerate our other plans.'

'How? The tunnel into Corinthium is not close to ready. A thin man can squeeze through, as the one we sent did, but ...'

'... not a horse, king. And we know you go nowhere without your horses.'

'We cannot conquer without them—'

'How long?'

'We already kill a dozen slaves a day in those mines.'

'Kill more. Kill them quicker. How long?'

A sucking of lips. 'Two passes of the blue moon.'

'Hmm. Seafarer, will your sea be sailable by then?'

'Perhaps. It would still be a risk.'

'It is all a risk.' A silence, then, 'This one I saw in the smoke. He was not physically strong, I felt. But his mind?' A deep breath. 'How many vessels were you going to take?'

'Fifty. Enough to conquer a divided land town by town.'

'Take a hundred. It may not be so divided by the time we reach it.'

'One hundred ships? That's a lot of men to raise in a short time.'

'Not when the prize is the whole world.'

'A whole world worth nothing unless the One is come.' It was the huntress who spoke and the other men joined her in her cry. 'Praise her. Praise him. The One!'

The rougher voice came again. 'Has my ship made the shores of Ometepe? Have you spoken to your emissary?'

'Who can tell of my sister Gistrane,' the woman said.

'And of my brother Korshak,' added the horse king. 'Have you heard?'

'Not in a week.' The man they called the priest sighed. 'The distances are vast, the storms between us … disruptive. I will try later. We will find each other eventually.'

'Do so. I cannot raise so many without knowing if the prophecy is true.'

'Have faith, seafarer.'

'I have the faith, priest. But my sailors are simple men and need some proof.'

'Then I shall get it for them.' A pause. 'And if I do? Can we advance? Complete the tunnel through the southern mountains? Sail through the mountainous seas in the north? Send the second fleet to Ometepe?'

'By when?'

'The zenith of the moons. The first day of summer.'

Three hisses. Then one voice, the woman's.

'Yes! Yes, by the One, let us begin the hunt.'

Another: 'Yes, by the One, we will ride.'

Another: 'Yes, by the One, yes! We will sail.'

'Yes, huntress. Yes, horse king. Yes, seafarer. And before your warriors we priests will raise the banners of our god.' Fleshy lips parted over black teeth. 'By the One, when the two moons ride equally in the sky, on that first day of summer,' black eyes glowed, 'let us go and conquer the world.'

4

The Sanctum on the Hill

Lara lay on the bowsprit of the ship, her hands gripping the netting, her thighs the wood, the water a cascade of foam a spear's length below her. She'd found this perch early in the voyage, a stormy refuge. At first she'd seek it to ease her sickness, for she'd never been to sea and the motion hit her hard. The cool spray and wind in her face, the ability to void out of sight of others the little she managed to get down of the ship's foul food, all made it a good place. Yet even after she'd gained control, and the nausea had passed, she still returned there several times a day and the rougher the sea the better. As the Black Cormorant bucked, rose and fell, it reminded her of riding Saipha, whose ears always stuck straight up and so was named for that horned moon. The pony had been her lover's first gift to her. He'd taught her to ride – but within a year she was near as good as her tutor and they'd race laughing over waves, though these were made not of water but of sand on the desert floor. She'd laugh sometimes now, as the boat leapt and landed. But she wouldn't laugh long, remembering too soon where this race was headed, before remembering the other reason she came there. Not just to be alone. To be away from the man in the cabin below, and the fear in his eyes.

'Ferros!' she shouted into the wind, knowing that would carry it beyond the hearing of any sailor or passenger. She also came here to say the things she could not say to him in that cabin. From the moment they'd met five years before they'd always said anything, everything. To not be able to or, if she tried, to get no response was a pain greater than she'd ever known. So she gave words here each day, to wind and water.

'Ferros.' She said it this time as a caress not a blow. 'Where have you gone? How far away are you?'

It had changed everything, the revelation of his immortality. For him entirely, of course, but for her as well. She'd understood the change as soon as she'd seen him on that infirmary cot; one far greater than the scar caused by an arrow that had ripped out his eye, ripped away his old life. Even in the three weeks of sailing, the scar was almost gone, the eye regrown and returned to its same, beautiful cerulean blue. But the old look within it – the self-belief, the swagger that she mocked sometimes and always adored – that had not healed, that had not returned.

The ship rose and fell, a set of ever growing waves drenching her. But the autumn had continued near as hot as summer, and the water was a cool relief. She'd tried to persuade him to take his turn there, but he claimed he had no time, he must be at his books. General Olankios had sent a tutor to accompany Ferros, a Timian monk called Gan; for Ferros had left schooling to join his regiment at ten and neglected all but war studies since. Now, for what awaited him in Corinthium, he would need to know more about books and quills and less about maps and blades.

Corinthium! She peered forward, as the seventh big wave passed over her and the next set began. She couldn't see the city, not yet. But they'd been told that with this following wind they would be there three hours before sunset. *Then what?* she wondered. *A life begins that I will have so little control over.* She didn't have much back in Balbek. But she knew the small town's every cobble and eaves. She had her brothers and sisters, all younger than her and in her thrall. She had her parents – or did she now? They had made it clear that if she did this, if she followed this soldier to the city – unmarried, for there was not time for all the ritual required – then she was their daughter no more. To make love to your chosen one before marriage was understood, if never discussed. To move from your parents' house into his was not. It offended both civil law and the gods. Yet the words her father had shouted were in the heat of that last fierce row. She'd always eased his darkest moods with her gentle voice, her laugh. Surely she could do that again if . . .

If? If what? Her parents and siblings had been only five of the voices raised against her course. Ferros had been the last, the most insistent. Wait, he'd said. I will return, he'd said. But she could not because she knew he would not. His destiny would take him away for ever, and the light he'd brought into her life five years before, when she was just sixteen, would be extinguished. So she'd ignored his reasoned pleas, shut out the sound of her mother's wailing, her father's fury, the tracks of Aisha's tears on her little sister's upturned, precious face. She'd waited for him at dawn on the dock. He hadn't said anything then. Simply shrugged and let her follow him up the gangplank.

He hadn't said much since. He hadn't *done* much since. In the four years since they'd started making love they had rarely stopped. Only in those times when she knew they risked a child would they halt . . . a little. For even then, there was always plenty to explore, a different map into a world of wonders. Only here, now, on this ship had they reached a featureless desert.

The thought of him, of holding him that way, of being held, had her sliding back along the bowsprit. When her toe touched the wood of the hull, she turned, climbed and slid over the gunwale. A sailor was bent over nearby, coiling ropes. He straightened and his gaze moved over her. Her simple dress was soaked and it pressed against her everywhere, like a second skin. The brown eyes in the sailor's tanned face widened. But she didn't fold herself demurely or drop her own eyes. She just looked past the man she did not want to the one she did.

Ferros stood with the captain of the ship, a gnarled seaman from the Acrana Isles called Mikon. He said something, moved away. Ferros stared down for a moment then turned, saw her. He came forward, as the sailor beside her stopped gazing, and returned to coiling ropes. Apart from Lara only his tutor knew that Ferros was immortal. But all knew he was a soldier, a veteran at twenty-three, gifted in killing – and that Lara was his woman.

'The captain says that since the wind's picked up, we are making even better time.' Ferros nodded his head forward. 'In two hours we'll see Corinthium rising from the water. The greatest sight in the world, he says. Not to be missed.'

He looked ahead. She looked at him. Despite spending so much time below decks, his desert soldier's skin was still deep brown, his eyes still a burst of blue against it. He wore the loose, green summer tunic of the army, revealing shoulders muscled from years of work with sword and shield, bow and lance; tight over his chest, the wind pressed the material against his flat stomach.

His gaze had moved from his future in the city ahead, to his present before him. He was looking at the swell of her breasts, straining against wet cloth. She watched his eyes move down, and rest where the dress cut across her thighs.

'Then we'd better hurry,' she said, 'so we don't miss it.'

She took his hand, pulled. He didn't move. 'Lara,' he said.

'No more words. We've had too many words and not enough. Come.'

*

68

Ferros was wrenched from his dream by a cry. Ashtan was calling him, urging him to wake and fight. He reached to his sword, sheathed and hanging from a hook on the cabin wall. But as he touched it he realised that Ashtan was dead, and that the cry came from a seagull. Which meant that they must be nearing land.

A softer cry came from beside him. He looked down. Lara was naked and sprawled across him, her light brown hair, still damp from sea spray, unbound and flowing in waves over his chest, one hand gripping his left shoulder, her stomach pressed to his, their legs entwined. From the first time they'd made love, it was always thus – she would strive to touch as much of his body as she could reach with hers; fall asleep on him, settle and match him breath for breath. At first he'd found it uncomfortable. Orphaned at seven, he was unused to gentle touch and the women he'd slept with before, all three of them, had been tavern girls, eager to please for the coins agreed upon, eager to be gone to get more. But Lara would not be shaken off, even in sleep. At the beginning he'd slip from under her, think her gone – and wake to find her joined to him again, at breast, hip and thigh. He learned to not only accept it, but revel in it, adjusting to find their perfect fit, a child's wooden puzzle, complete.

He reached down, combed his fingers through her curls. She muttered something, turned to his hand. He pinched one tress between thumb and forefinger, rubbed, froze. A phrase came into his head. He thought it was the general who'd said it, though he'd been slipping into the poppy's embrace when the words were spoken. 'Claimed by time.' Had Olankios said that? Was it him the general had been referring to? Yes – and no. Time claimed everyone, no one shook its steady grip. But it would claim him far more slowly, if at all. Perhaps he would age, imperceptibly. It was one of the questions he needed to ask. But the tress he held would certainly change. Silver, thin, whiten ...

He let it go, rubbed his fingers as if to cleanse them. He'd tried to leave Lara in Balbek, a great hurt to spare her the greater one to come. But deep down he knew he'd been lying to both of them. It was himself who wanted to avoid the pain. There was so much he did not understand about immortality. Gan, his tutor, would tell him almost nothing, only push him to studies of things he thought he'd long done away with – geometry, faith, philosophy, none of which were needed in a night fight. But this he did understand: that he could not bear to watch the only woman he'd ever loved *claimed by time*. It would kill him, even as it killed her. And yet, of course, he would not die.

He tried to slip out from under her now without waking her. She woke on the instant. 'Stay, love,' she murmured, pressing into him. 'A little longer.'

He could not. 'Listen. Sea birds,' he whispered. 'We're getting close.'

She opened her eyes. 'Of course!' she said. 'The greatest sight in the world.' She leapt up, grabbed his hand. 'Come on, lazy! We mustn't miss it.'

It was a matter of a moment to fling on their one-piece clothes: his tunic, her damp dress. They ran up the short stair to the deck. They turned forward, halted, tottering on bare feet. Gasped and clutched each other.

Corinthium.

They'd been making love when the city had first appeared on the horizon. Slept while it grew from the sea. Now it was close, perhaps half a mile away.

He couldn't breathe! The city overwhelmed him. He'd known it as facts on parchment, sketches and maps and statistics. None of that came close to summing it up. In Balbek the tallest structure was the donjon of the fortress, its ramparts three storeys high. It would have been a squat footstool to the gleaming towers before him. Soaring edifices filled the sky like the jagged teeth of some gargantuan monster, faced in coloured marble that gleamed green, blue and white, yet all burnished red-gold now by the sun setting behind the ship. Each tower had been built by one of the families that had ruled the empire for centuries – Lascartis, Gonarios, Trebans amongst them – outdoing each other in height and splendour, striving to reach the clouds and shake hands with the gods. Only when the immortals took control near five hundred years before did the competition cease, and edicts limit the height to protect the citizens, too many of whom had died when ambition yielded to gravity and towers tumbled. And even if some families still lived in them, the towers were no longer fortresses to be fought from. The immortals had brought peace as well as building codes to Corinthium and a web of walkways now passed between the towers, where arrow, spear and stone once flew.

Balbek was a sprawl along a shore. Yet five Balbeks could have fitted easily into the frontage before Ferros. He knew, though, that the front was small compared to the city's depth. Corinthium went back for miles through a labyrinth of streets and alleys spread over six hills, all narrowing back to the seventh, the smallest, highest. It was so far back that he still couldn't see it. Yet the sense of it dominated everything before it. It was a city within a city, sacred and secret. The main arena was there for the games and the sacrifices. The council chambers too, where laws were made and wars declared. Unlike the ant's nest confusion of the six other hills, their teeming life, relatively few lived among the seventh hill's parks and plazas. Only the immortals and those who took care of them.

It was called Agueros. At its summit was a palace made entirely from red marble. This was the Sanctum on the Hill and it was both his destination and his destiny.

Ferros was looking so far ahead that he didn't notice the wonders closer to. 'Oh beautiful!' Lara cried, digging her fingers into his arm. The ship was approaching the entrance to the harbour. Two long stone jetties curved like bull horns from the land beyond. Atop each, hundreds of men and boys wielded fishing rods, casting into the blue-green waters. At both jetties' ends stood a giant stone figure, each three times the height of Balbek's donjon. They were men, carved in simple, graceful lines in the style favoured three hundred years before. The man to their left was a bare-faced warrior, wearing the simpler armour of those times: breastplate, an open-faced helmet crested with horsehair, a pleated tunic that reached mid-thigh, steel guards on his shins above low boots. He held the short stabbing sword called the glaive in his right hand. His left hand was stretched out, clasping the right hand of the man opposite him.

Stone curls flowed over this man's head, blending into a short clipped beard. He wore a long gown that reached his bare feet. His arms were uncovered and in his left hand he held an unfurled scroll, writing upon it too cramped for Ferros to read.

The words upon both men's forearms were clearer. They were in the ancient tongue, learned but hardly spoken at all these days. Nevertheless he'd had it drilled into him at his first school.

'What does it say?' Lara asked. For a weaver's daughter, reading was not a skill thought worth learning. Ferros had taught her some, but none of the old language.

He pointed at the warrior. 'You could guess that, given his role.'

'War?'

'Strength.'

'So the other is ... weakness?'

He smiled. 'That wouldn't be very inspiring. No. He is a scholar. His word is Wisdom.'

'They have the same face, don't they? One has a beard but—'

'Yes. They are "the Twins".'

The ship was getting close to passing under the stone bridge of the joined hands. 'Why do they not look at each other when they shake?' she said.

'They face away because, between them, they guard against all the world's dangers.'

'And that word?' Lara pointed, almost directly up now, to the carved word shared by the two hands. 'Is it "peace"?'

'It is.' He remembered the quote from his schooldays. '"Between Strength and Wisdom lies Peace."'

She reached, took his hand, squeezed it. 'So shall we find peace here, Ferros?'

He didn't answer her. That look, that she had taken from him for a few moments in the cabin, was back. Suddenly they were in shadow and she shivered. Then they were warm again, having passed beneath the stone hands and out again into the sunshine.

'Welcome to Corinthium,' he said, dropping her hand, turning away. 'We should pack.'

They didn't have much, so it took very little time. When they came back onto the deck again, each wore their one spare, and slightly better tunic. The *Black Cormorant* was already deep into the basin, its mast a single, small tree in a vast forest. Vessels of all sizes, from mighty seafaring three-masted galleons to skiffs with nothing but a brace of oars, jostled for right of way. Curses came in every language of the empire, from the guttural bark of the Wattenwolden, the northern forest tribes, to the sibilant hiss of the Southern Great Lake dwellers. Their captain, Mikon, showed his experience, threading a course for the main docks, that grew rapidly nearer. Though it wasn't simply skill that sped them through. Glancing up, Ferros noted the red flag of the Sanctum now flying from the mast. No other captain wanted to impede government business, not when fines could cost him a quarter of his cargo.

73

Similar considerations saw them swiftly at the dock, though they were roundly cursed by the captain of a carrack that was all but tied up when they approached – until he too noticed the red at their masthead. Speedy hands made the *Cormorant* secure, the gangplank was run out fast and they descended it. Lara swayed, sea legs unsteady, and Ferros caught her, held her. The noise, especially after two weeks at sea, was extraordinary, an assault in all those languages, as ships were swiftly unloaded and goods whisked away onto carts drawn by ass, bullock and man. 'What now?' she whispered.

Gan the tutor had joined them. As black as midnight and from the Xan people of the mountains below the southern desert, he was even taller than Ferros, stood a head above the crowd, so was able to answer her. 'They come,' he said, and soon they also saw what he had – a palanquin, borne by three men at each corner pole. Its walls were four squares of emerald silk, sloping up to a gold-topped centre crown. It was a moving tent and, like their ship at sea, with the red banner of the Sanctum rising from its apex, the crowds parted for it.

A curt command came from within, and the palanquin was set down. A hand, heavy with topaz, emerald and ruby, opened a gap in the shimmering silk. A rich turquoise sleeve followed the hand and then a face appeared. It startled them both, because its original features were hard to discern so enhanced were they in paint. Dark eyes lay in deep vermilion pools, thickened silver lashes opening and closing over them like curtains. Fair skin glistened in gold dust, rising over the dome of a forehead to a wide shank of hair dyed red as blood, and flowing down bare shoulders to curl onto a similarly shimmering chest. Or breast. Ferros could not detect whether this was a man, woman or something in between, and the voice, when it came, gave no further clue.

'Welcome, warrior of the west, loyal servant of the empire,' the emissary trilled, stepping from the carriage. 'May the gods bless your coming, may the two moons shine kind light, may the seven hills not trip your feet, may your path to the Sanctum be bright.'

Ferros swallowed. He'd learned in his long-ago schooldays that Corinthium had elaborate etiquette and rituals for every occasion. Greetings and partings were some of the most complicated. He also wasn't sure if what had been spoken was a poem and whether he was required to reply with another. But his schooldays were indeed long ago, and poetry for him was a horse galloped bareback along a dune. He couldn't think of a phrase to reply with except, eventually, 'Thank you.'

The eyelid curtains fell. Opened slowly, with the gaze becoming keener. 'You are Ferros, officer of the Ninth Balbek Riders?'

'I am.'

'Oh.' The eyes swept up and down him, narrowing as they took in the simplicity of his clothes. 'Well, well,' was all that came then. Finally, the ... person looked up and said, 'I am the poet Streone Lascartis. Also the Innovator of the Great Theatre. And I am *sent* ...' the word was laced with distaste, 'to bring you to the Sanctum. Come,' a jewelled hand parted silk again, 'you will join me in here. Your servant girl will be guided with your bags to your quarters. They are close by.'

Streone. It was a name applied to both men and women. 'Sir?' Ferros ventured.

'Hmm?'

The query gave nothing away in terms of gender. Ferros continued, 'Lara is not my servant but ... but my wife.' They'd decided on the voyage that even if it were not true it might be safer for her to be so named.

'Wife?' Streone looked Lara up and down differently, though with equal contempt. 'Well, well, she will have to wait for you at your lodgings. I am to bring only you to Lucan, and no other. There is no room.'

'Uh ...'

Ferros peered, could see that the palanquin was large, even if its main occupant also was. And with three burly men at each pole –

Streone could obviously read that thought. 'We do not go to the Sanctum in this. Through the streets that would take a day. No, we go by the Heaven Road. And there's only room in that carriage for two.' To Ferros's blank stare he added, 'Up there! Up there!'

Ferros looked. He hadn't noted it before, the roofs of the different towers and lower buildings being so conjoined. Now he saw two parallel cables running between towers that rose up and vanished over the first hill. And as he looked, a large woven basket appeared not far from them and began a climb to the first tower.

Heaven Road, he thought. Someone had mentioned it once, some trader drunk in a tavern. He'd thought the man had been trying to take advantage of a gullible provincial soldier. He swallowed again. 'Nevertheless,' he began, 'my wife—'

'Go,' Lara said. 'You wouldn't get me up in that anyway. You'll return later, will you?'

Ferros turned to Streone. 'Will I?'

'Once I have delivered you, you are no longer my concern.' The emissary shrugged. 'Yes, probably. If you request it.'

'And you say someone will see my wife to lodgings?'

There was no reply, just a click of fingers. A small man in a simple white tunic appeared, clasped his hands before him, and bowed over them. 'It is an inn nearby,' Streone said, 'the Haven,' adding, as he saw Ferros's look, 'a respectable one, trust me.' He leaned down and whispered to the small man, who nodded. 'Now, come. We have delayed long enough.'

The emissary climbed into the palanquin. Ferros turned, pressed Lara's hand, and followed.

She watched the vehicle borne away through the parting crowd. She turned back – Gan the tutor had gone, she didn't know where. Only the servant was there, and he already had their few bags in his hands. He nodded his head in the direction they should take and set off.

'Gods help me,' she murmured, and followed.

Once he'd got over the terror of flight – he'd never been off the ground higher than the top of a cedar tree before – Ferros found he enjoyed the sensation … and the view. Between the fourth and the fifth hill was a deeper valley and the basket – it really was little more than that, with Streone filling more than half of it and pointedly ignoring him – rose high above it. So high that Ferros was able to take in the whole city – from the Twins at the harbour entrance to the Sanctum, their destination, its walls glowing like a lit hearth in the sun's last beams. Here at the centre of the world, the sun set fast. Maybe a half-hour passed before they glided onto a stone terrace, and already the city below was dark, and glittering with lights, like a million dancing fireflies.

They stopped. A servant opened the door set in the wicker. 'Follow,' commanded Streone, stepping from the basket, and Ferros obeyed. His guide led him down passageways and through chambers large and small, all softly lit by torches in sconces made of huge pink clam shells, flames flickering within. He – or she – moved fast and Ferros had little time to study what he passed through. All was made, or faced at least, in marble of different shades. From niches statues peered, nymphs, satyrs, gods, warriors. Some rooms had furniture: desks with scrolls upon them and other scrolls, thousands of them, lining the walls. There were no fires anywhere. It was autumn, the

77

evenings drawing in, and the hill was high up. Wearing only his light tunic, Ferros felt cold for the first time in an age.

They paused before a door set in a wall, flush and almost invisible, at the end of an oblong chamber with padded benches rising in four ranks either side, some kind of meeting hall. Streone opened the door and, with a sigh, started up the stair beyond it. It curled up and up, spiralling around a centre column, and the guide's breaths came more and more heavily as they mounted. After a score of turns around the spiral, Streone halted before another door, gasped 'Thank the gods,' and knocked.

A man's voice came, soft yet clear through the wood. 'Come.'

The room they entered was different from all before it. It was warm, flames in a fireplace set into one of the walls. Eight walls, Ferros noted immediately, and each one faced not with marble but with wood. Aliantha, he could smell it immediately, the scent making him suddenly ache for his home and the coastal forests near Balbek. Unlike the sparseness he'd passed through, this room was comfortable, a place to linger – and to work, certainly, for there was a long oak desk opposite him against one of the eight walls, between two curtained doorways that gave out onto the night. The desk was covered in paper, maps weighted open with small statues and knives, scrolls in neat ranks, pens in stands. But there were also places to rest in the room – a divan piled with furs before the hearth between two low chairs plumped with cushions.

A man stood before the desk, holding a piece of parchment. He was tall, near as tall as Ferros, dressed simply, richly, in a blue, ankle-length wool tunic. Flamelight flickered in reflection on the dome of his black, shaven head. He had a city beard, neat and trimmed around lips and jaw. Laying the parchment down, he spoke.

'My name is Lucan,' he said, crossing the room, his voice from the city too, cultured, rich and resonant. 'I am the leader of the Council of Lives. Welcome, young man. Welcome to ...' He paused, and Ferros waited for the name of the city. But the man smiled and continued, '... immortality.'

Ferros knew what he was now. He thought he'd accepted his fate. But hearing it pronounced by this man, from whom power radiated like heat did from his hearth, in an eyrie at the top of the world, made his knees buckle. He fought for balance, stepping forward. But the man had immediately taken his arm and, if he noticed the stagger, did not say so.

'You must be exhausted from your journey,' he said, using Ferros's motion to guide him forward to the divan. Letting him sit – lowering him, truly – he continued. 'I will send for refreshment. Streone,' he called, without looking, 'be so good as to tell Graco to bring a tray.'

'Of course, Lord Lucan.'

Ferros, still slightly dazed, remembered his courtesy, and turned. 'Thank you for your guidance here.'

'It was a ... pleasure.' The pause and tone indicated clearly that it was not.

His guide was at the door when Lucan spoke again. 'Do the preparations for the festival go well, Streone?'

'Very, lord.' The considerable chest was puffed out. 'I believe it will be one of the greatest ever seen.'

'Not like last time then?'

Streone sagged, face crimsoning. 'No, indeed. As you know the ... mishaps were not my fault. I—'

'The tray, Streone? Our guest?'

'Indeed, sir. Indeed. Thank you.' With a short bow, the emissary stumbled from the room.

'Was he *very* rude to you?' Lucan said, moving round to hold his hands out to the fire.

He, thought Ferros. *So*. 'He was ... polite,' he murmured.

'Polite? That is most unlike him.' Lucan chuckled and

turned. 'But his rudeness is compensated for by a great talent for spectacle. Have you heard of our early winter festival? The celebration of Simbala?'

Simbala, Ferros thought. Gan had talked of her. Goddess of death and birth. 'I ... no ... maybe ... some.'

'You will enjoy it. There are plays, epic poems, races on horse and foot. Perhaps you would like to take part?'

Ferros felt his tongue like a wedge of wood in his mouth. He couldn't get it to move properly and respond. It annoyed him, this dread that held him, had done so almost from the moment he'd known his new truth. He, who would launch himself alone into a fight against half a dozen Sarphardi warriors, with a battle cry on his lips and joy in his heart, behaving like a schoolboy on his first day, staring at the rod in the tutor's hand.

Speak, he commanded himself. Are you an ox?

The door opened. Someone came in. Lucan waved a hand and Ferros heard a tray being placed, footsteps, the door closing again. Lucan moved away. 'We have ice wine from Tinderos?' he called. 'Brandy? Ale?'

'Ale,' replied Ferros, adding, 'please.'

Lucan returned, handed him a goblet, raised a small, exquisite crystal glass of his own. 'To eternal life,' he said, and sipped.

Ferros drank off half the goblet, and smiled. He was used to the light wheat beers of the dry south. This was a northern ale, malty and sweet, full of complexities. Strong too, he felt that in a moment. It was as if his neck lengthened and relaxed. He wondered if it was laced with anything, distillations of poppy or hemp. He decided not to care.

Lucan came and sat in a chair beside him. 'I will not keep you long. You have had a hard journey and I know how this city can ... overwhelm at first. It did me, when I first came.'

'When was that?'

'Over four hundred years ago. It took me twenty to fully grasp all that had happened to me. One moment, forty years old and dead of plague in a filthy fishing village in Valraisos, the next,' he shifted, 'reborn.' He nodded. 'When I arrived at the Sanctum, I couldn't read, write, hold a conversation – about anything other than nets and tides. Now,' he raised his crystal till firelight danced in its facets, in the purple liquid within, 'I can tell the subtleties in different vintages of Tinderos wine.' He smiled. 'Oh, Ferros, the wonders that await you!' He drained his glass, smacked his lips, stood. 'I will let you go and get some sleep now. Forgive me for wanting to meet you immediately. We get so few new immortals. It is a day to celebrate. Tomorrow your wonderful journey begins. You will have questions—'

His tongue was freed. Ferros didn't care that it was the ale that did it. 'I have a question now.'

Lucan, who'd stepped towards the door, paused. For the first time, something other than pleasant welcome was on his face. 'I am sure. Many. They will all be dealt with by your tutors when you return to the Sanctum to begin your studies.'

He waved his hand at the door again. Ferros ignored it. 'I'd like one answered now, if you don't mind.'

'Speak then.' Lucan's tone had turned as icy as his wine.

'Can I die?'

Lucan stared at him a moment, opened his mouth. But it was someone else who answered.

'You can. It is not easy. And what a waste that would be.'

She came through the silk curtains that were blowing in from the terrace with the sea breeze. A simple emerald dress encased her but was cut in places that revealed near as much as it concealed. The skin that showed at face, shoulder, neck and above the plunge of breast was, like Lucan's, a brown just a shade from midnight black, and given by birth, far darker than the brown of Lara, given by the sun. He glimpsed more as she moved into the room, for the dress was slit down the sides to

81

show each long, muscled leg. Her thick black hair was gathered in profuse disorder atop her head and when she stopped before him – and Ferros realised he was standing without any memory of doing so – he looked into eyes as green as a forest in the autumn, speckled with autumn's red and gold.

'Roxanna,' she said, stretching out a hand. And Ferros, who had never done such a thing in his life, bent and kissed it.

'My delight these three hundred years,' Lucan said, and Ferros felt as if he'd been kicked in the stomach, all his breath taken by a vision of these two immortals entwined – until she restored his breath with her next words.

'Oh, Father, don't you know,' Roxanna laughed as she squeezed the hand still holding hers, 'that you must never reveal a lady's age.'

Lucan laughed too while Ferros stammered, 'You … you are … ?'

'Yes. His daughter and immortal. It happens sometimes, rarely. My mother wasn't, alas.' She took her hand back, gently. 'So trust me when I say this: there *is* a way you can die. But you will not want to. Not when you discover so many reasons to live.'

Ferros wondered again at what was in the ale. He had never felt like this. Because he was looking at the only reason he could ever want to live for ever and yet not find it time enough.

There was a silence of stares, broken at last by Lucan. 'My dear, we must send this poor boy to a bed.'

'Yes,' she murmured. 'Indeed we must.'

Ferros found his tongue, and a form of words. 'Healthy rest. Happy awakenings.'

They both smiled at the old mother's phrase. 'Sleep well, Ferros. Tomorrow your work begins.'

Graco, the servant, had appeared again, unnoticed. Ferros followed him to the door, resisted the urge to look back, though he felt her gaze upon him. As he circled the stairwell down, he cursed himself. '"Happy Awakenings"?' he muttered. 'Piss in a pocket!'

His smile, though, lasted back through the Sanctum, into the basket, and all the way back to the port. Only when he stepped from it did he frown, as the servant led him from the platform towards the Haven Inn and the young woman who awaited him there.

Back in the room, father and daughter stared at the closed door and did not speak until the echoes of footfalls faded.

'Well, child?'

'He has promise.'

'You think so?' Lucan clicked his tongue. 'He struck me as so many from Balbek – bovine, dull, uneducated.'

'And yet did not General Olankios's letter speak of a natural soldier, gifted in all the ways of war? Of tracking, hunting. Killing.' She moved to the tray of drinks, poured herself a glass of ice wine. 'Did we want a wit or a warrior?'

'You know what we want. And we both know that we have not much time to get it.' He went to the desk, picked up the parchment he'd been reading when Ferros first arrived. 'Olankios also writes of a woman, possibly a wife. The servant who brought the letter said she arrived with Ferros on the boat.'

'So?'

'Might she not interfere with your plans?'

Roxanna laughed. 'When has a wife ever stood between me and my desires?'

'True. Though he is from Balbek. Loyal, dependable—'

'Ah, but Father, you did not feel his lips upon your hand.' She looked back to where they'd stood before the fire. 'I saw something different in him. Unformed, yes. But there and waiting to be shaped. Beyond his courage, his skills, his loyalties. And

he was handsome, no? That broken nose? Those scars? Rough –
but I have never concerned myself with that. Indeed—'

Lucan, who had not minded his daughter's ways in over two
hundred years, felt the faint echo of an old anger now. 'I do not
wish to know,' he said sharply. 'Do what you must. Just keep
your desires to yourself.'

Roxanna looked at him, one teased and painted eyebrow
rising. 'Oh, I will, Father,' she said. 'Which reminds me.' She
lifted her glass, drained off the ice wine. 'I must go and indulge
another.'

Lucan stepped towards her. 'Tonight? You go to destroy
Maltarsus tonight?'

'Why not?'

'It is all arranged?'

'All. The workers' noble leader is even now being made drunk
by my agents. Not too drunk. Enough to leave him … amenable
to my charms. Or rather, the charms of the famous courtesan
Andropena.'

Something of that echo of irritation from before remained in
Lucan. 'Isn't it easier just to kill him? Why fuck him?'

'If it was easier, I would.' She set down the glass. 'But we do
not want a martyr to the dock workers' cause. We want a scandal.
We want him disgraced, ruined.' She smiled. 'Besides, possessing the body of one as gifted in deviant practices as Andropena
is rumoured to be will bring its own rewards. Perhaps I will
learn something new.' She laughed, adding, 'Though I cannot
imagine what.' She moved to the doorway, stopped in it, turned
back. 'Perhaps what I learn will be the very thing that makes
Ferros fall entirely. For there's always something, isn't there?
You remember that well enough, don't you, Father?'

She left. Lucan stared at the doorway for a long moment,
then turned back to the desk to re-read the letter from Olankios.
Roxanna was right – the boy, for all his ox-like responses,

sounded promising. And she was also right in this – they didn't need another poet like Streone. They needed a blade.

Though she had raised herself from the fish-gutting tables of the docks, and was as strong as the ropes she used to bind her clients, the harlot Andropena was no harder to possess than anyone else. There was brief shock and a briefer struggle when Roxanna barged her way in, dissolving into the whore. It was the workers' hero, Maltarsus, who was the most surprised, for Andropena was on top of him at the time and seemed just briefly to flag in her efforts, to sink down with a cry of desperation, not passion. But when she rose up again there was new fire in her eyes, and she flung herself from him to return with the snares and bindings that were her trademark.

In forty years of marriage he had never betrayed his wife. But when their ninth child had died of the sweating sickness one year before, Marya had turned to the gods to preserve the other eight. She would have no more, nor indulge in the act that could create them. It was her sacrifice and he thought it would be his, switching all his energies to the cause of the dock workers whose leader he'd become. The strike he'd organised was bringing concessions. The immortals in their Sanctum were about to crack; rumour was they would give in tomorrow. But when Andropena offered to reward him, because she believed in the cause too, seeing as she was a daughter of the docks, and having drunk rather more than his usual in anticipation of tomorrow's victory, he'd found it impossible to resist her.

It was only when he was stripped, bound, gagged and Andropena was whipping him that he wondered if he'd made a mistake. When she mounted him again, he reconsidered that. But he was only certain, utterly and finally, when his brothers-in-law burst into the room, their sister, his wife Marya, in their midst.

85

It took them some time to free him from the clever bonds, the tie-er having vanished, but by then it was too late. For his marriage. For his reputation. For his cause.

From a shadowed doorway opposite the tavern, Roxanna watched the furore through Andropena's eyes. She could possess a body for a day and a night, longer than any other immortal she knew, even Lucan. But she wasn't especially enjoying this experience. The whore was diseased, which was hardly surprising, and parts of her ached. But it was her mind that disturbed the most, filled with a bitterness Roxanna had rarely encountered before. She remembered how surprised she'd been when she first possessed another, hadn't imagined that other people could harbour and retain such anger, such enmities, such . . . self-loathing. On the rare times she doubted herself, or her actions, or her morals, she moved rapidly to thoughts, then actions. Fucking was good for doubts. Killing was better.

These people bursting now from the tavern with their wails, their fury, their sense of betrayal? Why didn't they simply choose what pleased or profited them then act upon it?

As she would.

Satisfied that all had gone to plan, Roxanna headed for the docks. The nearer the water, the rougher the taverns. She knew she'd find some playmates there to try some of Andropena's skills upon. She'd learned early that it was pointless possessing someone unless you drained them of their specialised knowledge. And this whore's knowledge, while limited to one arena of life, was very specialised indeed.

As she walked, she smiled, remembering earlier in the evening and another man's touch. Ferros's lips on her hand had been a sweet caress. It had stirred a memory of her first male lover, Chiros, who had been as inexperienced as she, and twice as gentle. He'd been beautiful – and, for three hundred years now, dust in the wind.

She stopped before a crudely made door, and sighed. She knew from his kiss, from his eyes, that this soldier would want something different from her. She also knew that she would become whatever he required. For a time.

Not tonight though. Pushing open the tavern door, she grinned at the wind-whipped sailors and hard-handed dockers who looked up at her entrance. 'Evening, boys,' she said, and slammed the door behind her.

5

The Raid

The serpent-prowed ships burst through the dawn mist.

It was only because he'd been awake most of the night examining the killer's body and unable to sleep afterwards that Luck was walking the cliffs at that hour. Reaching to the elk horn at his waist that all by decree must carry, he brought it to his lips and blew the four-note alarm.

The first ship grounded, leaned. On its one sail a dragon, woven in gold, roared. Its two eyes were stars, it clutched four more, one in each of its talons, while a last one was impaled upon the tip of its barbed tail.

Seven. The raiders were from the Seven Isles. Not Askaug's closest enemy, not their furthest either. As he kept sounding his notes, he saw a huge, familiar shape drop from the ship into the water. 'Stromvar,' he groaned. Of course the Lord of the Seven Isles would be first ashore, a god seeking what all gods sought: gold and glory.

His call found its echo almost immediately. One horn, three, five. The warriors and gods of Askaug might have been sleeping off the effects of the spring feast but Death had come to their town and they roused to meet him.

'Shit!' Lowering his horn, Luck hobbled back to the

snow-choked path as fast as his weaker leg would let him. 'Not now. Not now!'

He lurched through the arming men and women, made for the hall. He found his brother-gods within it, arming too. 'Luck!' Bjorn yelled, all harm from last night's mead dispelled by battle fever. 'Are you going to fight this time?'

'No. Hovard, we must talk.'

'Talk?' His elder finished strapping the cross-belts across his chest which held the quiver of javelins on his back, then picked up his short axe and waved it at the sounds coming from beyond the hall – battle horns, shouting. 'They, whoever they are, have not come to talk.'

'It's Stromvar. He—'

'Stromvar? That boar-faced bastard?' Bjorn tipped back his head and yelled in joy. 'He killed me the last two times. He's mine. Leave him to me, Hovard. I demand it!'

'He's yours.'

'No. Both of you, listen. We need him—'

'Need him on my point.' Bjorn hefted Sever-Life, his lean and supple sword, and swirled it through the air. 'Though perhaps I'll slice him a dozen times first.' He swung low, cut high. 'Here! Here!'

'Quiet!' The ferocity of Luck's shout halted even Bjorn's swinging. 'You know what happened here last night. That ... stranger, trying to kill Einar.'

'As I will kill Stromvar.'

'It's different. You'll kill him, and he'll be reborn in hours. He'll kill you next time. Hundreds of years of that. Killing. Being killed. Being reborn. And meanwhile mortals die around us for this ... sport,' he spat the word, 'while their families weep—'

'Weep yet know they have gone to glory in the mead hall of the gods. Where they too are immortal.' Bjorn picked up his shield. 'It is our way, brother, and has always been so. Why are you questioning it now?'

'Ways change. Must change. If what I've seen in my dreams, in the mirror of water and the cast of stones is true, we are going to need every warrior, man, woman and god, here and alive.' He thumped his fist upon the table. 'I told you last night – the gods are being killed!'

'And your proof is the attack on Einar?' Hovard threw up his arms. 'One god. One time.'

'I think you need to listen, my love.'

They all turned – to Freya, standing in the doorway. Like the men, she was in breastplate and helm. Instead of shield and axe though she held a bow. 'Luck told me some of this last night. Hear his thoughts.'

Hovard looked past her. 'The fight?'

'I've seen the mothers and the young into the caves. The war maidens are armed and gone to the gate. It is being held. The enemy are bringing a ram up from the beach but that will take some time. You have that. Listen.'

'Thank you.' Luck turned back to Hovard. 'I wasn't going to tell you until I was more certain. Now I have no choice. Because of last night.' He put two fists on the table, leaned. 'That face I saw in the smoky glass? It was the face of evil – but it was also the face of a man. He sent the one who nearly killed Einar. He has sent others who were not thwarted. We are being weakened, slowly and surely. I do not know why yet. But I know that to deal with what is to come we must be united. Not just Askaug, and the west.' He drew a deep breath. 'All Midgarth.'

Hovard stared, silent. It was Bjorn who yelled. 'United? Midgarth? That has never happened. Never could. We fight each other. Gods and men, brother, this is what we do!'

'It *has* happened. You know it has, for you know your history.'

He spoke to Bjorn but kept his gaze fixed on Hovard. 'Haakon the King.'

'Not history! One who was neither god nor man but both? Who laid down the Laws then vanished into the mists?' Bjorn snorted. 'A myth to be told on a winter's night – like the coming of Gudrun Gift-Bearer. Though not even as good a story as that one.'

'Perhaps the time has come for us to start believing in myths again,' Luck said, his eyes not leaving his eldest brother, adding softly, 'and in a king.'

Hovard stared back. 'That is a lot to draw from dreams and stones and a face in smoke, brother. A change in the whole world.'

'Better that, brother, than the loss of the whole world.'

'Believe in him, my heart,' Freya said. 'I do.'

Hovard looked from his love to Bjorn, and lastly to Luck. 'What would you have me do now? With the enemy at our gate?'

'I have a plan.' He smiled. 'And the enemy is exactly where we want him.'

'Does this plan involve fighting? Please say it does.'

Luck turned to his aggrieved brother-god. 'It does, Bjorn. Just not killing.' He leaned down to rest his elbows on the table. 'For this is what we must do.'

Stromvar the Dragon sat on a rock on top of the low hill that faced Askaug's gates. He was excited.

Today is going to be a good day, he thought. The tala stones cast by his seer said so. His guts said so, his stool that morning firm and long. Even if they had not surprised Askaug because of some fucking sentry on the cliffs – who posted a lookout the morning after the spring feast, for the gods' sake? – he knew his enemies at the gate ahead of him would be suffering the feast's effects. He'd denied his own warriors their celebration and some had grumbled. But a wonderful speech he'd made as they rowed had reassured them. For there'd be plenty of feasting in Askaug when they took it that day.

And take it he would. He'd brooded on it throughout the long winter which did not want to end, which was already colder than any he could remember. He was fed up with the Seven Isles. He was fed up with mere raids. Why should he and his people huddle on barren rocks in the ocean, which the winter storms swept over without hindrance, while the Askaugers sheltered beneath cliffs and with unlimited wood from their forest hinterland to burn? He was fucked if he was going to do that any more. He would take Askaug, rule its people, blend them with his own – and the resident gods could have the Isles if they wanted. See how they liked them.

The resident gods! Another reason to feel happy. He'd killed that stag-fucker Bjorn in their last two encounters. Only once before over all the years had any god killed another three times. He was that god. But it was more than a century since his triple defeat of Petr the Red. He was confident he would equal that today with Bjorn. But he had greater ambitions still. Take the town and he'd take Hovard too. Kill him as well. A brace of gods in one day? They'd sing about that in fires across Midgarth for a score of years at least.

Stromvar laughed on another thought. Why stop at two? Why not three? Kill the elder gods and Luck would be easy prey. He wasn't even a fighter. Three gods in one day would make a song they'd sing for a century. Though he'd make sure his skald amended the song's words a little. Made Luck as fierce a warrior as the other two instead of the useless little cunt he was.

A warrior ran up. 'The ram is in position, lord.'

Stromvar looked down at the ram from his rock, then over at

the gates. The tower above them did not have as many warriors in it as before. Cowardly fuckers had probably noted the size of his ram and run off.

'Attack,' he grunted.

The warrior ran down, took up his position at the ram's butt end, still in the shelter of its sloped wooden roof. At his command, archers fanned out, their shield men beside them. At another shout, all began to run forward. The ram, pushed by twenty men, started slowly, then picked up speed.

Stromvar lifted a buttock off the rock and farted. May need to vent another turd, he thought. And no doubt it will be just as firm and long as the first one.

In the square behind the gates, all was ready. Hovard, in the tower, had sent back the guards, in threes and twos. As soon as the ram began its run forward, he waved off the few who remained, ducked under the first flight of arrows, and descended the stairs. He'd observed the strength of Stromvar's forces, twice as many as he'd bring on a common raid. If he was to guess, his old enemy was there for conquest, not goods or glory, especially as he was striking the day after the feast. You had better be right, little brother, he thought, glancing up at the balcony of the house to the left of the gates as he ran across the square. And your plan had better work.

Crouched behind the wicker wall of that balcony, Luck was thinking the same. It was risky, all of it. Uncertain. Yet he knew this: succeed and his people might still be doomed. Fail and they certainly would be.

Freya was beside him, bow in hand, a quiver full of arrows before her. He hoped she wouldn't need them. She smiled at him – but he saw his same doubts reflected in her eyes, where her smile didn't reach.

He handled his own weapon again, the only one he'd ever

93

been any good with: rope. Like many others, it was a weapon drawn from the farm. If swords were beaten from plough blades, spears straightened from scythes, and axes repurposed from the chopping of wood to the chopping of limbs, rope could be transformed too – into the slingshot that boys and girls would hunt with and give up when they were grown. He'd retained his into adulthood; his left arm and shoulder had grown doubly powerful because his right was so weak, while his aim was so keen that he could put a stone into a bear's eye at fifty paces. He could also flick a fly off a wall at ten with a whip, or coil a noose over a bull's horns, wrap a length around its legs, and lower it to the ground.

None of which will serve me here, he thought, checking and rechecking the two loops he'd tied, following the thick rope from his feet up and over the balcony and through the metal wheel of the building's winch.

He licked his lips in sudden panic. *This is madness. I should get Hovard to reoccupy the tower.* But then he heard the ram's first crash into the gates and knew it was too late.

He rose, peered. Arrows were still flying up, though fewer as the attackers realised there was no one shooting down at them. The ram came again and again, each crash splintering the gates and cracking the bar that lay across them. A last rush snapped it, burst the gates. They flew open, the ram withdrew, warriors with shields raised ran screaming in … and stopped, a dozen paces into the square, those following running into the backs of those who'd halted, realising, spreading wider, till they'd reached both sides of the square, formed a shield wall two ranks deep …

… to face the one-ranked shield wall before them.

Men and women stared at each other in the near silence, some of the attackers muttering, one man yelling 'Cowards!' then going quiet as if embarrassed by his noise. No one was looking up, but Freya had nocked an arrow and was ready in case someone did, and came for them. She and Luck looked down – and watched the biggest warrior yet march through the shattered gates to halt behind his men.

'What the fuck is happening here?' Stromvar shouted.

Silence held. He put a hand on the back of the soldier before him, leaned forward to peer. 'Bjorn! Where are you, you arse-licking coward? Skulking as ever, are you? Too scared to fight at the gates? Two deaths enough for you, are they?'

Luck looked at Askaug's wall. Saw his brother in the middle of it lower his shield and raise his head. Careful, Bjorn, he thought, sending the words out. Remember the plan. Keep your temper. Use your wits.

Then he heard his brother's laugh. This could be either a good or a bad sign. 'I have a death here for you, Strum-bum,' Bjorn called. 'Care to come and get it? Just you and me?'

The silence, broken by the two voices, was now shattered by many. Askaug's men and women let forth a chorus of catcalls and jeers. Those of the Seven Isles responded in kind. It was only when their leader began hitting some, and bellowing at all, that they quietened for him.

A signal suddenly cut off those around Bjorn. So Stromvar shouted, perhaps too loudly at first. 'Why should I fight you alone, Bjornie?' he jeered. 'I have near double your forces here, and many more outside. Why not overwhelm your ranks and kill you at my leisure?'

'Why indeed?' Bjorn gave out a large, exaggeratedly fake yawn. 'Then do so, Stromvar the Dragon. I'm sure you can whip your skalds into writing songs that celebrate your bravery and that they will be sung . . . oh, right into the middle of next week!'

With a roar, Stromvar started jerking aside the men before him. 'Songs? Let's see what songs you sing, Bjorn the Pretty, with Death Dealer in your throat!'

He'd broken through his own ranks, waving the sword he'd named. Bjorn stepped from his. 'Come on then,' he called.

'Are you certain, quite certain?' Freya nudged Luck with her foot. She'd pulled the bow string back halfway. 'I could kill him fast. End this.'

He still wasn't certain – but he had to be for her. 'You will end nothing. His warriors will still fight for him, reclaim his body to be reborn, kill many of us. As many of them will die. And we are going to need every man and woman in the fight ahead, if I am right.'

'I pray you are,' Freya said, and released the tension in her bow.

The sound of the first clash came from below. Luck looked, and watched his brother being driven about the square. Stromvar was in a temper, which could mar a less experienced fighter. But the Dragon had scores of kills to his name. He used his anger to add power to his blows, raining them down from height, for he was near half a body taller than Bjorn. His brother deflected the cuts with his sword, used his litheness to slip from side to side to avoid them. But when he took a blow direct on his shield, the force of it crumpled him, and he staggered, only just avoiding the cuts that followed.

Luck knew also that his brother was fighting without using his main talent: the swift dart and lunge, an adder's strike and kill. His sword was lighter for that purpose, his shield too. But he could not use that skill, not if he wished to serve Luck's purpose.

The men of the Seven Isles were cheering. The men and women of Askaug were largely silent – only releasing a great groan when Stromvar, who'd missed a downward cut when Bjorn had slipped to the right, swung back – and slammed the flat of his blade into Bjorn's face.

His brother fell back, blood exploding from his nose. He probably couldn't see, but somehow must have sensed, the next falling blow. He managed to roll away, as the great sword cut the dirt where he'd just been. Rolled again, staggered back ... towards the balcony.

'Get ready,' said Luck. Freya laid down her bow.

The blows came even faster now, over and around, lunges and slashes. Bjorn dodged them all, deflecting with his shield, with his sword, with the movement of his body a finger's width from falling steel. His staggers took him back, ever back – until a last cut across his chest scraped his breastplate with a high, sharp screech and his fall away sent him reeling into the building's wall.

Stromvar paused to gloat. It was his mistake. 'Pretty boy ...' he began.

'Now,' said Luck, and on the word, he and Freya put a foot each into the plaited loops, grabbed the rope above them, and hurled themselves over the balcony. There was an awful moment when they hung there from the winch, when Luck thought their combined weights might not be as great as their enemy's, or would snap the machinery. Only a moment though, before the noose he'd stepped into tightened around Stromvar's left ankle. He flipped upside down and rose past them roaring, while they fell as fast to the ground.

'Now,' came Hovard's quiet command. As one, the ranks of Askaug ran out, and re-formed to encircle the front of the building, while a dozen archers ran onto the balcony above and leaned over it with arrows drawn to their ears.

Stromvar was spinning, roaring, pain and fury making most words unintelligible. After the sudden shock, those of the Seven Isles swung their shield wall to face the other. 'We'll fight you!' one of them cried out. 'We'll not stand by and watch our chieftain slaughtered.'

'No one need be slaughtered this day,' Luck called. 'We only wish to talk.'

'Talk?' That word was clear at least, in Stromvar's anguished yell. 'You've broken my fucking leg and now you wish to talk?'

'If you please,' replied Luck.

Bjorn rose and stood beside him, staring up at the suspended god. He wiped some blood from his nose, then spat. 'Oh, he's very big on talking, my little brother. You'll soon learn that ... Strum-bum.'

'So you are telling me,' said Stromvar, his broken leg up on the mead hall's table, 'that my cousin Beornoth was murdered last summer by this same black-eyed bastard whose corpse you showed me?'

'By him or one like him. Yes,' replied Luck. 'I would have to see the body but—'

'You can't. We burned it, of course. The trunk anyway, since the head was gone.' For a moment the five gods in the room all shuddered. A head could survive a little time away from the body. It was not anything any of them wanted to experience.

The fifth god, Einar the Black, who had taken no part in the fighting while recovering from his wound – as a visiting god he'd have fought with his hosts – now ran his finger along the faint line of it around his neck. 'But why me? Why Beornoth? Why kill the gods? The people love us.'

'Not all the people,' said Freya, refilling the six goblets from a large jug of hot mead. 'Could this not be resentful mortals, Luck? There was that group, a hundred years ago, from the northern lakes. They beheaded their god.'

'Yes!' Stromvar slammed down his goblet again, half empty. 'Why should these bald, black-eyed fuckers be from a foreign land we've never heard of, as you suggest? Einar here is dark enough, as are most of his people in the southern mountains. Perhaps a group of them live in caves, inbreed—'

'No. He is from away. I know this for certain.'

98

'How?'

'I have ... examined him.'

'Shit.' Bjorn hawked, spat. 'You didn't?'

'I did. I had to.'

'Did what?' Stromvar asked.

'Luck has always been curious. About life, and how it works.' It was Hovard who spoke now, softly. 'He ... takes things apart. Birds, beasts, fish. Dries them, reassembles them.'

'That's fucking disgusting.' Stromvar grinned, and leaned back. 'So what did you find?'

'First I examined his possessions. The craft he came in, of which no man has seen the like? It was made of tanned seal skin—'

'—which we use.'

'But it was wrapped over a frame of the lightest, strongest wood I have ever seen. Almost unbreakable. One not found in our forests.'

'Yet,' said Einar, 'there are forests in the south so vast even my people have not penetrated to their hearts.'

'So a forest people would build an ocean-worthy boat? It is made to survive being rolled in big waves, the paddler sealed in. It is also designed to be pulled over snow. It has runners on its base. I think ... I think a man could ride over snow in it as he could ride a wave.'

'Like a sled?'

'Like no sled we've ever seen, Freya.'

Even Stromvar was silent at that, so Luck pressed on. 'And then there was what he'd eaten.'

'Eugh, brother!'

Bjorn stood and left the table, making a show of being sick. Luck continued. 'In his stomach were seeds of fruit we've never seen here. His sack contained dried meat that tasted like no creature that I know, flavoured with a spice also not found in

99

our lands. There's more I could tell, of what I found and where I found it – but I'll spare Bjorn's delicate stomach. Then there's these.' He reached into his sack and pulled out the globe and the stoppered vial, set them down, looked at Stromvar and Einar, who stared, fascinated, at the smoke swirling within. 'He brought these. I saw things here. A prophecy of sorts, I think.' He shrugged. 'I can't know. But I also saw another black-eyed man.' He sighed out a long breath. 'Never have I felt such evil in one man in my life.'

'Show me this fucker,' said Stromvar.

'No. I doubt you would see. I think I only did because … because I have spent years staring at things that are and are not. Also, look.'

Luck bared his teeth. Stromvar peered. 'They're dirty. You need to scrub them with a pine stick, sap and needles,' he said.

'I have. Scrubbed and scrubbed. The black has faded, a little. But only a little.' He tapped the stoppered vial. 'I think if I were to use this often, soon my teeth would never be anything but black.' He leaned back. 'Though I … I desire to use it again. There was something in it, in the scent of it, that makes me *crave* it.'

'Like mead?' said Bjorn, turning back.

'No, brother. Nothing like mead.' He tapped the globe. 'Somehow they communicate with this. Over a long distance.'

'Who do you think "they" are, Luck?'

'I don't know, Freya.' He shook his head. 'All I know is that I must go and find out.'

Bjorn returned to the table. 'Where will you search, little brother?'

'East.'

'To the mountains?'

'Beyond the mountains.'

'Impossible,' said Stromvar. 'No one has climbed them, ever.

Even as a god in an eagle, or running as a wolf, none have gone over them.'

'No one has tried in fifty summers. And the weather has changed. Besides, the killer did.'

'You said he came by boat.'

'The last stage only. Even his boat could not have survived the northern seas in winter. None of ours, the finest in the world, ever have.' Luck opened the drawer under the table. 'This,' he said, pulling out the piece of supple dried skin, unrolling it, 'we found amongst the killer's possessions. We think it is—'

'A chart,' said Stromvar, reaching down, spinning the skin towards him. 'That's Askaug,' he said, tapping a finger on the end of an indent. Tapped again. 'Here's Peersoo. Tamauk. These cuts are my home, the Seven Isles.' He peered closer. 'I have charted them myself, for the whale hunt. Though this,' he tapped again, 'is better work than I have ever done.'

'This is Molnalla the tallest of all mountains. See this cleft below?' Luck laid his forefinger on the chart. 'I think the killer pulled his boat over the mountains there, sledded down them, to here. Then he put his boat in the water,' he hesitated, then moved his finger, 'here.'

A silence as all stared. Hovard broke it. 'But that would be ... that is—'

'The Lake of Souls.'

It was Freya who breathed it softly. But all of them there, save Luck, raised their hands, two middle fingers thrust out, to ward against the evil of the name.

'No one,' said Hovard, licking his lips, 'not even a killer in a magic boat, could survive the Lake of Souls.'

'I think he did,' replied Luck. 'Paddled across it, then down the Serpent River, the only one that does not freeze, to do his killing.' He sat back. 'So I must do the reverse.'

Voices exploded.

'You cannot!'

'Are you mad?'

'Brother!'

But it was the softest voice there that came clearest. 'Hovard is right, Luck,' said Freya. 'No one survives the Lake of Souls. No one even ventures close to it. Those two young hunters were the last, ten years back.' She looked up. 'What were their names, Bjorn? They were friends of yours.'

'Karn, and his brother Rukka the Handsome. I hurt my leg chasing the same huge bison Karn had wounded.' Bjorn leaned down. 'I shouted at them to stop, that we'd gone too far already. But they were young, it was Karn's first bull, they kept the chase. And they—' He broke off, shook his head.

Einar spoke. 'If the marsh gases didn't get them, the ghosts who it is said live there would have.'

Hovard leaned across the table to be heard. 'How can you be certain he came that way, brother? The killer may have crossed the mountains further in the north, circled down.'

Luck shook his head. 'No. He came from the Lake of Souls.'

Bjorn thumped the table. 'But how can you know this, brother? How?'

'Because of the last thing I found in the killer's craft. It was attached to the prow. Almost like a serpent head on our longships.' He drew something out of his satchel. 'I am sorry, Bjorn.' He held out what looked like a fist-sized piece of balled leather, then placed it on the table. All stared at the object, puzzled, until Luck spoke again, softly. 'It's Karn,' he said.

Bjorn did go then, not just away from the table; outside, where he threw up, loud and long. It was the only noise, as all the others stared at the shrivelled monstrosity on the mead-hall table.

It was Stromvar who broke the silence. 'If this is ... is who you say ...'

'It is.'

'Then why the fuck would you go anywhere near this place?' Stromvar roared. 'No insult, but you are small enough already.' The huge warrior licked his lips. 'Go south, to Einar's land. Let him guide you through the great forest, then come back north to cross the mountain.'

'It would take too long. Even if every second day I travelled as a beast – and you all know how that drains us – even if I managed that, it would still take three months.' He looked up, straight at Hovard now. 'I don't think we have three months.'

Stromvar grunted. 'You are brave, little man,' he said.

'I am not, believe me,' Luck replied. 'I never have been. But I must do this. At least, I must try.'

Einar ran one thumb around his healing scar again. 'I can see – feel! – that you are right about the killings. I can accept that the one who did this to me was from beyond our world.' He thumped his hand down upon the table. 'But are you certain – certain now! – that this means that he and others are coming to conquer us?'

'Can you think of a better way of preparing us for conquest than by killing those who could unite the people against them? The best fighters too?' Luck looked around at all of them. 'I believe it – but I cannot be certain until I have gone to look for myself.'

Silence again, as all stared at the mute and shrunken head before them. Wiping his mouth, Bjorn returned. Saying nothing, he picked up the remains of his friend and tucked him into the folds of his cloak.

Stromvar stood, testing the weight on his broken leg, now nearly healed, as was the way of the gods. 'And us? What do we do while you journey? Just wait for your return?' He shook his head. 'For which, I have to tell you, the odds are not very good.'

'You cannot wait. Whether I return or not.' He looked at his eldest brother, largely silent throughout all the talk. 'Hovard?'

He stood too, faced Stromvar. They were nearly of a height, the two warrior gods. 'We have talked of this – Einar, Luck, Freya, Bjorn and I. My brother here,' he pointed at Bjorn, 'was especially hard to convince. He'd rather keep fighting you—'

'And beating you – as I would have done today!'

Hovard took Stromvar's arm to still his response. 'But even Bjorn is convinced now.' He took a deep breath. 'All know how deep the ancient rivalry runs between Askaug and the Seven Isles. So if you and I can make a truce, others will too. We will spread word of it throughout the land,' he looked once at Luck who nodded, 'and gather all, every god and principal mortal of the land ... atop Galahur.'

Stromvar stepped back, eyes wide. 'For a ... Moot? Why not wait for the regular one? The last was, what, thirteen years ago? So ... seven years. Nothing to a god.'

'Have you not been listening, Lord of the Isles?' Luck said sharply. 'We do not have seven years. I don't think we have one.'

'So, a special Moot.' Stromvar shook his head. 'There has only ever been one special Moot before. When our fathers went to Galahur to decide the Laws of Combat for the gods.'

'Rules, surely,' muttered Luck. Now he'd got his will he felt no elation, only a deep exhaustion. 'It is, after all, a game.'

Einar and Bjorn glared at him – but Stromvar tipped back his head and roared with laughter. 'Little man, I do not know why you say you have no courage. You have just mocked the entire reason for living of all the gods! Before two of its greatest killers!' He wiped tears from his eyes. 'Ay me! Well, if you can do what you plan to do, perhaps your brother and I can do this.' His face changed, his voice lowered. 'But tell me, Hovard of Askaug, do you think to make yourself king over us all? Like Haakon from the legend?'

Hovard's voice was as even. 'Perhaps you will be king, Stromvar the Dragon. Perhaps none of us will. It will be for gods – and the people – to decide. The living and the dead.' Hovard stepped closer again, held out a hand. 'At the Moot on Galahur.'

Stromvar looked at Hovard for a long moment – then reached out and gripped the other's elbow. 'Then let us do this,' he said. 'Do we bring men?'

It was Luck who replied. 'The ancient rules of a special Moot state that each god will bring the twelve principal men or women of their kingdom. For at such a meeting, the outcome will be for both gods and mortals to decide.'

'A dangerous precedent, to give mortals an equal say in the dealings of the gods. But if it is the way of the Moot—' Stromvar shrugged, stretched. 'I will return to the Isles and prepare for the journey.'

'No, lord.' Luck stood. His head came to the large man's middle and he stared up. 'Others must prepare. You five gods must bear the summons throughout the realm. For the Moot must take place in ten days' time.'

'Ten days? Ten—?' Stromvar's jaw dropped. 'That's impossible.'

'No. Difficult, of course. But each of you will bear one of these.' He reached into his satchel and pulled out a slim white ash stave the length of his forearm. 'I have carved the tala of summoning into them.'

Stromvar's mouth was still wide, as if he sought flies to trap. He took the stave, stared at it, perplexed. 'Bear it? How?'

'Why, in your beak, of course.' Freya smiled. 'Choose whatever bird you like. Though the dove always flies the fastest, I have found.'

'And is easiest taken by a hawk.' Stromvar closed his mouth, never shocked for long. 'I'll go as an eagle, thank you, as I always do. Let a hawk try to fuck with me then.' He tapped the stick on the table. 'But transformation is wearying, as you know. How far do we have to bear this stave?'

It was Hovard who replied. 'We will pass the stave on to the first gods we tell. They will hand it over to the next, till all of Midgarth has the news. Since Galahur is in the middle of the land, at the joining of the four great rivers, and the six droveways, all should be able to reach it in time.'

'Since I now appear to be taking orders,' Stromvar shook his head, 'is there a place you wish me to go?'

'Einar goes to his home in the far south-east,' Luck replied. 'Freya and Hovard to the towns north and north-east. Bjorn to the southern peninsula. Would you take the south-west? Lorken?'

'Lorken? I've raided it often enough. Should be able to find it. I'll go tell my men.' Stromvar moved away, still limping slightly. At the mead-hall door he turned back. 'The noose you caught me with was clever, Luck. But I think you will need all the power of your name and more than your cleverness where you are bound. There is a reason no one has returned from the Lake of Souls. Good fortune on your journey.' He looked at each in turn. 'All your journeys. By the favour of the gods, we will meet again ... in ten days' time. On Galahur.' He nodded, and left the hall.

'I'll see him to his fleet,' said Bjorn, following.

'Bjorn?' Luck called and his brother turned. 'Do not pick a fight.'

'Me?' Bjorn grinned, and left.

The four remaining gods were silent for a long moment. 'So, it has begun,' said Einar the Black.

'But what has?' Now he'd got his will Luck felt as empty as a drained mead butt. He sat down heavily. 'What has?'

*

The great thaw started the next day and came fast. A sudden hot sun melted snow and ice, turning the streets to muddy slush. Children ran laughing through the town, while their parents stopped to turn their faces to the returned light, close their eyes, and smile.

It took till late afternoon before Luck was ready. Behind his hut he'd packed and repacked the killer's strange vessel – it had done the journey once, so he would take it, and fill its storage holds forward and aft. There were hard choices to be made, for though it was spring near the sea, the high mountain passes he hoped to cross would be deep in snow for a month yet, and the highest would never be clear. Since he was not gifted with weapons, he need not weigh himself down with much metal, save for a small cooking pot, and an axe that was more a hatchet for wood. The one weapon he was good with, his slingshot, weighed almost nothing being rope and leather and he took only twenty of his small, shaped hunting stones. His food was light, dried fruit and meat; he would forage along the way. Clothes were easier. Half the time he would possess animals to travel and they, of course, had their own clothes upon them.

It was midnight. He would leave with the sunrise. Hovard had stopped by, just before he set out himself. He'd given Luck his best knife. They'd talked, but Hovard had never needed much advice when dealing with gods or men. Bjorn hadn't come, sent his wish of fortune with Hovard. He had always hated farewells. For such a hard warrior, he was strangely soft about his brother god.

The last god of Askaug came later, close to midnight; the one he most wanted to see, the one to whom he least wanted to say goodbye. She came as he was standing in the doorway, drawn by a sound he loved – the first cuckoo of spring. 'He's too keen,' Freya said, striding up the narrow pathway between his herb beds. 'Can't you hear the desperation in his voice?'

'Hear it? That's me calling. What you're talking to here is just my shadow self.'

They laughed, and she moved past him, into his hut. It was always crammed with things. He lived alone, after all, and rarely had the desire to tidy. Animals that he'd killed, torn apart, dried and reassembled peered life-like from shelves; birds flew again from strings attached to the beams. The jumble was worse because of his packing.

He came in behind her, looked at the mess, suddenly embarrassed. 'Let me get you a chair. I know I have one ... somewhere.' He rooted about, found it under a pile of skins and furs, threw them onto his bed, beckoned her to sit. She did, and he sat on the thrown furs, their knees almost touching.

'You leave with the sun?'

'I do, Freya. And you?'

'And me. You have everything?'

'No.' He shrugged. 'I cannot know all I will need, because no one has been where I must go. I have chosen the essentials and will figure it out from there.'

Freya looked beside her. On a shelf was the globe that the stranger had brought, in which smoke still swirled. 'Do you take that?'

'I had thought not. But then I realised, since it is how they ... communicate, in ways I do not understand, that I may need it to—'

He broke off. She finished for him. '... to communicate with them? Whoever they are?'

'Perhaps, yes. I may have to. After all, as we know, I am better at talking than I am at fighting.'

'That is true.' Freya took her lower lip between her teeth, sucked in a breath. 'I have been thinking. They – this unknown "they" – will have an advantage if they can speak to each other over distance and we can't.'

'It is true. But there is nothing to be done.'

'There is, though.' She leaned closer. 'You know I have my gifts, as you have yours. Some, not so dissimilar.' She looked to the open door. 'That cuckoo that still calls? He is barely a year old. This will be his first spring, the first time to try for a mate. But there is another older bird, five years old, a male also, who will not give up his territory easily. He is wily, does not call yet and is, even now, stalking his young rival.'

'You know because you have possessed them today, one, other or both.'

'I have not. I know this because I can send my mind. But birds are simple creatures, want little, driven by simple desires.' She reached out a hand, laid it on Luck's cheek. He could not help the slight lean he made into her palm. 'Mortals are different, it is almost impossible to read their thoughts, which are always in such a flurry. And immortals,' she added, her fingers running down his face, 'are the hardest to read of all. But there is a way.'

He wanted to move his head away from her caress. It ... hurt too much. But he found he couldn't. The words he formed half caught in his throat. 'What way?'

'This.' She leaned closer then and brushed his lips with hers. Pulled back a little so she could see into his eyes, his unblinking eyes. 'When two gods are joined in love, their bodies and their spirits entwine and their minds follow. If I choose, I can know where Hovard is any moment of any day. If he's at sea, on a hunt, in battle, even in beast, I can send my mind to enfold his. I can talk to him over distances that matter not at all. And he can talk to me.' She raised her left hand, showed Luck the faintest of white scars already nearly healed upon the palm. 'You saw me do it, when I spoke to Hovard to get him to stop the killer.'

Luck didn't dare move, barely dared to speak. 'So you are saying that if we ... that what we need ...?'

109

'I am. You see? Even just a touch of lips and you already can read my mind.' She smiled. 'At a distance we will need blood, a little pain. Here—'

She leaned in again. He leaned away, but only a little. 'Hovard?' he said, a final, weak protest.

'He knows. And he doesn't. But he also realises that for you to succeed in what you do, you must be armed with every weapon we can give you. He brought you a knife. I—' She stood, looked past him. 'So – is there a bed under all that?'

He reached back. Swept the bed clear. Things fell, things broke, he didn't care. He had loved Freya for a century, in every way it was possible to love her but one. Now he had that too and it was everything he'd ever dreamed of, and more. Much more.

Afterwards, they lay naked under the furs. He'd lit a whale-oil lamp so he could see her, needed sight as well as touch to believe in the truth and the wonder of it. She stroked the bulk of his shoulder, ran fingers down his bunched back, his weaker arm. It was the first time since the passing of Gytta that anyone had and he found that, as with his wife, he didn't mind the touch.

'You know,' Freya said, 'my mortal friends will tell me how hard it is to be with one man for a lifetime. I tell them: try five!'

She laughed and he did too. He didn't often and it felt good. She stopped first, turned his face to her. 'You will be careful,' she said, 'and you will let me know how you are?'

It took him a moment to realise that she hadn't spoken the words aloud.

'I will,' he replied, in thought. 'And you the same.'

They slept. He woke and she was gone but it hadn't been for long, there was warmth beside him still. He stared up until the roof beams of his hut came slowly into sight and he knew that dawn was there. Then the cuckoo began to call again. He wished the young bird well in his quest. Sometimes love will win, he thought.

He rose, dressed swiftly. Only the first light was in the sky and the town still slept. The strange boat was all but packed. There was a hole through the prow stem, just below where Karn had been placed, and he'd run a thick leather cord through, knotting it. Now, after stowing the last few things, carefully wrapping and placing the globe with its vial of liquid, he slipped a rope through the prow loop and began towing the boat. His hut was high up in the town, there was still snow on the ground here and he moved as swiftly as a man with only one really good leg was able.

Puffing heavily, he came eventually to the first downward slope. A trail ran along it, swooping down the valley before rising again and climbing east. He knew that a long, hard winter had brought hungry animals closer to the town than in other years. Soon, in the forests ahead, he would possess a beast, and place its foot in the loop. Then he would limp no more, for a day at least, before he grew tired and the beast too strong.

'Bear or wolf, do you think?'

The voice, in that deep silence, made him jump half out of his skin. Luck yelped, threw himself sideways into a pile of snow, looked up. There, perched directly above him on the branch of a tree, was a god. 'Hello, brother,' he said, with a grin.

'Bjorn, you half-brain! I nearly soiled myself.'

'And you probably haven't got many changes of leggings, have you?' With his usual grace, Bjorn swung his whole body around the branch then dropped lightly to the ground. 'So, bear or wolf?'

Luck sat up, brushing snow from his beaver-fur coat. 'What are you talking about?' he grumbled.

'I think wolf myself.' Bjorn scratched at his beard. 'Bears are stronger but so much harder to control, don't you find?' He looked down into the valley ahead. 'While I was waiting for you I spotted a she-wolf and her mate.' He turned back. 'Play throw-sticks for who gets which?'

Luck's head was perhaps still a little fuzzy from the night behind and the task ahead. 'Are you saying—?'

'That I'm coming with you? Of course I am. And before you ask, it was my idea not Hovard's, though he agreed fast enough.'

Something stirred around Luck's heart that he was not used to. But this was no time for sentiment. 'Bjorn, I'd like your company of course. But your task is to fly the summons south.'

'Strumbum agreed to do it.' His brother grinned. 'I mean, his mouth's certainly big enough for two staves. And the peninsula is only a little past his destination, Lorken.' He stopped smiling. 'Besides, Stromvar knows, as we all do, that your wits will only get you so far. There may be times when Sever-Life will be needed instead.' He reached up, tapped the hilt of his sword, strapped across his back. 'Besides,' he added, looking to the east, 'there is someone I need to speak to, at the Lake of Souls. The one who decided to use my friend Karn as a boat decoration.' For a moment he stared ahead, into the forest's depths, beyond them. Then he looked back, and his smile returned. 'So wolf it is. But which one for you? Oh see, I just happen to have some throw-sticks with me. Best of three?' The grin widened as he held them up. 'Your call, little brother. Noggin or bum?'

6

City of Women

'One more. One more,' urged her guide.

Nak was from these mountains – short, browner than her, with the narrow eyes of the mountain people – and could speak rapidly to the wagon driver, Bok, in a tongue that had nothing in common with Bunami, the language spoken on the coastal plain and, with slight variations, in the volcano city, Toluc. Atisha suspected that the two words were all Nak had of her tongue – and that he did not know what they meant. He used 'One more. One more,' on her like he used his sharpened stick to goad the llamas. If she was flagging near day's end he would point to the crest ahead and say it. Reaching that, he would say it again, gesturing to the next one. A week after setting out, once she'd regained some strength, she'd decided it was better to walk than sit on the lurching, bone-jarring wagon – the trails they took were strewn with rocks the size of apples. At the start his words were agony, disappointment at the top of every rise. Now, two and a half weeks later, she welcomed them. She didn't know what awaited her in the City of Women that was her destination, but she knew she'd need her body to be strong to face it. Between the walking and the diet – llama milk, llama butter, dried llama – the little weight she'd put on in pregnancy had largely gone. She was getting lean again – unlike little

Poum, fat on mother's milk, of which she had an abundance.

The child gurgled now in the cloth sling on her back. Nothing had changed in the baby's anatomy. But though Atisha had given the child a name that could belong to either sex, she had decided she had a daughter. She had to. The opposite was unthinkable.

The path steepened, narrowed, entered a defile, walls of rock rising each side of her, curving in to meet ahead, like an entrance. Her breath came harder. This high up the air was thin for a coastal girl. She paused for a moment, leaned against one rock face. Fant flopped beside her, long pink tongue out, panting hard – for he was as much a creature of the lowlands as she.

'One more, one more,' came from behind them. She glanced back. Nak was, as ever, behind the first llama in the line of six, all linked by rope and weighed down with supplies. Four more were yoked to the small wagon, also piled with goods, Bok atop them. With a grin, Nak waved his stick, then jabbed the long bone needle at its tip into the lead llama's haunch. It started, spat, began to climb. She'd been trodden on before, didn't want it again. Heaving a breath that hurt – the air this high was iced as well as hard to come by – she pushed herself off the wall, climbed to the gap, stepped through it …

… to wonder!

It was the first and only time 'one more' was right. For there, on the next peak, was a city. The city. The City of Women.

She stopped so suddenly that Poum jerked awake and began to cry. For once Atisha didn't instantly reach to comfort her, she was so stunned. All in her sight for near three weeks had been the grey and white of the ranges and high plateau. Here were greens and yellows, some reds, on terraces that girdled the mountain like fecund belts. These narrowed as they climbed to a great stone citadel, with towers, gateways, houses, their roofs made of dried lake reeds, the thatch an arm's length thick.

At the centre was a two-storeyed hall, its huge wooden doors flanked by giant lamps that burned with the blue flame of oil. Even as she watched, a bell sounded and immediately other lamps began to appear in the embrasures and windows that studded the walls, stars in a granite sky. She looked down and saw a bridge spanning a gorge, woven from reeds and suspended from wooden towers, two at each end.

She felt the nudge of a llama's snout in her back. The beasts had probably known for a time that their destination was close; that rest, fresh straw, to eat and to lie upon, awaited. But for a moment longer she did not move, her breath held, not by chill nor mountain height but by sudden fear.

She stepped aside and, reaching around, plucked Poum from her cloth cage. Delving under layers she brought out a breast and the baby eagerly fastened on. As the caravan passed her, she turned again to the City of Women. A journey ends, she thought. Another begins. But what is our destination now?

Beside her, Fant sank down and laid his head on his huge paws with a sigh.

'You are the latest One? You?'

The hall was alive with flame, in sconces on pillars, and in the full hearth. But it was still cold – as cold as the woman who sat in a carved chair on a raised dais, peering down at Atisha.

Muna – so she had announced herself, governess of the City of Women – studied the paper she held, and looked at Atisha again in exaggerated disbelief. 'Are you sure you did not steal another's clothes and life?' She laughed, a sound without humour. 'In my day, the Fire God loved women with some flesh to them. I myself was … voluptuous.' She raised fleshy arms, and a multitude of bangles slid from her wrist and stuck halfway down her forearm. 'He did not favour girls who looked like boys.'

Atisha stayed silent. There was no point disagreeing with the woman who now controlled her life.

Her silence irked. 'Proud, are we? I wouldn't be. We have three other "Ones" here and they earn their keep like anyone else. I would have been the fourth, of course,' she lowered her arms and the bracelets jangled down, 'if Intitepe had not chosen as one of his twelve a witch from the Shadow Islands. I would!' She looked around the hall for contradiction, at the dozen women who stood in a half-circle before the dais, all with their hands folded before them and their heads bowed.

One raised hers. 'Of course you would, Muna. Intitepe was bewitched.'

'Bewitched,' Muna repeated. 'But she got her reward, the bitch. Insatiable, she was. Took a lover from the guards! Imagine! But Intitepe swam them both in the lava, them and their bastard son. I remember him saying to me as I comforted him afterwards, "I should have chosen you, Muna, I should—"'

She stared above Atisha. Moments passed until the woman who'd spoken coughed softly. Muna focused, looked down again at the letter. 'It says here ... well, I think it's best we keep what it says here between ourselves, don't you?' Silence still. 'Yes?' she snapped.

Atisha looked directly at her. 'Yes.'

'Very well.' She considered Atisha again. 'Can you do anything?'

'Do?'

'Work, you stupid girl.' She sniffed. 'You look like a peasant.'

'My father was a farmer. I learned something of—'

'Can you sew?'

It was a new voice that interrupted. Atisha looked at the women with the downcast eyes, did not see who had spoken.

Muna knew. 'Really, Besema? You would take this peasant on?'

116

'I will if she can sew.'

Atisha saw her now. The woman had raised her head to speak. Within a covering shroud, she saw hair as white as mountain-peak snow and a face puckered by wrinkles. The voice had been old too, like dry leaves rubbed together. Yet the eyes that turned to her now were young, as young and blue as dawn on a summer's morning. And beyond their colour there was something in them, some appeal, some offer, some ... hope. 'I can sew,' Atisha said quickly. 'I won prizes for it in my town.'

It was a lie. It was her friend Asaya who'd been the seamstress. Perhaps the governess guessed the lie. She hesitated, and for a moment Atisha feared she'd assign the peasant to work the terraces. Then she shrugged. 'Very well. Take her, Besema. You always like the outcasts, don't you? But be warned,' she raised the letter and pointed. 'This one has displeased Intitepe. Displeased him greatly. Praise him!' She glared around and all the women, even Atisha, echoed her.

'Praise him!'

Muna waved her hand. 'Go. All of you. You tire me. Go!'

The women bowed, shuffled out. Poum waited in the lobby of the hall, squirming and whimpering in the arms of the servant Atisha had been forced to leave her with. In the three weeks since her birth, she not been separated from her mother, even in sleep. Fant, who'd accepted the silent command to watch over the babe, rose now and came forward, his tail wagging.

'Come, pretty one, come.' Besema stepped close, took Atisha's arm. Her voice dropped to a low rasp. 'Oh yes, you are a pretty one, and your child too. Whatever that bitch in there says.' She moved away to a descending stair and Atisha, crooning soft words to Poum, followed, the dog at her heels.

The old woman led them through a labyrinth of stairs, hallways and chambers, across gardens open to the night sky, and finally through an archway and along a winding terrace that

117

curved around one edge of the mountain. In her first glimpse of the city, Atisha hadn't taken in its immensity. The towers didn't only reach three levels into the sky, but had depths far below the surface. There was a long, low structure on one terrace they passed, white-walled, reed-roofed, light spilling through gaps in shutters. Within, Atisha heard the clank of plates, the tock of wooden spoons dropped on tables, the glug of liquid into mugs, some laughter. 'Supper time! Supper time!' Besema sang, and giggled, and Atisha was suddenly aware of how completely famished she was. Beside her, Fant echoed her with a hungry growl.

Eventually, they halted at another stone arch. 'Is he good, your hound?' Besema asked. 'Will he obey you, keep quiet, keep still?'

'He ... will,' replied Atisha, puzzled.

'Good. Wait just the other side.' She opened a wicker gate set into the archway, they passed through, she followed and closed it behind her. This terrace was darker, no torches set in walls as the others had. Starlight, and the two half moons that held the sky, revealed a little. There were tall, dark shapes in the gloom. Fant growled – and the shapes moved, fast, separating then coalescing. Atisha grasped the collar she'd put on him for safety when they'd reached the city. 'What is this?' she asked.

Besema stooped inside the arch then stood, holding a gated lantern in one hand, something else in the other. She opened the lamp, and a small, guttering light shone ...

... on a llama! It had its teeth bared, dark eyes wide over its furry muzzle. But it was just one of many, dozens of them, pushing forward into the light spill. These were bigger than the pack animals they'd travelled with, had much thicker wool coats. Atisha, who'd never feared llamas, was frightened here by this mob. Fant, who'd been kicked by one in the mountains, slunk behind her legs.

'Here,' said Besema, thrusting something up, 'this is what they want.'

Atisha saw what the old woman was offering – a bucket of small, wizened apples. She lifted one, held it out. 'No,' Besema snapped. 'She'll have your finger. Throw them. Throw them!' She put the bucket down, reached in, grabbed one, tossed it into the air. Llamas moved quickly, competing. Atisha grabbed, threw. 'Faster!' said Besema. 'More.'

They passed through the herd, which scattered as the beasts chased the apples Atisha hurled. After a hundred paces they came to another wicker gate, set into a fence. Besema let them through into a small herb garden. Beyond that was a large, one-storey, white-walled, reed-thatched house.

Behind them, the llamas shifted, snickered and stamped. 'How many are there?' Atisha asked, looking back.

'I keep a hundred here. But I get the wool from many more. Wool and … other things.' She opened the front door onto a room already lit. 'Because of this.'

In the centre of the room was a huge loom, bigger than any Atisha had ever seen. Coloured threads ran from dozens of spindles. In the loom's centre, held like a spider's prey in its web, was a multicoloured tapestry, filled with dozens of squares, triangles, loops.

Besema placed the empty basket inside the door, then moved into the centre of the room. 'You sleep there.' She gestured to a pile of skins in the corner of the room. 'That door,' she pointed to one at the back, 'is mine alone. You do not go in there, understand?' The words were sharply spoken and Atisha nodded. 'Good.'

The old woman moved away, to the hearth, and the cooking pot there. She swung it over the fire, which she bent to and coaxed back with breath, then twigs then sticks then logs, into full life. Dipping her finger into the pot, she raised and licked it. 'Hmm, guess what's for supper? You never will. Llama stew!' She laughed in her dry-voiced crackle then pointed to the baby fussing in the sling. 'It will be a while. Feed your child.'

By the time they sat at the table a little later, Poum was sleeping on the pile of furs, Fant happy nearby, gnawing a bone. Atisha had sighed when she thought of more stew. But her first bite filled her with wonder. It was savoury, spiced with herbs and chillies, delicious and deep. She swiftly finished it, scooping the last with a slice of crunchy bread. She felt she could not ask for more – and did not need to, Besema filling her bowl again with a smile. There was liquor too, a sharp distillation that had little taste but brought tears immediately to Atisha's eyes. She sipped while Besema drank, two tumblers, three. It didn't seem to affect her words, few of which were spoken anyway. It brightened her blue eyes still more, and they became ever more fixed on Atisha.

A third bowl, and even Atisha was done.

'Water runs from the mountain, at the edge of the house. Go clean the bowls and spoons. The pot too, you've emptied that.' Besema followed Atisha's glance to the babe in the corner. 'The child sleeps. I will watch. Go. You earn your stew here, girl.'

Atisha rose. Fant did too, but she waved him down to his duty. He would not let anyone harm the child.

Outside the night was cold, a sharp contrast to the room. She shivered, hurried to the edge of the house. A stream did fall from the mountain, filling a natural stone basin before cascading on. She used a clump of moss to clean everything. The pot was encrusted, and took longer. She was almost warm by the time she finished.

When she came back inside, she looked straight to the furs. Fant was there. Poum was not. She looked wildly about – and found her baby on the bench of the loom, in Besema's arms. Atisha dropped everything she held, pots and bowls clanging to the floor. She drew her obsidian dagger from the sheath flush to her spine. 'Give her to me,' she shouted, striding forward. 'Give her now, or—'

She stopped at the loom's right beam. Poum was naked, lying on her back, giggling. She circled her legs in the air, revealing and concealing the petals, the this and that at her core. 'Of course,' said Besema, holding her up, one hand under her bottom, one under her head. Atisha sheathed her knife, took her, checked her. She was fine, giving the smile she'd only just started to make.

'She was fussing. There was a smell. I thought I'd—' She broke off. 'I am glad I did.' Her voice sharpened. '*Can* you sew?'

'What?'

'Can you *sew*?'

'I …' There was little point in lying. The old woman would find out soon enough. 'No.'

Yet instead of the expected anger, a chuckle came. 'Well, you will learn. That, and other skills too.' She took her upper lip between teeth still white and strong and inhaled loudly. 'And you will need to learn fast. Because from all I know of Intitepe, he doesn't take risks. *She*, as you call her, is a risk.' She shook her head. 'He must have loved you very much, to let you go. But the memory of that love will fade fast, in time, and in the arms of others. Soon he will remember only one thing: the prophecy.' She rose, adding, softly, 'I think you may be the one we have waited for all this time.'

Atisha stared at her. She'd been the One, of course. No more. But she also knew, instantly, clearly, that the old woman wasn't talking about her anyway.

The girl – Napocha? Was that her name? – gave a last great cry and slipped him from her, shuddering, to fall beside him into the pool.

Intitepe had wearied of her attempts to please him, so he had given a small grunt, pretending to be satisfied when he was not. He could not understand this latest failing. For as soon as he'd seen her again, he remembered why he had chosen the girl. She had the fairer hair of many in the northernmost province of Palaga, and a body of perfect symmetry – tall, but with large, high breasts, a slim waist, a pleasing swelling at hip and thigh. Her body was near milk white, unlike the browner girls of the coast, and he'd picked her for that contrast. It wasn't even that she was poor at her task; she was willing, enthusiastic, keen to learn. But with the other ten in his marana, it had been the same. He'd worked his way through them, south to north, every few days for three weeks now. He'd not invited any back for a second night, nor allowed any to stay that first night beside him – he was having enough trouble sleeping as it was. Besides, none had shown any sign of being the next One.

His hip hurt. 'Move, Napocha,' he snapped.

'Natara, lord,' the girl said, shifting, then looked up at him, startled. 'I ... I ... I am sorry to correct you.'

He glanced into her deep blue, fearful eyes, then away. Fear bored him. It took all delight from what he did. He didn't want it, nor its cousin, obligation. He only wanted to be desired as he desired.

No. I know what I want, curse it. I want Atisha.

He stared up into the heavens, found her, down from the spider's left eye, past the cluster of seven monkeys. The sky was clear tonight, the star bright and winking at him, as she would wink at him when she laughed at him, cried out for him, made him cry out for her. In the afterglow she would question him, her mind agile and curious. And he would tell her things, of the world and how it worked, share some of the knowledge that a five-hundred-year-old fire god had acquired. Yet she never received it in awe, in obligation, only in delight and with ever more questions.

Until the night had come when she'd asked him about the prophecy, the same night she'd revealed her betrayal. For what else was it? To allow herself to get with child? To give up all they'd been, and still could be, for that? For what any animal could do? She should have remained twelve years by his side not two, then returned to her village at the Festival of Change, wealthy beyond dreams, there to marry some lump of a farmer who would not believe his fortune and would give her as many children as she could want. Instead ...

His eyes searched the sky again. Only one other had ever betrayed him like that, shared the same joys and laughter – then gotten with child and questioned him on prophecy. There she was, at the head of the line of stars they called the Snake, at the top tip of its forked tongue. Besema. He remembered her name well enough. Was she still alive, in the City of Women? He doubted it. It was sixty years since he'd named the star for her. Sixty since she'd questioned him in this same pool.

Sixty since he'd given the son she'd made to Toluc, his brother god in fire.

He wished he could unname the star he'd given her, blot it from his mind. He'd tried – but he never could. As he knew he would never be able to unname Atisha's.

Yet, he realised suddenly, clearly, there was something he could do.

'It was a mistake,' he said aloud.

'I am s-sorry, lord, that I offended.'

'Not you.' He rose from the pool, dripping. Grabbed a blanket to rub himself down then strode to the door, jerked it open. 'Fetch me a runner. And find Tolucca. Send her here,' he commanded the startled guard.

He turned back. The girl – Natara, of course that was her

123

name! – had risen from the pool, stood there now like a river goddess dripping water. She was magnificent. And he felt absolutely nothing for her.

Relay runners would get to the City of Women in seven days. They would bear his command to separate Atisha and the baby immediately. Tolucca would arrive two weeks later. She would take her raven mask and her obsidian dagger. She would return with his son – if son that *thing* had already become – and in a great ceremony the child would be offered to the lava. It had been too long since the last sacrifice. The people needed to be reminded who he was.

The Fire God.

He moved past the dripping girl to the window, and stared up at the stars in the southern sky. This time, though, he sought none. Three weeks for Tolucca to reach the City of Women, he thought. Three weeks to return. So in six weeks I will know – and be free to love again.

In six weeks I'll be able to sleep.

Intitepe should not have been looking south as the focus for all his fears. He should have been looking north. And not to a mountain top but to the sea ...

... to a part of his realm where, beneath towering, jungled cliffs, fishing villages lay scattered along beaches of black sand like ill-fashioned pearls on a chain. Off one of those villages, so isolated that its people only knew it as 'the Place', a vessel was drifting towards the reef. Its main mast was sheared, its few sails shredded, most of the oars that also could power it were snapped in half or lost to wave. Of the crew who'd set out six months before only half were alive, and those barely – and they had only survived by drinking sea water and eating their dead.

If Intitepe were attuned to more than one danger at a time he might have seen, as his father might have seen, as Saroc,

priest-king and last immortal rival would certainly have seen ...
a fisherman, who'd had a poor day and so was the last out on
the evening tide. Seen him look up suddenly from his empty
nets at the ruined ship. Mistake it for a moment for one of the
giant tree trunks that sometimes drifted to their shores. Change
his mind when a figure in black rags rose from the prow and
beckoned to him.

He paddled fast for the shore, threading the reef passage
as the ship drifted closer to its doom. He roused the villagers
and they had a swift debate. Some thought the black ruin was
filled with devils. Some that it bore emissaries from one of
their seventeen gods. All agreed that nothing this exciting had
happened in the Place in even the oldest man's living memory,
nor in any tale passed from father to son.

The canoes reached the vessel just before it foundered on the
reef. They lassoed it, lashed it, pulled it with hard strokes of their
paddles through the gap in the reef and into the calm waters of
the lagoon where it grounded and tipped, ten canoe-lengths
from the shore.

Creatures – these black-ragged skeletons could not be called
men, not yet – dropped into the water. Twenty made it to the
beach, while three, who could not get so far, lay in the shallow
sea, spinning in the slow circles of the drowned.

The survivors lay face down on the sand until, watched by
the entire village – men, women, children, babes in arms – the
fishermen turned them over one by one. They were not devils,
or if they were at least they had human form. Men then, most
small and stringy much like themselves. Only one man was
taller, wider, with strange scarification on his face and arms,
and legs that bowed, as if he'd sat astride logs all his life. The
second to last they turned was a woman. All were famine-thin
and covered in scabs and welts.

Only the last was different, and he was very different. His

head was like a skinned coconut, his teeth blacker than burnt wood – as were his eyes. When he opened them, they shone like sable pearls in a red clam's shell.

He was a god, or he was a devil and they didn't much care which. When he pointed at his mouth they gave him water. When he pointed at the others, they gave them water too. Then they brought them all mashed flesh of mango, and raw fish. At last the man spoke, and though they understood nothing, the sound was a song, beautiful as a bird greeting the rising sun and as compelling as breath. Finally when he brought out, from a fold within his rags, a thing the size of a coconut but that swirled with smoke within, they knelt as one in the black sand and worshipped him.

All this Intitepe, the Fire God, might have sensed, if he had been facing north, not south; if all his intuition had not been consumed by five hundred years of peace, and a single prophecy. Yet it had been. To his and his realm's eventual and perpetual sorrow.

7

The Race

It was a sound that Ferros loved – the snort and stamp of horses on a cold, bright early winter's morning. Three weeks of rain had ended and below the window of the room in which he studied, someone was preparing to ride.

'The answer, young man, is to be found in the pages before you, not written in the sky.'

Ferros turned away from the window and his longing, and back to the man on the other side of the desk. It was the first time in his three weeks of study that Lucan, leader of the Council of Lives, and the man he'd met in the Sanctum on his first night, had come to instruct him. To begin he had still worked with Gan, the tutor who had accompanied him on the voyage from Balbek. But Gan's limits were soon reached, and specialists were brought in. One man had taught him of potions, of the plants of power. Another had lectured on geography. Neither subject thrilled him, though he found that despite leaving school at ten to join his regiment, he was swift to pick things up. He retained little, however, from two excruciating mornings spent with Streone, his first guide in the city, who spoke of festivals, of art and theatre, subjects in which the soldier took little interest. He also learned far too much about the man's triumphs, first as an actor and poet then, once he'd discovered his immortality, of the producing of the spectacles that all immortals delighted in. He was, by his own frequent admissions, the greatest impresario that had ever lived.

It was better when an initially taciturn general called Parkos had come to explain the development of the army, and the wars that had been fought to manage the tribes on each of Corinthium's frontiers. Ferros had known some of this, especially the war histories of the Sarphardi hills where he'd served. His enthusiasm, and a jug of heated ale, had melted the older man's reserve and the two had quickly dropped into the ease of the barracks. Alas for Ferros, the general had come for only two days, to be replaced ... by the man who sat opposite him now.

That morning, Lucan had told him of the history of immortality. How the gift had been brought to a village of squabbling peasant fishermen by 'the visitor' who was known thereafter as Andros the Blind. How anyone 'gifted' then journeyed across the seas to reach the place they turned into Corinthium.

'May I meet them, these First Ones?' Ferros had asked.

'No. Because they came, stayed long enough to found the city about five hundred years ago, then vanished. No one knows where they went – though since immortals are born all over what became the empire, this indicates that they travelled widely after they departed from here. Sowing seeds.' Lucan nodded. 'Because aside from laws, and the first temples, they left that legacy in the blood. The birth of others like them. So rare. So prized. As are you, Ferros of Balbek.'

The history lesson had taken a day – an overview of the history of Corinthium from that founding to its present glories. Now, another day had begun – with philosophy. But as he turned back from the window, from the sound of horses, and the sense of escape that it conjured, Ferros struggled to remember the question Lucan had asked him. 'I—' he said, looking for clues in the text Lucan had handed him. Five-syllable words rose meaningless before him.

'I asked you ...' Lucan began, irritation plain in his tone.

One of those words came clear. 'Paradoxical,' Ferros said. 'You asked about how we deal with the paradox of Immortality. How even the ever-lived may die.'

'I did,' Lucan conceded. 'And does your text explain it?'

Ferros looked down. The text in question was from some mystic, an immortal called Hypethus who'd lived as a hermit in the caves near Cuerodocia for three hundred years. He'd tried starving himself to death – only to be reborn, famished. Thrown himself off a cliff – just once, the pain of reknitting so many broken bones an agony he chose not to repeat. Eventually, to spare himself suffering, he'd gathered a small band of similar immortal questers to die and live for him. Some had drowned in the sea – and swum to the surface and thence the shore. Some had been shot with a hundred arrows – and pulled each one out, an experience Ferros recalled with a shudder.

Seeking now, as Lucan sighed, he found the answer – in a paragraph he'd read and misunderstood, so couched was it in ancient terms of near impenetrable meaning. And understanding, he decided to speak with a soldier's candour. 'We can dissolve in fire,' he said, 'and we can have our heads hacked off. As long as they are kept away from the body for a time—'

'That is all you glean from the intricate philosophies of Hypethus?' Lucan interrupted. 'Burning and hacking?'

'Pretty much,' Ferros replied, picking up the smooth stones that anchored the scroll open and flat, letting it spring back into its cone. He sat back in his chair and stared at the older man. 'And it wouldn't have taken me one hundred years of suicide in a desert to prove it either.'

Instead of a frown or a word of chastisement, his usual response, Lucan smiled. 'Ah, the soldier speaks! How bracing it is to hear bluntness again. Everything in Corinthium, and especially in the Sanctum, is always so ... weighed. With truth a secret to be winnowed out of words.' He looked to the window, to the world and its noises. 'Little wonder my daughter finds you so ... refreshing.'

She does? Ferros wondered, keeping his expression bland even as his heart skipped. He had only seen Roxanna twice since that first meeting, the day he'd arrived in the city. Once from a distance, staring at her from this same window as the back gate opened and emitted her. Once closer to, as he took the Heaven Road up to the Sanctum from his lodgings near the port and she passed in a basket going down. She'd seen him too then, smiled and tipped her head. But before his dry mouth would let him raise some spit then try to form words she was gone. About what business he could only – and did – wonder. How does an Immortal occupy herself in Corinthium? Who does she occupy herself with?

He stared at the man before him, his black skin, the trimmed grey beard. Saw nothing of her – except in the viridescence of the eyes. But his greenness was as still and calm as a pond. Hers held fire and—

He shifted, under Lucan's returned scrutiny, with the sudden and uncomfortable feeling that the man could read his thoughts. Maybe it was another of the benefits of immortality. He'd been told that there were several – apart from the obvious one. Some had been hinted at – to be revealed when he knew more of the basics. Which he realised, again, that he needed to do. His ignorance, his bluntness, however 'refreshing', was holding him back. From what, he was still not sure. From whom, he was.

Then Lara replaced Roxanna in his mind. Unsettled, he unfolded another scroll, weighed it down. More long words to decipher. Someone whistled outside the window, a descent of musical notes. A horse snickered as if in reply. And in that moment Ferros did believe that Lucan could read the run of his mind because he said, 'And speaking of my daughter—' He rose, walked around the desk. 'Come, young man,' he said, and crossed to the window, pushed it all the way open, leaned out. 'Greetings, child,' he called.

Ferros joined him. There were two horses in the courtyard below – a stallion, large, sleek and sheeny black, the other smaller, shaggy-coated, a mare. A groom was at their heads, holding the two sets of reins. At their rumps, a hand on each, stood Roxanna.

'Greetings, Father. And Ferros,' she smiled up. 'A fine day for a ride, is it not?'

Lucan spoke before Ferros could reply. 'Our soldier is a student today, daughter. We are exploring the musings of Hypethus.'

'Oh, you poor man!' Roxanna's laugh was as musical as her call to the horse had been. 'Then do not consider this a ride. Consider this a rescue – from the third way to kill an immortal. Boredom!' She took her lower lip between her teeth. 'Do you want rescuing, Ferros?'

'I would consider it an honour, lady.'

'An honour? Hmm. You might not think that by the end of the day. And after all, Father, I am not interrupting his studies, just continuing them.' She smiled. 'Or did you want mere mortals to beat us in the race, yet again?'

'The race?' Ferros asked, turning to Lucan.

The man shrugged. 'Every year, at the festival of Simbala, various races are run, including one on horseback between immortals and mortals. They have many more to choose from while we have few who can ride. For myself, I can't bear horses.' He shuddered. 'They delight in beating us and have for twenty or more years.'

'Many more,' said Roxanna. 'So it may be worth seeing if Ferros is good enough to halt that run.'

The challenge in her gaze switched back to him, stirred him. 'Lady,' he said, 'I shall be delighted to prove that I am.' He turned to Lucan. 'Can you spare me for a morning, lord? Perhaps some air will clear my head and cure me of my ... bluntness.'

The leader of the Council of Lives studied him for a long moment – before he shrugged. 'Go then,' he said, and waved his hand. 'But have a care for him, Roxanna. I need him at his desk again this afternoon, not lying in the infirmary with a broken neck.'

'A gentle canter through the hills, Father, that's all.' She smiled. 'I'll have him back, barely sweating, by midday.'

'I'll come down.' Ferros turned from the window, dipped his head to Lucan, left the room. What did she say? he thought as he descended the stairs. *I'll have him ... barely sweating?* 'What are you?' he muttered to himself. 'Fourteen?'

Still, he was grinning as he walked into the yard at the back of the palace. Roxanna was facing the door, had moved to the horses' heads, taken their reins from the groom.

The very first time he'd seen her she'd been dressed in flowing emerald silk. Now she was all dark brown leather. A strap of it across her forehead tamed her corkscrewing black hair, a long-sleeved laced jerkin contained – but only just – her breasts, tight trousers did the same for her long legs, ending in boots. She wore a short riding cloak. None of it was new, much of it frayed in places. Well used, supple, easy to move in. 'This is Shadowfire,' she said, and the black stallion snorted, and jerked its head up and down at the sound of his name, while she let the reins slide between her fingers without releasing them. 'This,' she said, turning, 'is Serrana.' The mare did not move – except for her long eyelashes, raised and lowered over her deep brown eyes as she regarded him. 'You may choose either, Ferros.'

Her tone was light, nothing but friendly. Yet there was

something in her gaze that paused his reply. From the moment he'd arrived in the city he'd been tested. Every day in the room above them. Here, in some way, in this yard. For what, he still did not know. But it was there, challenge in those green, green eyes.

'Do I choose for a gentle canter in the hills?' he asked. 'Or do we race?'

'Do you wish to race?' she replied, the challenge moving from eyes to voice.

'Why not? I mean, if you are testing me ... for this contest against the mortals?'

'The mortals. Of course.' She studied him then looked above him, to the window from which, Ferros knew, Lucan still watched. Her gaze returned to him. 'Why not?' she echoed him. 'Let us race. So ... choose.'

He looked again at Shadowfire. The stallion was Sarphardi, bred in the same hills as him, used by tribesmen and cavalry alike, made for swiftness across sands and over dunes. The sort of horse that would run for ever and break its heart if you asked it to. He'd ridden such horses since the army had taken him in as a boy. 'How long? Over what country? Do we gallop from this gate to the first hill beyond the walls?'

'We could. But the first part through the streets would be dull. Anyway I prefer something more challenging, don't you?' She smiled. 'Besides, the race against the mortals involves jumps as well as sprints and,' she gestured with her head to the side, 'javelins.'

He saw them then, what he'd missed before: hunting javelins hanging in two quivers from Shadowfire's saddle beak. He liked javelins. 'And the distance?'

'There is a valley close by. Fields, stone walls, streams, a forest.' She shrugged. 'It is easier to show you than explain. If you will only choose.'

That gaze was on him again. He looked away from it, to the horses. The stallion was a natural choice for him, of a breed he knew so well. Bold, fiery, fast. And yet, from the moment he'd discovered his immortality, everything that had been natural no longer was. So he looked again at the mare, who continued to regard him steadily. She was a tawpan, bred for the forest and mountain trails of the north. Her coat was a shaggy contrast to the smooth-flanked stallion. And the type of terrain Roxanna had just described? After all that rain? Serrana was sure-footed, calm – a platform for the precise throwing required for javelins. And yet ...

All his yearning for the life he'd left behind made him wish to choose the stallion. But that was his life that was, and it was no more. So when Shadowfire tossed his head, and Roxanna calmed him with a word, Ferros knew. 'I'll take her,' he said, stepping forward, reaching to stroke the starburst of white between the mare's eyes.

Roxanna's eyes widened just a little, a betrayal of surprise. Yet all she said was, 'Good,' and nodded to the groom who came and took both sets of reins. Hands free, each rider turned to their mount, to adjust their tack, stirrups and bits.

They rode from the yard, Shadowfire trotting in front in a sideways gait that showed how he yearned to gallop, Roxanna keeping him on a tight rein. Serrana followed slowly, head lowered, and for a moment Ferros wondered if he'd made a bad choice. Then he pulled back a little on the reins, moved the horse left and right with pressure at thigh and hand. Serrana was biddable – while beyond that Ferros sensed a contained energy within the mare, quite unlike the one the stallion ahead was demonstrating in his dance, and he was happier again.

The avenue, with offices for administration on either side, led to a small gate set into the towering white walls that protected Corinthium on its landward side – though from what, he did not know, for the city had not been attacked by the Wattenwolden, the forest tribes, for three hundred years, since the time of their last great leader, Caradocius. Two soldiers descended from the gate tower, bowed, then slipped the crossbar and swung the gate open.

They rode out. Ferros, dressed for study, not sport, in simple wool trousers and short jacket, had been cold within the stone of the city. But they entered an early winter sunshine that still held some warmth and the vista before him – recently cropped wheat fields rising to a treed ridge – sent heat through his body. He inhaled deeply, the first breath he'd taken in weeks untainted by city stench. It cleared his head of all desire bar one: to ride, the faster the better.

'Come then,' said Roxanna, and tapped her heels – spurred, he noticed with a moment's unease, aware of his own sandalled feet. The stallion moved into an easy canter. Ferros tapped, and was relieved when Serrana reacted instantly, soon catching up to her bigger stablemate.

They entered the forest on the ridge side by side and soon enough. An avenue of maple and beech stretched before them, autumn's bounty carpeting the ground in red and gold. Roxanna slowed to a walk so he did too. On her huge mount, and with her height nearly the equal of his, she looked down at him, one leather-swathed breast almost level with his face – something he swiftly decided not to study. She jerked her head towards the light, like a tunnel opening, about two hundred paces away. 'This track swings wide out to the right, then comes back in, leading eventually to our goal. But straight ahead, there are two fields – corn, but harvested, and bounded in hedgerows. In the meadow beyond them the land slopes straight down with a stream cutting across it. There's a ford, and a bridge further up to the right where this track joins again. You'll see it. On the crown of the next hill there's a ruined Temple of the Sun. The bell tower still stands and on its eastern side, of course, there's the remnants of the Dawn Window. There's a bale of hay in that, sculpted into the rough shape of a man.' As she spoke she untied one quiver from her saddle beak and passed it over. 'There's a circle painted here,' she ran her fingers around her left breast, pushing out the leather, and this time Ferros chose not to look away. She pressed her finger into the very centre. 'Aim your javelins for the heart, Ferros.'

'Always.' He took the quiver, tying it swiftly to his saddle beak. 'Three javelins,' he stated.

'Three. The javelins decide the race. If you get there first, you can dismount, take your time.'

He nodded. *If?* The way she said it told him that she was certain he would be second. 'Any other rules?'

'No other rules,' she replied, her eyes piercing him. 'There is only winning.'

'I see. And when does the race begin?'

'Now,' she said, and kicked in her spurs.

Shadowfire broke into an instant gallop. But so did Serrana as he dug in his heels and cried, 'Yah!'

He was pleased to discover that the mare was fast – yet nowhere near as fast as the stallion, who burst from the avenue's end and vanished down the slope with Ferros still ten lengths back. When he cleared the trees he reined in, had to squint against the brightness – to see Roxanna halfway across the field that had been corn, her mount's hooves shooting clods of mud up amidst the stalks.

'Yah!' he cried again, urging Serrana forward. He felt it straight away, in the beast's adjusted gait – the early winter rains had been heavy, and mud was flung from hooves as she strode. But she was lighter than the stallion and a glance ahead showed Shadowfire slowing a little as the land sloped upwards. 'Yah!' he called again, lowering his head flush to the mare's neck.

136

He'd nearly caught up by the first hedge. Watched the stallion clear it by half the height of a man. Ferros had never been much of a jumper, it was not a skill often required on the desert flats. But he knew the essentials – and that Serrana would know them better than him. With a jab of his heels he flattened still more, let slip the reins, and gave the horse her head.

She cleared the hedge, not by the same height but handily enough. Landed and was off again, making up still more ground on the stallion in the second muddy field. As they approached the next hedge he was maybe three lengths behind. I'll look into your eyes this time, Roxanna, he thought, and grinned, kicking harder ... and nearly flying off!

Serrana had baulked. He was up and on her neck, feet clear of the stirrups. Desperately he grasped her mane, just held on. Slid back, found lost reins and stirrups. Cursing himself for an arrogant fool – he'd held her back on the jump, like an idiot – he turned the horse, retreated twenty paces, turned again, kicked her hard and headed again for the hedge, letting her control it now.

They landed easily again, the downward slope pulling them on. But Ferros could see that his slip had given Roxanna a better option – rather than drive for the stream at this valley's muddy bottom, she had swung right and headed back up to the track that swung out of the forest and now swung back – to a bridge. It was wide out, she'd cross it and have to come back. But once on it, the big stallion would take the track fast, faster than his mare if he followed them.

Which left him no choice. He could see the ruined temple on the crest of the hill, almost straight ahead. She'd talked of a ford in the stream. He would have to try to find it.

Yet when he reached the water he saw that the stream was now a small river, swollen by the recent rains. He scanned it – again, rivers were not his expertise, raised as he was in the sands. It all looked like an even turmoil, no white cresting to show a shallower place. He glanced up, to see Roxanna covering the last of the wet slope to the track and the bridge.

Had he lost? Would she be waiting with three javelins buried in a straw heart, and that smile on her face? Then he sensed something, up through his seat, into his body. He might know little of flowing water – but the tawpan was bred in the northern forests which were threaded through with great rivers. 'Yah!' he cried a third time and, making sure that Serrana had her head, he urged her into the flood.

She did not baulk. Took to the water like a sea eagle – and plunged like one, for the water was immediately deep. Rider and mount went under. Cold shocked him; he gasped as they surfaced, reins gone, clutching the thick fur at Serrana's neck. But he'd been right, she was a swimmer and struck out strongly, ears back, head high, eyes wide. There was some current and it pushed them downstream. Suddenly Ferros felt the horse's body change, rise up. Hooves had found the riverbed; found the ford. Gathering herself, she scrambled them to the other bank.

The desert son had rarely been so cold. But there was no time to consider that. He wiped his eyes clear of water, the tawpan shook herself. A swift glance showed that Roxanna had cleared the bridge. He saw her flatten herself on Shadowfire's neck and kick for the temple.

'Let's go!' he cried, digging in his heels.

The slope was gentler, grassy, and Serrana took it fast. But as he crested the hill he saw the black blur peeling in from the side – the eastern side, he realised with a curse. The temple's eastern window would face the rising sun, and Roxanna was galloping up to it.

He applied rein, thigh, heel, Serrana leaping forward as he bent, snatched up a javelin ... and saw that there was only one left in the quiver. He'd lost one in the river. Yet there was no time to consider that for he saw Roxanna jerk her stallion to a stop, bend, heft and throw in one smooth movement. He didn't look to check, though he did hear the whisper of metal entering hay. He knew she'd have hit her target. As she bent to her quiver again, he pulled Serrana to a sudden halt, leaned back, sighted and threw. His javelin made a louder noise, sliding in beside hers, scraping metal and wood. He bent and drew his second shaft, even as he heard his first enter true.

As a horse soldier, he'd spent years training with javelins. She'd spent centuries. It showed in her easy heft of the weapon, the casual lean and effortless throw. But even as he watched he was turning himself, hurling, his greater strength sending his bolt as true as hers and only a heartbeat later.

'Yah!' he called and heeled Serrana forward. He might have chosen not to ride the stallion – but he knew them. And Shadowfire did what stallions do when another horse, a mare no less, comes suddenly near. He jerked his head, throwing Roxanna off balance even as she reached for her final shaft. Cursing, she had to leave it, grasp the reins with both hands, control her mount. The beast swung around, and Ferros, who'd got his toes onto the metalled edge of his stirrups, used the pivot to vault straight forward, over Serrana's head. He landed just as Roxanna got control. Reached before she could realise. Snatched the last javelin from her quiver, turned, and threw it. This time he followed it with his eyes, watched it fly as true, to slide in beside the others, straight in the bale's marked heart.

He looked up at her. Wonder had sent her eyes wide. Fury narrowed them. 'You ... you cheated!' she cried.

He left it a long moment before he spoke. 'How is that even possible,' he replied, 'when winning is the only rule?'

Fire filled her eyes and her knuckles whitened on her reins. For a moment he thought she was going to bring the stallion rearing, to dash his brains out with its front hooves. Then the fire faded, she tipped back her head … and laughed, long and loud. 'It was nearly a century ago,' she said, finally, 'that a man last bested me … in anything.' She nodded. 'I knew you were the right choice, Ferros.'

Raindrops hit him, an instant deluge. And he was cold already, from the freezing river water and with the heat of the chase fading. But her words sent a different kind of shiver through him. 'For what?' he said. 'It is time I knew. What do you and your father want with me?'

She nodded. 'You're right. You deserve to know.' Her gaze moved down him. 'But first,' she added, 'shouldn't we get you out of those wet clothes?'

There was no mistaking the change in her tone. He felt the heat in it, which transferred to his chest, and spread fast down to his groin. He grunted, took a step towards her, as she swung one long leg over the saddle horn and dropped to the ground. Straightened and waited for him, a different light in her eyes now, a smile on her lips, as he moved slowly forward. Almost as tall as him, and her in boots, their faces were level. He leaned for a kiss.

She placed two fingers on his lips. The expression in her eyes now was cool, amused. 'One thing I've learned: making love against a wall in winter rain is fine for the time of the love-making … and swiftly uncomfortable afterwards.' She ran her fingers from his lips, along his jawline, up to his forehead, brushing away the water drops there. 'But if we ride fast before you freeze, we can have heat. Hot baths, warm towels, the best mulled wine. We can make love on silken sheets and lie beneath them afterwards in the fire glow.' She leaned closer, her green eyes shining, her voice lowering. 'Don't you think that the first time we make love, Ferros of Balbek, we should make love as immortals with an infinity of time before us? Not like peasants with a snatched moment in a wet field?'

He wasn't sure he agreed. The heat and swelling of his body told him differently. But he also knew that Roxanna was in charge of him. Of him here, and of his uncertain future. Until he knew what that was, he would do whatever she wanted. So he stepped back. 'As you please,' he said. 'I would like to be warm again ... in some manner.' He reclaimed Serrana's reins, for she waited where he'd left her. 'Do we race again?'

'I don't think I could bear being beaten twice in one day. But let us go quickly nonetheless, before you die on me – and I have to wait for my pleasure till you are reborn. Here,' she said, reaching to the cloak clasp at her neck, sweeping the garment off, 'at least this will keep off the rain.'

He put up hands to refuse. 'But you'll be wet.'

'True. Then I will be dry again, soon enough.'

They took the bridge road, an easy canter that broke into a gallop when they reached the avenue. The city gates opened without a command. By the time they reached the stable yard, though, the chill rain was falling even more heavily and Ferros found it hard to dismount, as if he were frozen into the saddle. It seemed the deep chill had taken over not only his body but his mind as well and the burn of desire he'd felt at the ruined temple was gone.

For a time he'd been free again: a soldier, a rider, a man, just a man. But as soon as he was back within the Sanctum, he was again an immortal, with all that meant, all that he did not understand.

A groom came and offered a hand but Roxanna waved him away, dismounted. 'Allow me,' she said, reaching up – her smile vanishing as she saw the expression on Ferros's face. Mistook it. 'You do not look well, Ferros. Let us get you warm.'

He ignored her hand, slid off the horse's other flank. Took a breath. He did need warmth, but he needed something other first – an answer, from the only person he'd met who might be willing to give it to him. Stepping around his horse's head, he looked into her green eyes and his look stilled the words on her lips. 'What do you want of me? What do you all want of me?'

'Let us get you to heat first, Ferros, then I will—'

'No!' She'd half turned away and his shout spun her back. 'Answer me! What am I being ... groomed for? Why should I care for the musings of Hypethus, or the three ranks of government? For the contrast between lyric ballads and Sonovian free verse?'

'You've been talking to Streone.'

'I've been *listening* to you all! And you have all given me lots of information – yet no reason. Why I should learn all this? Why I should care?'

She murmured something, stretched a hand to him but he jerked his away, stepped back. He was shivering uncontrollably but he knew that cold was only a part of the reason. 'I had a life, Roxanna. One life. And it was plain enough. To fight for a cause I believed in: the empire. If such was my fate, to retire eventually to a vineyard and watch my grandchildren play. If other, to die in battle, for honour ... for my comrades, the only family I have ever known. And now—'

'You may still—'

'And *now* you ask me to do it again. And again. For ever. To watch everyone I know and love grow old and die. Those grandchildren. Lara—' he choked on the name, forced himself to continue, 'to watch Lara, her youth, her beauty, watch it fade, watch her ...' the phrase that the general in Balbek had used came to him, '... claimed by time. While I—?' She reached for him again and he stepped away, hands raised. 'Immortality,' he spat, 'it is a curse! I only ever wanted one life, to seek all that I could be within it. Warrior, husband, father. That was going to be enough. To be remembered for a few years by a few and then be forgotten by all, my name fading on a family tomb. A family I created, for I am an orphan. But this curse robs me of all that. Robs me of—'

Tears came, the first since Ashtan, his brother in arms, had died, with those the first in a decade. His arms fell then, and Roxanna stepped between them, whispering words, gentling him as she had her stallion before the ride. He let her grasp him, hold him, allowed her words. 'You are right, Ferros of Balbek. Because you are a soldier we thought it would be easier for you. To simply accept and obey.' She pulled him closer, until their faces were a hand's breadth apart. 'But you are different. And you are being "groomed", as you call it, for the same reasons you were raised to be a soldier. To fight for the empire against a danger greater than that empire has ever faced. Ever! It could mean the end of everything we know, of all this.' Her eyes swept around the world before settling back on him. 'For there is evil rising in the east—'

It was as far as she got, before Lara stepped out from under the dripping eaves of the barn.

From the moment she'd heard he'd gone riding – without her, with someone else – Lara had refused to seek the shelter and warmth offered in the stables. Preferred to shiver outside, and watch the water cascade off the roofs. Try to draw him back through the rain by the force of her fury.

He'd invited her! Three weeks it had taken him, telling her only a little of his days in the Sanctum. But even that little intrigued and her imagination did the rest, sketching a world so different from the dull, noisy neighbourhood near the port where they lodged. She'd explored those alleys and squares, even ventured where he'd warned her she shouldn't, into the darker streets and warehouses of the docks. Yet though her own city of Balbek was smaller, life in both places was much the same – people hurrying and hustling to live, too busy to pause and talk. She'd made only one friend – an aged former whore called Carellia who'd survived the years of violence and disease with half a dozen teeth and a thousand stories. Lara would buy her hot, spiced wine, listen to the tales, wonder at how randomly life handed out its favours. Carellia had lost her one true love when he'd killed himself. Not from despair – from his desire for immortality. Suicide cults, using dark rituals that promised everlasting life, had sprung up and waned over the centuries. They were always supressed by the natural immortals in their Sanctum as an obscenity, even though rumour said that immortals sometimes were born in those ceremonies. Indeed, the ritual that day had produced one – but that one was not her lover and Carellia had turned whore the morning after his death.

Aside from her, Lara talked to no one. She knew she over-whelmed Ferros with questions when he returned each day, chattering as if she'd only just discovered the ability to speak. She suspected it annoyed him though he never showed it, was patient, took her out despite his tiredness to see the local sights, to visit taverns, archery contests, once a strange performance where masked dancers chanted to drums and pipes, which nei-ther of them understood. But always, at night's end, she asked him to bring her to the Sanctum, to share some of its wonders. Last night he'd told her that he'd arranged it.

She hadn't enjoyed the ride on the Heaven Road; clung to the basket's sides and stared ahead, never down. She'd been relieved when it had broken, a problem with a tower, and she'd had to walk the last stretch, in the rain. But all discomfort vanished when she climbed the last hill of Agueros, and saw the red-walled Sanctum at its summit. The beauty of the world beyond the gates! From narrow winding streets where linked wood and plaster houses leaned so far over that their eaves nearly joined, to these wide, straight roads and single stone structures; from cracked and broken cobbles underfoot to smooth paving stones; from elbowing crowds hurrying everywhere to men and women, singly and in pairs, strolling under the shelter of awnings along tree-lined avenues. Chaos against calm. The man who guided her was happy to pause and smiled indulgently at her gasps and exclamations, patiently answering her many questions.

It was when he brought her to the innermost sanctum, in the entrance hall of a building he called the Study, that the warmth of her excitement had left, cold returned, with the greatest chill around her heart. For a man came, someone noble and high up by the way her guide fawned, a man as dark as night with a small grey beard and eyes like algae-filled ponds in a forest. He'd told her, as if it were a favour, that Ferros was not there to meet her. That he would return ... sometime. And that she could wait there, or return later, as she wished.

His manner annoyed her. 'And where is he?' she'd asked, forcing the man to turn back. And he'd answered with the words that brought that deeper cold to her heart.

'He is riding.'

When he'd gone, she asked her guide to do her a last kindness – and take her to the stables.

Riding? Riding was theirs, a shared joy from the moment he'd taught her, their escape, their delight. How dare he do without her the thing she most longed to do? She'd been cramped in a ship's cabin, cramped in their lodgings, squeezed in by people and walls. She dreamed of home, of letting Saipha have her head, of racing Ferros across the dunes outside Balbek. Was he going to ride and not tell her? She'd have smelled horse on him the moment he returned. In some ways it would have been worse than perfume.

Then he had returned and her anger and her hurt had doubled. It was like a hoof in the chest, when he rode into the stable yard ... with a woman. A tall woman with skin so dark it

145

was almost black, like the man who'd been rude to her before, eyes as green, swathed in glistening leather and riding with an ease that Lara, for all her skills, knew she'd never possess.

Ferros had not just been riding. He'd been riding with another woman.

She watched them dismount, talk feverishly, watched them move towards each other. She stepped out and she saw him see her, his eyes widening in shock.

'Lara,' he said.

She feared she would explode. Took too many shallow breaths before managing a deeper, longer one, then another. If she let out half the things she wanted to say, she would embarrass herself, embarrass him: Ferros's jealous, foul-mouthed provincial girl, here in the beauty of the Sanctum. Worse, before one of its queens. Even though there was no longer such a title – had not been since the immortals had come to Corinthium – this giantess carried herself like one.

Ferros came to her. 'Lara, I am sorry.'

'For what?' she asked, proud how her voice disguised her emotions.

'I ... forgot that today was the day we arranged for your visit.'

'You forgot.'

It was a statement, not a question. And her eyes were on the queen when she said it.

'I was offered a ride. I—' He raised his arms, let them fall. 'I am sorry. This is—'

'Roxanna.'

She said it coming forward while behind her a groom led away the two horses. Roxanna, Lara thought. So this is her. Ferros had mentioned the name once, as someone he'd met. Just once, and in passing – yet even then Lara had noted the way he'd uttered the name, the too-casual way he'd said it. She pondered later, thought she'd been too sensitive, seeking nuance where there was none, overwhelmed by all the new experience. Now she knew her instinct had been right, confirmed by the stunning beauty she gazed up at.

She knew that, in Balbek, many called her beautiful. Ferros did – had – often. But standing there, she felt like a weed beside a rose. 'Lara,' she said, resisting the urge to curtsey.

'Have we met? It seems to me we have.'

Roxanna's voice was honeyed, with the clear, clipped accent of the city's elites. Lara was aware of her own Balbek speech, tried to suppress the worst of its wide-vowelled excesses when she replied. 'I don't think so. This is my first time here.'

'I hope to know you now. Ferros has been keeping you a bit of a secret. Now I understand why.' She smiled, revealing gorgeous, bright and even teeth. 'There are too many in the Sanctum who would seek to corrupt such simple beauty.'

Bitch, Lara thought, held back saying, said instead, 'Is there much corruption of that kind here then?'

'Too much. It is a game around here.'

'Well, I don't play games.' Having been so focused on the woman before her, she suddenly noticed that Ferros was shaking. He was soaked. 'What happened to you?' she asked.

'I ... I fell in a stream.' He turned to Roxanna. 'You said I might find clothes?'

'I did. Go to the grooms' room here. They have a fire, some blankets to dry yourself with. I will send the clothes. Farewell, for now. And to you, Lara.' Roxanna turned, then turned back. 'We will ... talk another time, Ferros.'

They watched her stride across the yard, enter the building. 'Talk?' Lara said, a question this time, not a statement.

Ferros swivelled, spoke as he crossed the yard. 'I asked her what my purpose here was. She said she would tell me.'

'I could tell you *her* purpose,' Lara said. But she said it to his back, as he'd already entered the small, warm room. She was

147

silent as he stripped behind a hung sheet. Silent still when the clothes arrived – simple, well-made wool trousers, jerkin and fleece-lined coat. A message came with them: he was excused more study that day. His soggy sandals he put back on and they squeaked as the two of them returned to the platform for the Heaven Road, repaired and running again. Ferros tried to talk on the way down, explaining the ride, excusing, though she made no criticism, said almost nothing; and eventually he too went quiet. Only when they reached their lodgings did she speak again. 'I'm going out for a while.'

'Wait,' he said. 'I'll change into my own clothes. Come with—'

'No,' she interrupted, the word sharp. She took a breath, forced a calm. 'I've made a friend. Promised I'd meet her, tell her of my visit to the Sanctum.'

'I am sorry again, Lara.' Ferros stood, came to her, took her hands. 'I will take you, show it to you properly. Tomorrow. The day after.'

'Of course.' She disengaged her hands. 'I will not be long. I made stew. Needs heating. Help yourself.'

She stepped onto the street, leaned for a moment against the door, then set out. The tavern where Carellia always lingered, nursing a mug of hot spiced wine and hoping to be bought more, was only three alleys over. When Lara entered the rich-scented gloom, she swiftly spotted her. Collecting a steaming jug from the landlord at his trestle, she crossed to her friend. 'Sweet Songbird,' Carellia said, looking up, smiling, then smiling more at the jug in Lara's hands. 'What have you got there?'

'The price of a few stories, I hope.' Lara set the vessel down, and a mug beside it, filled both hers and Carellia's.

'Oh yes!' The woman drank greedily, smacked her lips. 'Lovely! The good stuff! That deserves the tale of when I was mistress to the King of Thieves, Sadakos Red Brow, and the time he—'

'Later perhaps.' Lara topped up the other's mug. 'Right now I'd like to hear a different story.'

'Which one, Songbird?'

'About your first love. The suicide cult he joined. How an immortal was born that night. What happened to her.' She picked up her own mug, leaned back into the shadows. 'Tell me, Carellia, something of life and death and ... life.'

8

The Lake of Souls

'Shh! Did you hear that?'

'Which "that", Luck? I hear birds, maybe a fish—'

'Shh! Stop paddling. Listen.' Both brothers lifted their paddles from the lake. 'Is that ... singing?'

They listened. But whatever it was he'd heard was gone again. *If* I heard it, Luck thought. Singing was only the latest noise in the mist that might or might not have been there.

'Forward,' said Bjorn, who was at the front, dipping his paddle again.

But Luck didn't join him. 'To where? How do we know we are even going forward now?'

'Then what would you suggest, little brother? Floating here till the foul mist clears? That could be days.' He coughed and spat into the water. 'Fuck, I have felt sick from the moment we entered it.'

'As have I. But paddling forward will not necessarily get us out of it. And we'll exhaust ourselves if we're going in circles.'

The brothers continued arguing in whispers. They'd already discussed one of them transforming into a beast, fish or bird, while the other remained with the craft. But possession required a god to see the creature he wished to possess; and there was nothing to be seen in this mist, which had been mere grey tendrils when they'd set out for the far shore, with the sharp rise of mountain above it, well lit by the afternoon sun. This also shone on the numerous small islands in the lake – and on one which was larger and flat-topped and from which the smoke of many cooking fires coiled.

People lived on the Lake of Souls – though the type of person that could survive there, could make their life amongst such foulness, they did not want to meet. No one did – and no one who did returned to tell of it. Bjorn's friend Karn had only been the latest who'd strayed too close. For all its horror, at least his parents now had a part of him, could give him the farewell of flame. Of his brother, Rukka the Handsome, there had been no trace.

When they'd set out, they'd chosen a course that would take them well clear of all land. But the fog had descended – or arisen – suddenly, pouring from both water and sky, obliterating everything in a few heartbeats. Their course was lost and so were they. To go on was as foolish as going back.

They were trapped on the Lake of Souls.

'It is better to act than to drift,' called Bjorn, ending the argument by immediately starting to paddle.

'I have always thought the opposite,' grumbled Luck, reluctantly paddling too.

It took no more than twenty dips before Bjorn yelled, 'Rock!' and back-stroked fast. Their craft swivelled, and Luck laid his hand against the stone that thrust up from the water. 'Just one or—'

'Hear that snuffle?' Bjorn interrupted. 'Otter, I think. There must be some land ahead. Give me one look at the fucking animal and I'll get us out of this shit.'

Bjorn dipped his paddle again. Reluctant still, Luck joined him and, in moments, the prow struck another smaller rock and, a moment later, ground onto pebbles. Bjorn was out and up to mid-calf in water straight away. The vessel tipped sideways. 'Heya!' Luck yelped, as he leaned towards the water.

'Sorry,' said Bjorn, pushing the vessel out till it floated again, swinging its back end around so Luck could hoist himself out.

So much shorter than his brother, the water came up to his mid-thigh. They'd already noted its strangeness. In a world still gripped by the last of winter the lake was, if not warm, at least not freezing. The meeting of warmth and chill led to the mist, he supposed, as impenetrable on the small pebbled beach he stepped onto as it had been on the water.

Bjorn dragged the craft higher up, then reached into the forward hold and slid out his sword. 'Now,' he said, 'let's see where—'

The man came silently, and running. They only saw him when he split the grey wall three paces away; saw, in the one heartbeat they had, the club raised high. Luck watched it descending, threw up his weak right arm to take the blow. But it was Bjorn's sword that took it, still in its scabbard, the god stepping in with a hand at each end, thrusting it high. Wood smacked onto leather-wrapped steel, Bjorn jerked his left hand down, and the man's own force caused him to stumble. His face came level with Luck's – he glimpsed white paint around furious eyes, teeth bared in a snarl. Then Bjorn swung his right hand up and over, and smacked the orb of his iron pommel right into the man's temple. He collapsed, with neither grunt nor groan, face down into the shallow water at Luck's feet.

'Your axe!' yelled Bjorn, ripping the sheath from his weapon, turning its point into the swirling mists and the direction the attacker had come from. 'There may be m—'

There *were* more. Two, also naked and painted around face and body, one with a spear, one with a sword. As his brother took them on, as metal clashed against metal and the only other noise in the near silent world was Bjorn's harsh breaths, Luck scrabbled for his short axe in the back hold. I hate to fight, he thought. Won't they talk?

But the next two who'd come, if they could talk, wouldn't again. Luck saw this in the swiftest of glances as he burrowed deeper through leather satchels of food and clothing. One assailant had lost his sword arm, severed at the shoulder. He was falling, fountaining blood – though still he did not make a sound. The second clutched his spear double-gripped before him, though now it was reversed and through him. As silent as his fellow, he glared at Bjorn before his eyes rolled up in his painted head, and he sat down.

Luck's fingers found not steel and wood but the rope and leather of his sling. With the ease of centuries, he slipped his forefingers into the loop at one strand's end, grasped the knot at the other, pulled a stone from the pouch on his belt, had it fitted in the leather cup and the weapon up and whirling.

Yet no other came – and the only sounds that did were the hum of his sling through the air and the hiss of two gods breathing. They both strained for noise, for warning grunts or the slap of bare feet on stone. Heard neither, and after a moment Luck slowed then stopped his sling, though he kept the stone in the leather cup with his thumb, and the cords at tension. Bjorn drove his sword into the beach before him and bent again to their vessel, swiftly undoing the straps that bound his shield to it, got it off and raised, and his sword again in his hand. As Luck moved into the shelter of the shield, Bjorn peered over its edge at the three dead men. 'There'll be more. And they may figure out not to come in ones and twos.' He licked his lips. 'Get the boat ready and let's get away from here, fast.'

As Luck turned to obey, he heard sounds. Human – but only just. It was the singing he thought had come before, though like no song he'd ever heard. Many voices made it, low and high, men and women ... and children. Especially, he thought, children. Moaning as if in agony; laughing the agony away in trills and runs of notes. The discord built and built, louder and louder, until it felt almost painful. Then suddenly as a flock of birds changing direction in the sky, all voices ceased.

Save one. And that one spoke just one word. An ordinary word, though extraordinary there because it was a word from their own tongue and one they were likely to speak every day.

'Now.'

'Who—' began Bjorn, then stopped, his eyes wide in surprise.

Luck looked at his brother and tried to decide what was different about him. It took him one more moment to notice the feathered dart that now protruded from the neck – the one moment before Bjorn closed his eyes and fell, shield and sword clattering onto the pebbles of the beach. Luck reached, but not quickly enough to catch him. For there was a whisper, a faint sting at his own neck, darkness.

Luck wasn't sure which pain woke him – his head, even worse than the morning after the night he'd tried to match his brothers at mead, half a century before, drilling agony and nausea both. Or the pain at his wrists, where slim but strong rawhide leather straps bound them tightly behind him. Or at his ankles, also tied and pulled up behind his body. When he tried to ease them, he pulled tighter at the wrists. Easing those caused sharp jabs in his legs. He settled again for the least painful, still painful, balance. He was trussed like a beast awaiting slaughter. Which thought had him moving on from his pain to his circumstances.

He kept his eyes shut. Opening them might lead to consequences. His body, never much use, was out of action now. At least his mind, his best weapon, could work. His senses could feed it.

So he listened. There was a chattering like bird calls, which he thought they might be until he heard a single voice respond and provoke more chatter. It was all coming from right before him and, raising his eyelashes a fraction, he first saw flames, then shapes moving before a fire. He'd always had thick lashes – blessed with them, Gytta had said, though he'd thought it another mockery, a soft and womanly thing for a misshapen brute such as he. But his dead wife had been right, for he was blessed in being able to see now and not look like he was seeing.

It was children who chattered – boys and girls, not one more than ten years old. All naked, all painted like the men Bjorn had killed on the beach, white hoops around their bodies. Some were on the floor, rolling small balls of woven reed back and forth, others in pairs were taking turns to pull long hoops of wool into different patterns, passing them between their fingers. Several chased each other around a raised dais on which was a huge chair. More children crawled on top of that – or rather, crawled over the man who sat upon it.

He was clothed at least, in a huge, sleeveless smock that covered but did not fully conceal a big body that was both muscled and fat. He reached to fend off the crawling children, or to pull one suddenly close to squeeze them against his chest, while they squealed in delight. The man's face did not change expression, which puzzled Luck – until he realised that it wasn't a face at all but a mask, a near perfect rendering of a man, made from some soft and pliant material. Real eyes reflected the firelight through slits. No feature moved, the lips parted in a fixed smile. There was something familiar about the face. The drug, Luck thought, still hurting his mind and gripping his body, as well as his neck, stinging where the dart had entered.

He focused again on the children, sliding over the huge frame. Noticed something else. They laughed as the man grabbed them, hugged them, ran his hands up and down them before letting them slide away. But their smiles were as fixed as the one on the mask and their eyes were dead.

Luck shuddered – and a voice came from behind the unmoving lips.

'You are awake. At lassst!'

The voice was high-pitched, sibilant; the words in the language of their land. A countryman, then. A beginning. 'I am,' Luck replied. 'My name is Strovyn, of Askaug.' He craned around and saw, a half-dozen paces away, the trussed, still unconscious form of his brother. 'And that is Hendrik. We are fur traders. We—'

'Oh, ssstop.' The hiss was soft, the tone amused, mock-hurt. 'When our time together is going to be so short, why ssspend it lying to one another, hmm?'

The children had stopped moving; all were staring at Luck now, their deadened eyes unnerving. He shifted, and agony shot through his lashed limbs. The pain in his head made thinking almost unbearable. But, tied up as he was, thinking was all he had. 'You are right,' he said. 'A guest owes his host the truth of himself. But a host owes something too and I was confused by the hospitality.' He pulled at his wrists, the pain immediate and intense. 'I can understand you taking no chances with visitors. We came armed into your country. But we mean you no harm. How about freeing us and let us begin again?'

'Free you?' His laughter came loud and high-pitched, and the children immediately joined him, laughing in trills and runs that sounded like the song Luck had heard upon the lake – instantly ending when the masked man did. 'I cannot have gods running free in my country. Sswimming free. Flying free.' A tongue darted out, to lick the rigid lips. 'Oh yess, I know what you are. Even who you are ... Luck of Askaug.'

It was a shock, his name sliding from that fixed mouth. Luck swallowed. 'How ... how do you know me?'

A little laugh, echoed by the children. 'We are cut off here, it is true. But occasionally a stranger will come by and talk before they … passss on. Tales are told. Less of you, admittedly. More of your brother gods.' The tongue licked again, withdrew. 'Who would have thought Bjorn Swiftsword would be here, in my hall?'

The more he talked, the more Luck was able to place him. 'But you are a stranger here too, are you not? Your voice tells me you are from the southern lands. Did you, perhaps, also hear tales of us there?'

The man stood abruptly, spilling a dull-eyed boy from his lap. 'I do not wish to talk about that!' he screeched. 'There was no life before. No land! No place! There is only here. Here! Now! Me!'

He stepped from the dais on which the chair stood – a throne truly, elaborately carved from black hardwood – and began talking fast in a language Luck had never heard, one made deep in the throat as if growled. The children scattered, snatching up their balls and ropes, and ran to crouch against the walls. He gave a shout and doors crashed open; there was the sound of running feet and in a moment the space before the dais was filled with painted, naked bodies – six men hurling themselves to the floor, their faces lowered, their arms raised high to the masked man, who called out more of what had to be commands. The six men grunted, shot up and turned to grab the two bound gods. There was relief as the cords around Luck's ankles were cut and he could stretch out his legs; pain returned as he was thrown onto some sort of board and lashed tight to it around chest and waist. He was then jerked upright and he could see the whole room.

It was the rough image of a mead hall, if one could be fashioned from woven reeds. Beside him his brother was thrown upright, similarly tied to a board, at the base of which Luck saw wheels. Bjorn had woken and the brothers exchanged a swift look that was part pain and part promise. They knew two things at least: that they were alive; and that it was hard to kill a god.

Then sight was taken, when cloth was bound over their eyes, and drawn tight.

The wheeled boards were swivelled, rolled. Luck hoped to feel night air – for there were beasts outside, of scale, fur and feather. It would be impossible to possess one while blind and strapped to a board. But blindfolds could slip, and cords loosen.

Night air did not come. They were moved, bumped over some threshold, but were inside still; doors closed behind them. They halted, and a near silence came, broken only by breathing – his own, Bjorn's, others', how many he could not tell. Then he heard the crackle of flame, and sudden heat came near his face. Luck tensed – it was one of the very few ways to kill a god, dissolving him in fire. But the heat passed, and that voice came again. Rage gone from it, excitement returned. 'Sshall I sshow you,' it hissed, 'wondersss?'

Luck's blindfold was snatched off. For a moment he still couldn't see, for he was dazzled by torchlight. He looked down, up at Bjorn, finally across to the man who held the torch. His 'face' was still immobile atop that big body, light still dancing in the eye gaps.

'You were right and I apologise,' the masked man said. 'I have broken so many rules of hospitality. It has been so long since I entertained. So I will begin again. First, I will give you my name. Not my old name, which no longer matters.' The tongue shot out, snake-like, then withdrew. 'I am Peki Asarko. Welcome, godss of Asskaug, to my realm.'

He bowed, stepped away. They were rolled after him, as Peki Asarko swept the torch through the room, a reed hall near as long as the first, not as wide. 'My realm!' he said. 'Mine – for I have made it. What savages they were, these people, when I first came here! Head-hunters. Cannibals. Why, they even wanted to eat me!' He laughed, and the men Luck couldn't see who pushed the boards laughed loudly too, stopping as soon as their leader spoke again. 'But there was some time between the killing and the eating. So, of course, I did what it is we do. I ... died.' He sighed the word, then shouted, gleefully, 'and then was born again!'

His laugh came once more, longer, echoed as before. Luck thought. A god? He knew few enough of those from the south. But this Peki Asarko – not a Midgarth name, it had to be taken from the tribe he ruled – was unlike any he'd met anywhere. The king-god continued, 'They were surprised at my resurrection, of course. It was almost enough to make them worship me. That, and a little, uh, animal magic, of course.' The tongue darted again. 'They'd never seen a god, which I thought strange, since some of us do travel. But after a day I started to choke on the marsh gases and realised why none had come here. The people had adapted, though many still died. Especially the children. My sweet children.' He sighed. 'I stopped that. Saved them. Led them here, to the big island's top, where the gases do not reach. They worshipped me then. And even more when I introduced ... the ceremonies.'

There was a swoop of the torch, a change of tone. From pompous to excited. 'Look here!'

Flamelight fell on the figure of a man – tall, naked, painted. Immobile. His eyes were wooden, painted too. At first Luck thought that he was a carving, and cunningly done. Until, with dread spreading a chill over his heart, he realised what he was seeing.

Peki Asarko put words to his dread. 'Flaying. We peel their skins off in large pieces. It's harder than you think. They don't live long after that. Well, some a little longer.' He gave a small laugh, unechoed. 'Then I ... put them back together.' He grunted. 'Do you know, in my home town, they didn't understand it. How I was doing it *for* the people.' His voice had gone into a whine, continued on the same note. 'It was the way to end the resentment of us, don't you sssee? This way,' he ran a finger up one painted arm, 'they are immortal too.'

He turned and walked further up the hall, using the flame he carried to light other torches in metal sconces on wooden pillars. All that was dark was now light, all that was hidden, revealed – a line of flayed men, women, children, right to the end of the room. The shock of it was like a kick in Luck's stomach, and the sickness he'd felt from the moment he'd entered the mists on the Lake of Souls surged up his throat and out. He'd eaten too little over too long so bile came fast, bitterness filling his mouth. Beside him he heard his brother spit and curse.

'There, there. I know. I know!' Peki Asarko had returned. Handing his torch to a man behind the board, he patted Luck's arm. 'I was sick the first time too. You grow used to it.' He giggled. 'More! You learn to love it.' He gripped. 'Now let me show you a sspecial wonder. My latesst . . . resurrection.'

He scampered ahead, the men again running Luck and Bjorn swiftly after – to halt before a figure set a little back in the shadows. 'Here! Here!' the masked god cried, lowering the torch he held.

From the moment he'd awoken from his drugged sleep, Luck had suffered shock after shock. But this was of a different level. From a different world. Because before him was another flayed man.

Bald. Black of tooth. Black of eye.

Peki Asarko leaned close. 'I know you've sseen one like him before,' he whispered. 'You have his boat, of course, that's how you came. And *why* you came, isn't it? To traverse our lake, climb the mountain, discover why the killers have come and what they intend? You worked out their route, didn't you, clever Luck of Askaug?' He clapped his hands, spoke louder. 'I have good news! I will ssave you the journey. I can tell you all that.

But first,' he swivelled away, and thrust his face into Bjorn's. 'The way you've been staring at me, Sswiftsword.' He ran his fingers over his mask. 'You know me, don't you?'

Bjorn didn't reply, just stared. Until Peki screamed, 'Answer me!' and hit him, backhanded. The blow sent the board sideways, the man behind struggling to drag him upright once more. When Bjorn lifted his eyes again, Luck could see hatred in them, as clearly as the blood on his lips. 'I know whose face you wear,' his brother said softly. 'His name was Rukka the Handsome, brother of Karn, whose head you shrank and gave to the black-eyed killer.' Luck gasped, sickened by recognising in his turn the preserved skin of the hunter, as Bjorn continued, 'So I tell you this: they were both my friends. And I am going to kill you, for both their sakes.'

'Wonderful!' Peki laughed, and clapped. 'The legend that is Bjorn Sswiftsword! Another heroic god, just like those who judged me, who drove me from my home. So noble. So ... dead!' He lifted his hand again, but Bjorn didn't flinch and Peki Asarko merely stretched out his fingers and patted his cheek. 'But not yet,' he said, turning back to Luck. 'I wouldn't be so cruel. First you must learn what you came to learn. Then you must die.'

He turned back to the flayed man beside him. 'This one,' he said, 'killed five of my people before they took him – so they hurt him too badly in the taking. I like to talk first, as you know. He died – but lives again.' He patted the man's face as he had Bjorn's. 'But his companion was taken more quietly – the one you must have met – we did talk. Did you discover that they can speak our language? That they have been studying it, us, for years? Preparing?'

Luck thought about the two spaces for paddlers in the craft, the duplication of many of the tools. Of course there had been two. 'Preparing for what?'

'Oh, gods,' Peki Asarko tipped back his head and laughed. 'Only the conquest of the world.'

'And you will help them?' Bjorn shouted. 'Betray your people? Your brother gods?'

'Who betrayed me? Exiled me? Just because my ... tasstes in death differed from theirs? Just because I chose to kill with poison not with blades?' He hissed this, his big chest rising. 'Besides,' he continued, his voice soft again, 'this is not betrayal. This is redemption. For they do not come to destroy the world but to save it. With a special place reserved for those who help them. An elevated place.'

'Amongst their gods?'

'Oh no! They have no gods. Or rather,' he raised his eyes to stare at the roof, 'they have but one.'

Bjorn growled again, about to rage. But Luck got in first. 'Is this one a baby? Neither man nor woman?'

Peki gasped then, his eyes shooting down to stare. 'How could you know what only the chosen have seen?'

The memory came, that blinding vision in the globe. 'I saw it – in glass.'

'You?' Peki's high voice rose higher in excitement. 'Then, *brother* ... you are chosen too. Rejoice, Luck the Lame, Luck the Well-Named, for it is we ... *different* ones who will have an honoured place in the new world, when all these warrior gods are gone.' He glanced back at Bjorn before leaning closer in. 'For I saw it too! In the glass! The one the other left me, before I let him go on to Askaug to ... continue his work.' He reached up now, fiddling with the straps that held Rukka the Handsome's face in place. 'Oh, and I saved one more surprise. Is it the best? The best for last?'

Peki Asarko took off his mask. The face beneath could have come from any town or village in Midgarth – red eyebrows and hair, a scattering of freckles, a thick nose, full lips. He was ordinary. Except for the eyeballs, lined in black circles. Except for the blackening teeth. Luck remembered the lure of the smoke that had risen from the drug he'd poured onto the globe. How he'd craved it again, though gradually the desire had dwindled. It was clear that for the god before him, the taste had grown along with its fulfilment.

Peki Asarko was looking at him as if expecting some bond of kinship. Which gave him a chance to learn more.

'Why do they want to conquer Midgarth?'

'Midgarth?' Peki gave a hoot of laughter. 'Midgarth is nothing. Our world is nothing. They have shown me worlds of wonder in their glassss!' He turned his black eyes to the roof. 'There is a city on an inland sea far in the south, where five times the whole population of our country live, with red temples and stone palaces that make our mead halls look like fishing shacks.' His eyes glistened. 'There is an island to the west, where a fire god rules who has killed all the other gods. It is in his land that the saviour will be born. *Has* been born already, perhaps. And the chosen people beyond the mountains are going to fetch this saviour ... to rule us all!'

Luck had suspected that there were other worlds – even before the black-eyed killers arrived and proved it. But so many? So different? His mind reeled, groping among questions. What people dwelt beyond the mountains? How numerous, how strong? He did not know how long Peki would remain talkative – or what would happen when he stopped talking.

'Tell me ...' he began.

It was the moment Bjorn leapt. Bringing out the hands he'd somehow freed – it would take a cleverer man than Peki Asarko to bind Bjorn Swiftsword for long – he jabbed his fingers into the throat of the man who was wheeling him, then grabbed him as his board fell to the floor. Luck's slammed down too, his own guard dropping him to lunge at Bjorn – who grasped one of the man's arms, snapped it, threw him aside.

Peki was frozen, staring at Bjorn on the floor now freeing the rest of the ropes around his legs. Then he jerked, screamed, 'Help! Help me!'

'I'll help you,' said Bjorn, 'for Rukka and for Karn.' He rose, stepped clear, reached. But Peki, agile for a big man, grabbed the flayed assassin and hurled him at Bjorn. His brother threw the tortured body aside, came again – and then was swarmed ... by children. Silent, they ran in from the door. One boy jumped onto his back, another leapt and grabbed him round the throat. Bjorn ripped their hands clear, hurled them away, reached again for Peki Asarko. But when a small girl slammed into his legs, he buckled, fell onto one knee. A dozen bodies hit him. For a moment he thrashed – until he was drowned by numbers.

'Blind them! Take them!' Peki screeched and now men rushed in, replaced the children, seized both gods, struck with clubs, knocking Bjorn out, binding him swiftly to the board again. The blindfolds were retied on both of them. Then they were rolled away fast along the mud floors, briefly out into the air then into another building. There Luck heard something different. Up to then, all sounds had come from wood, reed, earth. Now there was the scrape of metal on metal, the familiar screech of bolts drawn, the smell of iron. Stripped from the boards, their hands tied again before them, though not their feet, they were bent and hurled forward, landing hard. A metal door clanged shut behind them. Bolts were shot home.

Peki's voice reached him, muffled but still high-pitched and clear. 'Sleep if you can. Live if you can. Die if you wish. It is six hours till morning, and with the dawn, one of you will join my parade of immortals. But which one?' He giggled. 'Play throw-sticks for it if you like. Oh no! Whoops! You can't.'

Shrill laughter receded, vanished. The silence itself felt

muffled, the air thick, like a weight pressing him down. But the men had rushed the retying of his blindfold and Luck was able to scrape it off on his brother's knots. Yet freeing his eyes did not return his sight. Lifting his head, he banged it into a metal ceiling a hand's breadth above him. Rolling, he found a wall an arm's length to one side. Managing to roll over his brother – so gone to the world he made no complaint – he found another. His legs were not bent behind him any more so after shuffling he swiftly reached one end. He decided not to bother with the other. He knew now where he and Bjorn were. Or rather in what. He also knew why.

Peki Asarko had fashioned a box of iron against this day – the one when he captured a fellow god. A sealed box, so no mouse or rat could enter that a god could become and escape. Yet Luck's first concern was not escape but survival. A box this small had almost no air, and what they had they were using fast.

'Brother!' he called. But the only response was harsh breaths, bubbling through bloodied lips and nose. 'Brother,' he whispered, the word a comfort at least. If they were marked to die in this box – well, out of it, for there was barely room for them inside, let alone a headsman – at least they would die together.

Not yet though, Luck thought. There is something I can do first.

He took some deeper breaths, released them slowly, allowing his body and his mind to ease. Even if he was caged, bound, even if no animal could come within the metal walls, there was still a way for him to be free. A part of him, anyway.

It didn't take long. He'd been practising for centuries, after all. A few more breaths from the shrinking store. A sinking down. His body slept in the prison. His mind leapt free.

Is it my mind any more? Luck thought, as he always thought, despite the countless times he'd done this. His body was certainly gone, bound and breathless in the iron box that was now ... below him. As a child, and long before he'd learned how to possess the body of a bird, Luck had flown in dreams. Soon he'd learned how to control the flight, what direction to choose. But just as when he took an animal and was always part subject to the beast's lusts and urges, so in flight he was aware, as now, that it was not only what he thought of as 'him' that was flying. Or perhaps it was a different part of him. He'd called this other he 'Haakon' – the name of a hero, the last king of all Midgarth who'd united the whole land, mortals and immortals both, until he'd disappeared. Some said his spirit still roamed, as Luck's could roam, waiting to return and reclaim his throne. That he lived in the winter wind, the sudden hailstorm, the crashing wave. Later Luck had thought it a second foolish name for a lame god, a childish fantasy alone. And yet when he flew, he was not crippled. He was the god of his dreams, as fierce as Bjorn, as beautiful as Freya, as wise as Hovard. That he could not lift a dove's feather, could touch nothing and nobody, did not matter. And it was his alone, for though he'd tried to show them the way of it, not one of his brother gods, not even Freya, could manage it.

The box is a little bigger than I reckoned, Luck thought, looking down upon it. And there was a grille of woven metal in its roof that would not let a hair through it, but would allow air in. Enough for two gods? They might not die ... entirely. But would they have enough strength to fight, when six hours were spent, and Peki came to behead or flay the skin from one of them? Besides, there was always the drug in the dart that had first overcome them. More of that and they would not be awake to fight.

Time to be doing, Luck told himself, and floated from the hut.

Outside, he saw that he'd been right – the square-topped island was where all these people lived. The settlement itself was set within a bowl, so that none of the reed houses would be visible from the lake and marshes. The gases these exuded surrounded the land, making it look like a bread crust floating in a bowl of goat's milk, or as if the island hovered in a cloud. Though even as he watched those mists started to fray, torn by winds. There were reed boats of various sizes on the beach where they'd come ashore, a path leading down to it; their own craft was among them. On the level ground, there were at least fifty long-houses, spread haphazardly about, each reed-roofed, each with clay chimneys spouting smoke. It was cold below, Luck-Haakon knew. Not so in the air above, with no body to chill.

There was one larger, longer hut, near the centre of the island. At either end, two chimneys gushed; two separate structures had been joined. Figuring that only the leader would have the luxury of two fires, that was where Luck went, sinking down with one thought to hover for a moment above the woven reeds before slipping through them on another.

He'd been right. It was the house of the flayed and he dropped to stand amongst them in the middle of the hall, between a woman and a boy. Her hand was on his shoulder and both were gazing from their sightless painted eyes into the other part of the house, that once had been a separate dwelling. He watched the life there – a cooking fire, some children with bowls clutched before them, staring at the large cauldron upon it, while an old woman with a ladle stirred the broth. All were silent, the only noises in both houses the snap of flame and the wood scraping the metal. Until Luck heard one more sound – a sigh, high-pitched yet somehow voluptuous. It came from behind him, at the far end of the house of the flayed, near to the other flames. He turned – and there was the god sitting before his hearth.

A thought took Luck there. He was standing beside the

chair, before a table, before the flames. And though he could not touch, he could feel – and did – the huge surge of desire that swept through him. For Peki Asarko was holding a small glass vial, tipping it carefully, pouring one drop of viscous liquid onto a small glass globe. Luck could no more smell than he could touch – but memory did it for him, and he was back for a moment at the table in Askaug's mead hall when smoke rose from glass and he felt suddenly, instantly, ecstatically better than he ever had before in all his long lives.

Voices brought him back. Peki's – high, light, sibilant. And another's, one he'd heard before, though then the man had spoken but one word. He recognised it though. Deep, measured, certain.

'Two of them,' Peki said. 'I took them.'

'You have done well.' Luck opened his eyes, looked into the globe, saw the bald and black-eyed man he'd seen in the glass before. He spoke Midgarth's language in a slight accent, his lips parted over his blackened teeth. 'You kidnapped them?'

'No!' Peki giggled. 'They came to me, fissh to my hookss.'

'Came? From your town?'

'No. These gods are not from the south but the west. From Askaug.'

'Askaug?' Black eyes narrowed. 'Who are they? Their names?'

'You will be pleased. One is a famous warrior, Bjorn Swift-sword. The other is his brother, Luck the Lame.'

'Luck?' The man roared the name and Peki flinched back. 'Where are they?'

'Safe. I have them—'

'They are not safe until they are dead. Kill them! Now!'

'I will. One, at least, in the morning, by—'

'No!' Some reflected firelight flamed in the black eyes as the man leaned forward. 'No delay! Now! Keep their heads, I will send for them.'

168

'But—'

'Listen to me. This Luck is one of the very few that concern us. Most of the others – mindless killers and drunkards.' The voice softened. 'Obey me – and when I send for the heads I will send more of what you crave. You must be running low.'

Peki had slumped at the commands. Now he straightened again, eyes widening. He held up the vial. 'Yess. You see? I am. I am! Ssend, please.'

'I will. You will be well rewarded. And when we triumph …' The man looked sideways. Said something in a tongue Luck could not understand. Turned back. 'Obey me,' he said. 'Go and kill them now. Swiftly!'

Smoke swirled within the globe, the man lost to it. Slumping back, Peki fingered the small bottle. His thumb lifted to the stopper and for a moment, one delicious moment, Luck thought he was going to open and pour again. Then he shoved it into a pouch. 'Later, later,' he mumbled, and stood. He turned towards the hall's end, the other room beyond. Took two steps, then stopped suddenly, stepped to the side, to place two hands on a flayed man – the black-eyed killer, Luck saw. Rubbing his fingers slowly up and down the skin, Peki muttered, 'Swiftly? Where is the fun in that?'

He swivelled, strode into the other room. The children scattered to the walls, crouched, bowls held before them like shields. Five guards came forward and knelt. 'I want soup taken to the prisoners,' he yelled at them. 'Free the cripple's hands, he can feed both of them. But do not leave the door open. Feed them, and lock them back in.'

Two of the guards snatched up soup bowls, dipped them in the cauldron, then with three others turned and ran from the hall. Smiling, Peki lowered himself into a chair by the hearth. He spread his arms wide, and immediately children rushed forward into his embrace. He pulled a fair-haired girl onto his lap, ran his fingers up and down her back. She giggled – a sound without a hint of humour. Lightly, he pinched her skin. 'So much softer when one is well fed, isn't that so, little one?' On her nod, he smiled and looked up at the old woman. 'Feed me,' he said.

The guards were swift – but not as swift as Luck. Returning with a thought, sinking into himself, he accepted the bounds of his body, and the bonds upon it. These would soon be loosened. If a chance was to come, it would be when they were.

'Bjorn?'

'I am awake.'

'But are you recovered?'

'Not entirely. They beat me pretty well.' He shifted, groaned. 'I woke and you had ... gone. Find out anything?'

'Plenty. But this for now.' From beyond the metal walls came the sounds of men. 'Listen to me ...'

When the door was opened a few moments later, both gods had their eyes closed and their breaths coming in tortured wheezes. Bjorn lay with his head near the door as if craving air, Luck's feet beside his brother's face.

The guards grabbed Luck by the legs, hauled him out, pulled him up to sitting, slapped him. He moaned, eyes blinking as if into wakefulness. The guards laughed; one slapped him again to more laughter and then untied his hands, while another crouched before him, holding the two bowls, muttering something in his own tongue. Luck shook his head, as if still dazed, so the guard put down one of the bowls, lifted a spoon, showed the actions of eating. It wasn't hard for Luck to conjure the symptoms of nausea, the foul air of the box not much improved beyond it. He got onto his knees, letting the retches build, as the guards stepped warily back. Stood, lurched forward, made a dreadful sound – and snatched the knife from the soup guard's waistband.

He turned fast; Bjorn lifted his hands, the leather strings taut

170

between the wrists. The knife was well honed and Luck sliced through the bonds. The guards ran forward.

Too late. They were only men, and Bjorn was a god who now had a blade in his hand. Luck rolled clear to the side, putting his back to the wall, snatching up another dagger the first dying man dropped. He didn't need it.

None of them made a noise before they died. No shouts for aid. Luck assumed that Peki's punishments for failing him were extreme. Perhaps that was why the last of them died as silent as the first.

Bjorn lowered the last of the men to the floor, pulling the dagger from his heart. 'You really are very good at that,' said Luck, pushing himself up the wall to gain his feet.

'I know.' Bjorn wiped blood off the blade onto his sleeve. 'As I plan to prove one more time before we leave here.'

He walked to the door. 'No, brother,' Luck called, halting him. 'I share your desire to avenge Rukka and Karn. But I saw other things when I was out of my skin. Vengeance must always wait for necessity.'

Bjorn sighed. 'Is that another of your famous sayings?'

'It is now.' Luck joined him. 'For our necessity is perhaps nothing less than the saving of the world.' He nodded to the door. 'So we leave this place, fast and silent.'

'Back to Askaug?'

'No. We continue.'

'How? Possess a bird and fly off this island?'

'No again. You know it is never easy with a bird. Anyway, we'll need the boat.' He opened the door a crack, peered out. Not far away he heard that strange singing again, the piping of children's voices. 'Come.'

'Wait! Look at this.' Bjorn bent to one of the dead men – he had a sheath strapped to his back and in it ... 'Sever-Life,' Bjorn whistled in wonder. 'That's good.'

His brother shook his head. 'And they call me Luck!'

They ran to the path-head. The mists had frayed still further and the two risen moons, one waxing, one waning, shed silver and blue light upon their way. At the beach, they found their craft, and their paddles beside it. Bjorn bent, searched. 'It's all here,' he said, puzzled. 'Why have they not stripped it of everything?'

'No one does anything until that black-eyed fucker commands it. Not unless they want to end up flayed and exhibited. And he had other concerns. Us.' Luck snatched a paddle. 'Let us—'

A screech came from the cliff-top. 'Find them! Find them!' cried Peki Asarko.

In a moment the brothers had the boat launched and powerful strokes drove them swiftly from the shore, just as men ran onto the beach behind them.

Winds had cleared the mists entirely. Once they'd rounded the island, they could see Sarkon, the eastern star, clear in the sky, so bright it was as if it trailed a fishing line in the water towards them. They took it, followed it, while behind them came more cries and the sound of oars.

Luck, in the rear, glanced back. Moonlight showed him at least five boats, and glimmered on spear points and swords. 'Will they catch us?' Bjorn yelled.

'Not on the water. I'd wager our seal-skin vessel is swifter than their reed ones,' replied Luck, dipping his oar hard, his strong left arm compensating for his weak right. 'It may be different on the land.'

They increased the gap between them and their pursuit, though it was hard work, with no rest. An hour, maybe more, before they saw the white foam of small waves breaking onto a beach ahead; by then Luck could no longer feel either arm.

The boat ground onto silver sand, Bjorn leapt out, dragged it higher, peered back. 'Still coming. How long do you think?'

Luck pulled himself wearily from the craft. 'Not long enough, with this.' He slapped his shorter leg.

'Do we still need the boat?'

'Yes. It's how the killer came. If we make it, we'll need it the other side of this mountain, I think.'

Bjorn faced forward again, staring into the forest. 'It's this side of the mountain that concerns me,' he said. 'Come on.'

The beach was not deep and ended in trees – stubby pines, with marsh grass between them, almost as easy as sand or snow for Bjorn, his foot in the prow loop, to drag the boat along. Then the land began to slope upwards, steepening fast, and it became harder, Luck helping to lift the vessel over sharp stabs of rock. Soon enough, they hit the snow line. Easier to pull the craft, harder because the snow was softening with the spring and their legs kept sinking. While behind them the cries were getting closer.

'Fuck this!' said Bjorn, throwing the boat down. 'We'll have to fight.'

'No, Bjorn, there are too many of them. Even for you.'

'Then what, O wise one! Hide? I think they'd find us.'

'No. I do not know. I—' Luck swung his head both ways – and caught it, a whiff in the breeze. There, gone – until the breeze suddenly gusted again and hit him full force. He gagged – then grinned. 'Smell that?'

His brother turned, sniffed. 'By the gods! Bear! Bear, still in its winter sleep.'

The cries on their tail came louder. Their pursuers had reached the shore. The brothers moved sideways fast across the mountain, through a stand of birch – hunters with the hunter's nose. In fifty strides they came to the source of the stench – a stone outcrop jutting from the mountainside forming a sort of entrance, snow piled against it. Bjorn put his hand on the rock and smiled. 'Ready?'

'Do I have a choice?'

The snow gave easily to their hands. As it flew, the rancid smell intensified. The white wall suddenly gave – to reveal not one bear but two. Both growled, as startled as those who'd woken them. But the bears were sleep-groggy, and the gods desperate.

Possession was a skill honed over centuries. Like when Luck flew in spirit, it required a moment of calm, of nothing, of not moving, of leaving. To vanish, absorb, be absorbed. A moment of greatest danger, because if the creature attacked, the god was doomed. Perhaps he would be reborn soon. Perhaps the beast would rip his head off. But these bears were slow. They had their moment, the leaving, the joining.

After all this time, it is always still a little strange, Luck thought, as his own body vanished, as he sank into the bear, feeling the creature's limbs and, immediately, its intense and total hunger. It had slept for months, losing its fat. *Her* fat, he realised. Then, from her eyes, he saw Bjorn rise up – bigger, undoubtedly male. His – *her* – mate. At the beginning, the instinct of the possessed beast always pulled hardest, then was lost for a time, until it began a fight for repossession that the god, however strong, would eventually lose – in a morning, a day perhaps. For now, though, the she-bear's will was lost. Luck felt it go, dwindling like the scream of someone falling off a cliff.

The last voice he'd had in his head had been Freya's, the night he left Askaug. Now Bjorn thought-spoke.

'Are you well, brother? Is the body sound?'

'I ... I think so.'

'Good. Let us go then.'

Bjorn-as-bear got to his feet, then cried out.

'What is it?' asked Luck.

'My bear. Strong in some ways. But weak in one leg. Broken,

I think, just before he lay down for the winter's sleep.' He dragged himself from the cave, limped a few strides. 'It's set wrong. There will be no running up this mountain for me.'

The cries of those who chased them were nearer now. Came from back through the birch stand, where they'd first smelled bear. Bjorn looked there, then up. 'There's another trail just here. Take it.'

'No, I am not leaving you. We'll fight.'

'There are still too many of them, brother. Too many for two – but enough for one.' He drew himself up on his hind legs, sniffed the air. 'You know, in all these years, I've never fought men as the hunted. A first!'

'Brother ...'

'Go.' Bjorn's eyes gleamed within the bear's while his voice was clear in Luck's head. 'If your visions are true, you have to go and find a way to save us. And I can give you the time to get away.' They heard a crack of stick on the path. People were coming through the birches. 'Besides, brother, you are a terrible fighter as a man, and I suspect it will be the same for you as a bear. You will only get in my way.'

'It is the truth. So I go.'

He shoved the bear's left foot through the dragging rope loop of the boat. 'Hear me though, brother. Hold them for a while. Lead them astray. But don't get taken again. Your pretty head may only be filled with bear shit and vanity but it is still best upon your shoulders.' He bent to the boat, picked up his brother's weapon in his mouth, dropped it into a bush. 'And with what I've learned, we are going to need Bjorn's swift sword in what is to come.'

If a bear could grin, it did so now. 'I love you too, little brother god. Now go!'

Luck obeyed. Entered one stand of trees just as the mortals came from another. He didn't see them – but he heard their

175

cries of terror, as a bear stood on hind legs before them, roared then ran at them. They, of course, would only have heard the bear. It was Bjorn's voice though that followed Luck up the slope.

'Come, jackals. I have your deaths right here.'

As roars merged into screams, Luck set his bear legs to the mountain and, dragging the boat, began to climb.

9

The Bridge

Every third night in the City of Women, a half-dozen would gather in Besema's room to card and spin wool, knit, weave. The llamas on the terrace beside the house supplied some and more was brought by guards from the countryside around. Muna, in charge of the city, allowed this gathering when she forbade most others because she liked what resulted: clothes, blankets, tapestries, all to be traded across the realm for the luxuries she craved that the city itself did not produce – jewellery, wines, sugared sweetmeats. Most profit went to please her and her intimates; but Besema did not resent this because she got what she most wanted: to be left alone to gather with friends, to feast and laugh the night away.

Atisha was amazed at the variety of food that each woman brought – spicy stews, smoked fish, dried fruits softened in tangy sauces. Of the five guests on each of these nights, three were always new while two always the same, Besema's closest, oldest friends, Yutil and Norvara. And they, in addition to rich dishes, always brought skins filled with distillations of fruit, corn, or cactus. The more of these that were consumed, the noisier the room got, filling with memory, with laughter, songs.

On her first night Atisha heard tales of men and their clumsy love-making that made her blush, even though she considered herself worldly in such matters. She also learned that many in the city loved each other in every way it was possible to love – including the three friends. When Yutil was reminiscing about a night they'd had – in details that again made Atisha blush – Besema claimed it was an age ago, and anyway she was too old for all such nonsense now. Norvara had guffawed at that, adding on a loud whisper to Atisha while gesturing at Besema, 'If Intitepe is the god of love, meet the goddess.'

Atisha had blushed a third time. She did not have those feelings for women. But perhaps she would learn to. She knew that she would need to feel again the way she'd felt with him. And the idea of any other man touching her . . .

At her first celebration, the night after she'd arrived, she'd attempted to keep in the shadows and nurse her babe. She was uncertain as to her status – was she a prisoner, a servant? She'd come forward to clear dishes, to refill gourds. But soon enough she'd been sucked into the celebrations, made to sit, eat. No story was demanded of her, though while the others told theirs she would often glance up to find one of the women, especially one of Besema's intimates, staring at her. She assumed her host had told them something of her. It was natural, she supposed. Like Besema, they were all older women from different parts of the land, so none would understand what it meant to have been 'the One'.

It was on the third such night of celebration, however, eight days after her arrival, that Atisha discovered how wrong she was.

It began with an argument at night's end. The other three women had just left and only Besema's close friends remained. Norvara was from the northern province, Palaga, and still had the height and strength of that land, though the long, thick hair that once must have been as bright as ripened corn was now a coil of spun silver. Atisha had been told that northerners were foul-mouthed and quarrelsome, and Norvara appeared to confirm this, under the influence of all the liquor she'd drunk that night.

'Goat shit!' she exclaimed loudly. 'It is called the constellation of the scythe because it looks like a fucking scythe.'

'And what does a Palagan know of scythes?' Yutil replied. She was a lowlander like Atisha, so also smaller and brown-skinned. She had matched Norvara gourd for gourd – and had reached the stage where if her closest friend had declared there were really three moons, she'd have argued for none. Now she continued, 'Palagans grow no crops to use a scythe on. Whereas we of the coastal valleys live by them. Is that not so, Atisha?' Without waiting for a reply, she forged on. 'The constellation you refer to is called the belt of aztapi. Because on the day when the blue moon is at her greatest height, it girdles her—'

'Girdle this!' Norvara made a stunningly obscene gesture of inserting something long and large into her mouth, her tongue bulging out one cheek. 'We may not spend all our lives kneeling in the dirt like you peasants – no insult intended, sweetness,' she added to Atisha. 'But we in the mountains are closer to the skies and so see more clearly the—'

'Clearly? When you are face down on a rock every night sleeping off the effects of that urine you call beer? Hah!' Yutil rose, swayed slightly, then strode to the door. 'Come, Atisha. Come, Besema. Let us show this Palagan drunkard the truth of the stars.'

'You all go.' Besema stood and moved to the back of the room, to the door there that opened onto a room where she spent most of her time, that Atisha had yet to see. 'I have something to show our new friend.'

The two others turned back. 'Really?' Norvara said. 'She is ready?'

'She is. And we will need her help if we are to—' She broke

off, waved them out. 'Go. Let Atisha the Sober rule between you over belts and scythes. I will call you when all is prepared.'

Yutil led the way, Norvara behind. After a glance back to make sure Poum still slept – she did, nested in blankets near the fire, Fant asleep before her – Atisha followed.

The air was sharp cold, the inhale like an icy dagger, the first out like smoke. But it was pleasant after the aromatic fug of the hut, and Atisha stood for a while breathing, slowly, deeply. It was a clear night, with neither moon too bright, and thus the stars glimmering clear. Another sparkle came from below to their right – lamplight in the window of the hut at the bridge's far end. Ten of the male guards would be in there around their hearth, three others walking and shivering until their turn at warmth. There were five more guards in the city itself. Eighteen men and close to three hundred women. Atisha had wondered from the beginning if that caused any problems but had been too shy to ask.

Atisha swiftly found aztapi's belt and would have ruled in her fellow lowlander's favour. Truly, the constellation would have made a very poor scythe for any farmer-god. But the argument had moved on by the time she joined the other two. 'There, I tell you,' said Norvara, pointing. 'She showed it to us only last month. Has corn wine destroyed your memory?'

'It must have yours. Or your sight,' Yutil replied, 'because you are pointing at an eel, not a snake.'

'Faugh! There is no difference between the two.'

'Again, spoken like a true northerner. Atisha and I could describe six types of eel to you, couldn't we, child?' Yutil leaned out over the parapet and spat into the darkness below. 'Could you even find your own now?'

'Of course. It's just … it's … fuck! Where is it?'

'And where the fuck is mine?'

Both women burst out into laughter. Atisha frowned, not

seeing the joke. She felt excluded, the stranger again. So she sought something else – her star, the one that Intitepe had named for her. Found it swiftly, hearing his voice as he told her where to look:

'Remember, my love,' he'd said. *'Find the Spider, its left eye, the leg below that. Follow that leg down, past the cluster of seven monkeys? There, the brightest one. You are immortal too now, for you will for ever be remembered ... in the skies!'*

She found it, closed her eyes to it – and to halt the tears that threatened to come again. Through all her fury, beyond the anguish of his betrayal, there was a part of her that still could not believe what had happened. That he whom she had loved so much, who she'd been certain – certain! – loved her with an equal passion in return, had cast her away. Six passings of the blue moon before, she'd still been in the paradise she'd found within his arms, gazing upon a world that he shared with her, revealed to her, with the power of his extraordinary mind. Now, where was she? On a freezing terrace in the City of Women, listening to the drunken laughter of two of them. Her eyelids failed to trap her tears.

'What are you crones cackling about?' Besema said, emerging to join them at the parapet.

'We can't find our stars,' Norvara cried. 'Where's your eel?'

'Snake,' Besema said. 'It is there.' She pointed and Atisha, following the arm, saw the serpent. 'Can you still hear him say it?' Besema continued.

'Could I ever forget?' laughed Yutil.

'Nor me,' said Norvara.

Atisha looked at her. Then at the other two, who, like Besema, also raised their arms and pointed into different sections of the sky. Dread took her, even before they began to speak all together, words that were so familiar.

'There. The brightest one. The one I named for you ...'

'Yutil!'

'Norvara!'

'Besema!'

They cried their names separately, then joined to speak again. Their voices changed, deepened. Became his. 'You are immortal too now, for you will for ever be remembered . . . in the skies!'

Their cries rang out into the night, echoed faintly off the granite cliff faces across the gorge. Died. And in their fading, something died in Atisha too. All longing for the time now past – on the knowledge that Intitepe had said exactly to her what he'd said to these, to countless others. These three had been 'the One' as well, and he'd loved them as such. Placed them in the skies, and replaced them in his bed. And in that moment all her tears dried up, and she exchanged all the love she'd felt for hate. She was shocked to discover that the two had only ever been but a single breath apart.

Besema must have seen it on her face. On her own, mockery passed. 'Come, little one,' she said, gently taking Atisha's arm, 'I have something that will make you forget everything else. Especially him.'

Atisha followed the others back into the house. She thought that Besema was going to give her strong liquor, though she knew she'd never found the distraction in it that others did. Yet the older woman reached for no gourd, simply said, 'Look.'

She did – and could not make any sense of what she saw; wondered if she *had* taken too much drink before. She gasped, which woke Fant, who saw in his turn, leapt up, began to bark . . .

. . . at the sphere floating in the middle of the room.

'I call it my Air Moon,' Besema said, stepping forward, bending close to the sphere, which allowed Atisha to get some sense of its proportions, for it was of a similar shape, though double the size, of the old woman's head. 'The skin,' she continued, tapping that, causing the globe to sway and move away from her, 'is woven only from the finest hair, the inner hair, of the llama's coat. I cover the outside with the fibre of the astami grass, also woven. This,' she tapped what looked like a small wicker herb basket, set below the globe and joined to it by strands of twined reed, 'contains the power.'

'How ... how can it hover like that?'

'Come closer and you'll see.' Atisha did, and Besema reached a finger into the basket's open top. 'See? It burns in here.' Atisha leaned over, saw that the basket contained a thin-walled bowl of metal, and within that embers glowed. 'For years, I watched papyrus, some quite large pieces, rise from my hearth and vanish up the chimney. I always wondered why, yet for the longest time never thought to try to answer myself. Until I fashioned some different shapes, watched how differently they rose.' She tapped the globe again, spinning it the other way. 'What I came to realise was that the hot air inside must some-how be lighter than the cooler air around it. Then I thought that if I contained that heat inside a surface, the object must rise through that cooler air.'

'It is ... amazing.' Atisha stretched out a finger and, on Besema's nod, touched the skin. The sphere spun away and she smiled. 'A wonderful plaything indeed.'

'It may be more than a plaything, sweetness.' It was Norvara who spoke, coming forward. 'It may be a way off this mountain.'

'For a mouse?'

'For a woman perhaps.' Yutil stepped up, and blew out a long breath that spun the globe again. 'Besema has been working on a much bigger one. Maybe in a few months we can try it out. Maybe even—'

The cry was sudden, loud – llamas squealing on the terrace beside the house. 'Better than guard dogs – I mean no insult, Fant.' Besema stepped up and grabbed the sphere, as the dog barked again. 'Someone's coming who does not care that we know that they are. That's not good.' As she spoke she was moving to the back room, whose purpose Atisha now understood. 'Clear all away. Try to make it look like we were working.'

They couldn't do much. The bowls and pots of the celebration were everywhere and llama cries were now joined by the crunch of boots on frosty ground. Poum had woken, to instant tears, so Atisha went and snatched her up just as someone grabbed the door handle outside. Yutil had shot a bolt at the first warning; the door was rattled hard. 'Open this door!' a woman called. 'Open before we break it down!'

'Muna,' said Besema, returning and closing the door behind her. She looked around, shrugged. 'Best obey the bitch.'

Yutil pulled back the bolt, stepped hurriedly away from the door as it flew inwards. Two male guards entered first. 'Why do you lock the door?' said Muna, stepping in behind them. 'Have you something to hide?' The bangles at her wrists jangled as she swept her fleshy arms around the room. 'What's this? A celebration?' She stooped, ran a finger around a bowl, licked it. 'Ha! You treat yourselves well, don't you? I allowed you to meet to work, not to – Pah!' She'd picked up a gourd, sniffed it, threw it down. Liquid spilled. 'Well, now you can celebrate this.' She looked back. 'Enter and say why you have come.'

Another man walked into the hut. He was dressed differently from the guards, in the thigh-length red-banded tunic and sandals of God's Runners. Where Atisha had taken three weeks to reach the City of Women, relays of runners would make it in one. They carried the important news and messages the length of the realm. They carried Intitepe's commands. Seeing the man, Atisha shuddered.

The man pulled out a rolled papyrus. It was held together by a wax seal, red and in the shape of a flame. He broke it, raised it to read aloud. 'Intitepe, God of Fire and the Light,

184

commands this.' He looked straight at her. 'That the woman known as Atisha will, with her child, be taken to a secure place and held there till God's daughter comes. Mother and child will both then be brought back to Toluc, for judgement.' He rolled up the scroll. 'He has pronounced and will be obeyed.'

The Fire God's daughter, Atisha thought. Tolucca. She of the raven mask and the obsidian dagger. Who'd sat beside the birthing pool, waiting to take any son born and keep him alive only till he could be given to the lava. Intitepe had spared her and Poum that, to await what he called 'developments'. It was clear that he'd changed his mind.

No one protested. There was no point, not with the guards and the runner standing there, hands on their daggers. Yet after Atisha had wrapped Poum up in her carry sling, Besema came and pressed some things on her – a wool blanket, a sealed jar of stewed fruits. Leaning close, she whispered. 'It will take two weeks before the woman comes. Believe . . .' she got out before Muna barked at her. Besema gave Atisha's hand a final squeeze then let her go.

That touch, those words and the look in her friend's eye were the sole comforts Atisha took with her, as she and her baby were led away to prison. Fant, with Besema's hand in his collar, began to howl.

Boring, Intitepe thought. How boring it is, putting down rebellions.

Crouched on the hilltop, he watched as the last of his soldiers marched quietly into the defile below him, before turning back to the plain ahead, and the rebel camp that lay there. It was scarce dawn and these rebels would be as predictable as all their forebears. A few would be in hide tents, most would be sprawled upon the bare ground, drunk on fermented cactus juice and on their petty triumphs – the burning of towns, the rape of women, the killing of tax collectors.

On a few occasions in the past they'd also been drunk on immortality.

Like last time, Intitepe thought, and yawned. It happened once every hundred years or so, some boy born in some peasant's hut who, nonetheless, had a god's blood in the veins. Hailed as a saviour, there were always some disgruntled people who would acclaim the child – or man, if the immortality had just been discovered – and march to place him on Intitepe's throne. But it was already occupied, as the child or man would discover as he died, the way all other rivals had, when the lava consumed them. Immortal women were sometimes born too. Though they were not prophesied to kill the god, he didn't like the idea of other immortals around, and had ... accidents arranged for them. The few he deemed truly harmless he let live. Like the Crone of Palaga, who'd died at eighty, been reborn, and lived to one hundred and seventy-seven before her latest relatives, bored with her ceaseless demands, cut her head off.

This present revolt, though, had the more common origin, starting in some isolated village of Iztec province – among fishermen this time, his spies had told him – where they had killed the Fire God's tax collector, marched to the next villages, killed whoever opposed them in those, added to their forces then marched on the province's main town, killing the governor and sacking it before settling down to drink it dry. That these had moved further south in search of more destruction, more plunder, showed that they were bolder – or drunker – than many. Most rebels, after their initial successes, scurried back to their homes and hoped that retribution would not follow – though Intitepe always made sure that it did.

Will I fight today? he wondered as he yawned again. He'd put on his full armour – interlocking links of supple hardwood from chest to thigh, lined in iron, arm and leg guards of pink clam shell, his helmet hewn and crafted from blackheart tree. He had his stone-tipped war club, Skull-crusher, and his obsidian long dagger, Slake-thirst. He supposed he could do with the exercise. He often accompanied his relay runners for the first stage of their journey but hadn't lately. A vague unease had kept him in his palace for some weeks now. Truly, though, how much exercise was there in slaughtering drunk peasants? How much of a thrill in a fight when the worst that could happen to him was a wound that would swiftly heal, or a fortunately flung stone that would knock him out for a few minutes? When had he last felt that thrill in combat which once he'd craved?

Over four hundred years before was the answer. On that early winter's day when he'd led his men, his elite, into the heart of that much larger army. In the midst of whom he'd felled the priest-king in personal combat.

'Saroc.' He said the name aloud, liking the sound of it. It was the sound of final conquest. Saroc, his last immortal rival. Who he'd then given to Toluc, the Fire Mountain, dissolving his enemy's flesh. The priest-king's eyes had gleamed to the end as he sank into the lava, fixed on Intitepe. Conveying the strength of his final prophecy: 'As you slew your father, so a son of yours shall slay you.'

Noise below him took away the image – his men were settling into their final positions. He turned again to stare at the sleeping camp he would soon destroy. Stared past it into the north, towards the distant mountain that he could only see in memory, where he'd laid Saroc low. *Yes,* he thought, *I will fight today. Men who dare oppose me will feel my anger. Some I'll slay here, some I'll have carried back to Toluc, to offer to the volcano. It has been hungry too long.* His people needed to be reminded that sacrifice was required for the happiness in their lives. Sacrifice . . .

He swivelled, looked south. He'd dispatched Tolucca to fetch that ... *thing*. The child that Atisha – curse her name! – had made. He'd save the prisoners he'd take today for a big ceremony. A dozen of them, men and women, the leaders of this rabble from the coast. They would swim the lava first. Finally *it* would be hurled into the flames. He would hurl *it* himself, something he'd never done before. This he vowed.

'Father?'

He looked down. Amerist was there, one of his three immortal daughters. The middle one. Tolucca, the slayer-priestess, was the eldest, near three hundred years old. Sayana, the youngest at a mere seventy, was a simple girl, delighting only in weaving and songs. Amerist, one hundred and fifty at her last birthing day, was most like him – a warrior from the moment she threw the poppet from her crib and tried to pull his sword from his belt. She was tall, lean, her body strong and supple – and revealed, because she delighted in wearing no armour, and barely clothes, exposing herself to enemy blades with an immortal's certainty. She held a bow, on her back was a quiver with a dozen arrows, at her loin cloth, a scabbard with her short stabbing sword. Her small, hard breasts were, as always, bare.

He'd once considered taking her into his marana as one of his twelve. Sayana, the youngest, would happily have come to his bed if he'd asked but he had no interest in her softness. Amerist had firmly declined when he'd hinted at it. 'What if we made a son?' she'd said. 'I'd have to kill you before you killed him.' Besides, her desires ran elsewhere, to women. She led a dozen of them, her personal guard, dressed and armed like her, in the forces below.

'Daughter?'

'All is ready. How do you wish to proceed?'

He looked into the defile, at his hundred armed and armoured men. They were joking in whispers with each other. They always enjoyed these slaughters, for the killing and especially for what would follow, because he let them do whatever they wanted to the surviving rebel women – or the men, according to their tastes. Behind these, squatting silently on the ground, were Amerist's female band.

Although he knew this was going to be little more than a massacre, the memory of Saroc and some vague sense of real warfare stirred in him now. 'The men to go in first on my signal. The women are the reserve. They follow a hundred paces behind and await my further command.'

Amerist's hazel eyes narrowed. She liked to be in the first ranks. But she never disobeyed her father-god. 'Do you fight?' she asked, her anger showing in the curtness of the question.

'I will go in with the men. Maybe I will fight.' He rose from his crouch, stepped to her, put a hand on her shoulder. 'Don't worry, daughter. Watch for my signal. I will call you forward before the slaughter is over.'

'Good.'

She preceded him to the defile floor. His men fell silent, ceasing their jokes and boasts as he moved among them. When he came to the front his grey-haired, much-scarred commander, One-Eared Salpe, grinned and said, 'Orders, lord?'

Intitepe felt again that slightest stirring of excitement. He'd lived for this, once. 'Spread out on the plain. Two ranks, two apart, two deep. Silent charge. Kill at will.'

'Lord.' Salpe turned and hissed the command back. It would have come as no surprise.

Intitepe felt the settling behind him. The hefting of spears in their left hands, the drawing of swords with their right. Why not? he thought. Maybe a little blood will wash away this unease. He looked up, and watched Tulami, the morning star, wink and dissolve into the pinkening sky. He drew his sword. 'Forward,' he called softly.

They went at a run, leaving the defile, spreading fast to left and right into two ranks of fifty men, running on, the only noise the drumming of their feet on the parched valley floor. It wasn't much noise, and the enemy were in a drunken sleep, but someone must have heard or seen, because before they were halfway to the rebel camp, still a hundred paces away, someone screamed, 'Attack! Attack!'

It was like an anthill, when boiling water is suddenly poured on. Figures shot up everywhere, a hundred or more, kicking aside blankets, untangling limbs. Yet none of them reached for weapons. All just turned and ran for a second defile – this one behind them, that led into the next valley.

'Faster!' shouted Intitepe, the need for silence gone. It was annoying, he'd have preferred to kill or take them all here on the plain. Still, no stooped peasant or bow-legged fisherman could outrun him or his guards for long. And the next valley would be as fit a slaughter ground as this one, no doubt.

The slowest rebels died first, a few of his men heaving spears into their fleeing backs. More were struck with swords as they bunched in the next defile, even narrower than the one he'd led his forces from. But terror and razor-sharp obsidian goaded them on, the rebels bunching before exploding like a cork from a bottle of over-fermented beer. 'On,' yelled Intitepe, pausing to let some of his men run by him, running again with the second wave. He was caught up in it now. This was more like the hunts he loved, with the traitors ahead the deer.

This second defile was short, the next valley they ran into not large, no more than a hundred paces across, with shallow hills rising at the back of it. A stream ahead bisected the plain, a thin line of green water he glimpsed over the dip of its bank. It didn't look very wide ... so he was surprised when the rebels halted at it, didn't fling themselves into the water and risk possible drowning rather than certain stabbing. He was delighted they didn't, though. He hadn't thought he'd fight. But now his blood was hot, and it could only be cooled in the blood of others.

He was still fifty paces away, readying spear and sword, when the sight before him changed. Figures that had been hidden by the lip of the bank rose suddenly from their bellies to their feet. One rank, two, more. Where there had been one hundred fleeing rebels now stood five hundred. Men and women.

Armed men and women.

Intitepe caught up with the first runners when they skidded to a halt, many of those coming behind crashing into the back of those ahead. His ranks dissolved, as men jerked to a stop, cursing, muttering. 'Quiet,' he shouted – but for the first time in hundreds of years, he was not instantly obeyed. Salpe, other officers, shouted too. The mutters diminished, until at last the Fire King's forces were as silent as those who faced them.

The silence lasted five heartbeats – till it was broken by a single voice, on a single word.

'Forward,' a man called.

As one the rebels screamed and charged forward.

As one, the royal forces turned – and fled.

This is impossible, Intitepe thought, running faster to overtake his men. Peasants thinking, not just being killed, but killing. Impossible!

He knew what he must do. He had not survived the wars against his seven sons, and against Saroc, without learning things. He would rally his trained men in the narrow defile ahead. They would form a smaller front, with Amerist's archers holding the steep hills on either side. Peasants, however bold, would bunch and die on spear, arrow and sword.

Yet as he followed the last of the faster men between the sloping stone walls, he saw his new plan was dust – for the hills were already held. Men were up there with bows of their own, with rocks, with logs, and they swiftly killed the first of his guard that tried to run through the defile. Leaping their falling, thrashing bodies, he ran on, as arrows whipped past his face. A flung stone hit his shoulder, knocking him forward. He stumbled, felt a sting in his back. Now someone was at his side, a hand to his elbow, lifting him. He glanced – Salpe was there, looking grim. 'Lord,' the old veteran cried, 'we must—'

It was all he spoke, before an arrow took him in the eye. He fell, screaming, grabbing at Intitepe's cloak. The Fire God shrugged out of it, ran on. There could be no stopping for anyone, and his men were pledged to die for him.

He staggered from the defile. In the hills beyond it, the path he and his forces had marched down that morning ran south through the trees. He took a step towards it.

'Father! Father!'

Amerist ran up, and he stumbled into her arms. 'Daughter! They—'

'I know.' She dragged him into a semicircle of women, facing the way he had come, bows drawn. He saw there were fewer of them now. 'Father!' she gasped, looking behind him. So he did too – and saw the feathers of an arrow shaft protruding between slats in his armour.

She reached for it, and he hissed, swung away. 'Leave it,' he commanded, and looked beyond the women to the defile. It seethed – with his men, some fallen and crushed, some swaying and desperately fighting the shrieking rebels who leapt among them with sickles, daggers, axes. For the moment the narrow gap was so choked with bodies that no one was coming through, while Amerist's remaining archers were now making the hilltop too dangerous a place to stand.

Intitepe grabbed his daughter's arm, pulling her close. 'Hold them here. Hold them for as long as you can. I must go.'

'Go?' Amerist echoed him, incredulous. 'Father, we must rally the men, fight—'

'This fight is lost. We must prepare for the next one. The only thing that matters now is us, you and me.'

The shrieking rose to an even higher pitch. He looked, saw more rebels leaping, striking, more of his men falling. He stepped away. 'Cover me for as long as you are able. But not too long, daughter. Forget everyone else, even your women. Save yourself. Return to Toluc.'

'You'll be there?'

'I ...' It came to him on the instant. This defeat? The sense of dread he'd had for a while now? It was all connected to Saroc's prophecy – and so to Atisha's child. Four hundred years of instinct told him that. 'No! That *thing*, born to Atisha—'

'What?' Stones flew above them and they ducked. She took his arm. 'Father, listen, he does not matter now. Only the fight—'

'He ... *it* does matter! It is everything!' He flung her arm off. 'Obey me. Cover me. Then ... *run!*'

He didn't hear her reply, amidst bow-thrum and death cries. He ran, more certain with every stride. He would go to the City of Women. End the threat against him in person. He would dissolve Atisha's child in flame – there; he wouldn't even take the abomination back to Toluc. Then he would return north with an army to slaughter every peasant rebel, all their families, and salt their earth. No one would ever dare defy him again.

After another hundred paces he dropped into the stride that the relay runners used, an easy fast lope. Soon he was in the trees, their trunks diminishing the shrieks behind him first to distant wails and then to nothing. The hill was harder to run on than the flat, though, harder still because with every pace he became more aware of the arrow in his back.

It couldn't have gone that deep or he'd be dead. Dead to be born again. He thought of stopping to pull it out, which would probably kill him. The last time he'd died and been reborn had been two hundred years before. Gored by a stag he'd cornered. He still remembered the pain of rebirth, didn't want to face it now. Besides, instinct told him he was not yet safe.

It was his hearing that told him why. A strange sound, close – too close! – an animal cry that came from no animal he'd ever heard in his realm. Slowing down to hear more clearly he felt, through the soles of his feet, a drumming on the earth.

Immediately he cut sideways off the path, into thick brush that tore at his legs, arms, face. Came to a tree and, with what suddenly felt like the last of his strength, scrambled up to a low branch on the side of the tree away from the path. Lay there, trying not to pant, peering around the trunk back to the path he'd left ...

... just in time.

Something *was* coming. He heard it in a snort, then in another high-pitched cry. But none of that strangeness prepared him for what came.

It was a beast. He'd never seen the like. A man's body fused into a creature's that had a separate, long neck like a llama's but was twice the llama's height and length. Man and beast seemed one – until the whole halted, close to the spot where he must have forsaken the path for the trees. Then Intitepe saw that the man was ... *apart* from the beast, that they were two, that the man had been ... riding the animal, like children would ride a llama for a few paces before they were bucked off, though adults never did. And once he'd realised that it was just a man, he studied him more closely – and again saw strangeness like he never could have imagined.

The man was a giant, head and shoulders taller than Intitepe, who was tall for his people. Long black hair fell from a single topknot on his crown to just above his waist. His clothes were black too, glimmering faintly – tanned animal skin from his boots to the band across his forehead. He had a face as pale as llama milk, in vivid contrast to the black beard that grew thick and swept up almost to the eyes ... eyes that now turned towards him. In the moment he had before he swung his face back behind the trunk, he noted those eyes were pale as ice.

He held his breath. For a moment he clearly felt both the man's and the beast's attention directed towards him. But then another sound came, distant, clear – a trumpet blown three times. Grunts came from the man; short, explosive. Perhaps they were words. Other sounds followed – that same drumming that had approached, now fading into the distance. Only when he was certain he was alone, when birds began to call again, did Intitepe finally peer again around the trunk.

Man and beast were gone.

He lowered himself to the ground, groaned. The pain in his back had doubled. But he returned to the path, and began again to run, grinding his teeth against the agony. He knew he would have to stop soon, pull the arrow out, die if necessary, be reborn. It would take only a few hours but he could not spare them. Not yet. He would not rest again until he'd put some more distance between him and those ... *things* that had followed him.

Truly, he would not rest until he'd gone to the City of Women and killed Atisha's child.

In the city's deepest dungeon, in the darkest hour of the night, Atisha woke from a dream of fire. It was the only warmth she had in her cell, and her only comfort too. For in her dream she had wrested a burning brand from the hands of Intitepe, one he was about to plunge into a pyre atop which, tied naked to a stake, stood the child they had made. Not a baby now – their offspring was fully grown. Yet between the child's legs lay nothing of man or woman. A flower was there, of a type unknown to her, blooming even as Atisha looked. And when she'd seized

195

the brand, when Intitepe fell to the ground and wept, Poum had laughed.

It was the laugh that woke her. Poum was still asleep though her mother was sure it wouldn't be for long. Atisha knew that babies changed as they grew, that the early days of ease and gentle slumber would pass. But she also knew it wasn't mere growing that now kept her babe crying and squirming through most of the day and long into every night. From the moment of her birth, each had reflected the other; ate when both were hungry, slept when both were tired, laughed when each took joy. But there was no laughter in a dungeon and Poum knew, because her mother did, that they might never know its comfort again. For Tolucca – immortal, immortal's daughter, priestess-slayer – was coming in her raven mask to claim them both. Maybe as soon as tomorrow. They'd been in the cell for two weeks since the runner arrived. And though it had taken just over three for Atisha to reach the city, she knew that Tolucca would travel faster than a new mother and her babe.

Moving gently so as not to wake the child, Atisha groped for the gourd on the floor beside the straw mattress. Their single oil lamp had long since guttered out and would not be lit again till the change of guard in the morning. Her hand found the smoothness, she lifted, unstoppered, drank. The llama milk was on the turn, souring, but she sighed and swallowed. She had no appetite, drank because she must to produce her own milk for Poum – who had as little appetite as her.

The baby mewed as Atisha lay back down. 'Hush. Hush, little one.' She stroked the soft down that crowned her head, and the child, with a last mutter, settled. But Atisha couldn't, just stared into the dark and thought on death.

She knew she was exhausted, underfed, desperate. Yet her mind kept circling back and back to her choices, which had come down to two – wait and watch her child killed before her and die the moment after. Or kill her child herself and die the moment after. Out there, on the journey back to Toluc.

Here, within the cell.

Her thoughts no longer dwelt on necessity – she would not give her child to Tolucca and Intitepe to slay – but on means. Killing her child was easy. Killing herself was harder. She had no dagger. She had thought of fashioning a noose from the blanket Besema had given her – but in her searching of the cell she had found not a single point, on door or wall, to hang it from.

She sighed, closed her eyes. Sleep, she commanded herself. Could not. She tucked the blanket tighter around them both, and shivered. Thick wool, it still was not thick enough for that freezing cell. Yet the blanket was not the only thing that Besema had given her. She'd also given her hope. With a word. 'Believe,' she'd said. Now, staring at the ceiling she couldn't see, Atisha thought that cruelty – for a last hope taken away was the worst thing in the world.

Her eyes closed – then shot open again. Noises came, loud enough to penetrate the thick wooden door. She sat up, jerking Poum awake, who immediately began to wail. Atisha thought of comforting her – but what comfort could she offer if the person who walked through the door wore a raven's mask? She thought again on murder – but could not do it. While she was alive she would fight, because this she knew: chances to kill or die would come on the road back to Toluc.

The door swung open. Torchlight dazzled her. For a moment all she could see were shapes at the door, one larger that had to be the male guard, one a little smaller, who could be Tolucca. Atisha stood, clutching her crying baby to her chest, as the man lurched forward then fell to his knees, and the woman spoke.

'Did I not tell you to believe, daughter?' said Besema.

Another woman came in – tall, silver-haired Norvara. She

held a bow, arrow notched, string drawn, and the guard peered around at her, his hands by his head, terror in his eyes.

'Come swiftly,' said Besema, moving the flaming brand she held to the side, offering a hand.

'Are you getting me out of the city?' Atisha said, stooping for the blanket and the gourd.

'Yes.' Besema's eyes gleamed in the light of her torch. 'But come. There is still much to do – and much danger in the doing of it.'

It was at that moment that Poum, fully awake now, laughed.

Shoving the whimpering guard to the floor, Norvara followed them out, bolting the door behind her. They climbed the circular stair, pausing before the door that led into the entrance hall.

Atisha had fashioned her sling again, and now tucked a gurgling Poum into it then placed her on her back. 'What can I do?' she said. 'Have you a weapon for me?'

Besema handed her a stone dagger. 'Stay here. Protect the child,' she said. 'Let us do the rest – for we have been planning this for years. We only needed a sign. You and Poum are that sign.' She looked at Norvara. 'Ready?' On her nod, Besema put her hand to the door handle, slowly turned it, then pushed the door open.

Lamplight glittered. The hall, the whole house, was quiet, the only noise the sound of snoring that came through the guard room's open door on the far side. By the hall's front door, the night guard sat, his head lolling against the chair back, eyes closed. Norvara crossed and stood two paces in front of him, the creak of her bowstring as she drew it back a loud noise in the near silence.

Besema went to the door, reached for the top bolt, looked around, took a deep breath – then flung the bolt down, bent and heaved the heavy door wide. It opened on a squeal of hinges.

The guard sat upright, shook his head, stared. 'Move and you die,' said Norvara.

'Poroco?' came a voice from the guard room. 'What's—'

The rush of ten women into the hall buried the rest of the question. They were all armed, some with a variety of blades from the field, sickles and axes, others with mallets, daggers or bows. Yutil was at the front and knew her task, leading half a dozen straight into the guard room. There were cries, the sound of blows. A few moments later two men carried a third out, laid him on the ground and joined the door guard with their hands behind their necks.

'Now, Norvara.' Besema gestured. 'The bridge and the gate-house. Go!'

Through the open door, Atisha saw some more armed women waiting. Norvara had taken a step towards them, when a scream came from the balcony above: 'What is happening here?'

Someone spun, shot. An arrow drove into the wooden balustrade – right between the hands of Muna. She yelped, staggered back – and a bare-chested man who'd appeared with her took one look down, turned and ran. Women rushed up the stairs. Some went in pursuit of the man, others seized Muna, dragged her down, flung her between the guards. She was dressed in some kind of pink night gown and her hair was wild. 'What?' she blubbered. 'What are you doing?'

'Quiet!' Besema ran to the bottom of the stairs, called up. 'Have you got him?'

A young woman appeared. 'No. He got to the tower.'

'The tower?' She looked up. 'Gods! The bell!' And just as she said the word, the bell began to toll; frantically, accompanied by hoarse male shouting. Besema paled. 'The bridge, Norvara! Now!'

The women poured out of the hall, joined the others before it. Atisha followed. The woven-reed bridge was directly in front of the hall's entrance and she could see, on its other side, men roused by the alarm and massing at the guard house – roughly the same number as the armed women. But the men were soldiers, trained to kill. And the first of them were already on the bridge.

'Arrows!' shouted Norvara, and the five women who had bows shot. Only one arrow hit, the man screaming, falling, as the others rushed past him. The bridge spanned the gorge. It was maybe fifty paces long. The men would be there in moments.

In moments, Atisha thought, my brief hope will be gone.

Unless . . .

Her dream came back to her, as vivid as if she still slept. Intitepe was the Fire God. He claimed to be one with Toluc, the Fire Mountain, and between them, they sought to dissolve her child in flame. But she knew now that Intitepe was just a man, weak; more, a man terrified by an ancient prophecy; knew also that the mountain was just a volcano. Knew that flame was not their sole possession but a force to be used by any who could command it.

Either side of the hall's front door, two huge lamps burned day and night, in honour of the god. To supply their continuous need for fuel, pots of oil stood beneath them.

Thought and action one, Atisha stooped, snatched up a pot, ran forward, raised it above her head – and hurled it hard into the bridge's wooden stanchion. It smashed, and oil poured onto the reed bridge. Snatching the torch from Besema's hand, Atisha leaned back then hurled it.

Flame came, blue and low – until it suddenly shot high and the bridge exploded in red fire. One man tried to run through the shimmering wall – though whether it was the fire or the two arrows in his chest that killed him no one could know. No other followed – couldn't, for the bridge swiftly fell, a mass of smoke and sparks and screams, into the gorge.

'Child, are you mad?' Norvara pointed forward. 'You have cut us off from the world!'

'I did not think, except to stop the soldiers ...'

She trailed off. Besema came and put her arm around her. 'No. This is good. No one can come – and we are blessed on our mountain with enough food to last, oh, for ever! That should give us enough time to figure out what to do next.'

Atisha laughed. 'I thought you'd been planning this for years.'

Besema nodded. 'We were going to capture all the guards, seize the city, get you to the coast, hide you in the villages there. Now—'

They both gazed into the conflagration. The smoke that rose was too thick to pierce with sight but above the crackle they could clearly hear the shouts of angry men.

'Now I ask you to believe something else, daughter,' Besema continued softly, turning to her. 'That this will be the spark that sets the whole country ablaze – and burns tyranny to ash.'

Atisha swallowed. Her fury had passed and fear returned. 'Brave words. But when Intitepe comes, as he will?'

'He will find us resolute.' Besema nodded, to the women who'd seized the hall, to others coming from all parts of the city. 'Nearly all the women in the city will rise with us. Beyond this gorge,' she gestured ahead, 'perhaps most of the women in the land.' She smiled, squeezed Atisha to her. 'For everywhere, women have had enough of men ruling them, don't you think?'

The first person to emerge from the hut was a fisherman. He came fast, and made it only half a dozen paces before falling to his knees and vomiting. Staggering up, he vanished into the darkness, in the direction of the rebels' camp.

The second person to emerge from the hut was the huntress.

'Well, Gistrane?' The monk looked up from the glass globe, raising his black eyes to her. 'Did she tell you?'

'Of course ... eventually. Then all at once. It was hard for our friend there,' Gistrane nodded to where the vomiting man had gone, 'to translate all, so swiftly did she talk. And since my grasp of the language is only fair, I had to have him slowly repeat many things.'

She squatted, throwing her long, tightly coiled hair over her shoulder, before stretching her hands to warm them at the firepit's flames. 'Mother and baby are in the south. In a place they call the City of Women.' She smiled. 'When I thought my sisters and I were the only ones in the world to have one of those.'

'How far south?' The horse lord had a stick and poked the embers. Sparks rose.

'She was a little unclear as to distance. Forgivable, as she was a little ... distracted.' She shrugged. 'From their capital, Toluc, which is two days' march south of here, you can walk to the City of Women in three weeks. Runners in relays do it in one. If we move between run and walk – twelve days from here?'

'Or five if I ride. Maybe I should do that?'

'No, Korshak. We go together, always. Our holy leader commanded—'

'Your leader, monk!' The horse lord hawked, spat into the fire, then turned to the black-eyed man. 'I am *commanded* by no one but my king.'

'It was agreed then,' replied the monk calmly. 'We stay together, till we find the One. All our respective ... skills have been deemed useful for that. Together we are strong.'

'Hmm.' Korshak grunted, but chose not to argue further. He pointed to the globe. 'And have you talked with your leader lately?'

'No. I glimpsed him, but lost him before he could speak. The distance is huge and the storms,' he shrugged, 'will pass. But I will talk to my brother who is with the seafarer. Tell him to take the ship south. When we know the land we can guide him closer.' He looked out into the camp where the rebels, men and women, sprawled. 'Will any follow us? It might still be useful to have an army.'

Korshak snorted. 'This rabble? No. There are scores less of them each day. They are scurrying back to their villages with what they've pillaged. When they've finished the last of that foul brew they call liquor, the rest will be gone too.' He nodded to the hut. 'Did she tell you anything else?'

'Some things.' The huntress picked up a brand, wrapped in oiled wool, one they'd use to light a room, and shoved it into the fire. 'She is Intitepe's daughter. One hundred and fifty years old. Oh, and he's headed south as well. To this city. Apparently he wants the child as much as we do.'

'He has heard the prophecy? There is light in this land too?'

'No, monk. His prophecy is different. It brings life to us. To him it brings death. His death. So he seeks to kill it first. Kill the One.'

'Praise the One,' intoned the monk.

'Praise him. Praise her,' said the huntress.

But the horse lord didn't add his voice. He was staring at the hut. 'Immortal, eh? Hmm.' He sucked air between his teeth, dropped his stick, then stood. 'I've always wanted to fuck an immortal.'

'You are an animal. Like all horse lords.' She shook her head. 'It was only because we'd cut the balls off so many of you that you stopped trying to rape us.'

Korshak leaned down to spit into the fire. 'We would never have stopped. But we'd had all the pretty ones. Only you uglies were left.'

Gistrane rose to a squat, and reached to the knife at her belt. 'Is that so?' she said softly.

'Stop it, both of you,' the monk barked. 'We know why you

stopped killing each other. Why we all stopped killing each other.'

They turned to him. Korshak spoke the words he should have spoken before. 'Praise the One,' he said.

'Praise him. Praise her,' the others replied.

Korshak looked once, long and deliberately, at Gistrane's hand, still on her knife. Then he looked again at the hut and licked his lips. 'Still,' he said, 'we're a long way from home now.'

As he went to move around the firepit, Gistrane lifted the torch from the fire, the flames upon it fierce now. 'So we are. Yet for all that she is my enemy, she is still a sister, and a warrior. And for her reluctant aid I promised her an easy death.'

'No!' snapped Korshak, moving.

Too late. Gistrane rose, turned and shoved her brand into the thatched roof of the hut, and then into its reed walls. The horse lord bellowed, stepped closer. But there was little he could do, the hut caught so quickly. Screams came from within it, cut off when the roof collapsed. All – reed, wood, flesh – was swiftly consumed.

Korshak, glaring at the huntress, muttered curses. She smiled back. The monk stood, put his globe and stoppered vial into his carry-sack, then ran his tongue along his blackened teeth. 'South,' he said.

IO

Monster

They had been hearing the single horn for a while, its low call growing louder with every river bend they rounded. Now as the serpent-prowed ship pushed through the drooping fronds of willows on either bank, it was as if a leather door-hanging had been moved aside, admitting the full roar of horn and people and, more shockingly, revealing the vastness of the gathering ahead.

'They have answered your call,' said Freya, peering forward. One hand rested on the carved snake, the other on the man beside her.

'Aye,' replied Hovard, shuddering, 'but will I have an answer for them?'

She looked at him. 'I was waiting,' she said.

'For what?'

'For you to admit that you felt even the smallest doubt.'

He turned to her. 'What do you mean?'

She smiled. 'My heart, from the moment you accepted Luck's visions and then his plans, through the time you dispatched us all with our white ash sticks to issue the summons, to when you and I met again at Petr the Red's camp and during every minute of our voyage here, you have displayed nothing but an utter and complete certainty. It is unnatural.'

His lips twitched. 'Why should I be natural? I am a god, after all.'

'You are.' She let go of the prow, put her arms around him, pulled him close. 'You are my god. And, my god, my husband, I have known you for three hundred years. So I can clearly see the uncertainty you mask so well. Tell me of it now, before it is too late.'

'Too late?'

She jerked her head towards the bustle they were fast approaching, the noise getting louder with every pull of the excited crews' oars, their destination at last in sight. 'Before we land, and certainty will be all you will be allowed to display.'

Hovard took a deep breath. 'It was so much clearer in Askaug. Luck told us what he saw in the smoke within the globe, pure, black-eyed evil. And I have learned over the years to trust my younger brother god's visions. We all have.' He exhaled and stared ahead again across the serpent's scaly wooden neck. 'But why should *they* believe *me*, all those gods and mortals? Fighting each other is all they have ever known. How can I get them to change their entire way of life with ... words?'

'Because you will make them good words.' She squeezed his arm. 'Stromvar believes you. Acted on your bidding. And the world knows him to be the fiercest believer in nothing but himself.'

'One god. Who was there. Who saw what we had found, what Luck had revealed.'

'He carries weight. His reputation is such that people will follow him.'

Freya looked where Hovard did. Never had she seen such a gathering. When her people raided, a fleet of twenty was deemed large. Here, hundreds of longships were drawn up on the strand, while many had also come by foot. Beyond the beach smoke from scores of campfires roiled into the air. Pavilions of hide and canvas spilled over the slopes that rose steadily to the base of Galahur – a giant stone bowl.

Sheltered by the rock ramparts, thousands could gather on the slopes within and hear. In the middle of the bowl was a simple mound of grass-roofed earth, the empty barrow of the long-dead king, upon which stood any who would speak at the regular Moot, which came every twenty years. Haakon, named the Great, was the last one to gather gods and men together in a Special Moot.

Thinking of him, Freya turned back to Hovard. 'Haakon, who was buried up there, saw what we saw on a day much like this. Arrived here four hundred years ago with exactly your doubts. With your same questions: how can I convince a stubborn people and their stubborn gods to change the way they live? How, when all I have is my belief that they must?'

'I am not Haakon, wife.'

'No. You are Hovard. Yet just as he was not "the Great" until he persuaded them, neither will you be until you do. As you will.' She took his face in her hands, pulled him closer. 'Luck knows that you can do this or he would not have left you to do it on your own. Bjorn would follow you into hell flames, if you said you saw a way through them. And I—'

She broke off and he reached and took her head, as gently. 'And you, Freya?'

'I always knew I had but one life to live. And however long that life would be, I would spend it entirely with you. Not just because I love you. Because you always know what is right.'

They held each other, eyes in each other's, for a long moment more. Then, as one, they leaned, kissed.

'Aw! Aren't you sweet? Enough, my cooing doves!' The voice that came was northern, rough. They looked back on the squat and powerful form of Petr the Red. The god was well named, for every part of him that was unclothed – unkempt beard, pillar of hair, knuckles, caterpillar eyebrows – bristled crimson. 'Soon you may find a place to fully express this passion. For now, steady for our arrival.'

They gripped the serpent's neck again, just in time, as a last powerful sweep of oars drove the ship onto the shore's gravelled and sloping bank. Immediately the vessel tipped sideways. Freya fell onto Hovard. He held them both and easily with one arm.

'Oh fuck,' muttered Petr. 'Here he is.'

The next words came on a bellow, from a different, familiar voice. 'Little Red Petr,' Stromvar cried. 'How good it is to see my old adversary! Tell me, hairy one, have your parries got any better in the hundred years since I last kicked your arse?'

Hovard smiled, though he hid it. Freya looked away. Their host had been kind to them on their five-day voyage from his native Kroken, where the Askaug gods had rendezvoused. In return, they hadn't mentioned Stromvar, the god who'd killed Petr in combat three times in a row, a feat never achieved before – or since – in Midgarth.

It was something that he obviously remembered all too well, judging how his skin coloured into a match for his hair. 'I won't need to parry you next time, you piss head. For you'll be too busy plucking steel from your head.'

'Ho ho! A challenge, you all heard it!' Stromvar always gathered followers wherever he went, such was the legend of the Lord of the Seven Isles. There was a crowd about him now, and more drawn by his voice. He looked around and grinned. 'But for all his brave words, Little Petr knows he is safe, the rules of Moot protect him: no combat for two weeks before and for two weeks after.'

Petr flushed an even deeper red. 'Fuck the rules!' he yelled, and snatched up his battle axe. 'Let us go ... Strumbum! Here. Now.'

Stromvar's eyes narrowed at his nickname. 'Indeed,' he replied. 'Let us.'

Hovard looked at Freya and sighed. 'And so it begins,' he said softly. Then he leaned around the dragon prow, so the Lord of the Seven Isles could see him for the first time. 'By all means, my lords, go,' he said. 'One of you slays the other. The rules of Moot are broken, the penalty is applied, so punishment ensues. Four hundred years since it last happened and memory dulls but I am certain death will be involved. It always is.' He looked around. Many had gathered on the shore to witness the exchange, more were coming. It begins, he thought, and I am not even off the boat. His voice rose. 'Meantime, those who threaten us, who would destroy us, rejoice. Rejoice as a divided people stay divided.' He lifted Petr's axe hand high. 'By all means, lords, go to it. And after your heads have been struck off, let the rest of us kneel down right here and offer our necks to the slave's yoke.'

Silence then, on the boat, on the shore. Until Stromvar broke it. 'Can you wait a few weeks, Petr the Red?' he said.

Heat faded from the smaller man's cheeks. He lowered his axe. 'I can if you can. Vengeance postponed tastes all the sweeter.' He turned and looked at his crew. 'But not as sweet as Kroken ale, is that not right, lads? The most prized in the land. Ready to be shared at the feast tonight, on the eve of Moot. That is, Dragon Lord, if you have brought some of that pickled whale you islanders so boast of?'

'I have. And the men of Lorken have already promised a dozen of their fabled smoked wild boars.' Stromvar grinned. 'So let us feast and get drunk together, Petr. Maybe I'll teach you a few parries afterwards, to make our next fight more of a contest.'

Instead of countering, Petr grinned too. 'Maybe I'll show you why I won't need them.' He turned to his crew. 'Let's set up our camp, lads,' he shouted.

Men on the shore turned away to their own tasks. Freya leaned in to Hovard and whispered, 'A good beginning.'

He nodded. 'But only the beginning. What will be the end?'

'My lady?'

They looked down. Stromvar had waded into the water which reached to his huge thighs. He raised his arms. 'May I offer a goddess a ride to the shore?'

'I can wade as well as you, Stromvar.'

'You could. But why get such a lovely dress wet?'

Freya smiled, grabbed her satchel already packed at her feet, leapt and dropped into the waiting god's arms. 'Ah,' Stromvar murmured, bending. 'I knew you'd have some heft. I don't like my women skinny. I like a bit of flesh on 'em.'

'Is this what passes for sweet talk on the Seven Isles?'

'Of course. The most charming folk in Midgarth, us.'

He turned and began wading to the shore. Behind him Hovard called, 'Will you return for me, Stromvar?'

The god kept his eyes on Freya as he answered. 'Do I look like a porter?'

They waited for him on the beach. When Hovard reached them, Petr and his crew close behind, Stromvar said, 'I have been here three days. Shall we walk the camp? There are things you should see.'

Truly, it was already more town than camp. The priests who tended the sacred and eternal fire of Galahur were few in number, no more than thirty. But part of their function was to provide shelter for pilgrims who regularly came to ask questions of the departed gods. There was a modest hall for meals and prayer, and all structures necessary to keep a small town functioning – a smithy, a brewery, a granary, a slaughterhouse. Every twenty years the Moot tested their resources and stretched the town's boundaries. Areas were set aside for the tents of the visitors and, by custom, each town or village had their own place, along rough tracks that ran over the foreshore and up the lower slopes of Galahur like spider webs. It was fortunate that the spring had come fast and hot that year. The last Moot Hovard had attended, thirteen years before, had been the wettest spring in even a god's memory, the tracks turned to rivers of thick mud.

They walked, and Stromvar pointed out the land's far-flung peoples: some dark-haired southerners gathered around the hearth of Einar the Black; fairer or red-haired northerners who acclaimed Petr and his men following behind – and acclaimed the many barrels of Kroken ale they rolled up even more. As they approached the westerners, Hovard and Freya began to recognise some of their neighbours. These were gods, men and women from island and inlet, from coastal mountains and forests. A blend of light and dark and red, they were distinguished by faces browned and toughened by sea wind and spray.

The tents and pavilions of the Seven Isles folk were pitched next to those of Askaug. Indeed there was little to separate the two camps. Folk who had faced each other over shield walls and sword not two weeks before, who would cheerfully have shed the others' blood, now mingled, laughed, drank, shared food and fire.

'It gives me hope,' said Hovard, gesturing to them, and acknowledging the greetings of his comrades. 'If old enemies like us can put aside our enmity perhaps the whole of Midgarth can.'

'I do not wish to diminish your hope,' Stromvar said. 'But walk a little further.'

The eastern fringe of the canvas town they entered was frayed, as edges often are. Most of the tents were moth-chewed and poorly patched; some were just sheets flapping over open ground. The clothes matched the habitations, and rag-clad people glowered up at them as they passed. Where their own folk had overlapped, these blended – red-haired, fair and dark, wind-roughened faces alongside those which looked as if they'd rarely seen the sun.

'Where are they from?' asked Freya.

'Everywhere,' Stromvar replied.

Hovard halted, stared. 'How is that possible? Each man knows his place, his land.'

'Not when they have lost their gods.' Stromvar swallowed as he too looked around. 'Part of me came here hoping that your brother's visions were wrong. That the gods of Midgarth were not diminishing in number, that they were simply … absent for a while. We do that sometimes, we gods. We need to wander, as beasts, as men.' He shook his head. 'But then I saw these people. In villages and towns across the land, their gods are gone. No, that's not right. Their gods have vanished. Not to wander. They have been killed. And for all our faults,' a small smile came, 'yes, I admit, we have them, for we are greedy, concerned only with our own desires. But at least we provide a centre for our world, an order to it. These,' he waved his hand, 'have lost their order. So they abandon their homes, their farms, their villages. Many come here. The High Priest says it has been so for ten years. More and more people coming, staying. He says most tell him that their gods have abandoned them. And that if you had not called the Special Moot, he would have, because he can no longer care for so many.'

Freya noticed a woman slumped in the entrance of a tent. Her shirt was open and she was nursing a babe. It was a sight that always reminded her, suddenly, keenly, of the babes she'd borne and suckled. Three daughters – Helga, Djorn and Raika. Three who had grown and thrived and aged and died even as she and Hovard lived on. It was too hard, laying a white-haired woman on the pyre who once she had laid to her breast. After the last, Raika, two hundred years before, they had agreed to have no more. Yet Freya kept each of them alive in her memory, with the strength of her love. And often, on some endless winter night, she wondered if it would be such a bad thing to die, so she could hold them again for ever.

The woman she watched did not hold her child with love. Just stared dully ahead, her gaze vacant before her. Then, as if she felt them, she glanced up, met Freya's eyes and her own hardened. She leaned forward and, without taking her gaze from the god's, she spat. Freya winced, turned. 'How many gods have come, Stromvar?'

'There is still today and tonight—'

There was something in his voice. 'How many, friend?' said Hovard, taking his arm.

Stromvar looked down. 'Only a few more than one hundred.'

Hovard and Freya both gasped. She spoke. 'One hundred? There should be double that!'

Stromvar simply shrugged. Hovard took a deep breath, then exhaled long and slow. 'I wish Luck was here. He always likes to know that he is right.'

As they turned to walk back to their own camp, Freya felt something hit her in the side. She glanced down, saw the brown lump that could be earth, could be worse, at her feet. 'Fucking gods!' someone hissed, and she looked back, could not see who had said it. It might have been any one of the sullen-eyed people, all facing their way now. It might have been the woman, still staring, and whose expression did not change as she plucked her baby from her breast.

'And that's another thing,' Stromvar said, leading them away. 'The mortals are angry.'

'Just these?' said Hovard, glancing back.

'No. Now you have noticed it you will see that mortals are angry everywhere.'

*

Uproar. Once more the priest tried to take Algiz, the white staff of speaking, back. Once more the holder waved it above his head and shouted; though, as before, this man from the north – a mortal – could not be heard above the yelling of almost every person in the bowl of Galahur.

Freya sighed, looked around at the swaying, quarrelling hordes. They were spread on the slopes of the bowl in a great horseshoe, looking down upon Haakon's Mound: a barrow beneath whose turf was said to be a stone chamber where the king's body had been laid – though the story went that it was found empty the day after his death. On the mound stood the priest, and each speaker was meant to come to him, take the staff, be listened to in silence whatever his argument. Now men and some gods swarmed around it, crying out to be heard.

Yet the day had begun so well. The reverent dawn procession threading the terraces of Galahur, ascending to its crest and down into the bowl, each people, town or village walking to the soft accompaniment of flutes and drums and their own chanting. The High Priest, in his saffron robes, purple sash and antler mask, had called the ritual welcome, the prayers to seasons and to the gods, living and dead. Invoked Haakon the King, neither man nor god, both, who had called the first Moot four hundred years before and vanished soon after, leaving peace behind him – or at least a peace that gods and men could live with. It was said that he would come again, in the land's darkest hour, to save them all.

This is it, thought Freya. So where are you, king?

The day had gone so wrong so quickly. The suppressed anger of the first speaker – a man from Lorken – had been released by every subsequent one. The first god to try to speak, Einar the Black, had been shouted down, even though none but he or she who held the white staff should make a sound. The priest had brought quiet for a time, for all listened to him. But the next

214

god to speak, Stromvar, had also been hooted off. He looked so angry Freya had feared he might run mad, return to his boat to fetch his sword – for no weapon was allowed in camp or upon Galahur – and start slaughtering. A few whispered words and her soft touch had prevented him but he stood beside her now, a geyser about to spout.

'Can they not see? Are they blind as well as foolish?' Stromvar waved at the slopes. 'At the last Moot here you couldn't see a patch of grass for the people. One hundred more gods, each accompanied by their twelve. Now,' he slapped his chest, 'perhaps half those here are god-less. And they are the ones who scream against us the loudest.'

On the other side of Freya, Hovard stirred. He'd been silent, watching it all. But he could see that the priest, who he'd spoken to last night and who had at last wrested the stick back from the last speaker – he might be old but he had power still – was casting around for him. They had agreed that a few would be heard before Hovard came forward and told of why he had called the Moot. Few *had* been heard, truly. But he felt that if he did not step forward and speak now, no one else, god or man, would be.

'Wish me fortune,' he muttered, and began to push his way down the slope and through the crowd.

'Fortune,' Freya called to his back.

A cutting wind had sprung up, borne from the eastern mountains, winter's last echo whipping the banners of each town and people. A near silence came when the priest raised the stick – though angry muttering, which had never really ceased during any speech, continued like sea surge tugging at pebbles on the shore. As he wove down from the Askaugers' place on the slopes, Hovard heard his name being whispered, along with other words, some complimentary, some not. Over his simple leather tunic, he had chosen to wear a cloak dyed in deepest indigo. Expensive, rich. Kingly.

'Who does he think he is,' came one harsh whisper in a northern voice, 'Haakon the Great?'

It was a gamble, his choice of colour, because the people of Midgarth, men or gods, all thought they were roughly equal. Gods might live for ever upon the land – or beyond it if they lost their heads – but mortals could grow as powerful as any with a strong arm and the right desire. For a time. Evoking the memory of one who could have been either god or man and had chosen to rise above them both was a risk. But Freya and Stromvar had advised him, and they were right. His short time at Galahur had confirmed it. The scattered peoples of the land needed a leader.

He ascended the steps to the turf roof of Haakon's Barrow. The priest held the staff in both hands, crossways before his chest. The man lowered his head, held the staff out. Hovard grasped it in his right hand, wrapping fingers around its middle. Its tip was an eagle, beautifully carved. Its base was shod in iron. Cut into its whole length were tala of warding, of prophecy, of power. Luck was the tala reader of the family, but he had taught Hovard enough to recognise the meaning of the shapes cut about the centre of the shaft. They urged the speaking of truth. I will speak mine, he thought, and began.

'I am Hovard of Askaug,' he called, his voice centred, deep, realising that here at the base of the bowl he did not need to shout. 'I am the son of Bryn and Marka. Mortals both. So though I am a god, mortal blood flows in my immortal veins.'

A murmuring came at this, no words he could hear. He continued, 'I tell you this because I see the anger here, dividing what has always been united. At least has been so since the day four hundred years ago when Haakon the Great stood where I am standing now and brought us together, gods and men—'

216

'And women! Don't forget us, god,' a woman called.

Hovard could not see where this came from. The voice was a little slurred and it brought some laughter. 'And women too,' he said. 'Gods, men and women. We are all at heart a simple folk, are we not? To till our fields, to raise our cattle and our children, to hunt in our forests and on our oceans and in our streams – these are our ways. But we are also a people who love to fight.' A small cheer came at this, and Hovard raised his voice a little to top it. 'Gods, men ... and women, how we love to fight! It was ever so and Haakon knew that. But what he also knew was that our thirst for the fight could lead to the destruction of all the rest – the tilling, the hunting, the raising of our children. And so he gathered our forebears here and made his laws.' He raised the white staff and pointed the eagle head over the crowd. 'Recite with me,' he called.

There were prayers that men uttered for fortune before battle or the hunt. There were departed gods called upon, and living ones cajoled. But there were only Haakon's *Laws* – plain ones for a plain people to live and die by. All learned them from the moment that speech was possible. All here recited them now, no matter where they came from, no matter whether they were from villages or wanderers, landless. Gods, men and women old and young, speaking as one.

'Gods fight gods, man fights man and none the unwilling.
Quarter is given when asked.
There is no dishonour in refusing a fight.
The victor only takes as much as he can give back.'

Hovard glanced at Stromvar at that – for the Lord of the Seven Isles had come to take Askaug, and would have offered only his barren rocks in return. The fairness of that exchange was the sort of thing that would be discussed and settled at Moots. Hovard wondered then if Stromvar, in seven years' time at the regular Moot, would have been willing to give up Askaug had he conquered it. Somehow he doubted it. But Stromvar only stared ahead and called, as everyone else did, the last of Haakon's laws.

'These, my laws, will stand in my memory. They must only be changed if all life changes ... at the twilight of the world.'

As the last cries faded, Hovard looked at Freya. She nodded. He'd brought them together. Now he needed to make them believe that the twilight of the world had come.

'People of the Land,' he called, 'Haakon's Laws have kept us safe and content enough for centuries. But Haakon also knew that life does change, however slowly, and that is why he gave us that last law. To be invoked only when it was needed.' He took a deep breath. 'It is needed now and I, Hovard of Askaug, invoke it.'

A louder murmur came then. More than one voice cried out, 'Why?' Hovard lifted the stick, raising the eagle above them. 'It was once thought that we were alone in the world. That the mountains that no one could climb, the seas that no one could sail, meant that there was no one else. Many thought this could not be true. My own parents drowned trying to prove there was somewhere beyond our boundaries. They failed – but others have succeeded.'

This produced the greatest murmur yet, voices querying in confusion, wonder, mockery. Hovard looked at Freya and nodded. Lifting the bundle at her feet, she headed for the barrow. Hovard raised his voice, needing to in order to be heard. 'For someone has climbed the mountains. Someone has sailed the seas.'

'Who?' came a near universal shout.

It was the High Priest's shout that came to him loudest, as he was also standing on the barrow. His wrinkled face was anguished. Not surprisingly, as his world was being turned upside down. 'Who has come?' he said.

'He has,' said Hovard, and stooped to receive the shroud-wrapped bundle that Freya passed up. He stood it up beside him, as his wife joined him on the bundle's other side. All could clearly see the vaguely human form within the cloth and the sight brought an instant, uneasy silence to the crowd. Hovard reached to the brooch pin at the base and jerked it free. He did the same to the pin at the shoulder. Then, with Freya holding steady, he grabbed the shroud in both hands and ripped it away.

Uproar again. People shrieked, some fell to their knees, others made warding gestures to avert evil, joined hands thrust before them. All had seen corpses before. But none had seen a corpse that appeared to be alive, with hair on the head and a glitter in the eyes that only the very nearest could see were black beads.

Luck did a good job before he left, thought Hovard, seeing the preserved corpse of the killer for the first time since he'd left Askaug. His brother had said that such evidence might be needed, that persuasion and belief might not be enough. Judging by the cries, he'd been right.

'You can see this man is not from our lands. We have clear proof that he came across the mountains to kill the gods,' Hovard shouted. 'He nearly did kill Einar the Black, as he will tell you and show you his scar. We believe others have been coming and killing for years. Look around you. Where are half the gods? You people who wander the land, where did your gods go?'

He hoped they heard him. It was hard to tell, the tumult was now so great. Men, women and gods were shouting at him, at the priest, at each other. The crowd was shifting, people moving as if they would soon run mad. Hovard lifted the stick, waved it back and forth, called. Beside the priest, a man lifted a horn and blared a rallying call, such as would warn a village of surprise attack, or rally a force in battle. Under its deep bellow, gradually, the noise slackened, falling at last to a silence that somehow still shrieked.

Hovard took another deep breath. Freya smiled. He had them. Now he had to lead them.

The clapping began a moment before his next word. Came from but a single pair of hands, and yet was shockingly loud in that uneasy silence. People jerked, looked around, seeking the source – and saw the strangest sight.

They had not been there before. They would have been noticed for the oddness of their dress – or rather, their lack of it, for the dozen men who walked forward were all but naked, save for the white and black paint stripes that covered them forehead to toes, and the cloth at their waists which scarcely concealed their maleness. All men, then – though the one who led them through the stunned crowd towards the barrow, the one doing the clapping, could have been man or woman. He or she – the bulk perhaps indicated a man – was the only one fully clothed, though his garb was different from anyone else's in the bowl of Galahur. Whatever region they came from, near ocean, mountain or forest, most people in Midgarth dressed the same – shirts, jerkins and coats of tanned hide, wool leggings and cloaks – practical clothing of darker hues. This person wore a tunic made of fur, and dyed with reds, yellows and green in random patches. Buttoned at the neck, it swept to his feet, there to pass not over boots but over strapped, painted skin.

It was only when the strange crew were at the base of the barrow that Hovard realised what had confused him more about the person than the gaudiness of his clothes. His face wasn't his own. He wore a mask, a near perfect replica of someone else made from a soft and pliant material, like hardened beeswax. The face reminded him of someone; but Hovard couldn't think who, distracted by the strange figure now climbing the turf steps cut into the barrow. Alone, for the twelve followers remained, silent and staring, below.

The figure halted. 'May I?' he said. It was definitely a man's voice, though high-pitched. And Hovard, as transfixed as any, found himself yielding to the gesture that came with the question – and yielding control of the speaking staff to the new-comer.

'Thank you, ssso much,' the man said, and turned to face the gathered people. 'Greetings, people of Midgarth. My name is Peki Asarko. I am a mortal, and I dwell on the Lake of Souls.'

A shudder passed through the crowd. All there knew of the lake – its reputation, if not its truths. No one believed that any but ghosts dwelt there, and all avoided it for that reason, and because of the marsh gases that killed. All had also heard stories of the few who strayed near, and never returned.

The mask face dipped, acknowledging the feeling. 'I know,' Peki said. 'None of you thought that your nightmares would join you at the Moot, did you? But believe this: we of the Lake mean you no harm. We are different, yes, lead different lives there. But we are not your darkest fears. For we are dwellers of Midgarth too and when our land is threatened, like any other people we answer the call to defend it. Defend it from those who truly threaten it.' He turned now, and faced Hovard. 'And those who truly threaten it now are its so-called gods.'

Hovard shook his head, to wake himself from the spell the man's arrival and appearance had cast on him. He didn't know what was happening here. But he knew that the people, who had been ready to listen to him after the reciting of Haakon's Laws, were being swayed away again. He stepped forward, held out his hand. 'We do not listen to men in masks, Peki Asarko,' he said. 'Everyone here, god or man, is prepared to show his honest face to the world and be judged.'

Instead of giving back the staff, Peki turned back to the people.

'You see how the god will bully a mere mortal? How he will stop us speaking? I wear a mask because my face is hideous – for many years ago a god tried to blind me with fire. I do not wish anyone to be distracted by my ugliness from the truths I would speak. Must speak,' he said, stepping away, holding the staff away from Hovard who'd reached again. 'Will you let me speak?'

'Let him speak,' a man shouted, the phrase taken up, swiftly becoming a chant. Hovard glanced once at Freya, still holding up the black-eyed assassin. She shrugged and Hovard lowered his arm.

Peki passed close to Freya then, the mask turned to the preserved corpse she held. 'Nice work,' he whispered, giggled, then turned to face the crowd again.

'Why do we call you a god, Hovard? Yes, you live ten lives to our one, or more. But during those lives? You eat, you shit, you fuck, you kill.' Some in the crowd laughed. He turned to gaze out. 'Is that any different from us mortals?'

'They can turn into beasts.'

It was a woman who yelled it. 'Thank you, ssister,' replied Peki. 'Yess. They can become animals for a time. And what do they do with that gift?' He put a hand behind his ear, gazed out. 'No? I will tell you. They eat, they shit, they fuck, they kill. Such are our ... *gods*.'

Hovard looked out. And it seemed to him that he could suddenly see all the gods, the hundred who were there, standing slightly clear of their twelve followers. As if all the mortals had taken a small step away from them.

'And now what do these gods tell us? When they sense that we are angry? That we do not wish to follow them any more? They tell us that there is an enemy ... *beyond*.' He waved to the east. 'A threat – *out there*. Killers coming for all of us. All of us?' He shook his head. 'Or did I hear him say that it was the gods who were dying? Did I hear him say that he wanted to change four hundred years of Haakon's Laws because his brothers and sisters are threatened? Their way of life. Did I hear him say his only proof was this,' he waved at the corpse, 'desecration?'

Hovard had not said that. But looking out at the faces below, he saw that many there believed he had. Peki Asarko, bringing the mystery of the Lake of Souls and harnessing a resentment that many felt, was swaying them to his cause. What exactly that was, he had not said. Whatever it was, Hovard knew it was against all he'd come there to do. He sought to unite gods and mortals. This man sought to divide them further.

He stepped, placed two hands upon the white staff, as the muttering on all sides turned to a growl. 'My turn,' he said softly, for only Peki to hear. 'For I can tell you—'

It was as far as he got – because suddenly the eagle head of the staff jerked – and struck Peki hard in the middle of his chest. With a cry, the masked man fell back, down, releasing the staff – and leaving Hovard standing over him – as if he'd just hit him.

The roar that came then was twice as loud as the crowd had made so far. Men and women surged forward, shouting. None were as quick as the twelve painted warriors, who ran up the steps and surrounded their fallen leader. Hovard stepped back, protesting, though none could hear him. The High Priest seized the staff, waved it aloft, tried to quieten the mob, who poured around the barrow yelling and cursing. Only when Peki Asarko was helped up and raised his arms for silence too, did hush eventually come.

Stromvar had joined Hovard and Freya, and the three of them faced the painted men and their wheezing leader, who reached and snatched the talking staff from the hands of the startled priest.

'Very brave, god, to try to end my right to speech with your violence.'

'I did not—'

'In doing so,' cried Peki, overriding him, 'you have left me no choice.' He turned to the lake of faces surrounding the barrow. 'All can see how the living gods accept those who are of a different mind. But we know that our gods in the sky, in the warrior halls and on the thrones of everlasting life, are wiser than their earthly offspring. With Haakon the Great the wisest of all. For there is one other law that has not been spoken yet. Not spoken since he left it to us four hundred years ago.' He turned to the priest. 'Tell them.'

'I . . . I . . .'

'Oh, you'll need this,' Peki said, handing over the staff. 'Now tell them of Haakon's wisdom and his seventh law.'

A near silence now, all muttering gone. Only the wind still made noise, in the flapping banners. 'The s-seventh l-law,' the priest stuttered. 'The seventh law states—' He broke off. 'It has never been invoked before.'

'It has never been needed before.' Peki nodded. 'Invoke it now.'

The priest drew himself up, took a deeper, steadying breath. This was the law, and he was its minister. 'The seventh law of Haakon states this: "If all cannot be resolved between gods and men at a Moot, then one god and one man shall fight – and the victor shall decide the course."'

Upon the field of Galahur, people looked at each other. Hovard who, like all the rest, had never heard this law spoken, suddenly calmed. Though Bjorn was the true fighter among the Askaug brother gods, he knew he was good enough. Good enough certainly to defeat this masked man before him, who played tricks with sticks, and swayed a crowd with lies. 'Do you challenge me?'

Eyes glimmered in the mask. 'Yes, Hovard of Askaug. I, Peki Asarko of the Lake of Souls, challenge you.'

'Good. So let us fight. Here, now. And let the gods who sit above decide between us.'

'Yesss.' The voice hissed. 'Let their power sit in your sword, just as they sit in the sword ... of my champion.'

Hovard, who'd started to turn away to Freya, turned back. 'You do not fight?'

'Me?' A soft giggle escaped through the mouth slit. Then the voice came louder, carried. 'Though of course I wish to, I cannot. For that god who burned my face also crippled my arm. But it is within the laws of our land to appoint a champion to fight over any dispute. You can do the same if you like.'

He giggled again. Hovard grunted. 'So where is your champion?' He looked at the painted men still crouched at their leader's feet. 'Is he one of these?'

'Oh no. He is ...' Peki swivelled to the front, and stretched out his arm to the lip of the bowl of Galahur, to the place where he'd first appeared, '... there.'

All turned, those on the barrow, those on the ground, following the swing of Peki's arm. For a moment, nothing stirred. Until something shifted and a man appeared, moving slowly over the crest so that he was only revealed little by little. The bald crown of his head. A face painted in black and white stripes like those who crouched upon the barrow. A neck – which seemed not to be there at all, for the head stood on shoulders that spread wide, bulging with muscles like thick, coiled ropes. The chest no different, the stomach the same, both looking like they could be armoured in leather, but which was just more painted skin. The gasps only got louder as he came – until the moment when the monster crested the hill and stopped, on legs that looked like oak trunks in a forest, bringing a complete silence.

Peki Asarko broke it. 'My champion. His name is Ut the Slayer,' he said, waving. And then he laughed.

*

Stromvar entered the tent. In its corner, Freya looked up from the sword on her lap, and the whetstone in her hand.

'Is it time?' Hovard asked.

'Almost.' The Lord of the Seven Isles tipped his head to the noise behind him, a buzz of voices that had scarcely diminished since the moment the challenge was issued, and the challenger appeared. 'It is a feast out there. The men of Kroken have sold almost all their ale. People are eating meat that is barely cooked. I've heard three ballads already, telling of the fight.'

'Did any of those ballads have me winning it?'

Stromvar's silence was his answer. Instead he said, 'You should appoint me your champion. Let me fight for you.'

'Why?'

'Because I have a better chance of killing that big fucker.'

'You do.' Hovard reached down again to his leather shin guards, and resumed tying them on. 'And if you do, I will for ever be the one who hid behind you. You will be the leader then, not I.'

Stromvar grunted. 'Would that be such a bad thing?'

Hovard finished the last knot, stood and crossed the tent to lay his hand on the other god's arm. 'We will need your courage, Dragon Lord. We will need your strength and your prowess at war. We will need these things most desperately, I fear, in the times that are upon us. The one thing you lack, forgive me, is restraint. Your power is in your instant actions. But in the time ahead we will need thought as much as courage. Truly, I believe we will need it more.'

'So let me act for us now, and you think for us later.'

'No.' Hovard squeezed the forearm he held, stepped away, back to the weapons he'd laid out upon the ground. 'I will need to be obeyed, instantly. Men and gods do not obey cowards, however wise.'

'They don't obey the dead either, husband.' Freya rose from

the corner, came forward, sword at her side. 'And this is a final death we are talking about. No rebirth this time. If you fall, the monster will cut off your head and—'

'My love!' Hovard raised his hands. 'I know what will happen to my head. I know I will be finally finished and if I am, well, it is my destiny, and I will join my parents and all my friends in the mead hall of the gods.'

Freya laid a hand on his cheek. 'But I like this head where it is.'

'As do I. So let me use it while I can.' He turned back to Stromvar. 'Did you find out any more about this Peki Asarko?'

'Not much.' Stromvar took the sword from Freya, ran his finger along the edge, grunted approval, then licked blood from his fingertip. 'The painted ones talk in their own tongue and won't answer questions in ours. Einar says his voice is from the south, close to Einar's own people. Other than that—' The god shrugged.

'And the monster?'

'Hovard!'

'Sorry, my love.' Hovard smiled. 'Freya thinks if we call him a monster he becomes one, and that makes him harder to kill. He is just a man.'

'I don't know. Slaying monsters is in our blood, is it not? Didn't Haakon the Great slay a giant serpent to become king, and bring his laws?' Stromvar laid down the sword, picked up a shield. 'I have not learned anything of use from studying the mon— the man. He sits and stares and the painted ones keep their distance.'

'Weapons?'

'None are near him. No armour either. He is huge, of course, so I suspect he will wield weapons that suit his strength. Axe. Club. You? Just this?'

Hovard reached to Freya and took his sword. Unlike Bjorn,

he had never named it. He had never thought it magical, with a life of its own. It had been a tool, little more, and it had been twenty years since he'd wielded it in more than play – for as he got older he found he preferred thinking to fighting. Yet as he hefted it through the air now, he remembered how good a tool it was. Forged from finest steel, it was pattern welded, the metal heated and coiled, hammered out and cooled, again and again. It was the length of his arm and half again – shorter than many, lighter than most. Freya had not only honed a fine edge – as Stromvar's glistening finger testified – but she had rebound the leather grip in alternating bands of green and red leather which swept up to the pommel, a ball of iron that gave the weapon its perfect counterweight and upon which was carved a single eye: the mark of the All-Seeing God. He was 'the nameless one', father of all the other gods, who saw everything with his one eye, and ruled all through it. 'Yes,' he murmured, raising the blade, kissing it. 'Just this.'

There was a bray of horn. Three times. 'The summons,' Stromvar said, unnecessarily, holding out the oak shield, which Hovard took. It was painted red, rimmed in a metal band with a boss of iron at its centre. Stromvar stooped for the conical steel helmet. Freya came and affixed his cloak with its heavy pewter clasp – a wolf, snarling – at his neck.

As she thrust the holding pin through the wool, Hovard sought her eyes. 'If this goes against us, leave fast. Do not stay to mourn.'

'It will not—'

She lowered her hands and he grabbed one. 'Freya, listen to me. This Peki has a plan, that much we can tell. He seeks to divide gods and men at a time when we must be united. But our people are not so easily swayed, I think. Have them and our ship ready. Flee fast. Get home.' He looked up. 'You too, Stromvar. Because, for a while at least, the West – Askaug and the Seven Isles – may be the last refuge of hope in all Midgarth.'

Instead of arguing, Freya raised his hand, and kissed it. 'There'll be no fleeing. For you will not lose.'

'As in all things, my love, you are right.' Hovard stepped away. 'But just in case – have the ship ready.'

A man came to the tent's entrance – Ulrich the smith, whose great-grandfather had forged Hovard's sword. He glanced at it, then looked up. 'The men are outside.'

'Good. We come.' Hovard nodded at Freya and Stromvar and led them from the tent.

The Askaugers were lined up, Ulrich at their head. All had the same look on their faces, a frown of doubt which they all tried and failed to entirely clear as Hovard appeared. He stopped, nodded at them, didn't speak. There was truly nothing to say now.

They swung about and marched off. Stromvar and Freya followed and Hovard came last. He had a strange sensation, gazing at the backs ahead of him – an urge, while out of any-one's sight, to just slip off, find a bird, transform, fly away. He'd always loved to be a falcon, to hover over men and gods and watch their doings. But although the desire made his first steps slow, he soon caught up. It was destiny he walked to now, his and Midgarth's, irretrievably linked in ways he could only partially see. At that moment, he missed Luck keenly, for his little brother god was the seer, able to sift through the workings of the world, and make the patterns clear. 'Wherever you are, Luck,' he murmured, 'spare me a thought and guide me now.'

They climbed the slopes of Galahur. A few stragglers followed, though most had already answered the horn's call, judging by the buzz of sound ahead. Just below the crest, they swung around to the right, circled. They had been assigned the left end of the valley, the position of the challenged, so they'd been told – since the seventh law of Haakon had never been invoked, even the priests were uncertain as to all of the rules.

They halted just below the ridge crest. 'Ready?' asked Freya.

Not really, Hovard thought, but in place of words he nodded. They climbed into the bowl.

It was different than it had been. The floor of the small valley was empty, though the grass where so many had stood was churned, slick and muddy now. All the slopes had people on them, whereas before the rear was clear, as everyone had faced Haakon's barrow. On the turf roof atop that the priest now stood alone, clutching Algiz, the talking-staff.

Hovard's appearance caused a surge of noise. Men and women pointed, commented. And the volume rose even louder when, at the far end of the bowl, the painted ones appeared and formed a funnel over the crest. First Peki Asarko came, still masked, still in his medley of colours. Halting, he turned and flung out an arm – to the monster – Hovard was still failing to see him as a man – who did not enter as slowly as before, just stepped up and over the crest. Yet such was his size people still gasped loudly, and many called upon the gods to protect them.

The priest raised the staff. Gradually, a near hush came. He pointed the eagle first at Hovard then at the painted giant, finally at the earth before the hut. Hovard handed his sword and shield to Stromvar and set off down the slope, needing to pick his way through mortals who stared at him before moving aside – though he noted, in one swift glimpse, how at the valley's other end a clear path opened rapidly for his opponent.

They stopped before the hut, and turned to face it, ten paces apart. Hovard had watched his opponent approach but it was only when they were still that he could truly appreciate his immensity. He was not small himself – yet the top of his head was level with the lower part of the man's bulging chest.

'You are here to face the judgement of the gods in combat,' the priest called. 'Yet even now one of you could choose not to submit to their will, choose not to fight. Shame may follow you, but life will not leave you, and life is precious.' He looked from one to the other. 'How do you choose?'

Hovard's throat was suddenly dry. As he went to clear it he heard the other say, 'I submit my life to the will of the gods.'

The voice was a low rumble, as if it came not from a body but up from the earth. A sigh followed, as the crowd turned to Hovard, who hummed before he spoke to make certain his voice was steady. 'I submit my life to the will of the gods,' he said.

Another sigh, some chatter – ceasing as the priest raised his staff again. 'Then arm for the fight. And know – when the two of you descend next time, only one will rise.'

Hovard felt the other's gaze upon him, turned. The monster said nothing. But he opened his lips over a near toothless mouth and smiled.

Hovard took his time climbing back up the slope. People stared but he met no man's gaze until Stromvar's. 'Well?' he queried.

'As I thought – no armour. He doesn't want to hide his size. I'm surprised he hasn't got his cock out. He's so muscled he'll be slow, which should help you. He's—' Stromvar broke off, peered. 'I was right. He lifts a battle axe and a club. That's it.'

Hovard took back his sword and shield. 'So your advice, Dragon Lord?'

'Advice? My advice is don't get killed.'

'Useful.' Freya had taken the helmet from Stromvar. Now she placed it on her husband's head, and swiftly tied the chin straps.

'Yours, my love?'

She finished the knot, met his eyes. 'My advice is similar, with this addition. Kill him.'

'I will,' he replied, trying to sound certain, failing. As she

231

reached to remove his cloak, he caught her hand. 'No. You wove this for me. It keeps me warm. You keep me warm.'

She nodded. 'Fortune,' she said, turning sharply away, just too slow for him not to see the tear that ran from one eye.

He swivelled, glanced up at the sun. It was at its zenith so neither fighter would be dazzled. He blinked, the horn sounded again, and both men set out through the shrieking silence for the valley floor. Both reached it at the same time, came forward at the same pace. The battle axe, Hovard saw, was not the shorter one to be used in one hand. This was huge, and would usually be swung with two.

They were twenty paces apart when the man Stromvar said would be slow proved he wasn't.

He went from walk to sprint in a heartbeat. Hovard just had time to brace, to lift his shield, draw back his sword before the monster was on him, sweeping both his weapons down. Hovard had his shield for the club, his blade for the axe, instinct making him angle the sword so that the axe blade smashed and slid rather than smashed and snapped his only weapon. The force of the blow carried the axe to the ground, to plunge into the mud. But the club struck the shield rim full on, buckling the metal, the shock splitting the wood and driving him to his knees. Hovard was holding half a shield and through the gap he saw the monster swing the club back and high in a great arc to drive it down ... into the place where Hovard had just been.

There was nothing graceful in his slide away. He knew it, the crowd knew it, and their jeers came loud and fast, before they were lost to shrieks as the axe rose and fell again. Hovard's next roll away might have saved his leg – but he ended up on his back, a crab flipped over. He jabbed his sword desperately up, sensing the onrush rather than seeing it. But it made the giant stop, step back, gave Hovard the moment he needed ... to sit up, twist then hurl the remains of his shield into the painted chest. It was an insect bite of a blow but it allowed Hovard one more moment to slide away, stagger up, set himself – before the giant came again.

Which he did – bellowing, windmilling his arms, both weapons lost in a blur of wood and steel. There was no parrying either, for if he tried Hovard knew he'd lose his sword then his life a moment later. So he did the only thing left to him.

He ran.

Jeers came louder, louder than his heaved breaths. When he'd got twenty paces away, he turned, braced. But the giant had not followed, was grinning toothlessly at him, swinging his two weapons alternately through the air. The noise they made was like hornets, mustering for the attack. It was almost mesmerising. Indeed, for the first five steps the giant now took, Hovard did not move, as if held in place by the lulling sound. Then, when he did, it was forward and as fast as he could go. He could not run away again. If he did, he was not sure he would ever stop. Besides, it was likely the monster would run faster. If nothing else, Hovard didn't want to die with a blade in his back.

Perhaps it was the surprise, the speed of his run matching the monster's, for suddenly they were together, and Hovard took the axe blade once again on a sloping sword. Steel scraped down steel in a scream that was almost animal, while the club driven down was a gale in his right ear, just passing him by. But as he ran on, he stumbled slightly; enough. Heard the shout of terror, thought it might have been himself, felt the blow coming, didn't see it, twisted ... in time not to die, yet also not to avoid the club which caught him on his flung-up shield arm, and snapped it like kindling.

There were groans from all around – but cheers too, and a cry of agony that could have been him, could have been Freya. Somehow he stumbled on, sank to his knees, turned, lifting his sword before him, knowing how easily the monster would pat it aside. The monster …

… who had not come.

Through blurry eyes, Hovard saw him, twenty paces away. He had both weapons lifted high in the air, shaking them, roaring as more cheers came. It was a moment, and Hovard took it, breathing deep. His one arm was broken, that much he knew. Agony now, it would heal fast, as was the way of the gods. But only if he survived. To do that, before he was put swiftly out of his pain, he had to master it, and learn.

His eyes cleared, and he looked at the man receiving the acclaim. Only a man. A big man, sure. But not a monster. And all Hovard had done so far was fear, and react. Now he needed to act.

His enemy lowered his arms, as the cheers faded. Turned, grinned again, came slowly, yelling taunts in the guttural language of the Lake of Souls. And Hovard noticed something he hadn't before: that the man was so huge, so bloated with muscle, he held himself tall, high, and swirled his axe and club at shoulder height. The lower plane, Hovard suddenly realised, is mine.

That was when he remembered that he had another weapon, though no one would ever have considered it so; and jamming his sword point into the mud, he reached to his neck, pulled the brooch pin free, dropped the pin, and twisted the heavy brooch itself deep into a swirl of fabric. Then, as the giant gave a great bellow and ran at him, Hovard leapt up, leaned back – and hurled the balled end of the cloak. The weight of the brooch carried the cloak for a distance before it fell out, while the material flew on, far enough, like a fisherman's net hurled for herring, floating into that whirl of weapons.

It was enough to tangle them – for the moment Hovard needed. Snatching up his sword, he ran three paces, then launched himself feet first and arse down on the wet mud, swinging his sword back, around. Kept sliding and, as he passed his adversary, he put his broken arm behind his sound one, levelled the blade that Freya had honed to such sharpness and sliced into the huge leg, just below the knee. He knew it hadn't gone all the way through, felt it but he didn't stop to watch, just used the momentum of the slide, twisting his wrist, wrenching the blade out and sliding past the falling, flailing, yelling man. Still sliding, he came up on one knee, cocking his wrist, then jammed both heels into the mud, using the sudden stop, and the velocity of that, to spin him around ... and slammed the blade into, and through, the heavily muscled neck.

The head hit the ground three heartbeats before the body.

The force of his cut had carried Hovard through the complete circle. He came to a halt facing away from the dead monster, looking up the hill to the place he'd come from. Sound, which had seemed to vanish in the slowness of his never-ending slide, returned now in people cheering, beginning to rush towards him. He ignored them. There was only one person he needed to see, and he looked for her beside the Lord of the Isles.

Stromvar's face was split by a huge grin, and he was striding down the slope. She wasn't beside him. Neither were the men of Askaug.

Where are you, Freya? Hovard cried, soundlessly.

Running. As soon as her husband's sword sliced into the knee of the giant she knew it was over. But she didn't wait to see more, though the shouts of acclaim and the cries of 'Hovard!' told her as she ran what must have happened. She just shouted, 'With me!' and trusted the men of her town would follow, as she had warned them they might need to do. She needed the extra moments because they had further to run if what she thought was going to happen, did.

It did. From the moment she cleared the bowl and ran down its far slope, she could see the painted ones, their black and white stripes vivid against the greens of early spring foliage. They were moving a little more slowly than they might have – if they hadn't had to half-carry the large multi-hued figure in their midst.

Freya sped up. Her men followed fast. Those they pursued were not far from their boat, one of the few drawn up at Galahur's small dock. When they reached the jetty's end, some aboard cast off lines. Some of the striped ones, hearing pursuit in the slap of feet on beach pebbles, turned. Their leader was not one. 'Stop them,' screamed Peki Asarko, as he ran on.

They could not. Weapons were not allowed at the Moot, but weapons were in hand nonetheless, the small knives that were allowed for food, curved and straight. The painted ones were split between carrying their leader aboard and defending him while the men of Askaug just followed Freya's run straight into the enemy's midst. Blades rose and fell, parried, cut. It was over fast. Blood flowed and blended black, white and red into the colour of death.

The last man between Freya and her quarry lunged too early. She slipped her body to the side, sliced down; the man dropped his knife and fell, screaming, after his three fingers. Only the last man remained, the one she'd come for. He had one leg over the gunwale of his boat, and one still on the dock.

Freya sheathed her dagger, and grabbed the neck of his robes. 'Who are you under there, Peki Asarko?' she said, and ripped off his mask. But as she did he wrenched away from her, fell onto the deck, looked up.

She gasped, but not only for the evil she felt pour off him like a wave. For if his face was not as hideous as he'd claimed, it did have black teeth, it did have black eyes.

'Seize him!' she yelled to her men, already jumping into the boat.

Then she saw what he held – a sparrow, bright eyes blinking, a tiny thing in that vast hand. Big enough. 'No!' she yelled, landing on the deck, grabbing cloth.

Too late.

The robe she grasped was empty. The body in it gone. There was a flash of white tail, lost swiftly to the brightness of the sun. All that Freya had left was a memory: of deep evil within black eyes. And the promise of a deeper evil to come.

II

Cult

'You look so handsome, my love. Like the first time I saw you.'

Ferros pulled the razor from his jaw, looked back at Lara in the mirror. Raised an eyebrow. 'The first time?'

'The first time – in uniform.' She smiled. 'The true first time? Well, I did not think much of you at all, then.'

'You took pity on us, nonetheless. Ashtan and me.'

She laughed. 'You looked so young and so helpless. And the man chasing you had such a big cleaver.'

Ferros laughed too, turning to her. 'Enormous! And he was determined to use it to cut off several of our bits. Bits we knew we'd need.'

'Bits you'd already shown to the man's daughter.'

'Not ... shown, exactly. Hinted at. Offered.' Ferros shook his head. 'I think her father was the only man in Balbek who didn't know that his daughter had slept with half the regiment.'

'A lie. It was no more than a quarter.' Lara raised herself a little off the bed. 'You and Ashtan, running down the street, giggling like schoolboys.'

'We weren't much older. First year in training.' He turned to her. 'But the butcher was gaining on us. You opened your door, "In here, you fools," you hissed. Then you—'

'Hissed? What am I, a snake?'

'... then you threw that blanket over us, threw open the back door, yelled, "There go those bastards!"'

'Ferros! I was far too innocent then to use the word "bastards".'

He stepped away from the mirror, came towards her. Soap was on half his face, while his eyes danced with memory. 'Not too innocent to give me a good whack on the head through the blanket.'

'You were laughing so loudly. I thought the butcher was going to hear and come back. I feared I'd lose bits too then for hiding you.'

'Ashtan was doing the laughing. I got the blow.' He grinned, leaned down. 'The first of oh-so-many!'

Lara lifted her hand, struck him gently across the cheek. 'Oh, you poor bullied boy!'

'That's me. A slave to love.'

He leaned down to kiss her but she pushed him away, settled back against the pillows. 'My illness, love,' she said.

'I'd risk it,' he said, not withdrawing. 'It's been two weeks.'

'I am getting better. Soon.' She placed a palm to his forehead and shoved him away. 'Besides, you have the festival to go to.'

He straightened. 'Dancers? Players? Poetry?' He said the word like it was a disease. 'What do I know of all that? I am a soldier.' He returned to the mirror, put blade to jaw. 'If you were there, you could nudge me when I fall asleep. Please come.'

'No.' Lara sniffed deeply. 'I'd cough and put them all off. Besides,' she looked at his reflected eyes, 'I am sure she would rather have you to herself.'

Perhaps he was prepared for that. The eyes didn't change, though the razor stopped moving for a heartbeat. 'I am sure *she* will not even see me. She performs in her own creation, remember. And there will be hundreds of people there.'

'Oh, she'll see you,' she said, but softly and he didn't look as if he heard. He didn't speak more, finished shaving, dipped his hands in a second basin, splashed his face, wiped away all soap traces on a towel. He grabbed his cloak from the door hook, swept it around his shoulders, fastened it at the neck with the Genian silver brooch she'd bought for him. Turned to her. 'Well?' he asked.

She studied him. The boy, who had appeared briefly again when they'd talked of Ashtan and escapades, had gone. Only the man stood there now. The soldier. Yet grander than she'd ever seen, for they'd promoted him as soon as he got to the city; he was a full captain now, not just a field one, and they'd made him the uniform to match. One for occasion, not battle. A purple tunic of finest wool that reached mid-thigh, fringed in the black fur of the panther. Leather armour that had required three fittings, moulded exactly to his form with eagles at the shoulders, grasping in their talons the javelins that crossed his chest. More leather swathed his forearms and shins, the greaves there tucked into calfskin, fleece-lined boots. Only two items weren't new – the sword hanging in its battered sheath at his hip. The tightly wound strips of leather on its grip were stained, not just with sweat. There was blood there too, of the men who'd killed Ashtan, for he'd not cleaned it since killing them. Those who'd dressed him had tried to give him a pretty ceremonial sword. It had been the one thing he'd refused.

A soldier stood there all right. Yet someone else stood there too. The immortal. And she could see again, as she'd seen from the first, that it hung heavier upon him than his winter cloak.

She'd stared too long. 'That bad?' he asked.

She rose, went to him, laid a hand on each bicep. 'Every fibre the fierce warrior,' she said. 'Those dancers and players and poets will run screaming when they see you.'

'I hope so.' He leaned down. 'Come with me?'

'I cannot.' She lowered her head so he kissed the top of it.

'Very well,' he said briskly, turning away to put on his new helmet with its black horsehair crest. 'I suspect it will take a long time for me to return. The Heaven Road will be busy tonight.'

'I will be here, asleep. Waiting,' Lara replied.

'Be well,' he said simply, and was gone.

She looked at the door he'd closed, listened as his footsteps faded. When, after a minute, they had not returned, she swiftly set about her own dressing. Threw aside the night shift, put on her day one. Even though winter now finally and fully gripped the city in freezing winds and icy rains, she'd been told that where she was now bound would be hot. Still, she slipped her feet into her winter boots and threw her heavy cloak over her shoulders. Those would be discarded later, but she'd also been warned that where she was going was a good walk away and she didn't want to arrive there chilled.

She glanced back at the room. When she saw it again, she would be different. *If* she saw it again. Tonight would decide that. Once she crossed the threshold, she was committed, she knew. So, for one long moment, she hesitated and gazed with some longing at the bed. She had stayed in it even though she was not sick, had only pretended to be for these two weeks, in order to put Ferros off, one condition of what she was to undertake this night. The hardest one – for to make love to him was her greatest joy under sun or stars. And since that moment at the Sanctum, when he'd come back from the ride and she'd seen her, Roxanna, seen them together, he'd wanted to make love to her in a way that he had not since he'd been … *smitten* with immortality. Perhaps he'd felt he must. For she'd seen again the look in his reflected eye when she'd spoken just now of Roxanna. Seen that same look whenever he'd avoided talking of her in the two weeks since the stables.

She would lose him tonight. Or she would win him back. It was all in the hands of the gods – and in her blood.

Or not.

Hesitation left her. Closing the door behind her, she descended the stair, lowered her head into the bitter wind, ran the few streets and alleys over to the tavern. It was crowded this night, people from the neighbourhood seeking free warmth in the tavern's blazing hearth, in the heat of the press of bodies and mugs of hot wine.

Carellia was at her usual table, a steaming jug before her. 'Songbird,' she cried as Lara sat, 'I didn't think you'd come.'

'Why?'

'Many – most – change their minds at the last minute. You still can.'

'No. I cannot.'

'Very well.' The older woman nodded. 'But are you prepared? Have you abstained from the flesh of beast these two weeks?'

'I have.'

'And the flesh of man?'

'I have.'

'And have you drunk of the vine or of brewed malt?'

'I have not.'

'Good.' Carellia smiled her gap-tooth smile. 'But have a drink now,' she said, pouring a mug, shoving it across. 'Because, my songbird, you are going to need it.'

'You look like you need a refill, young man,' said Lucan, beckoning a servant. Though Ferros would have preferred a clay mug filled with heated winter ale to the chilled, sweet Tinderos wine, it was all that was on offer. Yet around the fourth glass he realised he was developing a taste for it – not for its sweetness, never that, but for its effect. Yet as the servant raised the brimming jug, Ferros hesitated. He was drinking on an empty stomach, barely filled with the mouthfuls of food other servants carried around the hall – trays of tiny quail grilled on skewers, morsels of marinated trout, cubes of ewe's milk cheese steeped in oil and herbs on slivers of flatbread. Perhaps he'd drunk enough?

Fuck that, he thought, and lifted the glass. 'Good, good,' said Lucan, patting his arm. 'I hope you are enjoying yourself?' He looked around, lower lip thrust out in concentration. 'Different than what you would see in Balbek, I suspect.'

'Somewhat. Men don't dress as women in Balbek. Nor dance as them. Nor sing with women's voices.'

'Ah, Streone!' Lucan laughed. 'Any excuse to get into a dress. Every year it is the same. Our creator of spectacles hopes that he will wear us down – that we will learn to love the form as much as he – or she, should I say?' He shook his head. 'But we never have. So Streone never wins. Well, hasn't in forty years.'

'Wins?' Ferros watched the servant move away, heading for the kitchens. Which was odd, because even though he had a full jug of the wine, he did not fill the glasses thrust at him on every side. He turned back to Lucan. 'Wins what?'

'The pieces which you have seen tonight, the last of which is still to come, compete with each other. They have been reduced from fifty to these ten. Strangely, Streone's always makes the ten.' Lucan laughed again, continued, 'The judges, of which I am one, award wreaths to three winners. Oak leaf for third place, holly for second, and silver leaf for the ultimate winner.'

Ferros grunted. 'And how do you choose? There's been poetry – if you can call it that, I didn't understand a word. That singing and … dancing, I suppose, from Streone. Two men shouted at each other pretending to be warriors – though neither looked like they'd ever wielded a real sword.'

'Blunt as ever, young man. We should have you as a judge next year.'

'I'd rather die,' Ferros replied. 'Which, of course, I can't.'

If Lucan saw the hint to talk further about immortality – the Tinderos wine was making Ferros bold enough to seek the answers he still hadn't received – he ignored it. 'And speaking of winning,' the older man said, running his hand over the shining dark globe of his head, 'my daughter tells me you were magnificent in the javelin race yesterday. The first time immortals have won in over twenty years.'

'You did not watch?'

'Alas.' Lucan shrugged. 'Affairs of state.'

Ferros nodded. He still felt the race in the delightful, familiar aching of his body. The four mortals they raced against had been formidable – Wattenwolden, huge bearded horse warriors from the northern forests who Ferros would have been pleased to serve with. Their two fellow immortals had been – adequate, losing their individual bouts, but only by a javelin's throw apiece. He and Roxanna, though; they'd been, he had to admit it, and as Lucan had just oberved, magnificent. In the last round they'd ridden better and thrown better than the top two tribesmen, with Ferros's last javelin – cleaving the bullseye – deciding it all. Roxanna, who he'd not spoken to since their ride two weeks previously, had still said almost nothing as they rode and threw. But at that throw, which gave the immortals their victory, she favoured him with a smile, a touch of her fingers on his arm, and one word.

'Superb.'

He'd looked for her, of course, from the moment he'd arrived at the Sanctum on the Hill this night. He was happy that she mainly ignored him now, of course he was. He'd decided, after that first ride, his race against her, that he would focus only on Lara. That a three-hundred-year-old immortal was beyond him. Yet when he did not see her he was disappointed. He'd have liked to be able to convey to her that he had made his choice. Truth be told, he would rather reject than be rejected.

'Ah. Here we are.' Lucan's voice, and the sound of instruments striking one chord in harmony, drew him from his thoughts.

'Perhaps, young man, this last piece will be more to your tastes?'

Ferros looked to the end of the hall, to the raised dais where all the performances had taken place. A dozen women came onto the stage. His sight, which had begun to blur a little after four glasses of wine, seemed to have been cleared by the fifth for he could see every detail. They all wore half-masks – blue, gold and silver – the lips beneath made fuller with crimson paint. They were barely dressed, with sheer silk over their breasts, a fall of shimmering cloth over their loins. Each body was stunning, any one could have been modelled in marble for a goddess. Only one was dark, so dark by contrast – and Roxanna's body, with those long legs, slim waist and full breasts, was the most stunning of all.

The dozen women moved onto the dais. Each adopted a different position there – crouched, prone, stretched high. Roxanna was in the centre, a dark sun to their bright satellites. She stood tall, her hands raised to the ceiling, head tipped over her arched back, long black hair flowing unbound behind her, reaching her waist. All the dancers held their poses for a long moment until, from somewhere hidden, came the sound of knuckle-bones whispering over stretched hide, and a single string plucked on a low note. Slowly, they began to move.

An unfolding of limbs, poses flowing gently to other poses, then flowing on. Each dancer's movements were separate, yet it was as if the same breeze moved them or they were caught in the same wave. Only Roxanna did not move, held her pose, the still centre to it all ... until all others froze and she straightened, head and hair rising, then reached to seize the long golden hair of the dancer before her, pulling it slowly down, down. The woman arched her back – and a cry slipped from her red, swollen lips. It was animal, it was human, it was pain and pleasure, and the sound brought an echo in Ferros's throat, growl and groan. His hand, which had held a glass, was empty. Whoever he'd been talking to had taken it. What he realized he needed was to be closer, to the white body that had given out that sound, that was being pulled hard and enfolded in the black one, who cried out as she received it before both were swallowed in a collision of hair, and flesh and moans.

More than one drum played now, more than one instrument was plucked, or sounded, the beat and volume building. The rest of the crowd was moving too, pushing forward. But they were courtiers, Ferros was a soldier. Swiftly he shoved his way to the dais. As he reached it, the women upon it split apart; were pushed apart by the force at their centre. By Roxanna, who stood tall again, raising her arms again to the ceiling. The women fell back, cried out as if struck; while Roxanna, looking straight at him, took her lower lip in her teeth and bit it. Blood ran down her chin.

Sound exploded – strings, drums, flutes. Moans. And the world went mad.

Within the maze of lanes down which she led Lara, Carellia had stopped twice already and asked the question.

'Are you certain?' she'd said.

'Yes,' Lara had replied, firmer each time.

The third asking was in the darkest of alleys, in a part of town she'd never been before, up on the rocky slopes in the east, where only the outcasts – the sick, the destitute, the deranged – were said to live. Whispers came from shadows, groans from roofless huts; there was a sudden scream, cut off. The rain fell, chill and pitiless. Her hooded cloak, long since soaked, hung heavy on her shoulders. She shivered, coughed. If she'd feigned sickness before, she would not have to soon.

If she lived.

Carellia pulled her into a doorway. Beyond its rotten wood, something scurried away. 'This is the last time I will ask you, songbird. Your last chance to change your mind.' The old whore's voice had got stronger, her eyes no longer danced, her grip on Lara's arm was firm. 'You do not yet know where the cult lives. No one can know but its acolytes. If you say no now, I will lead you back. You will drink hot wine, sleep in a warm bed. Life will go on for whatever span the gods have chosen for you.' She leaned closer. 'But if you say yes, your old life is over. For we will enter the sanctum that none but believers may enter. Once entered, there is no going back. You leave as an immortal – or you do not leave at all.' Her voice dropped to a whisper. 'So I ask for the last time: are you certain?'

She wasn't. How could she be, how could anyone? But she also knew she had no choice. There was no life back there, however hot the wine, or warm the bed – for Ferros would not be in it with her. She'd known, from the moment she'd seen him with Roxanna, that she would lose him to her. Unless she said yes now. With that word, she had a chance. She had none if she said no because there was no life without him.

'Yes,' she said.

Something bright came into Carellia's eyes. 'Good,' she said. Reaching past Lara, she pressed on the door. It gave and Lara, who'd been leaning against it for strength, stumbled in. Into a heavy leather curtain which she pushed against, past. Beyond it was heat and a dim, flickering torchlight that was yet so bright compared to the wet, cold darkness outside that she had to close her eyes. When she opened them again she saw that the door, which Carellia shut behind her before passing her, had concealed something unexpected – a long narrow cavern, hewn into the rock face of the hill behind the street. It was filled with people whose gender she couldn't tell, for all were hooded like her, their faces in shadow despite the torches that burned in sconces along the walls.

These people shifted to either side, forming a rough, narrow alley leading to the cave's end. It was brighter there, for five torches flared, lighting two figures who stood on a small, shallow platform, watching her approach. Both wore white robes and were masked, one as an eagle, one a bear. The eagle held another robe which he or she draped around the one who joined them now – Carellia, bending her head for the mask that the bear fitted to her, to become a lioness.

She beckoned and Lara walked between the silent watching lines, to join the two others who stood before the dais: a young man, with a terrible disfiguring growth over half his face, and an old, stooped woman.

Carellia opened her arms wide. The voice that came from beneath the mask was hers, and not hers. She stood straight, different from the slouching whore who'd told her tales in a tavern for wine. 'Welcome, last of the seekers,' she called. The eagle dipped a goblet into a pot that stood on a brazier behind him. Then he handed it to Carellia. Steam rose from it, and she held it high. 'Simbala, Goddess of Birth and Death and Birth, here is your blood, your sacred juices. Placed by you in the vine of life. Visit us now, through it. Join us here, with it. Offer your blessing in its taste.'

She raised it to her lips, took a big sip. A sigh ran through the crowd, and people came forward. 'Wait!' Carellia called, and the people froze. 'The seekers first.' She bent and held the goblet before Lara's mouth. 'Enter, Seeker. Enter the world. Meet Simbala.' Eyes glimmered within the mask. 'Drink it all.'

There was no question of disobeying. There could be no hesitation now. Bending to the cup, Lara drank.

Ferros was unaware of the exact moment when it happened. When the dancers and those who watched them, the two groups, became one. He'd been there, at the very front, all his focus on the extraordinary things that were occurring on the

248

stage. He'd never seen bodies move that way, never experienced music and movement blended like this. He was a soldier, and dancing was something that happened amongst the tribes on the wilder fringes of empire. He'd observed it, mocked it as primitive. Yet he could not mock it now, for he was dancing, everyone was dancing. There was a freedom in his limbs they'd never had before. In his mind too. He did not care how people danced around him, nor care if they saw how he did. For the first time he understood the power of Tinderos wine. If this was what it did to him, he'd never drink beer again.

Then, the merging. Some dancers descended to the floor of the room, some who had been the audience were now on the stage. The music was a frenzy, tune lost to rhythm, notes from flute and strings like the cries of beasts, caught and held in the net of drumbeat. He whirled, staggered. If he came near to falling, someone was there to push him up. Though each danced separately, all took care of those around them. He felt, for the first time since he'd come to Corinthium, that he was part of something greater, with a kinship to those around him that he'd thought he'd lost for ever when he left his regiment. So many in the room, in this crowd, were immortals. He was immortal. And he knew, suddenly, certainly, and for the very first time, that if this was how life could feel, he would happily live it for ever.

He threw back his head, howled his delight. Others howled around him. When he lowered it again, she was before him.

Every dancer was superb. Roxanna was beyond them all. He'd been mesmerised by the way her long limbs could move, how she threaded her darkness through the light that surrounded her, separate, until totally entwined. On the stage, though, she'd been dancing with others, for others. Here she was dancing only for him.

With him. For the longest time, though their movements

249

were fast and they came so close, they did not touch, as if their bodies had a layer of warm air forcing them apart. Until the moment they did, when he reached and ran one white finger up one dark inner thigh. Then all that was apart was together, they were joined at shoulder, chest, hip. Parting, linking again, spinning away, spinning in. The dance took him entirely and he lost himself to it, lost what was him, what was her.

He didn't know how what happened did. But the crowd was gone, the room had changed, he was alone with her and their dance had become something else – or rather it had become the promise that had been there from the moment she first walked out and arched her back upon the stage. No, the promise made in the moment when she entered from the balcony on his first day in Corinthium. The music was gone, yet somehow still throbbed in his mind, the pulse of it in his blood, in hands that moved all over her, as hers moved all over him.

Everything was shed – his armour, his tunic, his restraint. He pulled the cloth from her breasts, his rough soldier's hands gently rubbing the silk across them before moving it aside, before sinking down and taking one huge and hard nipple softly in his mouth. But she didn't want soft, she didn't want gentle, she cried out, pulled him up to her, bit his lip just before she sank her tongue deep into his mouth. They were still dancing but it was different, it wasn't just feet on a floor. There was a couch, there was a chair, there was him above, there was her above, there was a time they both faced the distant sea, steam rising into the winter air, with her belly on a wooden balustrade and him behind her with his hands around her neck, squeezing. Delight came and went and came again, more intense than he'd ever felt, all joined and as inseparable as their bodies. Somehow they found a bed, and their movements slowed, slowed until the dream that had held him since that last glass of Tinderos wine merged into a dreamless sleep. They were still joined, at every point it was possible still to touch. And when they parted it was like losing a limb. Yet though he reached with a moan, he did not wake, for her voice was in his ear, soothing him with, 'But a moment, love.'

'Lara,' he murmured, as deeper sleep took him.

All senses merged, each into other. She could touch sight, taste scent, see sound. Waves of that rose from the people who lay about the room – all, like Lara, curled up with arms wrapping their knees to their chests. All moaned, but no longer in the nausea that had first come. In ecstasy now. In wonder.

She thought she might have been lying there for hours but she couldn't be sure. Time had dissolved also, along with the earth and her body. She had flown across the sea to visit her parents. They were no longer furious with her, for leaving with Ferros. They understood now, gave their blessing. All their concern was about what she was doing now.

'Are you sure, little one?' her mother asked.

'Is it safe, my darling?' asked her father.

She had reassured them, she thought. Even though she wasn't sure – if she should do this, if it was safe. It wasn't – and she had to. Because the next place she'd travelled had been Agueros, the Sanctum on the Hill. Where her reason for life was. She'd found him, seen him in a way she never had before. He was dancing, staring at the woman who danced before him, joined to him. Roxanna. She could see that he was lost – to the dance, to her. There was but one way of getting him back.

Not safe. Not sure.

The only people not prone were masked. The eagle, the bear and the lioness moved among the moans, checking, reassuring. Lara knew that there were humans under the masks but the bodies had long since been given up to feather and fur.

The lioness bent over her. 'It is time.'

Lara sat up, swayed. All around her, people did the same. Clutching each other, they rose. A man helped her to her feet, held her while she steadied. He grinned. 'I have seen them, sister,' he said. 'They live in Simbala's palace. They wait for me.'

He didn't explain who waited with the goddess of birth and death and birth. Turned, just as she did, to the gong that was being sounded by the bear on the dais. All shuffled forward, though they left a gap right at the front where Lara now saw the disfigured boy and the old woman who'd stood there before. She joined them.

The bear struck the gong three more times, then set it aside, though the final note clung in the air, as visible to Lara as the smoke that guttered from the torches. The lioness stepped forward. 'Did Simbala show you wonders?' she called.

'Yes!' came the called response.

'And do you believe she has more wonders yet to show?'

'Yes!' This cry came even louder and the mouth beneath the half-mask – Lara could see it now, changing shape, teeth withdrawing, fur receding, until it was human again – shaped a smile.

'Yes,' the lioness – Carellia – said. 'For we know that Simbala's gifts never die. We dwell here, or we dwell in her palace – for ever.' She looked down, and laid her wooden stave on the young man's left shoulder. 'Why do you seek that choice today?'

He started. Half his face was covered in scar and scab. 'You see me,' he cried. 'My body is eating itself. No doctor, no apothecary, can cure me. But if the goddess will only favour me, if I can die and be born again,' he looked up to the roof, 'then I will be healed and live for ever! Either that, or dwell for ever in Simbala's palace.'

Cries came at that, joyful shouts of praise. The lioness nodded, then laid her staff on the old woman's shoulder. 'And you?'

The woman's voice was rough, from the local streets. 'Three

husbands I've given to the sea. But the fourth is still alive – and thirty years younger than me!' Some laughter came at that, and she joined it. 'So what choice do I have? Live till he gets old enough to appreciate me? Or go and join the ones I've lost, in Simbala's palace?'

More cries, more support. Carellia raised the staff, lowered it again. Lara closed her eyes as the wood touched her, readied herself to speak. 'And you, child?'

She breathed deep, answered. 'The man I love is an immortal. It is either join him here – or wait for him for ever in Simbala's palace.'

Louder cries came at this. Another smile from beneath the lion mask. 'You are all worthy. You are all ready. Simbala awaits you, one way or another.' She turned, gave her stick to the eagle, took something from the bear. When she turned back, Lara saw that it was a long, thick-bladed steel dagger. She raised it high into the air – and men rushed forward, seized Lara's arms, seized those of the old woman and the youth beside her. From around the cave low voices came, one word, one name, chanted. Building. Summoning.

'Sim-ba-la. Sim-ba-la. Sim-ba-la.'

Again and again the word came, louder and louder, the crowd pressing forward behind the three, drawing close to be part of what was to happen. She tensed, struggled against those who held her, then went limp. For memory came, of Ferros dancing. He had never danced for her, with her. Now perhaps he would.

With a great cry, the lioness raised the dagger higher still, then swept it down across the boy's neck. Blood spurted onto lion fur. A second swipe opened the old woman's neck, red fountaining high. Lara saw the knife raised again – but this time it paused for a moment ... and she saw something else. A change in the eyes within the eye-slits. And she knew suddenly, certainly, that it wasn't Carellia, the old whore she'd befriended in a tavern, who was scything the dagger down. Lara knew who it was, but it was too late to cry her name, or to do anything about it.

Too late to do anything but die.

Ferros woke alone, in a room he didn't recognise, with no memory of how he had got there. He was shivering, lying naked on a bed with a chill wind blowing over him from a door open to the morning, curtains streaming in on the breeze. He got up, winced. He felt tender all over, as if he'd been in battle. Looking down fed that idea – there were scratches on his body, and a bruise the size of his hand on his right thigh. But the sight brought no clarity, nor did the view from the balcony he hobbled to – by the sun, it was late morning, and he was in a room high up in the Sanctum, in one of its eastern towers. Only when he laid his hand upon the wooden balustrade did a memory come, which could have come from a dream. It brought the faintest stirring at his groin – which, he realised, ached as much as the rest of him.

He walked back to the bed, sat heavily upon it. What had happened? The last thing he remembered was talking with Lucan and then Roxanna taking to the stage with her troupe of dancers. No, he remembered going forward to the stage to get a closer look. At her. But then? He looked around seeking other clues. The sheets were a mess – torn in places, traced in blood. What he'd worn was scattered over the floor. His sword was out of its scabbard. There was blood on its edge too.

He went over, picked up his dress tunic. It was torn at the shoulder. He put it on anyway, then sat on the bed to pull on his boots. Got one on, stared at the other. His head didn't hurt exactly but it wasn't right. As if there was a piece of it missing.

There was noise on the stair. He pulled the other boot on and stood to face the door.

Roxanna entered. She wore a simple, long-sleeved dress, was covered from neck to ankle. She carried a tray. There was a pitcher on it, fruit. 'So,' she said, stopping and looking him up and down, 'How is my lover this morning?'

Her words, the smile in her voice and on her mouth, the purpling at her neck above the dress, brought a little more back. 'Did we—' he began, broke off.

She frowned. 'Oh Ferros! You are not going to claim you don't remember? Especially when it was so ... memorable? A woman could feel insulted.'

'I ... of course, I ...'

'Come,' she interrupted. 'Sit, before you fall over.' She put the tray down, sat beside it, patted the bed.

'Perhaps ... perhaps I should go.'

'Running off?' She thrust out her lower lip. 'Again, should I feel insulted?' Then she smiled. 'If I was an ordinary woman, I might. Soon you will remember that I am not, and that what we had was not ordinary but ... extraordinary.' She stretched back. 'It has been ... many years since any man, mortal or immortal, made me feel close to what you did last night.'

Ferros sat. Memory was returning. But though he remembered pleasure, he also remembered something else. 'I have to go. There is someone who will be worried about me.'

'You forget this too, Ferros.' Her voice was a little harder now. 'You told your someone that you would have to stay the night here. You are to receive the answer to your question as to your purpose here, this day.'

'I ... am?' It came out as a question. He thought he'd told Lara that he would return late and he could not recall being told that today was the day for an answer. Shaking his head, Ferros picked up a mug, drank. It contained squeezed pomegranate juice and it restored him a little. He put it down, looked at Roxanna. She had settled back onto her elbows. Her breasts were thrust up against the silk of her dress. The bruise at her neck was purple under her black skin. He glanced out to the balcony, coloured.

She saw the look, laughed. 'Good. I want you to remember, Ferros.' She sat up, slid a hand under his tunic, onto his thigh.

He let it lie. 'Lady ...' he began.

Footsteps on the stair. The hand withdrew and he stood to face the door. 'Master,' said the servant who rushed in. 'There's been a message from the city. A ... an accident. You are to come immediately.'

'An accident? To whom?' He stepped closer. 'What kind of accident?' he roared.

The servant stepped back, frightened. 'Forgive me, master, I don't know. That's all I know. You are to come.'

Ferros stooped, snatched up his sword, sheathed it, slung the belt around his shoulders. He turned to Roxanna. 'I must—'

'Of course you must.' She stood as she spoke, laid a hand on his arm. 'I'll tell my father. Return later, when you are able. For we have so much to discuss.'

Without another word, he ran from the room. He didn't look back, so he didn't see her smile.

A week had passed. Ferros knelt at the altar, his lips moving in unaccustomed ways. In prayer. The only time he prayed, and those times rare, was before a battle or raid, his words supplicating Mavros, God of War. Here, though, he was in a temple of Simbala, Goddess of Birth and Death and Birth. His goddess now, he supposed, even more than Mavros had been, since he'd become immortal. But he did not say his prayers aloud for each started with her name. Lara. And her name was forbidden now, she was outcast, a violator of every law of man and god, and those around him would know it and clamour against him.

'Lara,' he thought, prayed. 'Let your spirit find rest in your journey. Lara, let your sin be forgiven. Lara … come back!'

His eyes watered. He who had only cried once and briefly when Ashtan died, and once again in the courtyard after the ride with Roxanna, but had not for his parents, nor anything else in all his life of struggle, could not stop crying now. Four days he'd wept, once he'd ceased shouting, ceased searching. He thought it would be different if he could see her body. That whoever had found her had not done enough to wake her up. But her body had been buried secretly, beyond the sanctums of any temple, in unblessed ground, and no amount of yelling or drawn steel could get anyone to show him where she lay. For suicide was the ultimate sin, against gods and men. The cults that promoted it, which were all thought to have been suppressed long before, had been persecuted, their leaders slain. Somehow, they always sprang up again. And his Lara had listened to their call, as only the desperate did.

Desperate! Why had he not seen? Why had he not listened? Why had he not been brave enough to leave her in Balbek, forbid her to come? He would have missed her, but she would still be living now, and for the rest of her natural life. Instead, she'd killed herself, for him. No. He'd killed her.

'Lara,' he sobbed. Too loud. A man kneeling close by glanced sharply at him, then turned to the man next to him and muttered. The name had become infamous in Corinthium, along with that of Stephanos, a young man who'd had a wasting disease, and an old woman, Thraxia. Their names were shouted at crossroads so all could revile them in their prayers. Two leaders of the cult had been caught, along with many members, and stoned to death by mobs. One leader, a woman, and some others, were still being hunted.

He glared at the man and his companion who both turned their faces away from the angry soldier, for he was dressed as such, in the garb he'd wear for a long march, his sword with its bloody grip at his side in its worn scabbard. But in their fear he remembered who he was, and then what he was to do now. So he looked up at the altar again, at the dried flowers he'd laid upon it, and spoke her name one last time, clearly, defiantly. 'Lara,' he said, before rising and walking from the temple.

They were waiting for him under an awning across the street, sheltering from the chill winter rain. Lucan still looked nothing but annoyed, as he had from the moment Ferros had insisted on stopping for one last prayer. Annoyed too, no doubt, by this exposure to the many who stopped to gawk – it was rare for an immortal to descend from the Sanctum on the Hill and stand, dressed in his fine purple robes, so close to the docks. But even more stared at Roxanna, wrapped again in full leather, with dagger and short sword at her hips.

Her face, however, showed nothing but compassion. She took his arm. 'Is it enough, Ferros?'

'It will never be enough. How can I ever atone? I will carry this for the rest of my life.' He grunted. 'No matter how long that is.'

She squeezed his arm. 'Perhaps atonement lies ahead, in what you do now for our people. For Lara and everyone else.'

'If you have finished,' Lucan rasped, 'the peasants are getting presumptuous.' He slapped away the hand of a small boy who'd managed to dodge the immortal's three hefty servants and had reached out to touch his beautiful robes. 'And tides do not wait for prayers.'

They set off down the street, Sanctum guards clearing the way, a small crowd following. Every time Ferros had passed a temple of Simbala he had insisted on stopping. But this last had been the final one before the docks, and they were soon upon them. A ship was berthed there, the *Goshawk*, a two-master, much bigger than the vessel he'd arrived on. Necessary, he supposed, to deal with the seas that few ventured upon this late in the year. The water was calm enough now, though the sky was dark and the wind gusting. The reason for this rushed departure was Lucan, who had been a fisherman before he'd died of the plague and become one of the first immortals, and who still recognised favourable winds. With a sailor's good fortune, these would bear them swiftly to their destination.

'Aboard,' he urged, snatching his daughter into a swift embrace. He turned to Ferros. 'There was so much more that we could have taught you, young man. But what you have learned must suffice. Roxanna has scrolls that I have laboured long upon, for you to read and discuss on the voyage. They will tell you more that you need to know about the dangers you are to face.'

He had heard some. Roxanna had tried to distract him from his grief by telling him of their mission. He had not taken much in, though a name came to him now, along with his anger. 'Dangers? From a wilderness messiah?' he snorted. 'We saw them come and go at Balbek. Men in dirty loincloths with thorns in their flesh, ranting about paradise. A sword dealt with them then, and a sword will deal with them now.' He patted his scabbard. 'Why should this "Smoke" be any different?'

'Because you cannot stab smoke,' answered Lucan. 'And to even try you would have to get past the hordes he is said to have recruited.'

Ferros scoffed, went to speak, but Lucan stopped him, raising his hand sharply. 'No more talk. The wind sits in your sails. But know this, young man. This Smoke is no ranting messiah. And his message is simple.' Lucan lifted his eyes and stared at the leashed sails jumping in the gusts. '"Immortality is dead," he says. "Now all we have to do is kill all immortals."' He looked at them again. 'Aboard!'

Roxanna and Ferros boarded. Ropes were swiftly cast off. The captain on his poop deck let tide and the wind in smaller sails carry the vessel a little way from the dock before bellowing for the big sheets. Hoisted fast, they bellied swiftly. Two men turned the wheel and the ship made way out of the harbour, vessels clearing before it as their captains noted the red flag of the Sanctum at its mainmast.

It swiftly reached the entrance formed by the cobs that curled inwards. No man or boy stood upon them now, casting lines in the water, for none would risk the wind and rain, both more intense as they neared open water. Roxanna left him when he wouldn't take shelter, just stood with his face raised, his eyes closed. He didn't open them, even when they passed under the joined stone arms of the Twins, those huge statues that he had explained to Lara only ... only seven weeks before.

The memory stabbed him, as every memory did, sharply through his guts.

He'd prayed long for Lara in temples of Simbala, Goddess of Birth and Death and Birth. Now he turned back to something more familiar: to Mavros, God of War. Though this time his prayer was short.

'Let it come.'

Lucan remained on the dock, ignoring the murmurs of the crowds who ogled him, watching the ship pass under the stone arms of the statues, with the words 'Wisdom' and 'Strength' carved onto them. My daughter has both, he thought, though sometimes she lets her appetites get in the way of her reason. Ferros? He'd learned that the young man was not simply the dull provincial he'd first taken him for. Indeed, with more time he could have been moulded – as Lucan himself had been moulded when he'd first arrived as Melankythios, a fisherman every bit as stolid and ignorant as the soldier, more than four hundred years before.

Four hundred? he thought, rubbing at an ache that came

suddenly in his right temple. Closer to five now. One of the first immortals to be reborn, gathering with the few others who'd had the same experience; and that, it was said, only a few decades after 'the visitor' – Andros the Blind – had passed through his fishing village. *It was said*, he thought, his lip curling into a sneer. All talk of the coming of immortality to the world was so lost to myth, there were no hard truths to be found any more. Personally, he believed that there'd been no Andros, no bringer of the gift. Immortality simply was. Some were chosen, born to live for ever so they could grow wise – and rule wisely for ever.

The *Goshawk* had vanished, blending into the grey clouds that stretched across the horizon, lost even to his long sight. He rubbed again at his temple – though the ache was within, not upon the skin. It was odd, because such aches – like death wounds, like hangovers – would usually pass quickly with an immortal's healing powers. This one was growing. Perhaps it was hunger. All he'd eaten that morning, in his haste to get to the port – a haste slowed by the soldier's interminable praying at every roadside shrine – was one dry crust of bread. He would take the Heaven Road back to the Sanctum, and feast.

He turned. His guards began to push through the gawking crowd. He took one step after them … and stumbled.

Someone had driven an iron spike through his head.

His left arm, his left leg, neither would move. He tried to speak, call out, but his mouth didn't want to work. He fell then, he must have done, because he was looking at a duck's feather, attached to a cobblestone by dung. Then that faded, as darkness flooded his eyes.

I'll be born again, he thought. As always.

And then he knew he wouldn't.

'Tell Rox—' he began, to the shapes bending over him. But he died before he could finish saying her name.

12

Flight

'Shh! Listen!'

'I tell you, there's nothing.'

'Be quiet, will you. I heard ... there! That!'

'That scratching?' Ravaya, older than Atisha, and her partner this night, peered down into the darkness. 'It is nothing. Or it is a monkey. They live on these cliffs.'

'Where a monkey goes, a man can go.' Atisha sat back. 'Fetch Besema.'

'No, child. Besema has barely slept since the siege began. Now she does, she will not want to be woken for a monkey.'

Atisha reached to a pile of rocks. Two weeks before, after she'd burned the bridge, the only true access to the crag on which the City of Women stood, the war council had identified three areas of cliff that desperate men might try to climb, and assigned guards to each, with rocks to hand. Two nights before, one spy had made it all the way up – a man Intitepe had sent fast ahead when news had been brought to him, on the road down, of the bridge's destruction, because this man was a renowned climber. But he proved less good at stealth and had been swiftly captured as he tried to sneak into the main building itself. At first, he'd stayed silent. But under inventive interrogation, he'd ended up gratefully telling all he knew – not least that after Intitepe's defeat by the rebels, other parts of the land were rebelling too.

She picked a stone up now, leaned over the edge. Swayed. Before the birth of Poum, she had never feared heights. But others had told her that giving birth changed much about a person. It had changed that in her and now she hated being high up. So, stepping back, she lobbed the rock. They heard it strike some jut of cliff. Eventually, there came a faint splash as it reached the river. There were no other sounds.

'You see?'

'You are right. Let's go.' Atisha gestured to the hollow in the rock face that they had made their guard house, the firepit in it. 'You sleep if you like. I'll wake you – but only if I hear men, not monkeys.' She toed a smaller stone over the edge and turned away.

The yelp was faint. The splash that followed a few seconds later was loud. The two women looked at each other and Atisha hissed, 'Besema!' As Ravaya ran shouting down the path, Atisha snatched up a thick stave wound with oil-soaked wool and jabbed it into the firepit. The torch flared immediately and she went again to the edge and thrust it out.

There were six of them that she could see, faces upturned, eyes wide and startled in the flamelight. Men with black-painted faces and knives held in their teeth. They were maybe five of her body lengths down and, like ants caught suddenly under an overturned rock, they began to scramble, moving fast and silent towards her. Crying out, she looked around her, placed the torch so its flaming end was over the edge, grabbed two rocks, leaned out, swayed, but flung them down. Both bounced off overhangs, missing the men, who came faster.

She tried again – one rock struck a man on his forehead, he slipped, flailed, held on. Kept coming. They were two body lengths below her now and they were spread wide. They would

263

arrive at the same time and she could not keep all of them off the ledge.

She grabbed another stone, flung, missed. She thought of running. But now she saw more faces below, ten at least, maybe more. If these men reached the top, the siege was over. The friends who'd saved her would die, and not quickly. More, Poum, her child, the reason for all this, would be taken and then—

Poum. The name in her head centred her. She stopped swaying. And when the first man placed his hand upon the cliff edge, she stamped on it.

He fell. There was another pulling himself over. She shoved the torch into his face. He shrieked, tumbled into darkness. A third grabbed at her ankle. She kicked him in the face with her other foot but he held on, pulled her sharply. She fell backwards, landed hard, breath knocked from her, though she used the last she had to drive a heel into his eye. He vanished. But now there was a man standing to her left, another to her right. She reached for the obsidian dagger at her belt, found breath. 'Poum!' she shouted, like a war cry, rising to her knees.

'Poum!' It came like an echo but it was made by women, the six who rushed down the path with spears and axes. There were three men on the clifftop now, others just hauling themselves over. But the women had their force and their fury and for now the men had only their daggers. The three who stood were knocked backwards into the dark. The ones who reached for the clifftop had their hands broken and followed. Rocks were lifted, hurled straight down. There were screams for a while, terrible screams. And then there was silence, save for the harsh breathing of the women, pluming the cold air before them.

Atisha sat. The whirl of combat had prevented her seeing more than shapes. Now she saw them clearly – three women, young ones, whose names she did not know; and three old ones, who she knew well. Tall Norvara, small Yutil. And, of course, the third of the three: Besema, her spun-silver hair loose about her shoulders. Besema, their leader.

She had the torch now and waved it side to side over the edge. 'Goat-fuckers are gone,' she said, and spat into the void. 'All gone.' She turned to Atisha. 'Are you all right?'

'I am … all right.' Atisha rose to one knee, took breaths to steady her heart. 'You came fast.'

'We were lucky. I was already awake, and coming to get you. So,' she jerked her head towards the edge, 'the gods continue to favour us.'

Atisha frowned. 'Why were you coming for me? My duty here is till dawn.' She started. 'Is Poum safe?'

'Safe, and sleeping. It is not that.' She bent, offered a hand which Atisha grasped, hauling herself up. 'It is this,' Besema continued. 'He has come.'

Atisha's breath was taken again. There was no need to say who *he* was. But she thought his name anyway, as she turned and stared into the darkness which, she saw now, was just beginning to streak with light.

Intitepe.

The Fire God stood at the blackened end of what had been the bridge, staring across the gorge at the City of Women. Creeping dawn was bringing its many buildings, its vast and flowing terraces, from shadow into sight.

They amazed him. Some three hundred years before, he'd stood at this exact spot, the last and only time he'd been there, looking back across a one-person rope bridge at the single, simple structure he'd ordered to be built. A gift for her who'd been 'the One' then.

'What was her name?' he muttered to himself. Cava, that was it. She was from this province and had asked to end her days there. He'd loved her, of course, but her twelve years were over. He happily granted her request; had even accompanied her there, seen to the building himself, furnished it well so she would be comfortable, alone with only women around her. Most of the women of his marana would return, after their time with him, to their home provinces; take husbands, raise children, their prestige high, having been loved by a god. Cava had been the first to say that no man would ever touch her again, for no man could come close to the touch of Intitepe. He'd understood – of course he had, how could he not? – and had granted her request. As others asked the same, he let them come too, then allowed other women to arrive as well, approved every new building requested to house them, provided the funds and the men to build them. When the city had grown to house two hundred, he appointed a governess chosen from his marana, to keep order, with soldiers under her command – for gossip had reached his ears, lurid tales of women and their night-time activities. He did not mind them, rather the reverse – the image of women he'd once loved loving each other gave him pleasure. But his subjects were simple folk, and rigid in their morality. The governess was meant to keep all such excesses within the city's walls.

What was her name, the latest one? Muana? No, Muna! Not a 'One', an uninventive girl in his bed, but clever and organised beyond it – or so he'd thought. But he'd been wrong, for she had failed him, utterly. Failed to enact his simple order: seize and imprison the girl Atisha and her child, her monstrous child. And then somehow, Muna had provoked a rebellion.

Intitepe leaned forward, spat. A rebellion of women? It was absurd. Well, he was there now, and he would end it. When he was done he would raze the place, knock down every building, salt every terrace, and give all these *rebels* to the lava of Toluc. What a day that would be! With the last to swim that cursed Atisha ... clutching her monster child!

Someone coughed behind him. He turned, winced. When he'd reached Toluc and allowed the physician to finally pull out the arrow he'd taken fighting those rebel fishermen, he'd died, of course. Been reborn hours later. But he'd healed more slowly than he had in the past and there was still some pain. Then the journey south had been hard, Autumn's rains with winter's chill within them. Another season he'd have sailed, lived in ease in his luxurious cabin aboard the *Sea Serpent*, converted from the warship it had been when he'd taken it to the Shadow Islands to kill the last of his sons, Santepe, who'd created a fleet there. But the winds blew from the south at this time of year, against him, forcing him onto the roads.

He shivered. Even immortals grow older, colder, he thought as he looked at the one who'd coughed – Tolucca, his eldest daughter. She was immortal, yet in this dawn's grey light he thought she looked older too. She'd arrived ahead of him, just after the bridge was burned. 'Well?' he snapped.

Tolucca swallowed. 'They failed.'

'Failed? Where are they?'

'Dead in the river. All d—'

She stepped back as he snarled and reached for her. He'd ordered the cliff attack as soon as he'd arrived. It was the obvious thing to do. And if the local commander, Tokat, had done it three weeks ago they wouldn't all be standing there now. Well, at least Tokat would have been one of those broken at the cliff's base. As he deserved for his failure.

He lowered his hand, turned back. The sun came up fast this far south and the buildings stood fully revealed. The biggest, right in the middle of the city, was faced in red stone and glowed. Even as he watched, the two main doors swung open. Immediately, archers either side of him raised their bows. Tokat had told him that he'd given orders to shoot at anything that moved – though it seemed no one had yet been hit.

267

'Wait!' he yelled. The men eased their strings and he looked again at the door. A face appeared, a voice called. A woman's.

'Will you talk, Intitepe?'

Intitepe? Only in his marana when he felt indulgent could a woman call him by his name. He was 'lord', 'king', 'god'! And talk? He ground his teeth. Kill was what he was there to do. But since Tokat's failure had delayed that, he might as well find out more of what he was dealing with. Who.

'Yes,' he shouted across the gorge, 'I will talk. But who is it that would talk to me?'

'Oh, Intitepe! I am of course heartbroken that you do not know me,' the woman called. 'For did you not say that you would hear my voice for ever? Every time you looked up at the star you named for me?'

He remembered then. Her voice. That star. 'Besema,' he hissed, under his breath. 'Besema, you bitch.'

They stood in the hall, Besema at the front, her hand on one door, Norvara and Yutil behind. Only Atisha sat, and that was because she was nursing Poum.

She had started when she heard his voice and the baby had started too, unfixing and staring up, her expression the one she wore before tears came. Atisha had latched her again before that happened, though she could not prevent the tears that fell from her own eyes. Part of her still did not believe that the man who had claimed to love her beyond all measure, who had demonstrated it for two glorious years, now hated her. That he who had been her teacher in all things now wanted to be her slayer. Worse, even worse, that he wanted to slay what they had made between them, this innocent at her breast. She wiped her eyes, with the thought draining any further tears.

'Why would you talk?' she asked. 'We know what he wants. What he's here for.'

'But we don't know how he plans to get it. I would find out.' Besema turned and smiled. 'Besides, I know how to make him angry – and an angry man, even if he is also a god, makes mistakes.' She bent, picked up a soldier's kite-shaped shield, and stepped fully into the doorway. 'Do I need this, Intitepe?' she called. 'Will you have one of your archers shoot me if I put it down?'

'I will not. Come to the edge and let us speak. Your archers could shoot me here just as easily.'

'I could,' said Norvara, hefting her bow. 'But he would only die for a short time, whereas you—'

'I do not think he will,' Besema said. 'And I would like to look into his face one more time. I will read the truth upon it, as I always did.' She turned to Atisha. 'Stay out of sight, little one.' With that, she laid the shield down, and walked from the doorway.

Norvara looked at Yutil. 'Shall we?'

The smaller woman smiled. 'I wouldn't miss it for the world.' She bent, picked up a shield. 'But I will take one of these.'

'And I,' said Norvara, snatching up another. 'Let us go.'

'Don't!' Atisha called, too late. Rising, still feeding Poum, she went to peer around the edge of the door, and watched three wives of the Fire God stride to meet him again.

'Who is it that comes?'

'Can you not see, Korshak?'

He grunted. 'Just tell me, will you, Gistrane?'

The huntress smiled. In their time together – the long, terrible voyage to Ometepe, the time in the land, she'd found so many ways to make the horse lord angry. His weak eyes were just one. She peered down from the crag they sheltered behind. 'Three women come. Two hold shields. They walk to the gorge, to where a bridge must have been. I can see burnt ends on each side.'

'Is she one of them? The one we seek?'

'No. These three are old. Strong-looking, though.' She licked her finger, raised it into the air. 'There's a bit of a breeze. But I think I could still kill two of them before the third escaped back inside.'

'And why would you do that?' Korshak snapped. Then he saw her face. 'Ah, I see. You tease me again. I would have thought you'd have got tired of that by now.'

'Never,' Gistrane replied. 'Now, be quiet. If your sight is not so good, at least you can hear what these have to say. Oh,' she added.

'What?'

'He is going down to this side of the gap. The one we fought. The one who ran. This god of theirs. Intitepe.' She smiled again. 'The one you lost.'

'I will not do so again,' the horse lord growled. 'Shall I call the monk? He speaks their tongue better than either of us.'

For ten years before Gistrane had made her voyage, ships had sailed to Ometepe. Few vessels made it through the tempests, the vast seas, but two eventually did and both carried monks, who'd hidden in remote villages, aweing the locals and sending back the language they learned using their globes. All who were to travel afterwards learned the language of the One as well as they were able. Gistrane understood a fair amount. Korshak, like his eyesight, was weak.

She shook her head. 'Leave him be. I speak it well enough. Besides, the monk is busy, trying to reach the seafarer through his glass.' She leaned forward sharply, her eyes afire, her breath coming short. 'Hah! And I think we will need the ship now, and fast.'

'Why?'

'Because I see another in the doorway, watching. And she is holding a baby.'

'*The* baby?' All resentment passed from Korshak's face. It was replaced by wonder. 'Are you saying you see ... Him and Her?'

'Perhaps.' Gistrane's voice had lost its edge too. 'Perhaps I do,' she breathed.

'Then I *should* call the monk.'

He made to rise. She put a hand on his arm, pulled him down. 'Leave him. Listen. They speak.'

Atisha's sight had always been good. So even though the sun was lost to cloud and a light rain had started to fall, she could still quite clearly see the expression on Intitepe's face change as he recognised the three who stood before him. Shock was swiftly displaced by fury. Calculation followed, covered by a smile.

'My Ones!' he cried across the gorge. 'Yutil. Norvara. And you, Besema. What joy it gives me to see that you all live.'

'So much joy, I am sure,' replied Norvara. 'As I am also sure you forgot about us the moment we were replaced.'

'It is not true,' he protested. 'Every night I look into the sky, and see each one of you in your star ...'

'... "for you are immortal too now, and will for ever be re-membered in the skies!"'

Their chorused reply made his face flush. Somehow he controlled his voice. 'You sadden me. You know what we had. Each of you knows it. For a time each of you was the One. The joy of that. The sadness too. For you each also know that while you are subject to time's laws, I am not. It has always been the way—'

'Your way, Intitepe,' Besema said. 'Your laws.' He started to protest but she cut him off. 'Why are you here?'

Once more Atisha saw him choke his anger back. 'This is my realm,' he said, his voice level. 'Every part of it. And in every part of it I have to be obeyed. That is the small price all must pay for the peace this land has known for nearly five hundred years. Obey me now. End this foolishness.' He nodded. 'Then I will forgive you all. Then I will let you return to your lives.'

'And the price for that, Fire God?'

'Obedience,' he swallowed, 'the baby, and Atisha.'

'Yes,' replied Besema, 'I thought it might be that.'

She said nothing more. But Intitepe saw no concession in what she had said. So he looked beyond them, and raised his voice. 'Atisha! Listen to me! I was wrong. Wrong to let you go. Wrong to threaten your ... our child. Come to me now and let me put the wrongs right. You both will live. I swear it. Live with me, in your old home.'

There was a time when Intitepe could have sworn that corn flour was gold dust and she would have believed him. Never again. Carefully laying Poum down on a blanket on the floor, Atisha stepped into the doorway. 'You are a liar. A murderer. And you are no god, only a cruel tyrant who has lived too long. I will never listen to you again.'

The rain was falling harder. 'You have heard her answer,' said Besema. 'Ours is the same. So what will you do? Even here we have heard the rumours. Your peaceful land explodes in rebellion. In every part of it, people are crying "enough".' She leaned forward and spat into the gorge. 'So hadn't you best go deal with that? For by the time you work out a way to cross this gap, you may not have a land left to rule.'

He stared at them for a long, long moment. Finally, he spoke, and there was nothing in his tone, no fury, no bitterness. Only certainty. 'You were the wisest of any of the Ones, Besema,' he called. 'None have surpassed you. But it seems age has taken its toll on your wisdom. Or you would have realised that I have not come all this way just to shout across a gorge. And that I have already worked out a way across it.' He smiled now. 'So I offer you a last chance to submit. If you do not, know this: that when we come, as we shall, my soldiers will have the freedom of all your bodies before they kill you. And I will fuck all three of you one last time before you die.'

He waited. When Besema didn't reply, he turned and walked away. Immediately, men ran forward. They raised bows and shot fast, though the shields Norvara and Yutil hefted as they backed off to the house, Besema between them, took care of the arrows.

Distracted as they were, it was Atisha who saw the other men advancing to the gorge. Hundreds of them. Some lowered ladders onto ledges within it, some brought beams and planks to its edge, many began hammering, sawing, working ...

... on the bridge that they began to build.

By the third day, the rain had turned to snow. Winter had come in sudden fierceness. But neither a world surrendering to white, nor the arrows that they sent, slowed the remorseless creeping of the bridge. Men died, clutching at a feathered shaft suddenly sprouting from their necks. But women died too, for when one arrow flew out, fifty were returned. So they stopped shooting, watched other men die, slipping from slick wood to plunge screaming into the gorge. But the Fire God had hundreds at his command, so there was always another man to step up and wield bow or hammer. The bridge came closer with every dawn. And it would be completed by the next one.

The meeting was called for midnight. Every woman in the city, except for the few who kept lookout – and the former governess, Muna, still wailing in her cell – was there. Every woman had a voice though only a few spoke, representing the different choices, which had come down, truly, to just two: give up the newcomers, Atisha and her child; or die fighting.

After all who would speak had had their say, and the room had begun to dissolve into separate, harsh arguments, Besema climbed onto a table and waited. One by one, everyone noticed her. Silence came. She spoke.

'I have heard you, all of you. In the end, each woman has a choice to make, each is in charge of her own fate. I cannot decide for you. But I can tell you this. For those of you who look for mercy in the tyrant, know that there is none in him to be found.' She pointed down to Norvara and Yutil who stood before the table. 'We three – no, we four, for Atisha was also his One for a time – know him as only his closest lover can. Know that his sole concern is himself. His long life. His rule over his realm.' She swallowed. 'The spy we captured also told us the news: his realm dissolves in revolution. As it does he will become again the savage he was all those years ago. He will kill all who oppose him, as he killed his father. As he killed his seven sons. As he will kill all of us.'

A few of those who would still surrender raised their voices at that. Besema lifted her arms and they quieted, as she continued. 'He will kill all of us. He will have to, and in as terrible a way as possible. Order his soldiers to rape and torture us to death then spread the story wide, so others will hear, and cower in their homes in terror.' She shook her head. 'But shall I tell you of a different story that can be told? One that will spread ahead of him through the land, and bring those people from their homes in freedom's cause? The story of women who would not kneel or lie back before the conquerors. Who fought to the last strength in their arms, died with one last word on their lips: Hope.'

Again a murmur came, though this was more a growl. She waited for it to rise and settle, then spoke again. 'This woman, this child,' she said, pointing to where Atisha stood with Poum, 'they are who the Fire God fears. If we gave them up now, we would still die. But our deaths are nothing, a few more grains of sand on the beach of time. But in their deaths dies his fear and so our hope.' The voices sounded louder; Besema raised her own voice above them. 'So again we come to that choice: die in terror before a tyrant. Or die with our sisters ... in hope.'

Many – most – crowded forward, that word on their lips. Only a few still stayed back. Again Besema raised her hands, gestured for quiet, again, more reluctantly, it came. 'I know that not all of you believe me. And I told you that each must decide her own fate. I tell you mine – and Norvara and Yutil have given me permission to tell you theirs, which is the same: to fight to the end of our strength and when that ends – to burn this hall to the ground and us with it. A beacon of defiance that will be seen across the land.' She looked across the heads of those who were pushing to the front to those hanging back. 'But to you others, those who doubt or fear, or who believe any life is better than none, to you I suggest a different choice. Either go out when the hall burns and offer yourself to the tyrant and his men, or ... at first light tomorrow, use the ropes and nets we have woven and hung over the cliffs and flee.'

'What?' A woman Atisha did not know pushed forward. 'This is possible?'

'Possible – and most dangerous,' Besema replied. 'Norvara here will tell you the way of it. If you are young and strong you may manage it. While we who are old will stay,' she smiled, 'and light the beacon.'

Using her friends' hands, she climbed down from the table. Many mobbed her, but Norvara and Yutil took them aside. Besema crossed the room, straight to Atisha. 'They must all decide for themselves now. I have made my choice.'

'And I?' Atisha sighed. 'I would like to defy the tyrant too. But I cannot make your choice, because of her.' She swung Poum gently back and forth, the child agitated by all the voices. She thought back to the cliffs, the men she'd watched falling off them, and shivered. Remembered too how her sense of balance had changed since her child's birth. Still, what choice did she have? 'I ... I will have to risk the climb.'

'You will not. For you there is yet another choice. One I could not share.' Besema pulled a burning torch from its wall mount. 'Come.'

They went the way they had the night Atisha first came to the city – from the hall, through the twisting passages, finally out into the night, though there was even less to see now, with the snow falling so thick. By touch and memory more than light and sight, they found their way. The llamas were white mounds huddled together against the wall of their enclosure and did not mob them for apples this time. The two women stumbled at last into Besema's room, gloriously warm and bright from lamps and a glowing fire. While Fant brushed against their knees, whining his joy, Atisha looked around her. She wished only that she could remain where she'd been briefly happy, eating rich stews, listening to women's stories, to their laughter. But she could not. Could not even sink down as she wanted to do, rest and feed Poum, because Besema had not paused in the room, nor set down her torch, but carried it to the back door, the entrance to her private space where Atisha still had never been. 'Leave her to Fant,' the old woman said, 'and follow me.'

With that, she pushed open the door, and went out. Atisha set Poum down on her nest of skins and blankets, Fant flopped down beside the child and turned his soft ears for the babe to tug at while Atisha rose, followed Besema.

She was surprised, for she stepped not into another warm room, but into the cold again. Besema waited in a shelter, wood-braced, its reed roof jutting out a little way into a large open space, with the fall of cliffs beyond. 'Look there,' she said, pointing to the ground.

The snow had ceased as suddenly as it had come. The light from the one torch Besema still carried and the two which she lit from it was not great. So Atisha found it even harder to understand what she was looking at.

A huge sack lay there, dusted in snow. It was shaped like a globe and at one end, on its side, was a woven reed basket the size of a table, with walls the height of a small man. 'What is it?' Atisha asked.

Besema took her arm. 'Come and see.'

Closer to, Atisha saw that the sack was also woven. Kneeling, her touch told her that the wool was the finest, the lightest, taken from the inner part of the llama's coat. She'd pushed her finger through slats made from thin reeds that spread over the entire surface like a kind of net. She rose, and Besema led her to the wicker basket which she now noticed was attached to the sack with spun hemp rope. 'But this,' she began, 'this is—'

'Yes, child.' Besema was beaming now. 'This is the same as you saw before in my room. The globe that floated. Only much, much bigger. And this is your hope. Your escape.' She took Atisha by her shoulders, pulled her close. 'Though since I have only tried it once, and discovered many dangers when I did, you may come to long for the simpler perils of the cliff.'

Dawn. A few snowflakes fell – slantwise, for there was a slight breeze now, blowing from the south.

'Perfect,' said Besema, returning to where Atisha stood, having positioned women all around the bag. 'The wind will be stronger up there,' she pointed straight up, 'thank the gods. We would not want you to rise and just hover right above us.'

Atisha looked up, swallowed. Poum, perhaps sensing her mother's disquiet, wriggled in her arms. Or she might have been too hot, despite the chill morning. Atisha was, for both of them were wrapped in many layers. Besema had told her that it got colder the higher you climbed. One of the many things she'd told her, so much advice from a woman who'd been up

277

only once, at night, and while tethered to the ground by a dozen strong ropes.

Still, she spoke like a veteran. 'Do you remember it all, little one?'

'All?' Atisha swallowed. 'How could I? There is so much.'

'Not so much, truly. You cannot steer this like a boat. The winds will take you where they will.'

'And what if they take me to the sea?'

'They won't. This time of year all winds blow *from* the sea. It is why no man fishes in the winter, just stays home and mends his nets. If you were a fisherman's daughter, like me, you would know that.'

'Well, I am not. Nor am I a bird, to ride the sky.' She shook her head. 'But I can control how I go down, you say?'

Besema took a calming breath. 'And say now again: I have calculated that the fuel already in the brazier will carry you for a few hours. The extra fuel maybe one more. As the heat diminishes the air in the sack will cool, but slowly. You will drop. And if you feel you would like to drop a little quicker – if you see a suitable open place to land, or people who might help you – you pull one of these ropes. They open vents above and let hot air out.' She toed one that reached into the basket. 'The bigger one a lot of air, the smaller one less. But be wary. Open them too high and you will fall too fast.'

Atisha's shoulders sagged. 'Oh, Besema! I do not think I can do this.'

'Atisha, I know you can. You cannot stay. You have said you cannot climb the cliffs like a monkey—'

'I cannot.'

'So soar like a condor. Away from the man who would kill your baby.'

Those words did it. Fear left her – not entirely perhaps; but it was overtaken by anger. And that brought determination. She nodded. 'Let us do this then,' she said.

Besema smiled. 'Good,' she replied, and turned, calling, 'Make ready!'

The others had been waiting. Positioned all around the sack, which they'd brushed clear of snow, they began shaking it up and down. Air inflated it a little, and Besema, together with Norvara and Yutil, took staves that had been burning fiercely on a pyre and held them to the sack's open end. It started to expand, just a little. Immediately, other women brought an iron cauldron beneath it, tipped it a little, allowing heat and smoke to pour in, till the wool lining pushed out against the reed webbing that contained it. It filled, spread, tightened, rose straight up. The next moment the basket lifted half Atisha's height off the ground.

Fant, who'd been quiet and watchful, now started to run around, barking wildly. 'Come, Fant,' Atisha called, 'let's go.'

'No, child!' Norvara cried. 'We'll keep him. There's no room.'

'There's always room for Fant,' Atisha replied, lifting the yelping dog and tipping him over the edge of the basket. 'Also he can't climb cliffs – and I'm not leaving him here for Intitepe.'

'In! In!' cried Besema, taking Poum, holding her till Atisha had clambered aboard and could take her back. 'With the dog's weight, the fuel will burn up faster. You won't be able to go as far. You sure you won't leave him?'

She looked down, at Besema, at Norvara, at Yutil. There were tears in all their eyes, a match for those in hers. 'I'm leaving enough,' she said. 'Thank you all.'

'Thank you, little one. For bringing us hope.' Besema looked a moment longer, eyes gleaming, then turned. 'Now,' she cried, and snatched up an axe. Yutil and Norvara already had one apiece. Each swung and, with single strokes, severed the three ropes tethering the globe to the earth.

It rose – so fast! She laid her baby down, risked a look, swayed, gripped the wicker rim and looked again. Already, Besema and the others were small, waving their arms wildly. She looked beyond them, to that different cliff where three days before she'd killed men who'd come to kill her; saw women like spiders spread out over the rock face; saw, the other way, the bridge that was so close to spanning the gorge. On the other side of it, men were staring up, all stunned to silence. She ducked down, only peering out through a small opening Besema had cut in the wicker. She saw a man emerge from a tent and look up. But Intitepe was as shocked and silent as any there, watching as the wind pushed her out of the valley, and beyond sight.

After a while, the gentleness of the flight, the quiet of the skies, made her terror recede, if not disappear entirely, especially when she realised that she was largely helpless. The wind decided where she would go, which was slightly inland and always north. Not entirely helpless, though, for when the globe sank a bit she remembered Besema's instructions and fed the brazier with the fuel – compact bricks of wood chips and dried llama dung. Heat lifted her. Knowing this, she didn't add much, letting the globe sink slowly towards the earth. She felt a little safer, closer to the ground, and there was a low ceiling of cloud she didn't want to enter. She needed to see.

See what, though? she wondered, one hand in Fant's neck fur to still his whining as she scanned the ground. Escape from the Fire God had been the only thing driving her to such desperation. Neither she nor Besema had given much thought to what would happen next.

It was hard to judge, but she felt she had to be travelling at least twice as fast as any running man. And though Intitepe might guess she was in the basket, he could not know. He would finish his bridge and storm the city first. So the further she got, the more chance she had to find somewhere to hide from him, perhaps with some people who would give a lost stranger and her baby shelter – but not if she descended upon them from the skies. How far she got depended on the fuel – which, she soon realised as the globe dropped and she fed more to the flames, was not going to last much longer.

Lulled by motion and quiet, Poum slept. Fant finally too. Atisha would have liked to have joined them, but she kept looking down, seeking she knew not what. Over this valley the skies had cleared, the snow was left behind; a winter sun reflected off the sea far to her left and glistened on the peaks of the low coastal range below her. The City of Women was built on a crag in that range, directly behind her. To her right was another line of mountains, also running parallel to the coast. The valley was between them, with the inland range much taller. She knew she didn't want to drift to that, to crash onto those rocky slopes. The globe was starting to sink again, the fuel diminishing fast, and the thought of what would happen when it came down was terrifying enough on flatter ground, let alone among jagged stone.

She looked ahead. A river threaded the centre of the valley, a track of sorts running alongside it. She could see dwellings, scattered farmyards, tilled fields. Land near one of them? Further up the sun shone on a larger body of water, a lake, with huts lining its edge. Perhaps there?

The globe passed over a last peak – and immediately it began to swing as if a rush of air had come from below. Atisha staggered to the side. Poum woke, began to cry, Fant to growl. Now they were being pushed faster towards those other, taller peaks, where disaster lay. There was so little she could do but she knew she had to try that little. So, grasping the thinner of the two ropes that trailed up the outside of the canopy, she pulled. A vent opened, hot air was expelled – but not enough.

The globe dropped only a little, kept driving too fast across the valley. So she grasped the thicker rope, pulled it – and the globe lurched down. She let the rope slide, closed the vent; the vessel steadied, swept east again. Her breath came in shallow gasps as she played with the two ropes, letting the hot air go, somehow controlling the descent. But the rocks were getting closer, the remaining valley space diminishing too fast. She was level with the tops of trees now, heading straight for them, the ground coming up towards her. Uncertain which they would hit first, she jerked both vents wide, then flung the ropes away, fell onto Poum and Fant and held them tight.

It was level ground the basket hit; bounced, rose, fell again, tipped onto its side. Things tumbled onto her, some of them burning. They were dragged along at speed, both her and Poum shrieking – until the globe smashed into a tree, there was a loud pop, and a sudden jarring stop. Feeling ground beneath her face, not wicker, Atisha clutched her baby, and rolled herself out of the basket. Fant followed.

There were embers caught in her clothes. Atisha staggered up, scanned Poum, set her down, slapped at everywhere she felt a burn. More heat on her face; she looked up and saw that the wicker basket was now afire. Crying out, she ran forward and tried to snatch her bag of food from the flames. But they were too intense, she had to give up, stagger back, pick up Poum and move fast away as the ropes crisped and passed flame into the fabric of the globe. It caught and burned in its turn, sending a column of black smoke coiling into the sky. Fant barked at it but Atisha was too bruised, too stunned to do more than stare. Then, as the last of the globe dissolved, she shook her head to clear it, turned and began to walk away from it, into the valley. There were people there. Farmers. She would just have to hope that they would help her. She was a farmer's daughter, after all.

She walked a while over rough, undulating ground, before

descending to the river she'd seen, and the track alongside it. It was easier going on that, and she headed north, towards that lake. But she hadn't gone far before she felt a tingling in her feet, a vibration. She looked about her, could see nothing that might cause it; feared it was the first rumblings of an earthquake, like the one that had wrecked her home, and killed many in her village, when she was a child. But the vibration was steady, grew – then changed, bringing sound with it, unlike any she had ever heard before.

There was a thump, a silence, another thump, the gap between them shortening as they grew nearer, ever nearer.

She'd just descended from a rise in the road. The sound was coming from the same direction she had. She stepped to the side of the track, clutched Poum to her chest, turned ...

... and watched a monster come over the hill.

Nothing in nightmares, in childhood tales of magical animals came close to what she saw now: a huge beast with four legs – and three heads. The front head had the long nose and ears of a llama but this creature was three times a llama's size. The two other heads were human, joined to human bodies that were fused into that of the larger animal. This was all she saw, all she had time to see, as the monster crested the hill and began to descend the slope – until all its heads turned to her. Then the beast let out a roar, rose up on its two back legs, its front ones flailing just above Atisha's head. She shrieked, and fell back onto the ground, just managing to seize a barking Fant by his collar before he attacked.

The monster separated into three parts – and only then did Atisha understand what she was seeing – though the sight brought no less fear. For a huge man and a tall woman now stood beside the creature that, for all that it was monstrous, was just a beast after all, but with so strange an appearance she found it hard to take in. Yet she couldn't focus on it, not

283

with the man and woman approaching, both as alien as the beast. The man, all in baggy black clothes, with a head shaven around a thick knot of black hair that dangled down his back. The woman, also in black, but her clothes wound tight about her body, and her long hair fair plaited and held by a strap.

They stopped before her. And though Atisha knew that she had escaped what Intitepe had meant to do to her and her child, she now saw that she had only delayed their dooms; swapped his murdering fire for whatever these three monsters intended for them. She also knew she had no strength left to run. It was almost, she realised as she closed her eyes, a kind of relief, now that it was all over.

Nothing happened. She heard noises, monsters moving in for the kill perhaps. Yet nothing and no one touched her. So, taking a deep breath, she opened her eyes.

The giant beast had moved away, to crop grass at the side of the track. The black-garbed humans, the man and the woman, were no longer standing but kneeling three paces away. And as she looked at them, they murmured some words, then stretched their arms out, reaching towards her, before lowering their foreheads to the ground. It was similar to the way some would approach Intitepe. But he was a god. She was just a mortal. *They* – she and Poum – they were just mortals.

Weren't they?

13

The Stone Fortress

No one had told the mountain that it was spring.

Deep breath of nothing, one, two, three ...

Luck moved. Stopped. Again. Peered up through the falling snow. Again. The summit had to be close, surely? A question he'd asked himself over and over, especially these last three days. He understood now why no one in Midgarth had ever succeeded in climbing Molnalla. There was almost no air up there. He'd take three steps, each one with his legs plunged to the knee in snow. Need to halt and breathe before trying again. Often he wasn't sure if he was even going up. If thick snowfall wasn't blocking his vision, icy mists were. And ever since he'd almost drowned in that avalanche, a week before, had been struck by a log or a rock within the white maelstrom, his balance had been off. He'd discovered that when he was this exhausted, healing was slow. Some steps he'd take and end up face down, choking on white.

He had been lucky to find the killer's boat again, for the force of the avalanche had snapped the towing rope. It was miraculously undamaged, which hadn't made him happy. To have an excuse to lose its weight, even if it didn't weigh that much? He'd abandoned it twice already, yet gone back for it each time – for the vessel itself was light, and the little he possessed sat as well within it as in the pack on his back. Besides, he still felt he might need it. The black-toothed murderer had brought it to their land. He was going to return it.

Time to go.

Deep breath of nothing, one, two, three.

He stopped, breathed as well as he could, listened for movement. Did any creature live this high? What could? When he'd left Bjorn to hold off Peki Asarko's warriors, he'd run fast up the lower slopes in the guise of the she-bear. But the creature he'd possessed was weak from a winter's hibernation, and he had been forced to let it go within a day, continue as himself. Since then, he'd only possessed one beast, a weasel. At least that had allowed him to hunt, kill three snow hares. He'd roasted one, consumed it as himself, smoked the others to eat later. But since then – two weeks ago? – nothing fresh. All he had left now was one strip of the dried venison he'd set out with. He'd promised himself that as a reward when he reached the summit.

Which was where? Perhaps it was better to eat it now? The summit could still be two days away – more! – and he might starve before he got there. He had found another way an immortal could die, one that was obvious, yet even so he'd never heard of it before. An immortal could die from starvation. Finally die, because how could the body be reborn if it had no strength to be born again?

Three more, he thought. Three times three steps.

Deep breath of nothing. One, two ...

He stopped, foot raised over the ground. Was that a cry? he wondered, sinking down. All his senses had brought him things that were not there. Men and beasts moving through the grey. Women crying his name. The stench of hibernating bear, that he also tasted on his tongue. So what was this?

There! He heard it again, the hunting shriek of some bird, a hawk, he thought. If it was hunting, there was something to hunt. Possess the bird? Or its prey? Also, if it was hunting then surely it had flown up from the other side of the mountain? Which meant ...

Go! Deep breath of nothing, one, two, three.

Deep breath of nothing, one, two, three.

Deep breath of nothing, one ...

Luck fell, sliding into thick-banked snow. For a terrible moment he thought that another avalanche had got him, that he was going to drown again. Until he realised that he had fallen *forward*. Down. Then, when he sat up and wiped his eyes clear he also realised that he could see. Not the arm's length of white or grey that had been so long in front of his eyes. All mist had been whipped away by the strong, gusting northerly wind he now felt. Suddenly he could see a world before him – the other side of Molnalla. Far below, at the base of it, was a vast plain that stretched to the limits of his sight.

He had found another world.

Luck began to cry. He couldn't remember the last time he had – yes, he could, when Gytta his wife had died, forty years before. He reached into his pack, pulled out that last stringy piece of cured deer. He thought it was the greatest food he'd ever tasted and at that thought he began to laugh.

His mind was dulled, by hunger and thin air, he knew. Because only after sitting and chewing for an age did he fully realise what he was looking at.

'Another world, Luck,' he said to himself, but aloud, a form of conversation he'd never indulged in before he'd come to this mountain. 'Well done, Luck. You were right all along.'

Another world! Most of the beings he knew, gods or mortals, believed that only Midgarth existed. That the world was flat, which the unclimbable mountains and the unsailable seas proved. That there could be nothing beyond those. He had believed it too, for his first two hundred years. But soon he began to doubt. It simply didn't make sense. There had to be something … beyond. Then the changing weather – long, colder winters, longer, drier summers, short springs and falls – had brought other changes. A type of whale appeared that had never been seen before. A different bird. His mortal parents had also believed in a world beyond and had set out to prove it – only to drown on their voyage north. One thing he knew, though – no one had climbed this mountain before him.

'Untrue.' He shook his head to clear it. 'The killer did. Other god-slayers must have. I am merely the first of my people to do so.'

He looked out again. Some clouds had returned but rents in them gave him glimpses of rivers, forests. What wonders existed out there? What people?

'The ones who dispatched the assassins, Luck. The ones who would destroy my world. The enemy.'

That shriek came again. It was an eagle, not a hawk, but of a type he'd never seen before. A big brown one, gliding along the ridge-line. He watched it, and the bird one-eyed him as it passed. Could he lure it down? Eagles were scavengers more than killers, he might play dead. But was he strong enough to possess an eagle? Not yet, perhaps. And birds were always harder than beasts. Insects, he'd learned to his cost, were impossible.

He needed to rest a while, lower down the mountain where the air might be heavier. He needed to get there quickly.

He looked at the boat. This was the reason he'd dragged it all this way – because he'd recognised that on its base were sled runners. He'd guessed by them that the vessel was made for snow as well as water. Now was the time to prove it. And the quickest way down the mountain, to that better air, was over the vast sloping snowfields before him.

On the waters of Askaug he'd paddled small craft close to the shore. On the slopes near the town he'd ridden sleds. This vessel was sleeker, lighter. But boats were boats – and sleds were sleds. He was sure he could steer it as one, as the other, as both.

The slope immediately below him was humped with what had to be boulders. To his right was an open flat field that narrowed into a gulley, or a chute. Mist obscured how long it ran. But it would be far easier to steer down that than around the humps.

He dragged the boat to that part of the crest. Paused for a long while as breath returned. When it had – enough anyway – he pulled the paddle from within the craft. Unlike the oars that he used at home, this one had gently carved scoops at both ends. He'd discovered on the Lake of Souls how useful that was, for propulsion, for direction.

'What worked on water should work on snow, don't you think?' he asked the eagle as it glided past him again. The bird did not reply, so Luck replied for him. 'Of course it will,' he said, and lowered himself into the small vent at the back of the boat. When he'd first done so, the sides had held him snug. Now he had room to move. 'The first thing I'm doing when I get you, bird,' he called after it, 'is the killing and eating of a cow.' He took the paddle in two hands. 'Follow me,' he cried and, shifting back and forth, slowly moved the craft forward till the front end was over the edge. He leaned forward, the boat tipped onto the slope and began to slide.

It was easy. He dipped the paddle to the left, swung that way. Did the opposite, swung right. It was … fun! When had he last had fun? Where was it stated that a god had to be serious all the time? And the joy of moving without his legs pushing him! It was like a longship with the wind filling its sail. He picked up speed – and then it was even easier. A dip of the paddle here, he swung; a dip the other side, he swung back. Since his right arm was weaker he had to brace and dig in a little longer on that side. But the method worked and he guided the vessel down the slope, into the mists, as stone walls narrowed around him, laughing all the while.

Until a wind gust whipped the mist away – revealing a gap ahead of him, the end of the chute, and only sky beyond it. Saw that in the one moment he had. Far too late to do anything about it.

With a great yelp, Luck launched into the air.

He had flown, of course, as a bird. But then he'd been in control. Here there was none. The prow of the vessel dipped and hurtled like a falling arrow to the slope that seemed so far away and came up so fast. He hurled himself back, his thrown weight jerking the tip of the vessel up just enough so it didn't spear the ground. It slammed into the snow nonetheless, sending a shockwave through him. He heard a crack, and wondered if it was a rib. His? The boat's? But he had no time to do more than wonder, for his craft slewed hard right, making for a hump of snow that could only be a boulder. He jammed the paddle in on the left, snapping its carved end off but swinging him anyway, enough to miss the boulder by a finger. But his slew now took him fast the other way, to another white hummock, and he jammed the paddle in the other side, snapped that end too, leaned hard away, missing again – but this time only by a hair.

The slope rushed up at him. He stuck what was now a pole left and right, somehow steering a course between disasters. He wanted to stop, but had no idea how to do it. He was going too fast. Velocity had him and he could only surrender to it. Jam the stick in – left, left, right, left, swerving through doom.

And then he felt it, the slightest decrease in speed. Focusing on the ground straight ahead, he saw an area of smoothness. He had reached some wider plain of snow. Stabbing the paddle in on his right he moved across that, slowing, slowing – not enough. Not enough for the other thing he saw ahead – a shelf of snow with beyond it only sky.

He jammed the stick down. It was ripped from his grasp. He thrust his left arm deep and his shoulder was nearly wrenched from its socket. The boat swung, still did not stop, hurtled onto the slightest of rising slopes, heading for flight.

Luck jerked his arms up before his face and closed his eyes.

Everything stopped. Wind on his face. He had to be falling. He had nearly drowned once before the avalanche, in the ocean when he was only seventy. He remembered the sensation well. The panic and then the calm. The sinking into oblivion. Here, though, there was no water to ease him down, simply air all around. Any moment now he would be smashed onto rocks far, far below.

Nothing. He lowered his arms. Forced open his eyes. Stared into the sky. Looked down. He was still in the boat, which was half on land and half in the air. He was on the land side ... but only just.

He took a breath. At least the air was better here. Then the tip of the boat swung a little down. He leaned back and it swung up again. Slowly, so carefully, he lowered his hands into the snow and began to push himself and the vessel back.

When the prow was above the white, he collapsed back. Once he was ready, he rolled himself out of the boat, and sat up.

The clouds had gone again. Winter sunshine revealed the land. Above him was Molnalla's crest – far above him: that mad ride had brought him a long way. Carefully he crawled again to the ridge he'd nearly plunged over. The mountain fell away below him, straight down to jagged rocks far below. He and his vessel would have been broken there, dashed to pieces. He'd have survived it – if the dashing didn't include his head being ripped from his body. No guarantee. After those rocks the slopes began again – steep, but not too steep, leading far, far down and all the way to the valley floor. The tree line began where those gentler slopes did.

He looked to each side. To the right was something not so sheer. He thought that if he could get his courage back and took it very slowly, he could descend there on foot and reach those easier, treed slopes.

And then he noticed something else. He'd passed over it before, thought it just another tendril of mist rising from a pine-top. Until he remembered that mist did not coil – only smoke did. With that he saw, down the mountain and halfway to the valley floor, so grey and black that it near dissolved into the granite around it, a huge building. It had walls, turrets, towers – the first building he'd seen in all his hundreds of years that was made not of wood but of stone.

Luck sat back. 'Found you,' he murmured.

He dragged the boat a little further away from the edge, then sat down. He needed to think. Hunger, though, made thought hard. What did he know of this world he had entered? He had glimpsed evil in it – twice. Once in the glass globe that the assassin had brought to Askaug and again in the one that Peki Asarko had at the Lake of Souls. But did that mean the whole world was evil? He doubted it. Like anywhere there would be good people here and there would be bad. With good people capable of evil, and bad people ...

'Philosophy, Luck? Truly? Now?'

He shook his head, tried again to focus. Thought of the drug, the power required for seeing in the glass, its allure. Yet he doubted he was now to encounter a world populated solely by bald, black-toothed, black-eyed cravers. Who would till the fields or tend the herds if all were lost to sweet smoke?

His heart had slowed to near normal, his breath was coming clearer. Only his stomach truly irked him, its emptiness. If he was going to use the only weapon he was truly gifted with – his mind – he would need to feed it. He hadn't come this far, survived what he had, to blunder into a stronghold and be taken.

Food. There would be none in the expanse of white that surrounded him. But there were trees below – and creatures dwelt in trees.

Without the paddle, he would be unable to control the craft over the snow. And his one experience of boat sledding did not make him wish to repeat it. Sighing, Luck slipped the loop on the prow over his right boot and started, in his ungainly lurch, to tow.

There had been a few times in his long life when he felt that his parents' choice of name had not been so inappropriate. When he'd met and married Gytta, and the wonderful years that followed. When he and Bjorn had discovered hibernating bears and possessed them to make their escape from Peki Asarko.

Those were two. The mountain goat limping past on a broken leg was certainly a third.

Exhausted, he'd fallen asleep when he'd reached the treeline, slept – and woken to the goat.

It limped through the trees – a female, not too old, with her back leg so badly broken she made no attempt to lift it, just dragged it along. Hurt in a chase perhaps, a misjudged jump, which meant that the chaser might not be far behind. If the beasts on this side of Molnalla's slopes matched those in Midgarth – and there was no reason to think they didn't – a lynx or a wolf might be close. Time to act.

Close to four hundred years of doing it made his movements smooth, silent and imperceptible. He had his slingshot out of his pack, a stone fitted, one finger in the loop and his thumb on the knot, without the goat looking up. She paused, perhaps twenty paces away, when the faint whirr of rope through air came. She even turned to seek the source and looked at him. Too late.

The moment the flung stone struck right where he'd aimed,

between the eyes, Luck had dropped the sling back into the boat and was up, shuffling across, Hovard's knife in hand. There was no need to hurry, though. The goat was already dead.

He crouched beside it. The fierceness of his hunger seized him. Feeling for the beast's rib cage, he drove his knife in just beneath it and sliced down. There was blood, guts spilled out. All his years of cleaning out the entrails of animals he would preserve made his search easy. Severing all that held it, he ate the liver fast, still warm.

Tempted though he was to go on, he stopped. He'd had enough for what he must do next. And he'd done enough too. The scent of death was strong in his nostrils – and he was merely a god. Those with a better sense of smell would already be aware and be racing for a meal. He pulled himself to the closest tree and awaited them.

He knew their cries – the single red kite circling high, soon joined by others; the high shriek of the eagle, perhaps the one he'd seen before. They would descend soon and he would take one if he must. But there was one he hoped for, one he'd taken many times before. His brothers always chose the hunting birds, hawk or eagle. For countless reasons, he always preferred another.

And it came. Luck heard it first with that distinctive beat of wings, almost like a slow hand-clap. It gave out its throaty caw – Luck always thought it more bark than cry – and the voices of the other birds went up in pitch. Angry, no doubt. For they knew the true king of birds had arrived. And it wasn't the eagle.

The raven swooped down. Glided over the goat's corpse, turned back, folded its wings and dropped to sit on its flank. Bending, it began to tear at the spilled guts.

Luck studied it, its blue-black plumage, the darkness of its eye. Generally, the bigger the beast, the easier it was to possess. A bear was easier than a wolf. A raven harder than an eagle.

But large or small, scaled, furred or feathered, all shared this trait: they were easiest to take when they were fucking, fighting or feeding.

Focusing within, Luck rolled his inner eyelids up, dissolved his body and entered into the raven's.

There was resistance. Ravens were powerful in flesh and in spirit. For a long, ghastly moment, Luck's Other hovered, as if pushing at a door that would not budge. Slowly, so slowly, then quickly, then suddenly, it gave. He was in, and feeling the world through feather and gripping claw. None of the possessed gave up entirely and they would always fight to regain control. The more powerful the beast, the shorter the time a god could reside within. Luck could be a mouse for a week if he chose. He knew that, given his own weakened state and this bird's power, he had but hours. He would have to use them well.

The first thing to do was eat more. The raven was hungry and so was he and both could feed, with his new body absorbing raw flesh better than his human one. So they tore at the goat's heart, ripping it from its housing with sharp jabs – and just in time. For other birds were descending now, and in moments kites, crows and that same one eagle were there. Snatching up the severed heart, Luck flew to a tree.

While he held down the heart with his talons and tore at it with his razor beak, he considered his next actions. He regretted that when he still had them he hadn't used his hands to hide the boat. He might need it again on the return journey to Midgarth. He would certainly need what it contained, especially his slingshot and the globe.

A sudden, raucous increase in screams. Luck looked up to see the predator he'd expected – a lynx – run snarling down the hillside to possess the kill. Birds scattered in all directions though none went far. The battle for scraps would continue until they all were gone. But Luck would not witness it. Swallowing the last of the heart, he regurgitated some gristle, spat that out, raised his wings and shivered them. He felt the power in them, and both the bird's, and his own hunger, abated. He was ready.

He swooped between the trees, down the mountain. Ah, the pleasure of flight after the agony of that endless climb! He only controlled direction; the bird took care of the flying. It was one of the joys of possession, this part surrender to the beast. Especially for him, who limped through the world. To soar! This was freedom ... and could not last. For the raven's superior senses soon told him: the smell came when he was still two thousand paces away. Sound swiftly confirmed scent.

Man.

It was a single bell, a deep, slow tolling. The scent was more complex. The tang of cooking meat made the man within the bird hungry again. Wood burned. Yet there was another smoke in the air, which a raven could smell when a man or a god could not. A taint that brought a different kind of hunger – a craving, sudden and intense. He'd felt it before – once in Askaug, once in the middle of the Lake of Souls.

Up ahead someone was using a seeing globe.

The trees ended with this thought. He settled into the last of them, upon a branch, for this far down the mountain pines and firs had at last given way to birch and beech. The land that still fell away beneath him had once been treed, judging by the greying stumps. It rose briefly again to a vast plug of rock. Atop that was the fortress.

The different tribes of Midgarth built their defences in different styles, depending on where they lived. In the south-west, in the wide valleys, tall walls of lashed trunks were erected around each town on four sides. In the vast northern forests of Palur, beyond Kroken, men built solid huts up in the canopy with as many arrow slits in the floor as in the walls. At Askaug, perched atop sea cliffs, they only needed the one horseshoe-shaped wall, with the gate tower on the landward approach. But wherever in the land they built, his people used what was abundant: wood.

This fortress was built only of stone. And yet it looked as if it hadn't been *built* at all; was another part of the mountain spur beneath it, thrust up whole by subterranean gods. Rock did not end. Walls did not begin. All were one.

It had different levels. There was a giant main building which could have swallowed Askaug's mead hall three times and spat out a fourth. This sat at the centre of a rectangular yard, paths bisecting it that led to buildings not much smaller. Huge walls surrounded the whole, following the top edge of the rocky outcrop, studded with cylindrical towers, each capped in a cone of black slate.

Luck launched himself, gliding down and around the fortress, so he could view it from the front. There was a gatehouse there – again of a size so massive that it made Askaug's look like an outhouse. Vast wooden gates – the first thing he'd seen not made from stone – opened onto a roadway which switchbacked down the mountainside towards the distant valley.

Sight and scent had held him. Now he used the raven's exceptional hearing. There was a low hubbub: both animal – cattle, chickens, dogs – and human. Though there were few openings in the walls of the buildings, through them voices came: the murmur of conversation through one, men singing – no, chanting – through another. The loudest noise was the bell, still sounding from the tallest tower which rose straight from the centre of the main building. At its apex, just beneath the conical cap, Luck saw the bell, large and bronze, rocking slowly back and forth, its ropes pulled by unseen hands in some hidden room below. Below that ...

Halfway down the tower there was a rectangular window, with tall wooden shutters standing open either side of it.

Lamplight flickered within the room. Something else was within it too – the taint of sweet smoke.

He circled the tower, glancing into the room each time. Flames stirred but nothing else. On his fifth circuit, he reached out his claws, grasped the ledge and thrust his head inside.

The room was unoccupied – but someone had been there, and recently, for steam rose from two mugs of spiced ale, placed on a large oak table with chairs either side of it. The vessels sat amidst many cured skins, some rolled in cones, some open and held down by stones. Like the one from the assassin's bag, Luck recalled, which Stromvar had realised was a chart of their land. Other cones on the table were white, looked lighter than the skins – shown to be so when a gust of wind came through the window and they moved. One of these was open too, also held by weights on its corners, and upon this one Luck could see different kinds of markings – rows of them, tiny symbols, some repeating, many different. They reminded him of the shapes he would carve to see the future, or tell someone's fate, his tala. But he never put more than seven tala together at one time. Upon this sheet were hundreds.

He looked about the room again. There was a door, opening onto a stairwell that spiralled up and down the tower. To one side of that was an alcove with a bed, blankets furled upon it. The ceiling was wooden, flat, beamed. It creaked rhythmically, had to be the floor of the room above where people were pulling the bell ropes, bending up and down, the toll still clear. Perhaps it was where the drinkers had gone, leaving their hot ales behind. With a raven's hearing he would note the men, if men they were, returning. With a raven's speed, he would be out of the room in a flash before they arrived.

He hopped into the room, and dropped onto the back of the chair behind the table. From this vantage, he looked around . . . and saw it.

The globe, far larger than the ones he'd already seen, was in an alcove opposite the one with the bed, beside the window. Not visible from it, or Luck would have seen it, been drawn to it, straight away. Smoke spun within it, and Luck felt an instant craving. He wanted to go forward now, gaze into the swirling depths. Would have done ... were it not for a man already standing behind it, whom he'd not scented, heard, seen, so well was he folded into the shadows, with his black hooded cloak, his black teeth, his black eyes.

Luck shot straight up, spread his wings for flight. But as he did the window shutters were slammed shut. Too late did he notice the ropes attached to them trailing to the stairs; while the four men who had pulled them now ran in. Each had nets. And though he eluded the first two thrown, weaving around the room, he could not dodge them all. Snagged, he fell upon the table, and the net tightened around him.

The dark man came forward, a raven's black eye meeting one even blacker.

'Welcome,' said the man, bending low. 'I have been expecting you.'

Luck blinked. He looked like the same man he'd seen in Peki Asarko's globe. But how could he know that Luck was anything other than a bird? Surely it was best to stay within his feathers and await the chance for flight?

The man smiled. 'I know you can understand me. How well do you think I speak your language, I am wondering. I have been practising it a long time. Waiting for this moment.'

The voice was low, smooth, the accent not from anywhere in Midgarth, not even close, though the words were clear nonetheless. Still, he didn't see that he needed to reply, not yet.

Until the man spoke again. 'Come now. You came here to learn us, yes? Easier if we speak, man to man. Or priest to god? For you are god are you not ... Luck of Askaug?'

The shock of it. How was he discovered? It was impossible.

He squirmed within the net. Luck ... and the raven too, which had begun to struggle even harder at its possession, trapped within the trap. Sharing its body had given Luck ... not fondness for it, exactly, but sympathy. He would like to see it free again.

Within most beasts, gods could only speak to other gods in thought. But in his boyhood, he'd kept all manner of birds. Ravens could be taught to talk. So in the bird's voice, he shaped some human words. 'Bird go.'

The man leaned closer. 'What did you say?'

Luck tried again. 'Bird go.'

'Ah, I see.' The man smiled. 'Yes. We only want one of you here.'

Releasing possession was always easier than taking it, the occupied so wanted to be free. The raven closed its eyes, Luck opened his inner eyes, and then there were two in the net, and the four other men in the room gasped, crying out in their own tongue, at the man and bird suddenly side by side upon the table. Only his interrogator seemed unmoved. He said something in another language, and gestured with his hand.

The men came forward at his command. A blanket was laid over Luck's head, outside the netting, while the bird was lifted from beside him. He realised why he was blinded – to possess you had to see. The leader here knew that – and Luck knew who had told him: that traitor, Peki Asarko.

He heard shutters opening, the sharp bark of the raven, calling as it flew away. Then the blanket was pulled back. The man was looking down. 'You see?' he said. 'The first bargain kept. The first of many, I hope. A truce shall be the second, yes?'

'Truce?' For a moment Luck's own voice seemed wispy to him, after using the bird's. He coughed to clear his throat. 'A truce for what?'

'For you to learn all that you desire.'

Luck looked at the other men, their normal, mortal faces. They could have come from Askaug, from the south, where the darker-haired people lived. The main difference was in the hair. His people let theirs grow long, braided it or let it fly wild and free. These had shaved theirs off, save for a short circle of it around the crown. They were also beardless.

They were staring at him, fearful. He couldn't blame them – he had just emerged from a bird after all. Their terror told him this was not something they'd seen before. Which meant that there were no gods there – or at least none that possessed beasts. Yet something else was also in their eyes, behind the fear. Hatred. Why, he didn't understand, one of the many things he didn't understand. And their leader had been right – to learn was why he had come.

'Truce, then,' he grunted. 'I will do you no harm, nor will I attempt to escape, until we both declare the truce to be over.'

'And you are a people who take truces seriously, are you not? So. I will not harm you – until a time you force me to. Which I hope will be never.' He shaped a smile, lips parting over his black teeth. 'That is the last thing I want.' He looked up, moved his hand again. Immediately the men bent and unwound Luck from the net. Two went to stand by the door, which one shut. Two went to close the shutters.

Luck rolled off the table, stood, swayed. It was never easy emerging from possession. Like waking the morning after a feast, still drunk. There was a chair beside him and he pulled it out, sat. On the other side of the table, the man sat too. 'Ale?' he said, indicating the steaming mug.

'What is in it?'

'Ale. Spices. Not—' he gestured to the globe in the alcove. 'Anything like that. That would not be in the spirit of the truce, would it? Drink.'

'Will the man whose drink this is not be angry?'

'The drink is yours.'

That was something to be questioned – but later. First ... the ale smelled wonderful, and he'd been frozen for weeks. Luck drank. 'It is good?' the man asked.

'It is very good.'

'I am pleased.' The man steepled his fingers under his chin, shaven like the rest of his head, without even the same small circle of hair the others had. 'I hope this will be the first of much conversations between us. You want information on us, so you can fight us. I want information on you so I can make you understand why you do not need to.' He gestured back and forth. 'You call this a ... deal, yes? But please, your questions first. You have many, yes?'

Luck studied the man. It was hard to guess at his age. The eyes, like those of the assassin, were impenetrable darknesses. The black teeth distracted, as if they were somehow fake. His skin was smooth, with few lines or wrinkles. He could be young or old. Or, he thought suddenly, he could be immortal. And the man was right. He had many questions. Settled on one. 'You called me by my name. How could you know that?'

'By the globe you carried with you. Which also told me you were near. So I was ready.' He smiled, waving at the beer, then again back to the alcove, where smoke still shifted within glass. 'It is far more than a way to talk over distances. It is, in its own way, alive.' He turned back. 'I have globes everywhere in the world. Have done for years. Through them I learn your language. I speak it good, yes?' He frowned. 'No, I speak it *well*, yes?' He waved again at the globe. 'I am aware of all of them, where they are, who is with them. As long as the bearer has tasted Sirene but once.'

'Sirene?'

'The sweet smoke.'

Everywhere in the world, did he say? Implying places beyond Midgarth, and beyond whatever they called this land he'd sledded into? That one answer led to dozens more questions. One more would lead to another crossroads, yet more choices. He must be careful with them.

To give himself time, he looked down to the tabletop. 'These,' he said, tapping one of the white square sheets weighted down with stones. 'These ... squiggles. They are everywhere. What are they?'

'They are letters.' The priest shook his head. 'I was surprised that in Midgarth you do not have them.'

'Why would we? What are they?' Luck repeated.

'They are magic.' On Luck's grunt of frustration he continued, 'Each letter is a sound, and a symbol.'

'Like my tala then?'

'Your way of seeing the world, the future, cut into stones or wood? Oh yes, I have seen that too. In a way they are.' He steepled his fingers under his chin. 'But imagine your tala joined together and used not just for fortunes but to explain the world.'

'Explain it how?'

Instead of answering, the priest bent over a sheet, placed a finger. 'You *read* your tala, yes? I *read* this.' He cleared his throat. '"Next month, on the day before Pregor, a shipment of iron will be sent to the foundry at Maak. It is lower grade, so only to be used for spear tips and lances, not swords."'

Luck gasped. 'You read that there?'

'Yes.'

'You could be lying to me.'

The priest laughed. 'Shall I send for someone to read it to you again?'

'One of these?'

The priest looked at the men in the room. 'These are servants. None of them read.'

Luck shook his head. There'd been times over the centuries when he'd wondered if somehow his tala could be joined together. Other seers read tala too – but no two ever got fixed meanings from them, as this *writing* gave here. It was magic, he saw the power of it immediately. How it could unite people. How it could ... persuade them.

It was as if the priest part-read his thoughts. 'Yes. I was puzzled that you did not have writing. Only when I saw how distracted you were – by fighting, by your spoken tales of heroes and gods – did I understand. And realize that for all your strengths as a people you were also,' he shrugged, 'weak.'

There was no need for defiance – partly because, Luck realized, the man was right. These joined symbols, this 'writing'? He felt a craving, as he always did with anything new, of exploring it immediately. 'Do many read in your world?'

'Very few. Power is best kept by those who know how to use it, do you not think?'

A crossroads of questions lay before Luck again. He took a swallow of the heated ale, took a deeper breath. But the man spoke first. 'May I ask you a question now?' Luck nodded. 'This.' The other leaned forward, fixed him with his black eyes. 'Are you happy?'

Luck blinked. This was not anything he'd expected to be asked. 'Happy?' he echoed.

'Yes. Are you happy?'

Happiness? It was not a state of being he ever considered. He did not strive for it, nor seek to hold on to fragile moments of it, as many men did, in drink or love-making. Because he'd learned: moments always passed. He'd been happy with Gytta for a time – such a short time, as he watched time take her away. Greying her hair, wrinkling her face. In the end, eating her body.

Luck was startled to find sudden tears in his eyes. He looked down. Too late.

'I know. I know!' The man's voice came soft, gentle. 'It is hard to consider it, when a lifetime's seeking does not produce it. It must be even harder for a god, when you have had so many lifetimes to try, and still not succeeded.'

He knew he was weak from the journey. This man would know it too. But pity was such an obvious tactic he would not fall for it. Instead, he took another deep breath and sucked back his tears. 'I am ... content. It is all I have ever sought to be. Is that answer enough for you?'

'For now.' The man smiled again. 'Sometimes answers come in forms other than words. But the seeking—' He shrugged. 'I am sorry to interrupt you. Ask what you will.'

Luck took another sip of ale before he spoke. There was a game they played in Askaug during long winter nights. A war game upon a grid, pieces moved to overcome the enemy, and capture his god. It was called Dagat, and it required careful strategies. It was a game you got better at the more you played it. And Luck was suddenly aware that, even in the short time that they'd spoken, this black-eyed man had got better in the speech of Midgarth. He would, Luck suspected, be very good at Dagat. As was he. So he made his next move, carefully.

'You said we might speak to each other as priest to god?'

'I did.'

'I know that I am a god. At least, that is what I am called in Midgarth – but, if you have studied us as you say, and as your speaking of our tongue betrays, you will know we are not so different from the people we live among.' He put down the mug. 'But how do you know you are a priest?'

There came a long pause. 'It is a good question, Luck. A deep one, behind its simplicity.' He grunted. 'You are wiser than I expected you to be.'

'I have lived four hundred years. You pick up one or two things. Will you answer it?'

'I … can?' The reply came out more like a question. 'Yet I do not think you crossed the mountain to talk about my faith. You came to discover us.'

'It is simpler than that. We are a simple people. I came to find out who is killing my fellow gods, and why. So you are right, idle talk can wait.'

The priest nodded. 'Then let us talk no more. Words are … a maze, yes? We can wander through it for days and still not find a way out. Instead,' he smiled, 'how would it be if I showed you?'

'Showed me what?'

Black eyes glinted. 'Everything.'

'Everything?' Luck grunted. 'That is a lot to offer at a first meeting.'

'It is. Would you like it?'

'Perhaps. I am always interested in knowledge. How would you do it?'

'In a way you will appreciate. You, who have already seen behind the veil of things as they seem. You, who have travelled in dreams, had visions. Oh yes, Luck of Askaug, I know some things about you.' He stood and for the third time gestured to the alcove beside them. 'I will show you in the smoke.'

From the moment he'd seen it, part of Luck's attention had always been on the globe in the corner of the room. 'Will that liquid be poured upon it?'

'It will.'

'So you would drug me?'

The priest shook his head. 'I would open a door. Only you can decide if you wish to step through it.'

'Do you enter with me?'

'I will be your guide.'

'To show me only the things you wish me to see?'

'Oh no, god of Midgarth.' He laughed. 'Sirene cannot be

controlled like that. Sirene ... controls. And she liberates. As you will discover.'

She? Luck took another gulp of ale then sat back. Ever since he'd first gazed into the globe in Askaug, and seen this man's face in it, he'd wanted to gaze again. Yet he'd carried the stoppered vial with him all the way from home and had not opened it. That first time had shown him the hold it could have upon him. He knew he would crave it more each time until ... until perhaps his eyes would be black, his teeth – and perhaps his heart too. Yet this he also understood: he had not left his home, climbed that mountain, suffered all that he had, only to refuse the very thing he sought – knowledge. To know the extent of the threat to his world. This man was offering it to him. For his own reasons, of course. However, Luck thought, I have spent four centuries reaching my own conclusions. And no drug, nor black-eyed priest, is going to alter that.

He lifted the goblet again, drained it, set it down, stood. 'Let us do this,' he said.

'Let us.' The priest rose too, saying a single word to the four men who had just stood and silently stared. They left the room.

As the last one closed the door behind him, Luck said, 'You do not fear that I will try to do you harm?'

The priest answered as he crossed to the alcove. 'Why would you, when I am going to give you everything you came for? Besides, and forgive me, you are not really shaped for harm, are you? Whereas, you see,' his black eyes glimmered, 'I am.'

The globe rested on a wooden stand on a smaller table in the alcove. There was a chair either side of it. 'Come. Sit.'

Luck did as bid. The priest sat opposite him, the large globe between them. 'Now,' he said, and reached into a drawer in the table. From it, he drew a glass vial – bigger, more ornate than the one Luck had brought with him. Its cork was sheathed in silver and attached to the neck of the bottle with a silver chain.

All Luck's exhaustion was gone. It wasn't simply the craving. All his years he'd delved into *all* life, never content to simply live it. When he carved his tala upon stones or wood and cast them onto the ground, he read the world in them, in trance, in dream. Here he was being offered another way in; or, as the priest had said, a glimpse behind the veil drawn over life-that-seemed. If he did not trust his guide's words, knowledge was the one thing that would give him the weapons he'd need to oppose him. Not physically. It was true – he was not really shaped to do a man harm with his body. But with his mind ...?

'What did you call this again?' he asked.

'In our tongue, "Sirene". In yours, of course, there is no word. Yet.' The priest pursed his lips. 'Perhaps the closest you have is ... "paradise".' He flicked the lid from the vial, and poured, not a single drop, as Luck had done at Askaug, but a spoonful. It hit the glass surface, sizzled, transformed to smoke. He could not hesitate, imitated the priest, leaned in, sucked deep. It was sweet, it was acrid, it was both. He choked, yearned, inhaled again ...

He was no longer outside the globe but within the smoke which swirled faster, faster, coalescing into a column, shapes forming within it – tala, writing like he'd seen scratched on the priest's table, rivers and mountains carved onto calfskin. Then these dissolved, the smoke cleared ... and he was standing on ground that had no colour, no texture, looking up at glass that curved all around him. Looking out at himself, looking in.

Luck gasped, staggered. Someone put a hand on his shoulder. He glanced at the priest beside him, who was also inside the globe. The hand steadied him, as did the voice. 'Look,' the black-eyed man said.

Luck looked. Everything beyond was now gone – the symbols, the room, their other selves. There was only the curving walls of the globe and people moving upon them. He saw men like those from the cell, with their cropped hair. He saw bigger men with long black hair in topknots, riding huge horses. He saw fair-haired women, drawing tall bows, shooting them. Riders, priests died. Women died too – not just on the land. For he also saw ships that made his own people's longships look like rowboats. Three-masted, with vast sides. They clashed, drove into each other. One dissolved in flames, sinking into a fiery sea.

The priest's voice came. 'Our land we called Saghaz – in your tongue its name could be two: Land of Eternal Sorrow; or Wilderness of the Four Tribes,' he said. 'And wilderness it was, for the four tribes within it, who you see here – the Women Hunters, the Horse Lords, the Seafarers and us, the Warrior Priests – we fought each other, and often amongst ourselves. Peace came sometimes and was broken fast. Those who could fight did, and often died. Those who could not fight died faster. It had continued for ever, and though all knew that it would only end when the last village burned, the last baby died, none would stop.' He took a deep breath. 'And then he came.'

The ship sank in flames, arrows flew, men and women cried out – and then all were gone. Luck was looking at someone's back – a man, he saw, as the man turned around. Bearded, with long hair that shifted in colour from black to fair. His face changed too. One moment he looked like he could have strolled the streets of Askaug. The next his face was blacker than darkwood. Suddenly the man dissolved into a woman who stood there but a moment, before shifting again into a man.

'Everyone who saw him – saw her, saw *them* – saw them differently, remembered them differently.'

'There were two? A man and a woman.'

'No.' The priest sighed. 'It is difficult in your tongue. *They* were one.'

'I understand.' He did. Moving between bodies was something Luck knew about.

'They stayed a year, vanished as suddenly as they had come.'

'When?'

'One hundred years ago.'

Luck found his voice, a question, as he stared at this man. 'What was his – their – name?'

'The Four Tribes also named them differently. To the horse lords he was Wind Rider, to the seafarers, the Bringer of Storms, to the women, she was Moonlight Hunter. But we, the warrior priests, gave them the name we all know them as now.'

'And that is?'

For a moment, the black eyes were hidden as the priest closed his eyes. When he opened them again, they glowed. 'We named them *azana-kesh* – the closest in your tongue would be: "The one who comes before".'

'Before? You mean another came?'

'No. Is yet to come. Is coming.'

Luck shook his head. 'I don't understand. "Is" coming? Is this a difference in our languages? Do you mean a god? A single god comes?'

'I mean the One. The only One.' The glow in the eyes grew brighter. 'He comes. She comes. They come.'

'How is that ...'

'Wait. Watch. See.'

The priest swept his hand before him. This *azana-kesh* vanished – but not before two things tumbled from his – her – hands: a silver-capped vial, and a glass globe. 'The one who comes before gave us Sirene. It lets us see. See the world, see how we were destroying it with our wars, our hatreds. Peace came with it eventually, a peace that has lasted. Saghaz, the Land of Eternal Sorrows, was changed to Saghaz-*a* – "Land of Joy".' He smiled. 'And then other visions came from *azana-kesh*'s gift. Of a world beyond our boundaries, which we could not know existed before. Your world. Other worlds.' His voice lowered. 'Terrible worlds.'

He shot his hand straight up above him. Smoke flowed through the glass again, then vanished to reveal ... Midgarth. But Luck's cry of joy at the sight of home was choked by what he saw. Men clashed, fought with swords and axes, died. Women clutched children and wept. Drunken warriors swayed in mead halls, singing battle songs. It was not his Midgarth, for he was not a warrior. But he recognised the way of his land.

Then his world was swept away, replaced by another. So different. In a land of such verdant green it hurt his eyes, atop a mountain of fire, a naked man lifted a squirming baby above his head – and threw it into the flaming mud. Luck cried out at this horror only to see it exchanged for another: in a place where stone towers reached to the sky, men and women were flung down, to a mob that screamed for them below.

The voice came again. 'The towers are in the city of Corinthium. It is far to the south of us here. The fire mountain is even further to the west, at the centre of a vast island its people call Ometepe. They do not know of us yet – or rather, they are just beginning to. For we are coming. We are going to bring them the peace they need, the peace we have found. We are going to share with them, with you all, *azana-kesh*'s dream. His last instruction to us. To prepare our world and then your worlds for the coming of the One.'

Luck found his voice. 'And you choose to share this dream by sending killers to murder us first?'

'We observed you. We brought someone from each land back here. Learned your languages. With Midgarth, we saw that many there would not be ... *amenable* to messages of peace. Not when their whole reason for being was war. And so we made that choice.'

Luck grunted. 'And if we do not wish your peace? If we oppose you?'

'Some will. Some did here. A last war was fought, the most terrible of them all, between those who believed and those who would not see. Before the vision of *azana-kesh* could be fulfilled here.' He waved up again, at Midgarth's rocky shores, the world of towers, the verdant land, his own world, all four blending at their edges with each other on the glass. 'As here, all who oppose the vision will die. Those who accept us will find peace. Will find what I asked you before if you had ever had: happiness. And the whole world will be saved.' Luck started to speak, but the priest raised his hand again. 'Look! One last vision!'

They were no longer on the ground. But this was not flight as Luck knew it, as he'd lately taken it on raven's wings. He and the priest soared as themselves towards a midday sun. Stopped suddenly, hovered, and Luck followed the priest's pointing finger. Saw, in the far north, a vast fleet of those extraordinary ships filling with soldiers, women warriors, black-eyed priests, preparing to sail ...

To Midgarth.

Yet before he could cry out his warning, he was spun around – and now he saw, far in the south yet with vision that revealed every detail, an army. They were camped on an immense plain, in the lee of mountains every bit as tall as the one which he had just climbed. But these men were not about to climb, as he saw when his vision went closer, deeper, sinking into the very rock, opening into a world where more warriors stood beside horses in a vast cavern, and men laboured in a tunnel, digging into the rock face before them. He saw how the tunnel was nearly through to the other side, a thin wall separating it from another world entirely. The same world, he realised, knew without seeing, where the tall towers stood, though this part was far from them. Even as he watched, he saw riders. Two groups, one in pursuit of the other. The priest was tugging at him again, at his arm, at his mind, but Luck shrugged him off, went closer to the second party.

They were mounted soldiers. A man rode at their head, a woman close behind him. She was striking, beautiful, like no one he'd ever seen, with black skin and eyes the green of a gemstone. The man was striking too, with the face of a warrior like his own brother Bjorn, yet with something in the blue eyes that reminded him of his other brother, Hovard. An intelligence there. A determination.

The tug, the voice, was too insistent now. He turned. 'Come,' said the priest. 'We have not got long. And I have saved the best for last.'

There was only a single ship there, though as big as all the others. Three-masted, it forged north through a violent sea. As with rock before, so with wood now. Luck's vision bored through the ship walls, into the ship, into a hold, onto a mattress. Two lay upon it – a woman giving suck to a child. Luck only had a moment to glimpse her face – exhausted, frightened. And yet, and yet ... there was something of the soldier he'd seen, his determination in her brown eyes. But when she laid the naked child down, Luck saw what he'd seen once before, that first time he'd inhaled the sweet smoke.

The child was not a boy nor a girl. The child was neither. The child was both.

The priest's voice was soft in his ear. 'He comes. She comes. They come.'

Sound, vision, scent, touch, taste, everything lost to smoke. He was not in the air, not on the ground. Not in the globe looking out but suddenly back in the cell, flung down upon the floor. The sudden change was too much and Luck rolled over and vomited.

Once again, he felt the priest's hand upon his shoulder. 'It can be hard, the return. You will get used to it.' He licked his lips. 'You will wish to get used to it.'

Turning to the door, he called, 'Come!' Immediately, the four men entered. He patted Luck's shoulder. 'More questions when you have recovered. When it will also be my turn to ask some of you.' He turned to the men. 'Our guest may need help to reach his room, brothers.'

'My prison cell, you mean?'

Lips parted over black teeth. 'Oh no, Luck of Askaug. You are not a prisoner but an honoured guest. For why would you leave when I am going to give you – show you – everything you have come to discover?' He gestured to the globe. 'Within the smoke and without it.' He nodded to the men. 'Help him.'

The men bent to him. 'Wait,' he said, and they paused. 'I have one question I would like answered now.'

It had been hard to tell a change of expression in the black eyes. But Luck had found other ways and saw the priest's jaw set.

'Ask then,' he replied stiffly.

'Do you have immortals here?'

Again nothing shifted in the black eyes. The mouth did though, shaping a smile. And when he spoke, the triumph in his voice was undisguised.

'No. We never have. Which means that we needed to find the way for *all* to live ... for ever.' He nodded, and the men bent again, lifted Luck by limbs he found did not wish to work, carried him from the room to the stairs. Spiralling down they went, then out into the large square courtyard he'd seen before, buildings on four sides towering above him. They crossed, entered one of those. On its first floor, they pushed open a door, which gave onto a small, simple room. A mattress on a frame, furs upon it; a chair and a table with water, fruit, cheese, bread upon that. Logs burned in the hearth.

314

They laid him on the bed, left. Their footsteps receded. Luck lay, mastering his heaving stomach. It took a while. The urge to sleep overwhelmed him. He closed his eyes.

And opened them again. 'Freya,' he mumbled. Carefully he swung his legs onto the floor. After a moment he stood, and swayed across to the table. There was a knife on it, for the cutting of apples and cheese. In all his journey, though he'd been tempted, he had not tried to contact her, to use this gift, born of love. Now he knew he must.

He sat. Laying the blade to the flesh beneath his thumb, he cut. There was a little pain, a little blood before a pathway opened.

'Freya?' he called, but only in his mind.

It took a while – and then suddenly she was with him in a thought.

'Luck?'

There were no more words, as such. Yet visions passed between them. He saw a monstrous man laid low, a brother striving to unite men and gods. Saw Peki Asarko transform into a bird. Then he showed her some of what he'd seen ... what had the priest said? 'Within the smoke and without'? But as he tired, as sleep tugged and images blurred, he focused on the two things that had given him a tiny hope. In his mind's eye he saw them again – a mother with a baby on an extraordinary ship ... and a soldier riding hard towards the mountains, determination in his eyes.

For some reason he didn't understand, as Freya faded and he fell face first onto the bed, those twin hopes made him sink into sleep with a smile.

14

Smoke in a Cave

'Oh, I can get you to him,' said the man with the scars across his face. 'What I cannot promise is that you will ever get away.'

Ferros studied the man again for a long moment, then looked beyond him. The tavern was of a kind he'd enjoyed in his youth – the filthy rushes on the floor, the walls stained with the hearth smoke of centuries, the strong ales, the greasy food, and the customers who, like the man before him, you would hesitate to follow into a dark alley. In his youth, with Ashtan ever at his side, he'd relished the scent of danger in places like this. But that had been in his home city of Balbek where they knew every tavern, their more dangerous occupants and where the back doors could be found in each of them.

Here, though, in the city of Tarfona, in the province of Cuerodocia, on the fringes of empire, he was a stranger. Dressed too well for this place. Some men did not meet his gaze when he looked at them now. Some stared at him, hunger in their eyes. Though more of that was directed at the one who sat beside him.

When Roxanna leaned forward, men's eyes followed her. She had made no effort to disguise herself, or to minimise her charms. Her leather bodice was open at the chest, loose straps crossed over her breasts. Ferros watched the scarred man's gaze move off them, as she spoke.

'We will get ourselves away. We only require guidance, and information. Which we will pay for.'

'Yeah, about that.' The man took a swig from his mug, wiped the beer foam from his mouth. 'It's not enough.'

'We agreed—'

'Fuck that!' The man slammed his mug down. 'That was before I found out where he is. Where he's supposed to be, for you never know with Smoke.' He looked around. 'Like his name, he vanishes, don't he?'

'And where is he supposed to be now?'

'There's one last tribe, the Assani, that hasn't given him their support. Rumour says that's where he'll be, tomorrow night, at some feast they have for one of their fucking gods.' He turned aside and spat into the rushes. 'Animals, that tribe. They live close to the mountains, fuck their own horses—'

'Not civilised, like you, eh?' Roxanna reached and laid her hand on his. 'We don't care who they are or what they fuck. We only care that you take us to them, at the price we agreed.'

The man gave a sudden yelp, jerked his hand back. Ferros saw red slashes on his skin, as Roxanna continued, her voice low. 'Do not underestimate us, Tarfonan. We work for the Sanctum itself and it has places in this town you could disappear into where your scars would be multiplied tenfold.' She leaned back. 'Or you could take what was agreed, more than you'd make in a year of thievery, and take us to this ... messiah.'

The man sucked at his hand, glaring at her. But Ferros could see his eyes change. 'All right,' he said, 'no need for threats or—' he waved his hand. 'I'll take ya.' He stood. 'Main gate, dawn. It's a long day's ride, won't reach it till after sunset. Bring your own food and water. I'm your guide, not your fucking grocer.' With that he turned and left the tavern.

'Charming man. Will he be there?'

'Yes.' Roxanna picked up her own mug, sipped, made a face, put it down. 'He'll come for the gold.'

'And the chance to double it when he betrays us?'

'Of course. But I doubt he'll do it until he can show this Smoke what he is doing. Even then, we have ways of dealing with that.' She turned to him. 'What else did you find out?'

They'd separated as soon as their ship had docked after the voyage from Corinthium, which had taken three weeks rather than two because a storm had snapped one of their masts half-way and they'd had to lie in the island port of Cresto while it was repaired.

He'd gone directly to the barracks and the letter bearing the seal of the Sanctum had seen him taken straight to the local general. 'At first he was happy to see me. Less so when he realised I brought no reinforcements – and very unhappy when he read the High Council's command that he must now obey me. I have his detailed reports here.' He tapped the satchel beside him, then lifted his mug, drank deep. She grimaced, and he smiled. He was more used to poor ale than she was.

'And his latest news?'

'All bad.' Ferros drained the mug, put it down. 'Every ambush he set, every camp he raided, all failed. Smoke always slipped away, warned in time. But what is worse – not only is this messiah rallying the tribes to his message, most of the native soldiers who come from those tribes have deserted. The general's forces are largely reduced to his regulars from other parts of the empire. Only one tribe's warriors still serve in Corinthium's armies – the Assani, who our guide talked about. The tribe that this Smoke is due to visit and win over next.'

'And that's why we are here – to make sure that he does not.' Roxanna reached for her sword belt, unstrapped and lying beside her. 'This "message" that Smoke carries to the tribes. Did the general say any more of that?'

'Little more than we know already.' Ferros grasped his own sword. 'A great storm rises in the east. It will break soon upon the empire and sweep it away. When it does, all peoples will be freed from the tyranny of the Immortals. Freed by "the One". Though what "one" it is, he is not certain. Some of the reports say it is a child.'

'This "One",' she said, standing, strapping on her sword, 'is who I want to meet.'

When Ferros followed her across the room, he could feel all those eyes tracking them.

They left by the back door, and he stopped her halfway down the alley that led to the main street. The alley was roofed, and had two gated lanterns, one back above the tavern's door, one ahead at its end. The street beyond was less well lit, and a cold rain was falling.

'You said, about our traitorous guide, that there were ways of dealing with him. Care to share them?'

She was silent for a moment, staring at him. Her voice, when it came, was softer. 'I need to, Ferros. I have for some time. There is something else about being an immortal, a power within you. In the end, it may be the only thing that can save Corinthium. I did not tell you of it on the voyage here, as you were still in mourning for Lara.'

Her name, spoken aloud, still cut him. But action, he knew, even if it could never heal him, would at least distract him for a time. 'Tell me of this power.'

'Not here. At our lodgings. When I—' The back door of the tavern slammed open and banged on the alley's wall, interrupting her. He turned – and saw five men step out.

'Quickly,' he said, taking her arm, pulling towards the main street.

She did not move. Indeed, she was smiling. 'No,' she said.

319

'Because, now I think about it, it may be easier simply to show you.'

'Show me what?' was all he got out, before the five men came. Ferros stepped an arm's length to the side of Roxanna to give himself room, and put his right hand on his sword's grip.

They halted a few paces away. Four of the men were big, with long dark hair and dark skins but with the startling blue eyes of the eastern tribes. They formed a half-circle behind the fifth who was smaller, paler, dressed a little better. A trader, Ferros thought, from elsewhere. One of the ones he'd noticed watching them in the tavern.

It was this man who spoke, his accent showing his origins on the streets of the capital they'd just journeyed from. 'We were so sad to see you go, my beauty,' the man said, staring straight at Roxanna, ignoring Ferros. 'So early too. How about we take you to a real tavern, where the drink's not swill, and we can all have some fun?'

If the man was looking only at her, his followers only stared at Ferros. Each had the same challenge in eyes glazed by beer. They were looking forward to a fight – one especially, the biggest and most scarred of them all. The small man was clearly looking forward to something else, his gaze lodged on the straps across Roxanna's breasts.

A fight was the last thing they needed. Five to two was bad odds, even back in the Sarphardi hills. If they could not die, they could still be killed. And they did not have the time required to be reborn. 'Friends,' Ferros said, stepping a little before his companion. 'Let me give you coin for that drink. It's late for us, though, and we—'

'We're not your fucking friends, pretty boy.' The small man's gaze was all on Ferros now. 'Though, now I think of it,' he continued with a grin, 'we are going to fuck your friend. Good, eh?'

He said this last while turning to his gang to seek approval for his wit. They gave it in grins and, for a brief moment, all their eyes were on him. A brief moment – which was all that Ferros needed for the third-best option in an alley fight. If you can't run, and you can't talk, take out the biggest fucker first.

He gripped his sword tighter then, sliding the weapon fast from its sheath, drove its fist-sized iron pommel straight up and into the biggest man's jaw. He crashed back, gone to oblivion. But the three other big men drew their daggers, turned on him, while the smaller man gave a shout of joy and lunged, open-armed, for Roxanna.

Ferros vaulted the fallen man, ran a few steps to give himself space. He spun, sending steel whistling through the air before the assailants' faces. They spread as far as the alley allowed. Each now drew swords to add to their daggers. So Ferros reached into his boot and drew his knife from there, making the odds about as even as they were going to get.

He dropped into guard, sword and dagger parallel and shoved straight out. But his concern was more for Roxanna than him-self. He glimpsed her between his opponents. Their leader had locked his arms around her.

And then she was gone. Not departed. Just suddenly, and completely, not there. The man stumbled forward, shrieked – and then jerked upright. His next shriek was so loud, so high-pitched, so … strange, that his three men half-turned. Ferros knew he should use their distraction, attack, but he was as held as them – by the small man swivelling slowly around in the empty alley, his eyes filled with a weird light. There was also a wild smile on his face. 'Friends,' he said and stepped forward.

Two of his men turned fully to him. The third, who still half-faced Ferros, looked puzzled, his guard lowering, an invitation. But again, even though Ferros knew he could move, should move, he was unable. Too transfixed by the small man, the dagger in his hand, how he used it.

Two of them fell, dead or dying. The third yelped, turned, ran at Ferros. He was probably trying to flee. But he was armed and swung his sword so Ferros ducked it, stabbed up, putting his dagger blade through the man's throat. He joined his comrades on the ground.

There were now just two standing in the alley – Ferros thrust his sword towards the small man, who lowered his dagger. Blood ran from it to the ground. 'Roxanna!' Ferros cried. Somehow, he'd lost moments. It happened sometimes in combat, time and perception distorted by fear and blood and killing. She must have fled the alley. She would return.

'Watch this,' chuckled the man, and laid the blade's red edge against his own neck.

'Stop ...' Ferros began.

But the man laughed again – then slashed his own throat. Blood spurted, a long arc of it, as he fell. Yet as he fell, he ... split. Or at least that is what Ferros thought he saw – a body dividing into two. Saw now two bodies there. One on the ground, kicking the cobbles as life left him. The other kneeling, then rising before him, alive.

Roxanna.

Ferros staggered, till his back was against the alley wall. 'How?' he croaked. 'How?'

She came to him. 'The second gift of the immortals,' she said. 'I will explain all.' She put a hand under his arm, lifted him straight, as the tavern door behind him opened and someone began to shout. 'But not here.'

He shook his head, sheathed his weapons. She strode away and, with a last glance at the small man, jerking and bleeding out upon the ground, he stumbled after her.

'Are you a witch?'

Roxanna smiled, and topped up his ale from her jug. Ferros

gulped it down. It was the second mug he'd consumed since reaching their room above the tavern, though he had no memory of the first. 'Isn't it interesting,' she said, 'how people always choose witchcraft to explain what they cannot understand?'

'Then you are not?'

'No, Ferros. I am an immortal. And you have just witnessed the second gift of immortality. The ability to possess another person.'

'Gift?' He took a sip, and put the goblet down. He could already feel the strong ale's effects and his heart had finally slowed. 'It is a curse.'

'Why? You do not have to use it. Many don't. But why would you not?' She pressed a hand into his forearm. 'To take over another's life? Not just their body – their memories, their beliefs, their whole mind? To see the world through someone else's eyes? Experience it through their being for a time?' She nodded. 'It is more than a gift. It is a privilege.'

He took his arm away. 'For a time?' he echoed.

'Yes. They will fight for control, even though for them it is as if they sleep. You can stay within a weaker person for perhaps two days. A stronger person for less than one. We leave and they awake, unharmed. After some interesting ... dreams.'

'Unharmed?' Ferros grunted. 'Like the man in the alley?'

Roxanna shrugged. 'That little shit got what he deserved. They all did.' She topped up his goblet again. 'You killed at least one, did you not? It is no different.'

It is, he thought, in ways he couldn't frame with words. But there was so much more here that he did not understand. 'But you were gone! Your clothes, your weapons. Everything. And then you came back ... with them all.'

She grinned. 'Convenient, isn't it?' She stopped his next outburst. 'I do not know the *how* of it, Ferros. Far wiser minds than mine have struggled to explain how and failed. It simply

323

is. You don't have to understand it. You just have to use it.'

A memory came. Of when he was lying in the surgeon's room back in Balbek, waiting to have the arrow that had killed him removed. When General Olankios, also an immortal, had visited him before he went under the scalpel, he'd hinted of something other to do with immortality. Something that troubled him. Was this it? He swallowed. 'Why was I not told of this before?'

'You would have been. But your lessons were cut short by necessity. I would have shown you, probably even tonight. Well,' she smiled. 'I did.'

He did not smile. 'So you can teach me this? Another lesson?'

'There is nothing to learn. All you have to do is choose someone, desire it, and you are gone.'

'That makes no sense.' Ferros picked up the goblet, then put it down without drinking. 'I could not do that. Not just by thinking it.'

'You can. You will.'

'I will not.' He shook his head. 'People are themselves. They should not be used like ... like slaves, for no reason.'

'I agree.' She took his hand. 'There was a reason I did that in the alley. To save our lives. There is a reason you will do it too. To save the empire.'

An empire ruled by people who do that may not be worth saving, he thought. He stared at his hand in hers. This time he did not have the strength to pull away. 'There is so much I do not understand,' he murmured.

'Save your questions for another time. For now, all that matters is that it *is*. And we will use it, as we will use your sword, and your wits, to accomplish what we must here.' She squeezed his hand. 'For how else do you think we are going to get close enough to this Smoke to kill him?'

He went to speak again. But she silenced him by rising,

pulling him up with her. He stumbled; the ale, the shocks of the night, weighing on him. 'Enough,' she said. 'It is deep in the night and we rise with the sun. If there is one thing lacking for immortals it is that even we must sleep.'

On the vessel that brought them they'd had separate, if cramped, cabins. He'd lain in his, mourned Lara, and Roxanna had kept away. In the city they were travelling incognito, as traders, husband and wife. There was one room. One bed.

She led him to it. He paused, stared down, and she looked at his expression and laughed. 'No fear, soldier. You sleep. I have the general's reports to read before I do.'

He nodded. Relieved. And yet ... Since that mad night in the Sanctum, at the festival, the closest they'd come to touch was when she'd had her hands on him at the table. But like him, Roxanna had obviously decided it was best things stayed that way.

He lay down. She went back, pulled out the papers from his satchel, leaned into the lamplight, began to read. He stripped down to his tunic, climbed under the coarse blankets. For a time he could not sleep, visions of an alley, of the fight there, of the man pulling a dagger across his own throat, prevented him. Then he did, slipping seamlessly from visions to jagged dreams.

One came and stayed. Memories of Lara, of their last love-making, blending with other times before; dissolving in their turn, as her body dissolved into another, very different one – white blended into dark, small and slim transformed to tall, voluptuous. Then the dream was gone with his tunic, slipped from him as she slipped under the blankets beside him. He murmured 'No,' but just once, as a naked Roxanna manoeuvred on top of him, down him, pushing his thighs apart. She took him then, all of him, sudden and deep into her mouth, into her throat, and though he was ready for her from his dream, he cried out. She moved differently then, combinations of tongue and teeth, fingers, the fall of long, black hair, in rhythms he'd never experienced before. She ... possessed him. Faster for a time, slower for an age; building, always building to a point that she never quite let him reach.

Until she did. He shouted again then, his hands gripping her hair, his flesh exploding in her. It lasted long and when it was finally over he lay sprawled, unable to move as she climbed up him and lay on top of him. The room was entirely dark, he could see nothing. Only feel her breath on his face; he tasted it. And then that too was gone.

Her voice now came again from the far side of the room. 'That was only another dream. You will wake from it too soon. Sleep till then.'

So he did.

It was still mostly night when they assembled at Tarfona's land gates, but once these were opened, Ferros could see ahead to the jagged ramparts of the eastern mountains, etched by the hidden, rising sun. No man of Corinthium had ever climbed them, though over the centuries many had claimed they had – and brought back tales from the world beyond, of three-headed giants, leopard-faced women, and flying snakes the size of ships. But these were fables for the credulous and for children. The reality that Roxanna and those of the Sanctum spoke of was of a darkness rising there, brought by men. Men who had somehow found a way to climb the unclimbable, though no one had told him how many, or how.

Men could be fought – and beaten by other men, Ferros thought, turning to look back at his forty soldiers, making their last adjustments to tack and weapons. All of them were Wattenwolden, regulars but from the Wattenwold, the northern forests, though now dressed like those they hunted for this covert mission. They'd cut their hair too, down to the Assani's single topknot; shaved off their beards. They were bigger than the local tribesmen, however, and would not bear scrutiny for too long. Still, it was the kind of patrol that would ride out every few days all over the fringes of empire, to deal with any mischief, the kind of patrol he'd led so many times into the deserts near Balbek, far to the west. When they'd first assembled, he'd watched their officer, Gandalos, walking up and down the lines of horse, commanding, adjusting, praising. Envied him his tasks, as well as his soldier's riding tunic and cape, his lance, bow and sword; his simple life, the only one he had ever wanted for himself. But Ferros had other clothes now, the civilian ones of a trader with the tribes, his disguise for this venture. He had another life. Lives, he corrected himself, and looked lastly at the other immortal there.

Roxanna was dressed much like him, in a merchant's simple attire: grey tunic and trousers, worn boots, cloak and wide-brimmed hat. The three packhorses were loaded with trade goods for the tribes. At least on top. Concealed beneath were more weapons, sheaves of arrows, and the bolts and bars of the powerful artillery weapon, the Bow of Mavros. This threw huge missiles and though it was used more often in sieges, it had been deemed useful for their mission. If subterfuge failed, awe might be required. Though, Ferros thought, scratching at the stubble on his chin, if we get to the point where we need to try and awe someone, we are probably already dead.

Gandalos approached, a servant behind him collecting the armour the young officer was now pulling off, beneath which he was as disguised as all of them; he'd only worn the uniform for the inspection. Done, he mounted his horse. 'Ready, sir,' he called. The officer was of an age with Ferros but had been informed who was in command.

But is that me or ... ? Ferros turned again to meet his fellow immortal's eye. She'd been gone when he'd awoken. A soldier had come later to fetch him to the gates. They had not spoken since his ... dream. She rode up beside him, and he spoke now. 'Are you ready?'

'I am.'

He turned to the guide. The scarred man's eyes were glazed from too little, ale-laden, sleep. 'Which track?' Ferros asked.

'To the left.' He grunted. 'To the left, between those hills, and straight towards the sun.'

Ferros turned. 'Let us ride,' he called softly, and tapped his heels into his horse's flank.

Beyond the hills, a vast plain opened before them. Winter rains had soaked the grasslands, turning verdant green to dull grey. In the distance, those mountains. Their crests were even brighter now and, within a few hundred paces of his reaching the plain, the sun rose. Not creeping gently but shooting up like a fiery ball hurled by Mavros, God of both Light and War. For a moment he was dazzled. But clouds loured above the peaks and the sun vanished swiftly into them, turning the world grey again. It wasn't raining for now, but Ferros could smell the rain to come.

Their mounts were of the local breed. Akin to the Sarphardi he was used to, tall and strong, they would ride these grass-lands as effortlessly as the Sarphardi did the sand dunes. They alternated canters with stretches of walking. At that rate, their scarred guide had said, they would reach the gathering place of the Assani by sunset.

As the day passed, and despite the rains that regularly came and soaked them, Ferros began to feel better and better. Ever since he'd been ... *smitten* by immortality – he could not think about it any other way – he'd been worried about the conse-quences of it, of all that would be demanded of him. He'd sat in classrooms, watched dances, drank Tinderos wine and resented nearly all of it. He'd let Lara come with him when he should have forbidden her, and so had let her die. Now, though, he had a fine mount between his legs, a sword at his side and he was riding to defend the empire. This had been his life before. Perhaps in doing his duty well now, he would begin to atone for Lara's death, somehow make it ... not worthwhile, never that, but at least not the futility it was.

His nature was to lead the column. But the troop had an officer and though Gandalos knew he answered to the new-comers, these were still his men. So when at one point Ferros got ahead of him, the other man again retook the lead – and gave Ferros a smile as he passed him. It was a challenge Ferros was delighted to take up – so whenever Gandalos ordered the gallop, the two would race. It was unspoken yet also clear, some distant feature of land laid out for a finishing post. They soon discovered that they were equal, these two cavalry officers from either end of the empire. And Ferros revelled in a camaraderie he had missed.

At a break they took to water, feed and rest the horses near the middle of the day, Roxanna drew him aside. 'You are en-joying yourself.' She raised an eyebrow. 'Should I be jealous?'

Ferros shrugged. Roxanna was another unanswered question he'd set aside as he raced. He knew she did not stir his heart as Lara always had. His loins, however ... 'Have you thought more on a plan?'

'You read the dispatches, as I did.' Roxanna took a bite of the cured meat they all carried. 'It was little enough to go on, to be sure. This "Smoke" rouses the tribes against us. He preaches, as so many wilderness prophets have before him, about salvation to come – to be found in rebellion. He has had more success than any before him. So we must deal with him as we have with all other such messiahs – with the blade.'

'If we can do what other assassins have failed to do – get close enough to use one.'

'That,' replied Roxanna, chewing slowly, 'is indeed the trick. And we will only know the way of it when we get there.'

They rode again, through alternating rain squalls and bursts of sunlight. Soon those were on their backs, and as the sun sank they entered a rising land, the foothills of the great mountains beyond. Grasslands gave way to scrub, then trees, finally to narrow canyons, the way forward lined in walls carved by wind and water, the path strewn with boulders. It was a place made for ambush and both Ferros and Gandalos walked their horses with wary eyes and hands on weapons. But their scarred guide soon came level with them, dismounted and shook his head when asked. 'They do not post sentries. Why would they when they are "loyal" to the empire? Besides, no warrior will miss the gathering.' He grinned briefly. 'This Smoke always provides fermented asses' milk and plenty of it.'

This latest, narrowest gorge ended, opening into a larger bowl of rock that rose steeply towards the walls of the mountains ahead. It would have been too dark to see their tops now, even if they weren't swathed in clouds. Ferros was only aware of an immensity that made him slightly giddy when he looked up. When he looked down, he realised the width of this last valley they'd entered – for what he took for fireflies were, in truth, distant campfires.

'The gathering,' the guide said unnecessarily, and spurred his horse forward.

The sound of it came soon enough – a distant drumming that grew louder as they approached, and was soon punctuated by the ululations the eastern tribes were known for – a cascade of notes rising from deep to shrill, ending in prolonged screams, like an animal caught in a snare.

They came to a crossroads of sorts, muddy tracks sweeping away to either side, with one going straight forward. To the right was a slight rise, a stand of small, scrubby pines. Calling a halt, Ferros dismounted, and led the troop into them. At its furthest edge they could see clearly into the camp about two hundred paces ahead. The drumming, the screams were building. Men were leaping over fires to shouts of acclaim.

'Truly?' he said to the man beside him. 'No guards?'

'With that going on?' The scarred man pointed. 'No one wants to miss it. Besides,' he leaned forward, spat, and Ferros thought suddenly, achingly, of Ashtan, 'this Smoke always appears when the tribe is at the height of its frenzy – and in a spectacular manner. No one wants to miss that either.' He tied the reins of his horse to a tree. 'I'll go in, come back, tell you what I see.'

He took a step. 'No,' said Ferros. 'You'll stay here.'

The scarred man whipped around. 'What? Don't you trust me, Corinthian?'

'Not further than my reach,' Ferros said, raising his hand to demonstrate. The man's sullen eyes followed the slow rising but not the sudden snap as Ferros changed his open hand to a fist and struck. The guide fell, unconscious before he hit the ground.

'Tie him to a tree,' Ferros called.

Two soldiers trussed the man. Meanwhile, Ferros led Roxanna and Gandalos out of earshot, to where they could see ahead. The drumming was even more frenzied now, the voices blending from separate cries into one chant, a rising and a fall on a single sound. On a word.

'Are they chanting a name?' Ferros asked.

The other officer shook his head. 'No. A number.'

'Is it "one"?' murmured Roxanna.

Gandalos nodded.

'I see.' Ferros pointed to where the biggest flames rose. A mob was dancing before them, more joining all the time. 'That looks like the centre of it, there. See the flat-topped rock above and behind it? A fine place to speak from. I'd wager that is where this Smoke will appear to speak to the tribe. So we need to get close to it.'

'How close?'

'So close you will not miss with a javelin.' He looked at Roxanna. 'Throwing at a man is different from throwing at a hay bale. Will you be as accurate?'

'Oh,' she replied, running a tongue over her lips. 'I have managed it before, once or twice.'

'Good. Two spears, in the heart, on my command. Then we—'

'Two?' Gandalos interrupted. 'Three, because I will be beside you.'

'You will not. You'll be here. Mounted. Ready—'

'I should be with you. Three javelins for certainty. I am—'

Ferros raised a hand. 'That is the second time you have interrupted me, soldier,' he said softly. 'Do not make it three.'

Gandalos stood straighter, stiffened. Then he said, quietly. 'I apologise, sir. It's just that I know these people—'

'Which is why I need you here,' said Ferros. 'Killing is one thing, and hard enough. Killing and escape afterwards is harder still. I do not wish to lose a single man in this. We will need you, your bows, and your knowledge to have any hope of getting away.'

Gandalos looked as if he would debate it further. But after a moment of staring he nodded. And the moment he did, the ululations, that had been building in noise, in frenzy, suddenly and totally ceased. That word, which Ferros now knew as 'one', echoed once more off the mountain, then faded to an unnerving silence. 'Be ready, Gandalos. It is time for us to move,' Ferros said.

'The guide?'

'Leave him where he lies.'

The rain had been coming in intermittent squalls. Now it

strengthened, came hard and steady. It was a blessing, for once he and Roxanna pulled the hooded tribal cloaks over themselves, and wrapped their scarves around their faces, there was nothing of the city showing about them, save their boots – and the quiver of hunting javelins they slung over their shoulders. But as Ferros turned to go, Roxanna grabbed his arm.

'There is an easier way. Why not possess two savages? We can get as close as we wish, then. Kill easily and as easily slip away.'

Ferros studied her a long moment. 'You may do as you wish, lady,' he eventually replied. 'I cannot see a time when I will ever want to ... use another man like that. So I am going to do what I have always done – serve the empire as myself.'

'Very well, Ferros of Balbek. We will do it your way – for now.' She smiled. 'But trust me – "ever" has a new meaning for you now. You will see that time, and sooner than you think.'

They set off into the heavy rain. Soon they had reached the first Assani – all men – for women in this tribe, Galandos had told him, had no sway or say, so would be waiting with the children in a camp nearby. They passed easily through at first, these men in singles and pairs. It got harder when the land began to funnel, slopes rising on each side, and the bodies before them pressed closer together. All were staring hard at the flat ledge ahead, on which another smaller fire burned, two huge men either side of it, cloakless, spears in hand. Some gave passage with a grunt, others snarled and had to be slipped around. Soon enough, and too far off for a safe javelin throw, the wall of cloaked backs became impenetrable. Ferros glanced at Roxanna, who raised an eyebrow, and looked at those blocking them, her meaning clear. He shook his head, sought around – and spotted a tongue of rock jutting from the cliff face to his right. Only a few perched on it, and these were mainly boys, for the approach looked hard to climb – but it was a finger of rock pointing towards the ledge. He indicated it with his eyes. Roxanna shrugged, but followed him.

It was the hard climb he'd anticipated. But youths reached down and helped haul them up, to grunts for thanks. Soon they found a slightly wider platform and squatted there, on their haunches, tribal style. Hard to reach, it was not only a thirty-pace throw from the ledge, it was the best view in the place. Ferros looked across the silent, staring crowd, spread between the canyon walls. The rain had now stopped again, and a few fresh torches burned in metal baskets clamped to rock faces. The fire on the ledge diminished to a glow ... which, even as he looked, transformed suddenly into a wall of flame shooting high above the hearth guards' spear tips, dazzling in that dark. Men cried out on all sides as, with a loud 'whoosh', the flames shot even higher and then were engulfed in a vast billow of smoke. It blew down over the crowd, over them on their perch, sweet and acrid at the same time, bringing tears, causing coughs. Yet even as he wiped his eyes, Ferros saw a man emerge from the cloud he had made, for which he was named.

Smoke.

He was nearly as tall as the spearmen beside him but that was the sole similarity. Where they were clad in the garb of their tribe, tight-wound strips of cloth about their chests in alternating colours, heavy wool skirts to below the knees, he wore ankle-length robes in layers, white on black on white. Their heads were shaven to a single topknot, his hair was long, falling in waves either side of his face. Their faces were clean-shaven, he had a thick beard that reached from his cheekbones to a hand's breadth below his jaw. A large curved nose stood proud of it, like a rock in a dark brown sea.

Roxanna gasped, leaned forward. Ferros looked at her. Her dark face had flushed, lightened, as if she were a chameleon. Her green eyes had shot wide, and there was a look in them that had never been there before. He'd seen fury, jealousy, lust. But he had never seen terror. And if she was terrified . . .

He suddenly needed the comfort of a weapon in his hand. He clutched a javelin, drew it out. But she reached out fast and grasped his throwing arm. 'No!' she whispered. 'We cannot kill him!'

'What? But that is why we are here.'

'You do not understand. We *cannot*.' She dug her nails in deeper. 'We have to take him. He—'

'One!'

It was the only word Ferros knew in the tribal tongue. And it was spoken softly enough now, by the man on the platform. Not softly at all by the Assani. They roared it back.

'One!'

The sound echoed off the canyon walls, once, twice, the third fading away. The man smiled, then reached behind him, to another man, unobserved till now, smaller, hooded, also cloaked. Turned back to the crowd holding . . . a glass globe. It was big, the width and height of his chest, and smoke swirled within it. A moan rose from the mob, from the boys below them on the rocky spur, echoed off the far walls of the canyon. Smoke the man smiled again – and this time his lips parted, revealing teeth that Ferros saw were not white, but blackened. The smaller man came forward again and placed a kind of stand before the fire. Smoke laid the globe upon it. Then he called out something else, something that sounded like a question. Ferros could not understand it but the crowd did, and there was yearning in their shout.

Smiling wider, Smoke raised a hand. He had something in it – a bottle of some kind, for something dripped onto the glass. Within the globe the mist cleared instantly – and the crowd gasped as one. And Ferros did too, couldn't help himself. For sitting within the globe, cradled in swathes of mist, was a baby.

It wasn't the further shouts that spurred him. The moans, the cries of joy, the ecstasy that the coming of the child produced. It was something inside Ferros – the sudden certainty that all that had happened to him – death, rebirth, Ashtan's death, Lara's death, everything – the reason for it all was moving in mist before him.

Fury took him. Throwing off his cloak as he rose, his left arm going forward, his right way back, he crouched, coiled and, unspiralling, used every part of his power to hurl the javelin.

Roxanna's cry of 'No!' came just as he released. She needn't have worried – for Ferros wasn't aiming at the Smoke without… but the smoke within.

Glass exploded. Fragments, jagged shards flew everywhere. A gush of grey shot not upwards but out. An acrid taint flooded the air and every person close to the ledge was suddenly coughing, retching. Slightly higher, Ferros's eyes cleared first, and he drew the breaths he needed. He looked. The baby was gone. But the bearded man now clutching a wooden plinth, whose face was cut and bleeding, was staring up, in wonder that shaded fast into fury. Not for him, Ferros realised. For the person beside him.

The word he spoke was clear, even if Ferros could barely hear it above the coughing. 'Roxanna!' Smoke said, hatred in the word.

Most of the Assani were still choking but some were recovering faster and these were turning, seeking. The youths on the rock below were the first to know where the javelin had come from. All turned, growling, and with daggers in their hands.

The trumpet blare came sudden and loud, its call cutting through the screaming – the same call used in the empire's armies wherever they fought. Somewhere nearby, a cavalry squadron was charging.

Instant mayhem below. Shrieks of surprise, of anger, warriors

336

shedding cloaks and grabbing weapons. Leaders amongst them must have recognised the terrible defensive position, for cavalry would massacre such a packed mob. Their own trumpet sounded, and men began to surge out of the canyon, towards the threat. The youths, torn, glared at the two immortals above them then turned away, scrambling down to follow their tribe to battle.

A blur whooshed over the crowd. A sound came, terrible but familiar: metal piercing flesh. It came from the ledge and when Ferros turned back to it he saw that death had arrived in a giant arrow from the Bow of Mavros. One of the huge guards hung from it, pinned against the stone wall. The bolt must have only just missed Smoke. He looked once at the dead man, once more at the two of them on their perch, then turned and vanished into the rock cleft.

'We must get him.' Roxanna was already scrambling forward, along a narrowing finger of rock that pointed to where Smoke had just stood.

Ferros followed. 'You know him!'

It was not a question. 'I know him. No time to tell. We must take him.'

'Not kill him?'

She took a running jump and made the platform, Ferros landing a moment after. Their boots crunched the fragments of glass. 'I told you – you cannot kill him. He is an immortal.'

'What?' Ferros stopped. But he would get no explanation for Roxanna had plunged into the rock wall.

The cleft he followed her into was a tight passage between sheer cliff faces. It was short, twenty paces taking them out into a narrow gulch at the centre of which flowed a stream. Their quarry was ahead of them – and already mounted. There were two of them and they didn't look back, just spurred their horses and galloped from the gulch.

Ferros and Roxanna ran to where they'd vanished. The high

337

walls dropped away, a valley opened, the land rose and they could see the stream beside them flowed from the granite wall of the mountain ahead. The riders were galloping straight for it, already about a quarter of the way there.

'Shit, we've lost him.'

'Not yet,' said Roxanna, who'd been looking the other way. For in from the side of the valley rode half a troop of cavalry.

Gandalos was at their head. He reined in, and one of the troopers brought two riderless horses forward. As they mounted he said, 'The rest lead the Assani away to the north, will return when they can. Like hornets, the tribes always chase whatever poked their nest. We swung around to the south. Which way for us?'

'Forward,' replied Ferros, mounting. 'We have to catch ... them.'

As he spoke, he spurred. The troop broke into a fast gallop. Gandalos was at his right side. 'Is one of them the cloaked bastard?'

'Yes.'

'I missed him by a hair.' He gestured back and Ferros saw the Bow part-dismantled and strapped to the side of one of the horses. 'I'd like another shot.'

'You're fast with artillery, Gandalos. Which I think you'll need to be again.' Ferros was peering ahead. 'The other man rides like a sack of turnips.'

He did, his legs flapping to either side. Smoke was not waiting for him, though, already ten lengths ahead. But their lead was enough that even the bad rider had reached the sheer rock wall of the mountain before the troop had got within five hundred paces of him.

'Trapped 'em now,' cried Gandalos, leaning his head down beside his horse's neck.

'No,' called Roxanna, on Ferros's other side.

338

He glanced at her, then looked back. The horses remained before the rock face. The men had vanished.

The answer was clear when they rode up – there was a small and jagged entrance to a cave. Ferros was off in a moment, thrusting his head into the dark. He couldn't see far but he could hear – the sound of scrambling men. He turned back. 'Ten men to stay here with you, Gandalos. Ten with us.'

'No, sir. With respect, this time I am coming with you.'

There was something in the way the young officer said it that made Ferros want him along. He nodded. 'Torches,' he called, and five of the pitch-tipped staves were brought forward, and strike lights used to set them swiftly ablaze. He grabbed one, Roxanna another, Gandalos a third, two soldiers the others. They went to the rear, Ferros to the front and he led them into the dark.

For the first dozen paces the passage was little more than the width of his body, the roof just above his head. Then it grew larger, and he was able to raise the torch nearly to his arm's length. The ground they walked on was sandy, almost smooth – and climbed, steadily at first, then suddenly and sharply. The climb didn't take long. There was an overhang to duck under – and they entered a cavern with glistening, encrusted columns rising as if supporting the roof on a place of worship, their torchlight lost in shadows above. It was wider for a while too, though they swiftly reached another narrowing – an archway that looked as though tools as well as nature had formed it. Ferros paused, ran his fingers along one smoothed section, grabbed Roxanna's arm as she tried to hurry past. 'So you know him,' he asked softly. 'This immortal?'

'I have known him all my life.' She stopped his next question, speaking fast. 'And catching him is more important than telling you about him now. Because listen. Listen!'

Ferros obeyed – and heard, over the sounds of feet slapping

on stone, a steady *clink, clink, clink*. Not just one tool. Many.

Roxanna shook off his arm, plunged ahead. Ferros now followed, Gandalos a pace to his rear, his soldiers behind them.

The next passage was wider again, its floor smoother. Roxanna was running, her torch a stream of flame behind her. So Ferros ran too, as did the others. Over their breaths he heard more – the men ahead. They were nearer, tiring perhaps. He sped up, till he was shoulder to shoulder with Roxanna.

They entered another cave – much larger even than the one before. And they could tell that, see more of it, because this cave had gated lanterns hung from clefts on the natural stone columns. The men they chased were halfway to another entrance – an easy javelin's throw. But both men were flagging and Roxanna wanted them alive.

That was the moment the immortal ahead began to scream. 'To me! Arms! Arms! To me!'

Summoned, a dozen armed men appeared in the doorway.

Their quarry stumbled past the soldiers. So there could be no hesitation. 'Corinthium!' Ferros cried, drawing his sword.

They crashed into men barely drawn themselves. There could be no waiting, only fast killing. Ferros thrust his flaming torch into one face, stabbed swift and sure into another's chest. He felt a blade cutting for his side, swivelled to parry it – but another parried it first, and finished off the man who'd made the cut.

'Obliged,' Ferros said.

'Perhaps,' Gandalos replied.

Men shouted, men killed, men died. Ferros swept his torch around, seeking danger; saw, on the floor, thirteen dead bodies – soldiers wearing a type of armour he'd never seen. Only one was from Corinthium, though another was failing to stem blood flowing from a gashed arm.

He sought her, found her – Roxanna, blood on her blade and her torch already thrust into the entrance to the next cave.

'Come on!' she yelled, and Ferros was behind her in a moment, and following her through.

And stopping, as suddenly as she did. They lowered their torches to the ground, had no need of them in a world so bright. They both swayed, clutched each other, needing to steady themselves – for they were high up in this new world, on a ledge that overlooked it. To their left, was a wide stone stairway. Their quarry was stumbling down it. Ferros did not take a step, however, nor reach for a javelin. He was too stunned.

This cave was huge – so tall that the roof was lost to shadow, so wide and deep that a small army could fit within it. As part of an army had. Scores of half-naked men stood by a ramp that was being built on the staircase approach – frozen now as they stared up. Tall men clothed in cloaks and wearing boots, with long topknots of hair, stood among them, holding whips. Beyond them, there were carts filled with dug stone, more half-clad men in traces. Spread out across the area behind them, wider than the wide cavalry ground he'd trained on at Balbek, warriors stood by horses.

Hundreds of them. Everyone staring up. Everyone immobile. Everyone silent. Until one voice spoke in a language he did not know, with a command he recognised.

'Seize them,' someone said, must have said, and men drew long curved swords and began running up the stairs.

'Back!' shouted Ferros. But Roxanna hesitated, still staring down. Ferros looked and saw what she looked at – the man called Smoke come to a halt at last, staring back … at her. Ferros saw their quarry smile, lips parting over those black teeth, before he grabbed her arm and, dragging her back through the gap, began to run.

Pursuers had become the pursued.

Yet even as he ran, as he leapt the bodies of the men they'd killed, Ferros was thinking like a soldier. He knew what he'd just seen – an invasion force. But however alien the warriors, he also recognised cavalrymen when he saw them. He was one himself and he would no more go to war without his horse than he would without his sword. It was unthinkable. So he knew that they were widening these tunnels to bring a horse army through them. Judging by the numbers of half-clad men who had to be doing the digging, they were not many days from being able to do so.

By the time they entered the last cave, the one before they'd leave the mountain, he had made up his mind. 'You three!' he shouted. 'Bows at the door.' Three men ran to obey him. 'Gandalos? Bring in the ballista. Set it up here.'

'Sir!' He ran.

'So we fight?' Roxanna had her sword sheathed and a javelin already in each hand.

'*We* do not. You have to go.' Screams came from behind him. His men were firing into the dark. He saw her hesitation. 'Go, Roxanna! Take five men. Only you can command the general at Tarfona to bring the garrison here fast. But with fifteen I may be able to hold them here till you do.'

She looked as if she was going to argue – then nodded. 'I will go. But this much, Ferros. I ride alone. I need no guard – and you will need all the men you have. If I meet the others who led the Assani away, I'll send them back too.'

A cry from behind. One of the empire soldiers staggered back, an arrow in his eye. Galandos ran past them with two men, began to set up the ballista. Ferros nodded. 'Go then. Return fast.'

'I will.' She leaned in, and kissed him hard. 'But hear me – if you are taken, and this Smoke gets you, do not tell him you are an immortal. Do tell him that we are lovers. It will amuse him – and it may save your life.'

He grabbed her as she turned. 'Why?'

'Because he was my lover once. Also my husband. And before his name was Smoke, it was Makron.'

She turned, was gone. And with Gandalos's warning cry, he had no time to think, only turn and fight.

The two men left at the gate had run out of arrows, and blades had driven them back. Six huge men were there, swinging vast double-handed swords. Ferros threw one javelin, Gandalos another, both hit, then both ran forward. Four fought four at the cave entrance.

Their enemy were hampered by the lack of space, their weapons suited to plain, not cave. Their steel drew sparks as they dragged points across the ceiling, trying for the high cut. So Ferros stepped close and opened a man's stomach with a slice, Galandos stabbed another through the eye, the other soldiers killed as swiftly and, for a moment, there were just the four of them there, heaving breaths.

Until another man stepped through the entrance and made it five. He did not have a sword. He had a bow. And it was aimed at Ferros's chest.

There was an instant, just a small one, during which Ferros thought he might do something. Knew that the hesitation had probably cost him a life. This one anyway.

But Gandalos did not hesitate. Just stepped in front of Ferros and took the arrow through his throat.

'No!' cried Ferros, catching his comrade's body as he fell, lowering him to the ground, aware of the two other soldiers as they stepped up and killed the bowman. Focused on the light as it left the young man's eyes.

Then he heard the voice. Recognised it immediately. Which meant that he must have been struck too, without even feeling it. He was dead, had to be. Because the person who spoke was dead as well.

'Rise, my love. Rise and fight,' she said.

He looked up at her. She looked down at him, in the moment before she bent and snatched up Gandalos's sword. For more of the enemy had burst into the cave and she turned to take them on.

'Lara?'

Glossary and Places

Corinthium:
taka – throwing knife
Sarphardi – desert peoples, made up of clans
Saipha, the Horned Moon
Blue Revlas, the Blue Moon
Makat – famed for its brothels
Buzuluk – slave market
Ganhar – copper mines
Trachamea – legendary whore with small breasts; patroness of
  brothels
Balbek – Ferros' home town
Lascartis, Gonarios, Trebans – elite families of the city
Agueros – Sanctum on the Hill
glave – short stabbing sword
Heaven Road – skyway to Agueros
Aliantha – hard wood/tree from the south
Ice wine (from Tinderos)
Valraisos – Lucan's birthplace
Cuerdocia – province
Tawpan – breed of horse
Temple of the Sun
Dawn Window in Temple
Sonovian free verse
Genian silver

Simbala – Goddess of birth and death and birth
Tarfona – capital, province of Cuerdocia
Assani – Cuerdocian tribe
Bow of Mavros – arrow artillery
Cresto – island and port
Wattenwold – the northern forests
Wattenwolden – Tribesmen from the north

Ometepe:
Palace of Waters
Toluc – volcano and main city
osako bird
heyame – the ball game
waytana – the sacrifice stone
paytaza – a healing plant
azatapi – the blue moon (Revlas in Corinthium)
marana – the house of Chosen Women
Bunami – language of most of realm
Palaga – province in the North
astami reed – for weaving
Iztec – rebels' coastal province
Rakama – the visitor (literally wave rider)
Shadow Islands – known for its witches

Midgarth:
Tala – Luck's fortune stones (like runes)
Telling – a cast of stones for prophecy
Molnalla – the fire mountain the east
Galahur – gathering place for the Moot
Lorken – Southern town
Sarkon – Eastern star
Tulami – morning star
Kroken – Northern town

Palur – northern forests.
Dagat – the game, like tafl
Persoo, Tamauk – West Coast towns
Algiz – white staff of talking at the Moot

Four Tribes:
Sirene – the drug of communication
Saghaz – Land of Eternal Sorrow
Saghaz-a – Land of Joy
Pregor – a feast day
Maak – a town known for its metal work
azana-kesh – the one who comes before

Author's Note

Those who have read my author's notes before will know that I think of each book as a journey. And as the cliché goes – one of course I would never use in any novel but allow here – every journey begins with a single step. Sometimes it's a flash of wild inspiration – an image on a wall, a person on a movie screen, a fall of light in a forest. Sometimes it's more prosaic – or even, dare I say, practical.

'Historical fiction is going through a bit of a dip in sales,' my then new agent, Mike Bryan, said. 'Ever thought of writing epic fantasy ... for adults?' he added, knowing I'd written some for teenagers.

'Not really,' I grumbled like a baby who has had his historical fiction soother taken away.

But I did what I do. I sat down with a new notebook, opened it to a blank page, looked up at the ceiling, looked down and wrote the word 'immortality'. Then I circled it – and began to free associate around it, each scrawled word sparking the next.

Monty Python famously did it with:

'Word. Association. Football. Match. Stick. Up. Yours'

Mine was different. In three minutes my mind map had shot off in all sorts of strange directions. In three hours, I had a five page synopsis.

The Immortals' Blood journey had begun.

It wasn't all such plain sailing. 'Just think,' the aforementioned agent said, 'with fantasy, there's no research.'

Ha!

When the plot had been fleshed out, I had three worlds to conjure – a Greco-Roman one, a Norse One, an Aztec one. All needed research to provide a base to them. Then there was the other world, Saghaz. Which itself had four very different tribes. So I needed to invent four religions. I tell you, I don't envy Gods! (Fortunately inspirational fantasy writer Guy Gavriel Kay gave me good advice: 'Be general on rites and testaments. Not too specific.') Then there was the whole concept of immortality itself. How it works, what sort of philosophy would underpin those who live an everlasting life, why can't an immortal be killed? There were two moons – I was going to have four but realized I'd then have to study astrophysics, which is not my natural bent. Throw in climate change plus a 1% vs. 99%, 'elites controlling the masses' subplots and ... argh! Research!

As far as I have a philosophy of writing, it is this – borrowed from the King in *Alice in Wonderland* when she asks how she should tell a story: 'Begin at the beginning,' he says, 'then carry on till you get to the end. Then stop.' The way I do that is through 'character in action'. Develop a central character or two in each world, throw loads of obstacles in their way and see how they clamber over them. They tell me who they are – eventually – while telling me the story. Joining all the different strands together is another, later part of the process entirely.

Along with my 'journey' idea, I also feel that in every part of any of my books, almost on any page of them, you can find *me*: something that's happened in my life. Something I've read, watched. Someone I've met, observed, heard. Or some adventure or accident that's befallen me. Often forgotten, lodged in some dark brain cavity, dredged up to be squeezed through character and plot to become something hopefully original. (Though when I tell people this theory they have been known to back away slowly. I mean, I assume you have just read this book, since you are reading this note. Would you want to be trapped in a room with me?)

Some examples:

When I travelled through Peru thirty-one years ago, one of the facts that lodged was a theory that the famed Nazca lines – a giant zodiac carved in the desert floor by people who lived between 500 BCE and 500 CE – could only be properly viewed from ... the sky. And that some materials were found that could have been from hot air balloons. In Peru. Fifteen hundred years or more before the Montgolfier Brothers. Hence, here, Besema's air globe.

Or the wild effects of different drugs – (N.B. this could be a reading thing, I make no claims, deny or affirm nothing) – how Lara could be hallucinating on a type of ayahuasca at the cult meeting, while Ferros is simultaneously tripping at a rave. Or how Sirene, the sweet smoke, could be a version of DMT.

Or ... the techniques of biblical slingshot use, learned by me when I played the role of a Jewish Zealot, gifted in the hurling of stone via rope, in NBC's 1980's Roman epic *Anno Domini*.

Or ... I won't go on. But if something strikes you, feel free to write and ask. I don't guarantee accurate recall – much is lost in those dark cavities – but I'll try.

What especially excites me now is that the journey you've just taken with me is only the first of several. Or perhaps part of a much longer one. You see, by the time you read this I'll be off into the wilderness again. I have some characters already, of course. I promise that I am going to treat them bad and see what stories they tell me next because of it. Yet other, new characters, will also arrive to add their tales. To be filtered through consciousness, memory, impression and emerge as prose. Sigh. I suppose this means there will be even more people backing away from me in small rooms, preparing to flee.

Hopefully not the following people though.

Thankfully, many colleagues came aboard for this journey, which could not have been undertaken or completed without all of them.

At Gollancz, I've had the wonderful support of a top notch house – part of Orion, who published my first eight novels, and whose fold I am so grateful to once more be sheltering within. Specifically Stevie Finnegan, who gets the news out there; Brendan Durkin, who organizes my everything; and most particularly Marcus Gipps, who took a punt on me, as they say, and who hugely aided in the writing from first conception to final edit, with his sharp mind and smart notes. Grazie tutti!

I have been blessed with great readers – the superbly generous, totally brilliant, and wickedly funny Diana Gabaldon who, despite being the busiest person on the planet, still finds time to read, comment and help. And also Sebastien de Castell, author of the Greatcoats and Spellslinger series, a terrific writer, who introduced me to my agents …

… who changed the direction of my career. Mike Bryan and Heather Adams of HMA Literary are super smart and thoroughly delightful, combining wit and insight with great taste in wine and an appreciation for life outside the closet of writing. I think we spend as much time discussing the English Premiership as we do my career. But it was Mike who suggested this genre, one I had always loved to read and never thought to write. Thrilled that he did. Though there's just one thing …

No research, Mike? Really?

Chris Humphreys
Salt Spring Island, BC, Canada
May 2019

BRINGING NEWS
FROM OUR WORLDS
TO YOURS . . .

Want your news daily?

The Gollancz blog has instant updates
on the hottest SF and Fantasy books.

Prefer your updates monthly?

Sign up for our
in-depth newsletter.

www.gollancz.co.uk

Follow us 🐦 @gollancz

Find us 📘 facebook.com/GollanczPublishing

Classic SF as you've never read it before.
Visit the SF Gateway to find out more!
www.sfgateway.com